World Without Love

Redemption

Book Three

Jaye Frances

A Note From the Author

Redemption is the third and final book in the "World Without Love" series. The series is a continuing story and meant to be read in sequence, beginning with Book One, **Betrayed**, followed by Book Two, **Reunion**. Both are available in Kindle eBook and paperback from Amazon. The "World Without Love" series contains mature content and is intended for an 18+ reader.

They would take your soul,
if they could . . .

Chapter One

"My name is Katherine. I'm here to help you get settled."

I wasn't sure how long I'd been unconscious. The last thing I remembered was Bobby pulling Annie and I apart and dragging me out of the cage. And then nothing . . . until a few minutes ago, when I'd woken to the soft white noise from an A/C vent.

Katherine had knocked lightly, announcing herself with, "May I come in?"

It was a token courtesy—saying no wouldn't have kept her out. And yet, I didn't fear the stranger on the other side of the door. There was something about the environment—the comfortable bed, the modern upscale room furnishings, the original artwork on the walls—that dispelled any suggestion of captivity. It extended far beyond the sterile ambiance you'd expect from a contemporary hotel room, the space had a welcome, homey quality that immediately replaced my fear with curiosity. And as I'd heard the click of the door handle, it wasn't apprehension that propped me up on one elbow, it was anticipation. If these people were really the sort Bobby had described, they could easily find out what happened to Annie. And more important, they might be able to help her.

Katherine was mid-40s, trim, and attractive. She wore a short, brown tailored skirt revealing legs that appeared to have spent plenty of time on a

Stairmaster. An ivory silk blouse—open to the second button—draped lightly over her breasts, then snuggled around her small waist. Flawless make-up accented deep green eyes. Her sandy-blond hair was cut in a no-nonsense bob, framing her soft, pretty face with a perky salute. She could've been a model in another life.

She smiled and leaned against the dresser, her clothes accommodating her movements like a second skin. Admittedly, it was an odd thought, especially under the circumstances, but I suddenly wondered if I if I'd ever see her naked.

"I'm sure you have a lot of questions," she began.

I shrugged my shoulders. "I'm just glad to be out of that place . . . the auction."

She grimaced. "You don't need to worry. Those people can't touch you anymore. Not here."

I ached to ask if she could extend the same protection to Annie, but it was too soon. I would have to wait for the right time.

"From what I understand," she continued, "Robert—oh, he probably asked you to call him Bobby—gave you some idea of what your new position entails, correct?"

Bobby. That asshole!

"He told me a lot of things. Unfortunately, not all of them were true."

Katherine's eyes narrowed. "I've never known Robert to intentionally misrepresent the truth, especially when offering an opportunity to serve with us here, in the department."

Unable to wait any longer, I blurted it out. "I'm talking about the other girl, the one in the cage with me at the auction. Bobby told me he would take us both, keep us together. Then he let someone else buy her." My voice cracked and I fought to retain my composure, determined not to break down in front of her.

"You mean the other American girl, the one bought by Gregory Housing?"

She knew.

"Her name is Annie," I said.

"Yes, we know about Annie. She was working on the *Kelsey* before the ship was lost at sea."

"Then you know Bobby promised to buy her, too."

"I assure you, it's a promise he deeply regrets."

I waited for more, but she stood quietly. That wasn't good enough.

"Bobby said he was outbid," I offered. "I think there's more to it than that. A guy who buys girls from slave auctions with government money isn't pinching pennies, and I doubt he ever runs short of cash. If he really intended to buy us both, the price wouldn't have mattered."

Katherine watched me carefully, making sure I was finished. "You're very perceptive. We'll teach you to hone that skill, how to use it accurately without jumping to unjustified conclusions."

"What does that have to do with Annie?"

"Your assumption that more than money was involved in Bobby's decision is correct. And before I go on, I want you to understand he fully intended to buy both of you. But the situation changed at the last minute. He had to get you out of the auction as quickly as possible . . . for your own safety. And because time was short, he couldn't tell you the whole story."

No amount of explaining would change the fact that Annie had been left in the hands of a madman. Now the only important thing was what could be done to help her.

"None of that matters," I said. "Gregory Housing is a killer, and Bobby knew it. He let that monster take Annie after he'd promised to protect her. If I'd known that's the way you do business around here, I would've refused Bobby's offer and stayed with her. At least she wouldn't have been left to die alone."

The cheery expression that had been a constant part of Katherine's demeanor changed to serious concern. "I understand your loyalty to your friend, and I'm not saying it's misplaced. Right now, you're speaking from emotion . . . from anger and fear. And those are poor substitutes for clear, accurate thinking, especially when negotiating for something you want. Remember this, Jewel. It's much too early for you to be making hollow threats to leverage your value." She threw me a cold, icy stare. "I'm going to give it to you straight. For me to do my job, I need your commitment. I can't have you second guessing your decision to work for the department, and I won't have you challenging me with ultimatums. Now, if you're ready to listen, I'll explain what happened."

I swallowed the lump in my throat. There was no point in arguing. She was right. I had no influence here. I'd shot off my mouth before evaluating my situation and the people around me—people who might be able to help me find Annie.

"I'm sorry," I said. "I keep hearing Annie's voice screaming at that bastard, begging him to let her go. It was the last thing I remember." I wiped at a tear streaking down my cheek. "I can't get it out of my head . . . Gregory walking into the cage, carrying a handful of straps and a coil of rope. And then hearing her cries, begging him not to hurt her. The worst part was not being able to help, and now, I can't imagine what she's going through." My voice broke. I couldn't continue. I dropped my head, half-slapping at the tears, mad at myself for wallowing in my own misery when Annie's was so much greater.

For the longest time, Katherine was quiet. When I finally looked up, her expression had changed. Not to the original façade of a cheery Polly Anna, but to one of compassion, not unlike what I might have expected from a concerned big sister.

"You and Annie went through a lot together. And it's only natural to feel the way you do, especially when someone like Gregory Housing is involved. I can tell you what I know, but it's important you understand it's *all* I know. If and when there's more, I'll share it with you. And if it becomes necessary to withhold something from you, I'll let you know that, too. I won't intentionally lie to you. From here on, you must believe we're on the same side. You can't work here under a guise of suspicion. You'll need to trust those around you, and they'll expect your trust in return." She paused. "Jewel?"

I was staring at the floor. I raised my eyes toward her and bit my lip.

"There are no exceptions," she added.

I collected myself as best I could. "I want to know what happened at the auction."

Katherine nodded. "Bobby is required to do his job with extreme discretion, maintaining a low profile. When Housing began to bid against him, Bobby countered with slightly higher bids, trying to dissuade Gregory with simple economic leverage. When he realized Gregory was determined to buy Annie, he had to back off. If Bobby had engaged in an all-out bidding war, it would have called attention to his identity and the amount of money he spends. And that's simply not acceptable."

"Why? What difference does it make?"

"Because sooner or later, someone will begin asking questions about who he works for and what he does with the girls he buys. Bobby's service to our department is very important, for all the wrong reasons. Too many questions can compromise his effectiveness." She stopped, hiked up her skirt, and pulled a cell phone from a holster-case strapped to her right thigh. Glancing at the screen, she looked up, finishing with, "Do you understand?"

"You're telling me the people who work here have to avoid doing anything that would create unnecessary attention."

She nodded. "It's called intelligent discretion, a kind of protective umbrella that maintains the department's political integrity."

I took a deep breath, feeling the sudden tension between us.

Katherine noticed immediately. Moving to the edge of the bed, she sat next to me.

"There's nothing scheduled for today," she said. "Use the time to become acquainted with your room and new wardrobe. Take a walk around the grounds if you like. This afternoon, I'll give you a tour of the cafeteria, the gym, and the main reception and office building. We call it the Fortress."

"And tomorrow?"

"You'll begin your training. Classes in the morning, lab work in the afternoon."

"Training?" My mind returned to the ship, where the men had taken turns with me on deck to break down my resistance, trying to desensitize me to the idea of providing sex on demand.

"We begin with three concentrated curriculums. You'll start with communication, learning to listen and use language more effectively. Occasionally, one of our girls needs to neutralize a regional slang or a distracting accent. In your case, that won't be necessary. Next, you'll work on interpretive skills, how to read and decipher basic code and hand signals used by agents and staffers." Her expectant stare made it clear she was waiting for a response.

"I understand. What else?"

"We'll work on improving your behavioral flexibility."

"My what?"

"Think of it as specialized skills. It means you'll learn to satisfy the expectations of our guests while working toward the desired *result*."

Her emphasis on the bottom line bothered me. "What kind of result?"

"Our job is to acquire information."

"You mean intelligence?"

"No, dear. Here, inside the wall, we gather *information*. Those working on the outside—agents and operatives—they obtain intelligence."

"There's a difference?" I didn't really care, but wanted to ask a question to let her know I was paying attention.

"The distinction indicates the source as well as the credibility. We assign a higher probability of accuracy to information. *Intelligence* must be verified from additional sources before it's considered credible."

I nodded, not really understanding.

"It has to do with the way the gen is collected," she continued. "When it results from *our* efforts," she tipped her head toward me, an indication I was now included as an official member of the team, "it's the outcome of using focused rapport, social skills, and our feminine attributes." She paused, her expression turning dark. "Outside the wall, I'm afraid the methodology is often less civilized."

Her words flowed with a kind of practiced precision, the way they would when someone doesn't need to think about what they're going to say next. She hesitated only when she needed an indication I was listening.

She looked at me expectantly. "Don't you want to know where you are?"

I silently scolded myself for not bringing it up before she did. My location should matter to me, as a part of normal curiosity. I quickly found my voice. "Am I still in Bangkok?"

"Yes, more specifically, you're in the diplomatic compound. I know you're feeling a little displaced. But don't worry, most of the girls feel right at home after a day or two."

"There are other girls here?"

"Usually, we're a family of six, including myself. Right now, we're in the middle of regional reassignments. Several of our girls were recently transferred to new projects. So for the time being, you, Marcie, and I are holding down the fort."

She noticed my eyes darting to the corners of the room, as if searching for a roommate in hiding, ready to spring out and introduce herself.

"Each girl has her own room," Katherine assured me. "A suite really. Your bath is through that door." She pointed to the six-panel oak colonial supported by four polished brass hinges. "This room is yours for as long as you're here. You may consider it private. You'll also use it to entertain, when appropriate."

I may not have fully understood everything she'd said, but I had no doubt what the word *entertain* meant.

"If there's anything you need—a particular brand of shampoo, moisturizer, lipstick—write it on the pad you'll find on top of the bath vanity. The staff does the shopping once a week. Anything that isn't stocked locally, we can have shipped in."

"Anything?" While I wasn't fishing for an exotic brand of body wash or a dozen bars of French milled soap, I was surprised at the latitude she was offering, inferring the staff was a bunch of inscripted genies popping in and out of their magic lamp in a puff of smoke.

"Except perfume and deodorant. Those will be provided to you based on the preferences of your assigned guest."

"You always know that much about the men?"

She smiled, her way of letting me know I had a lot to learn. "Men leave lots of clues. And they're consistent. If a man liked a particular fragrance or color ten years ago, chances are he still likes it today. Women, on the other hand, are far less predictable."

"Women?"

I saw a sudden flash of concern on her face. "Is that going to be a problem, because if so—"

"No," I interrupted. "It's not a problem. I didn't realize there would be women . . . guests."

"It's not as rare as you might think," she said. "Dignitaries and political figures often travel with their wives. And some of those women have an influence on the business and political decisions their husbands ultimately make. So we do our best to give the ladies a positive experience during their visit. It's often as benign as needing a companion for the day, someone to eat or shop with." She paused, her eyes darting upward as if remembering someone in particular. "Occasionally, they express a preference for more."

I couldn't ignore the obvious question. "And I suppose if a woman wants a man, there are male hosts, too?"

"Our job is to ensure our guests are safe, comfortable, and entertained. In that order. Along the way, we hope to gain their trust, and bring their objectives and interests into alignment with ours. To accomplish those goals, we don't think in terms of limitations. It's more about doing whatever it takes."

Her expression didn't change, but I could tell she wanted me to understand the extent to which I could be called upon in performing my job. *Whatever it takes,* she'd said.

Katherine had done most of the talking, yet I'd begun to recognize a sense of give-and-take between us. But I wasn't ready to trust her—at least not yet—and I was pretty sure she knew it. I figured it was part of her job, to read me, detect the tiniest tell—a muscle contraction, an adjustment in posture, a hand gesture—that conveyed far more than words ever could.

I decided to risk it and ask if there was anything she could do to help Annie. And this time, I would try to control my emotions. "Can I ask you a question?"

Katherine raised her eyebrows, suggesting her readiness to listen.

"How much do you know about Gregory Housing?"

"We keep tabs on him."

"Is there some way to find out where he's taken Annie?"

Katherine fell silent, her gaze fixed on my face. For a moment, I wondered if her training allowed her to peer inside, beyond the limitations of skin and bone.

Finally, she said, "While we could make those inquiries, and eventually have them answered, I'm wondering how prudent it would be?"

Prudent? It was like asking me to evaluate the importance of drawing my next breath. I wanted to challenge her, break through her sudden veneer of polished indifference. Yet the metered calm of her voice, the absence of any argument, stopped me. Her words were more than a veiled threat. She didn't like repeating herself, and this was her way of telling me— *again*—that it was far too early in our relationship to discuss what she could do for me.

For now, I would let it drop. But from what she'd told me, information about Annie—including her location—was something the people who worked behind these walls had access to. And if they could get it, so could I.

One way or the other.

Chapter Two

Katherine had left abruptly, excusing herself to answer the earlier text on her cell phone. I wondered if the message had been planned, a pre-arranged signal to insure our first meeting was just long enough to provide a brief introduction and not overwhelm. Perhaps that was one of those things beyond my need to know.

It was time to explore my new home.

My room was far different from the cabin Annie and I had shared onboard the *Kelsey*. Appointed with contemporary furnishings, my queen-sized bed was flanked with large maple nightstands, their deeply polished end-grains confirming solid-wood construction. A matching dresser and velvet cushioned chair completed the room.

Katherine had mentioned a new wardrobe.

Wondering what century had influenced the department's sense of fashion, I opened each dresser drawer and began scrounging through the neatly folded tops, shorts, jeans, and socks—casual wear.

Inside the large walk-in closet, the balance of my clothing was organized by type and color. A full-length rod was filled with cocktail dresses and evening gowns. Another held blouses, sweaters, skirts, and slacks. In the back, a built-in rack displayed fourteen pairs of shoes—each dedicated to a specific function—including a pair of sneakers, three each of sandals and flats, two pairs of casual pumps, a pair of three-inch heels in black, brown, and dark blue, and two pairs of four-inch, fuck-me stilettos.

Everything was a perfect fit. Even the heels were comfortable. Although I wouldn't find out until much later, the stilettoes were custom-made at fifteen hundred a crack, the built-in gel support allowing me to stand for long periods during cocktail parties and other social functions, when presenting my assets in full length was not only expected, but a requirement of the job.

It was time to check out the rest of the building. This was my new home, at least for a while, and I was curious.

The door to my room was unlocked, as I'd expected. I would have been suspicious of everything Katherine had said if I'd found myself a prisoner. In fact, the handle had no lock of any kind, at least not the type readily accessible to the room's occupant. It meant anyone could enter any time of the day or night, regardless of my state of dress or what I was doing.

I wasn't sure how I felt about that. I would take it up with Katherine later.

Throwing on light cotton shorts and a pullover top, I stepped into the hallway and closed the door behind me. Scanning both ways, I didn't see a single indication of life.

The carpeting, the artwork on the wall, the occasional accent table along the corridor reminded me of the San Francisco Hilton, where Carl and I had spent two nights of our honeymoon.

I counted eight rooms, including mine. Each had a small brass nameplate over the door, numbered from C101 to C108—a reminder of our government's compulsive obsession to systematically identify, number, and map every square inch of occupied space. In this case, it made sense—especially for someone like me who, without it, would be counting doors until I was familiar with the location of my room.

I made a mental note of the number— C104.

As I walked toward the far end of the hall, one of the framed pictures distracted me. Appearing to be an original oil, the scene was a restful pastoral. It wasn't the artist's skill that caught my attention, it was the subject—a young bare-breasted girl relaxing alongside a meandering stream beneath a large canopy of oak trees, the landscape suggesting a cool haven on a lazy summer afternoon.

I felt a tinge of voyeurism. And it made me realize that, just as I was watching her in that distant, frozen moment in time, someone was surely watching me. A government facility of this importance would have video cameras in every nook and cranny of every building.

I scanned the ceiling for camera housings or protruding lenses. The lightly textured finish appeared smooth and unaltered. The crown molding, however, did not. The grain pattern of the wood looked artificial and repetitive, with a recessed quarter-inch cavity dotting the finish every ten to twelve feet. Too large to be the puttied heads of recessed nails, they were most likely openings for pin-hole lenses.

I wanted "Big Brother" to know I was aware of their monitoring and that, frankly, I didn't care. I smiled and waved as I passed each dot in the molding, hoping to convey a little innocent whimsy and not the compensating actions of a snooping newbie who'd realized her every move was being scrutinized.

Reaching the opposite end of the hall, I'd expected to find a group of small offices or an open bull-pen with desks, chairs, and filing cabinets—usual fixtures for any government operation. I was surprised to discover a large reception and gathering room.

I was also relieved to find it empty.

Vastly different in appearance from the casual sprawl of the typical middle-class living room, the expanse of polished oak flooring was highlighted with large Persian rugs, each one strategically placed in front of beige leather couches and overstuffed easy chairs, creating separate areas for conversation. French Provincial end tables flanked each sitting area and supported vases of mixed flower bouquets, the carefully coordinated spots of color adding a sense of civility to the room. The soft glow from wall-mounted, bound-glass lighting sconces left the twelve-foot coffered ceiling uncluttered by the usual geometric pattern of recessed incandescent floods.

Every picture on the wall, every precisely placed cushion on the leather couches appeared to serve the gods of design and style, the final result presenting an image that could easily grace the cover of Architectural Digest.

Katherine had been right—anything and everything was a phone call away. And in a day or two, I was certain that same degree of availability would also apply to me and the services I could provide to "guests" of the embassy.

On the opposite side of the room, a pony-wall flanked by twin columns created the illusion of a formal entry. More functional than grand, its understated design was enhanced by a set of eight-foot-tall paneled oak doors. The room had no windows, leaving me to guess what waited on the other side of the twin slabs of polished wood.

Growing accustomed to my new freedom, I tried the handle of one of the doors. The deadbolt retracted in near silence, the smooth mesh of spline and gear no less precise than that of a fine watch.

The neutral scent of the reception room was immediately overwhelmed by the fragrance of blooming jasmine and new-cut grass.

I didn't hesitate.

Standing under the covered breezeway, I took my first look at the embassy compound. In some ways, it was like pulling back the curtain on another time and place, where poverty, strife, and conflict had been eliminated.

An immense landscape of Bermuda tiff stretched out before me in manicured perfection. Accented with stately maples and huge oaks, the trees presided over curved stone pathways, their granite edges softened by low-lying hedges highlighted with rows of pink and yellow asters.

From my vantage point, it appeared the system of ornate pathways provided access to every building in the compound, including the largest and most architecturally ornate structure centered a hundred yards away. With its elaborate mix of columns and decorative façade, it was the obvious centerpiece of the embassy. Katherine had called it the "Fortress." By the end of the day, I would learn the twelve-thousand square foot reception and meeting facility was the initial arrival point for visiting dignitaries and diplomats.

The more generic structures appeared dedicated to less glamorous functions—storage rooms, the motor pool, and staff dormitories located around the perimeter of the compound.

Breaks between the buildings provided a glimpse of the nine-foot concrete wall that completely enclosed the two-acre facility. Apparently, security was tight.

While my residence hall had been empty and quiet, the outside grounds were bustling with activity. In the distance, gardeners and groundskeepers were busy cutting, trimming, and sweeping. Other personnel—campus staffers wearing navy-blue blazers, white dress shirts, burgundy ties, and tan slacks—scurried from building to building with obvious urgency.

Everyone appeared to be on a mission of importance. Even the leaves were raked with authority.

After being kidnapped from the Morrison home, I'd been a continuous prisoner—hog-tied to the floor of a van, kept under lock and key in a ratty hotel room, my every move under constant supervision. My new freedom was intoxicating.

I had to explore.

With the exception of the Fortress, the dozen or so buildings within the compound reflected the priority of utilitarian function over architectural form. The flat facades were augmented by heavy cornerstones and wide window pop-outs, the features barely breaking the basic four-square design. I imagined the interiors to be just as stark and sterile. Dull gray signage identified each structure with letters and numbers rather than purpose. Two of the buildings stood out as unusual, their large metal doors, huge strap hinges, and keypad entries offering clues to the importance of their contents. I imagined their obvious bunker-like construction provided a secure location for computers and sensitive communication equipment, especially with their banks of roof-mounted microwave dishes and exotic pendant-shaped antennas.

Without a destination in mind, I started walking the interconnecting system of pathways, wondering how long I could continue to encounter the constant stream of staffers and maintenance personnel before someone stopped me. But instead of evaluating stares and a quick order to return to my room, I was greeted with "Good morning," and the occasional, "How are you today?" Even those approaching in a distracted daze managed to break from their trance long enough to speak.

After twenty minutes of strolling the grounds, I discovered all paths eventually led to the main reception hall—the Fortress. As I stood in its growing shadow, I was fairly certain I'd arrived at the rear entrance and not the more stately façade that surely graced the front. It was, none-the-less, intimidating.

The double-door entrance was recessed behind a deep portico, and on either side, armed guards stood at attention.

I felt out of place. Everyone I'd seen, even the gardeners and maintenance personnel, conformed to a dress code. With my tan shorts and blue pullover, I appeared more like a lost stray from a tour group than the government's newest inductee. I wondered if it was a good idea to test the limits of my new freedom, especially on my first day. Even if the guards allowed me to pass, what business did I have wandering around inside the embassy's headquarters?

Several blazer-wearing, badge-brandishing staffers whizzed by me. An older gentleman in a three-piece suit took the five shallow steps leading to the portico in two short strides. None of them offered a greeting. Apparently, those with business *inside* the Fortress were far too focused on affairs of state to acknowledge a loitering vagabond.

I was ready to walk back to the residence dorm when a young woman with a ream of copy paper under her arm slowed as she approached. "Do you have an appointment? Appointments are received at the front entrance."

"No, I don't have . . . I mean, not really," I stammered.

She didn't respond. Resuming the same frenetic pace as the others, she was through the doors before I could say any more. No doubt she'd been summoned to reload the main printer, hopefully arriving in time to prevent World War III.

No longer a transparent visitor, I was beginning to feel conspicuous. The guard on the right had never taken his eyes off me.

My decision was impulsive and spontaneous. I hoped I wouldn't regret it as reckless, or brash.

I took a step, then another. Unchallenged, I walked up the stairs toward the entrance. Before I could touch the doors, they opened—not electrically from sensors—but from the immediate attention of a second set of guards, positioned inside the foyer.

"Where's your badge? It needs to be visible when entering the building."

"I didn't get a badge."

"Your destination?"

"I guess I don't have one of those either." The inside guard was immediately talking on his radio, his left hand raised like a traffic cop, indicating I was to stay right where I was.

"She's with me." The male voice came from behind.

I turned around, curious who was offering to take responsibility for my unauthorized entry into the embassy's central sanctuary.

At just over six-feet and two-hundred well-distributed pounds, he was dressed in a dark gray suit and maroon tie, his firm jaw and confident expression making him as impressive as he was attractive. His light brown hair was neatly trimmed, with no indication of a part.

I glanced down at his shoes, thinking it odd they made no sound as he approached.

Removing his aviator-style sunglasses, the guard immediately stepped back and offered a half- salute.

"I'll take a guess and assume you're the new hostess." He smiled, revealing a row of perfectly spaced, gleaming teeth.

"The only thing I'm sure of is the *new* part."

He offered his hand, the sudden flip of his jacket revealing the handle grip of an automatic pistol peeking out from a waist holster. "My name's Mark."

"Jewel."

"Let's take a walk to security. You can't go anywhere in this building without ID."

"It's all about the badges, huh?"

"Procedure and process, the government thrives on it. It's the glue that holds this place together."

"Conformity to the hive?" I asked.

He smiled again. "I presume you've met Katherine?"

I nodded. "I think I like her. At least I'm *trying* to like her." I cringed as I said it, realizing Katherine would no doubt learn what I'd just said.

"She's been on assignment here for two years. Been with the service for over fourteen. She's the best at what she does. Don't be afraid to ask her anything."

"She has all the answers?"

"It's a good place to start."

"Anything off limits?" I asked.

"She'll let you know. Of course, you may not like the answer, but don't question what you're told."

His sudden change in demeanor put me on edge. I wanted to get back to the flirty give-and take we'd had just seconds before. I'd already decided seeing more of him wouldn't be such a bad thing.

"What do you do here?" I asked.

"Work."

My first impression suggested he was placating me, dismissing me as a novice. I would learn I'd received the customary answer offered by those engaged in sensitive activities. Even seemingly benign information was distributed judiciously, with co-workers told only what they needed to know to accomplish their job.

"My new bird leave the nest?"

I recognized Katherine's voice. She was suddenly behind us. I doubted it was a coincidence.

"Just stretching her legs," Mark said. "Pretty serious infraction, though, wandering around without a badge. I suppose we should have her shot right here on the spot."

Katherine turned to me. "And now you know how important it is to always have this with you." She handed me a laminated plastic card riveted to an alligator clip. The front displayed my picture, first name, ID number, and a barcode long enough to label a double-marked-down flat-screen from Walmart. The edges were finished with a light blue security border, inset with Eagle holograms. "You'll receive several," she added. "At least two with a magnet, so you won't damage your better clothing. Remember, never wear it outside the compound. The guard will remind you to surrender it as you leave the gate. But if he's distracted, he might miss it. Outside the embassy, you're not to reveal your position or association with the government."

"It's our version of the Twilight Zone," Mark chimed in. " . . . a place that exists between shadow and doubt."

I started to ask him how long he'd been waiting to say that, then decided against it, noticing his smile had returned, interestingly, with Katherine's appearance.

Katherine pinned the badge to the upper sleeve of my pull-over. "You'll receive your thigh holster tomorrow."

"I'm going to carry a gun?" My voice carried a hint of surprise, but the idea appealed to me.

"No, dear," Katherine smiled. "It holds your badge, cell-phone, and a few essentials. You'll use it during official functions, when you're wearing a cocktail dress or evening gown."

Mark squinted, his eyes on my legs. "So that's where the girls keep them, close to their—"

"Close to their hearts," Katherine interrupted, finishing his sentence.

Probably an old joke, reserved for first-timers.

Katherine reached out and touched my arm. "Come with me. I've give you a quick tour. Mark has other business to attend to."

I looked at him, hoping he would object. Instead, he took a step back. "It was nice to meet you, Jewel. I'm sure we'll see each other again."

I mumbled goodbye as he left. Apparently, he *did* have other priorities.

"So what does Mark do here?"

Katherine's expression fell stern, as if evaluating my need to know. Apparently, she saw no harm in telling me, perhaps ready to trust me with a bit of privileged information.

"He's an outside agent . . . communications."

"You mean like a spy?"

"Like a telephone repair man."

Confusion tugged at the right corner of my mouth.

"He makes sure we have ears when we need them," she added.

I nodded, a little stunned over Katherine's ability to interpret facial cues.

"You'll learn more about this in training," she explained. "Here's the short version. Some agents work strictly on the compound. They report each day and work their assigned shift. It's no different than any other job." She paused. "And then there are the *others*, agents who have outside assignments."

Others. She'd used enough emphasis to convey the idea their jobs were steeped in clandestine subterfuge. And apparently, I had just met one of them.

I wondered if Katherine could sense my attraction to him. She seemed to be a walking antennae system, easily detecting my thoughts and intentions. *So what?* I hadn't been with a male lover of my own choosing since enjoying the forbidden delights of young Logan's lean and muscular body.

The thought began to move through me . . . the pulse-quickening anticipation of Mark's sculpted chest pressing against my breasts as he settled between my legs.

I noticed Katherine tip her head, like a bird listening to the call of its mate. Was she picking up the sudden shift in my heart rate and blood pressure? I didn't know how, but something told me she knew exactly what I was thinking.

For a split second, I considered admitting my attraction to him. It would be an attempt at girl-talk, sharing my feelings in a first-time bond with a new friend. From the look on Katherine's face, now was not the time.

I promised myself, if she ever asked, I wouldn't deny it—I wanted to fuck him.

Chapter Three

My second day started early. Katherine met me in the cafeteria for a quick breakfast, then shuffled me off to a small corner office in one of the buildings adjacent to the Fortress.

"Do you want me to take notes?"

"No, I want you to listen and learn. Here we use our memory instead of paper."

I felt my stress level rising. I'd anticipated a few challenges, and now, meeting Katherine's expectations would be one of them.

Today's lesson was brief—two hours—and consisted of an overview of the department's mission and how it operated as a "shadow" organization within the embassy's allegedly transparent political environment.

"Any questions?" she'd asked.

"How does all of this take place without someone finding out? I mean, aren't there politicians or public watchdogs for this kind of thing?"

"Always."

"And that doesn't bother you?"

She squinted at me. "Does it bother *you?*"

I decided to tell her the truth. "I could give a shit."

The left corner of her mouth lifted in frustration. "We'll have to work on that."

The rest of the day was all about the paperwork.

Looking over the shoulder of a data specialist, I verified page after page of personal online information, then watched as he methodically made revisions to reflect my new identity—one far more vague and obscure.

"We'll add a few shadows and eliminate some of the details. It's all for your safety." The guy tapping away at the keyboard—he'd introduced himself as Ronnie—was surprisingly friendly and efficient. He was also young and geeky, probably hired right out of college with a killer degree in computer science. "I'll also do a little image manipulation on the photos," he added. "The more doubt we can cast on your past identity, the less likely you'll be surprised by someone who takes an interest and tries to research your history."

"What do you mean by *takes an interest?*"

"Could be anything. Infatuation, curiosity, even someone who recognizes you from high school."

I couldn't imagine the odds of bumping into someone from San Diego, here in Thailand. He answered my question before I could ask it.

"It's rare, but it happens. I see your husband was in the Navy. Even though his discharge occurred prior to your marriage, he still keeps in touch with several of his friends from the service. Some of them you've met. The ones you haven't may have seen pictures of you. And if you ran into them, they might recognize you."

"From a picture?"

"It's the impression they formed *from* the picture. Because you're attractive, they would *want* to recognize you. If you passed them on the street, it might trigger something in their memory." He paused. "And then there's always simple fate. It's hard to predict what the future has waiting for us."

I was a living testament to that.

"But not to worry," he continued. "By the time we're finished, you'll have a new background and a plausible reason to explain your presence here. In fact, after a few weeks, you'll begin to believe it yourself."

He was erasing my past. My life before arriving at the embassy was quickly disappearing. The person I used to be no longer mattered. If there was such a thing as a new beginning, this was it.

"I need your signature on these." Katherine had re-entered the room with a handful of pre-printed forms—a government service application, medical history, and a list of family contacts. All the blanks had been filled in with bar codes.

"How do I know what these say?"

"Most of it refers to your employment, pay grade, employee rating, that sort of thing. The civil service manual doesn't contain a job description or GS rating for a hostess. Your official title and duty assignment is administrative assistant."

For all I knew, I could be signing away my citizenship. But Katherine's no-nonsense attitude confirmed I was expected to cooperate.

Katherine tucked the completed forms into a plastic file folder.

"Will I get a copy of everything?" I asked.

"What do you need it for?" Katherine snapped.

"Just asking. Force of habit, I suppose."

"They say old habits die hard," she said, then added, "Let's hope that's not the case with you."

Ronnie stopped typing. He'd heard it, too—the implied ultimatum. I almost let it go.

Turning to Ronnie, I asked, "Does she treat all the new girls this way or is she just playing hard to get?"

His face flushed deep crimson. Sexual innuendo was not one of his strong suits.

Ignoring my question, Katherine set her hand on his shoulder. "Have everything you need?"

"Yep, I'm done."

Katherine headed for the door. "This way, Jewel."

Outside, a bank of thick, gray clouds was quickly extinguishing the setting sun, the retreating orange-tinted sky coaxing the first hints of twilight from the horizon.

I checked my watch. Nearly 7:00 PM.

"Guess I lost track of the time. Are we meeting again for breakfast?"

Katherine never broke stride. "Are you hungry? If you'd like, we can grab a quick salad in the cafeteria before we continue."

"I thought we were done for the day."

"This would be an excellent time to explore the Fortress. The dayshift has left, so our presence won't be as intrusive."

"Oh."

I was tired. I'd had enough spy-school for one day. But Katherine looked like she was ready to butt heads with a buffalo.

"If it's okay with you," I said, "I think I'll pass on dinner. The sooner we get started, the better."

Chapter Four

Katherine had been right. Without the usual complement of day-staffers, the Fortress was more like a mausoleum than a citadel of international goodwill. Last night's visit had given me the opportunity to really *see* it, to completely tour the entire building, with its large formal dining room, small press theater, and bank of offices and conference rooms.

Although the primary mission of the embassy was to provide a sovereign U.S. presence, its real purpose was far more broad—and clandestine. Its function was best described by the commonly used acronym R-U-N, the letters standing for *Right Under their Nose*. The embassy compound provided a relatively safe location for operatives to receive their assignments and exchange sensitive information—far preferable to the dangerous backstreets and high-risk alleyways of the city.

The facility was larger than most. Occupying the grounds of a former Thai military installation, the U.S. had obtained it in exchange for providing Thailand with protected status, essentially making them an unofficial ally within the intelligence community. The acquisition enabled several outlying operations to be moved to this location and consolidated under a single security umbrella.

The embassy was a place where deals were struck, power and money exchanged, and the business and information community conducted less-than-transparent negotiations affecting everything from the importation of technology and weaponry to choosing the best location for a new Burger King.

Upstairs, Katherine showed me the hallway leading to the director's residence, a 1600-square- foot windowless apartment with three bedrooms, two baths, and a small study. Although designed to comfortably accommodate an average-sized family, two of the bedrooms were vacant. Preferring their children grow up in a more traditional environment, the director's wife and two daughters lived in the states, resigning themselves to a life with an absentee husband and father.

On the opposite end of the building, we toured the guest wing—six suites furnished and decorated to meet the highest expectations of visiting heads of state and their immediate staff.

"These are also often used as hospitality rooms," Katherine explained, "where you can take an important dignitary or other influential VIP for a private chat."

Apparently, this was where I would be expected to do some of my finest work.

"Most of the time," she continued, "you'll know in advance if a guest expects to be entertained. We'll do our best to brief you before they arrive, but always be prepared for the spontaneous request."

The idea of sexually accommodating a stranger took me back to the deck of the *Kelsey,* where crewmembers had taken their turn fucking me, simply because they could.

It was depressing as hell.

Katherine picked up on it immediately.

"You have a concern with something I said?" she asked.

"I suppose I'm still getting used to being a whore. You know, letting anybody fuck me, anytime, anyplace."

Katherine bristled. "Jewel, I don't ever want to hear you talk like that again. What we do here is persuasive manipulation. Sex is one of our tools. So is being a good listener or a concerned friend. We use our assets and skills to establish rapport, build relationships, and obtain information."

I hoped she didn't think I was being argumentative. "Yeah, I get all that. But the bottom line is the same. If someone asks, I'm expected to drop to my knees."

She shook her head. "The embassy is not an on-demand brothel. When someone makes a spur-of-the-moment request for sex, bring it to me. If there's a reason, and I mean a damn good one, then I'll green-light the activity. Otherwise, you'll treat an overly amorous guest like any other, using discretion, tact, and diplomacy."

"Anyone ever get upset?"

"Very seldom. But if it happens, I'll take care of it."

I heard the subtle inference of a protective mother hen. Maybe she was on my side after all. But sometimes, it was hard to tell.

This morning, my first stop was the embassy's version of an in-house counseling department—a small office tucked into the rear of the human resources building. After accepting a cup of coffee, I sat back in a large, plush chair and began my "interview" with the facility's psychologist, a lovely woman in her mid-fifties named Sherry, who began our meeting by telling me I was in for the adventure of a lifetime. When I asked her to elaborate, she simply smiled and asked if the coffee was hot enough.

I'd expected the third degree. And while her questions were surprisingly personal, they seemed relatively benign.

"Have you ever had an out-of-wedlock pregnancy?"

"Do you still carry a torch for an old boyfriend?"

"Before you were abducted, was there anyone with whom you maintained correspondence?"

I continued shaking my head, then stopped to reconsider her last question. "Does Facebook count?"

"Yes, dear. Everything counts."

"Then, no, not really. After Carl and I left the states, internet access was spotty. I got tired of using the slow public Wi-Fi, and there was too much going on in our normal life to bury my head in a computer."

I tried to remember when my life was normal. Was it only a few weeks ago? A month? I tried to recall the last time I had enjoyed my ritual Saturday morning breakfast at the Kalu restaurant, or watched the afternoon sun shimmer off the wet sand of Arugam Bay as Carl emerged from the ocean after trying unsuccessfully to ride a three-foot wave all the way to shore.

Sherry reached out and touched my hand, not offering comfort as much as wanting to make a physical connection.

"Do you miss your husband?"

Jesus, another mind reader. "After what he did to me?"

"In spite of what he did to you."

I took a deep breath, releasing it in a long sigh. "Honestly, I don't know. I could sit here and lie to you, tell you I don't care if I ever see that bastard again. But we spent a lot of time together. And at the beginning, when we were starting out, things were good."

I waited for the next question. After a few uncomfortable seconds of silence, I said, "Your turn."

Her words came with a calm and soothing rhythm. "Sounds like that part of your life is still an open chapter, needing to be resolved."

"I suppose there are some things I'd like to say to him, questions I'd like to ask."

"Ever see yourself going back to him, living together?"

That one threw me. Why would a clandestine division of the state department put me to work as a sex toy—or to use Katherine's term, a *swallow*—if I planned on returning to my husband? The idea was insane. And it pissed me off.

"Oh, yeah, I plan to hook up with him as soon as I finish my five-year hitch with the department to see if he'll take me back. Been craving for some of that fine hubby cock for weeks now."

Why the hell did I say that? She's just doing her job.

"I'm sorry," I added quickly. "Since my husband bet and lost me in a card game, I've been forced to have sex with over a dozen men. My life has been turned upside down, and I'm not sure why." I paused, hoping that would be enough. From Sherry's piercing eyes and continuing silence, I realized I would have to tell her the rest.

"When I was held captive," I continued, "I met someone. We became friends. And right now, she's in the hands of some lunatic who's wiring her up and pumping her full of electricity so he can listen to her scream." I wiped at the tear streaking down my face. "It would be nice to catch a fucking break, you know?"

Sherry reached out and tapped the back of my hand, the same way she'd done when she'd asked about Carl. "Maybe that's why you're here, Jewel. To catch a fucking break," she said, her face full of concern. "In fact, maybe this is where you were meant to be all along."

Chapter Five

The next three weeks of training were intensive and time-consuming. Anticipating a classroom setting, I was relieved to find the sessions in the form of one-on-one coaching.

With my instructors recruited from various members of the embassy staff, I watched demonstrations and roleplay in persuasion techniques, effective listening, and congruent conversation. Feedback and correction were immediate and on-the-spot. Unless I had questions or experienced difficulty with the subject, we moved on to something else. Some of my tutors spent only a few hours with me, covering particular aspects of their work having a direct influence on my duties. Others spent the entire day bombarding me with questions meant to uncover gaps in my comprehension from previous lessons.

Even the culinary staff took part in my education. During a tour of the kitchen, the chef briefed me on typical menu choices in this part of the world, and explained how agents, operatives, and staff were served dishes identical in appearance to those of the guests, but missing the additional fat and sugar typically added to enhance the flavor of the food. 'That's why you are never to offer a guest something from your plate. The difference in taste will be obvious.'

'You'll get used to it,' he'd assured me. 'And

when the guests are feeling the effects of a fat-rich gravy, you'll still be sharp-witted and light on your feet.'

Katherine handled general protocol personally, often leaving me with homework in the form of computer-based lessons designed to acquaint me with the traditions, customs, and practices of the host country. She amazed me with her expertise in bureaucratic decorum, showing me how to elegantly diffuse a potential argument between guests who had fallen into the political abyss of discussing partisan policies or radical religious sects.

Finally, I was briefed on the *two-faces* strategy, which advocated the practice of appearing politically correct and above suspicion while effectively accomplishing the business at hand, even when the "business" was in direct violation of the host country's laws.

I found the training process interesting, and I tried to be a good student. Yet, I was constantly distracted by thoughts of Annie. I kept telling myself she was still alive, and that once I established the contacts and resources I needed, I would be able to help her.

Chapter Six

Katherine was making an unusual night visit. It wasn't a bed-check—the room's infrared and motion sensors provided a constant update on occupancy. I'd stopped myself from asking about video cameras. I didn't want to put Katherine in the unpleasant position of admitting my every move was being monitored.

Like all of Katherine's visits, she was there for a specific purpose. This would be the final briefing before my first official shift on the main floor of the embassy—a cocktail party followed by a formal dinner.

I was more than a little nervous. At first, I had no idea why Katherine thought I was ready to attend—and perform—at an official function. She'd assured me this was the perfect situation for my debut. Even so, I was certain this was some kind of test to evaluate how I would handle myself in a public social setting.

I had to admit, part of me found the idea exciting. I was bored with the training. I wanted to end the pretend roleplay sessions and do something real. I'd even caught myself fantasizing about the conversations I would have with guests, using charm and flirtatious banter to create a positive buzz about the *new girl* at the embassy. And while I wouldn't let her know it, I wanted Katherine to be proud of me.

"Any last minute advice?" I asked.

"Keep the conversation flowing by asking questions," Katherine said. "Then listen to learn more about the guests."

"You'll give me some ideas of what to talk about, what subjects to avoid . . . right?"

"It doesn't work that way," she said, shaking her head. "You can't approach a guest with a preconceived agenda. Your job is to make them comfortable, and talkative. Above all, be aware of everything going on around you."

"How many guests are expected?"

"Around two hundred. About eighty percent will be men."

"And you'll be there, too?"

"Yes, and so will Marcie. She's back from an off-campus assignment. You'll meet her before tonight's event."

At least I wasn't being thrown into the lion's den alone. I felt some of the pressure lift.

"And Jewel, this is important. When introducing yourself, only offer your first name. If someone asks for your last name, you will provide your alias . . . Harlow."

"Harlow? Really?"

I remembered my father talking about Jean Harlow, a film star and sex symbol from the thirties and, at the time, a vampy seductress without equal.

"A lot of foreign nationals are American film buffs. It could provide an immediate topic of conversation."

"But the reference is so dated. You think people will get it?"

"Americans underestimate the influence of our entertainment industry on the rest of the world. For many, it's a source of fascination, and it isn't limited to a single generation or era."

"So, am I supposed to be related?"

"You can allude to the remote possibility, but only for the purpose of creating a sexual undertone."

I didn't like the idea and I wanted her to know it. "We never talked about changing my name."

"It's part of establishing your new identity. I saw no point in bringing it up until you were ready to start meeting embassy visitors."

Tomorrow night's dinner was beginning to feel more like a marriage ceremony . . . a formal affair complete with my assumption of a new last name.

"What if a guest asks about my background, my family? Do I use the department bio?"

Katherine's disappointment was obvious. "It's not the department's bio. It's *yours*. From now on, it's who you are."

I'd memorized the specifics of my newly-created persona. But it still seemed alien, as if belonging to someone else. That worried me. If I hadn't been able to convince myself it was real, how could I convince others?

"Now listen carefully." Katherine waited long enough to create a dramatic pause. "If you find yourself in an awkward situation or if a guest asks you a question you don't know how to answer, bring your left hand up and touch your ear. Someone will approach you and interrupt your conversation."

"How long will that take?" I was beginning to feel panicky again.

"Marcie and I, and at least a half-dozen staffers wear ear-buds. One of us will always be close by."

"Here's your assignment." Katherine handed me a letter-sized envelope. As I took it, I made contact with her wrist. The touch surprised both of us.

Maybe it was nerves, needing to connect with her to calm myself. Whatever the reason, my next move was completely spontaneous.

I leaned in and kissed her on the cheek. "Thanks, Katherine."

She immediately pulled back.

"What's wrong?" I asked.

"When you can show affection without requiring it in return, then you can come to me. But not before."

Still in training mode, she was using a moment of vulnerability to prove a point. I had kissed her out of need, wanting her approval, hoping she would respond the same way. And from her perspective, that was unacceptable.

She'd rejected my honest affection and it hurt, even though I understood why she'd done it. After a few seconds, I realized she was waiting for me to break the silence.

"I think I understand," I said.

She tilted her head slightly to the side. "Convince me."

"There's a big difference between my own needs and the needs of others. I have to learn to keep them separate and not get them confused, even when I'm lonely . . . or horny."

Katherine looked pleased. "You're going to do well."

She brought her hand to my face and brushed the side of my cheek. My breath caught in my chest, a surge of adrenalin setting my heart to pound. The thought of pulling her close overwhelmed me. Instead, I remained still, looking into her eyes, hoping her powers of acuity were working overtime.

They were.

As she pressed her full lips gently against mine, I opened my mouth, giving her tongue access. Instead, she pulled back again.

"Crap! Is this another lesson?"

This time, it didn't hurt, though her insistence on pulling my strings was more than frustrating.

She smiled softly. "I want you to enjoy yourself. But never let it stop you from listening, or from learning. The goal is to remember everything when you're in the presence of a guest, regardless of the nature of your activity. And when I say *everything,* I'm talking bigger picture, including their tone of voice, gestures, and facial expressions. Can you do that, Jewel?"

"Yes," I answered without hesitation.

She walked to the door, then turned to face me. "You know, I asked that same question of the girl you replaced. In fact, this was her room."

"What was her answer?"

"I'll try."

Chapter Seven

I hadn't slept much. Nervous about tonight's party, I'd met with Katherine over lunch for some last minute advice. But I still had a strong case of the butterflies.

"Be on the floor at 6:15," Katherine reminded me. "Guests will begin arriving at seven. We'll use the forty-five minutes to go over any final details."

"Anyone specific you want me to pay attention to?"

"Not this time. Consider it a dry run. Have fun with it. As you chat with the guests, ask yourself what you could be doing to give them a better experience."

Seeming to know how uneasy I felt, she added, "If you run out of talk or don't know what to say, smile and wait for the other person to speak. A little silence can be very powerful. It often conveys the idea you can be trusted."

"Expecting anyone important?" I wondered if I would have the opportunity to meet the president of a first world nation or a notorious dictator from South America.

"Tonight it's mostly low-level politicians and vendor clients. We have a firm guest list, but there are always a few tag-alongs. The guard reports any *black sheep* from the front gate. We pull a quick bio and, unless it's someone known to be a problem, we generally allow them in. It's good PR, and occasionally we pick up a new contact on the outside."

From my orientation, I knew what she meant by a *quick bio*. Every person not on the guest list had to be vetted to determine the security risk, and it had to be done in ninety seconds—approximately the time it took to drive through the entry gate and briefly stop the vehicle in the "safety net," where ground-mounted sensors swept the underside of the car for explosives and electronics. And while a minute-and-a-half was plenty of time to complete a background search, the guest's political and philosophical alliances also had to be "interactively scanned" to determine the likelihood of volatile exchanges with other guests.

Katherine was suddenly on her feet, waving at someone on the other side of the cafeteria. "There's Marcie. I want you to meet her before you leave."

I turned and saw a tall, well-proportioned brunette waving back. As she headed in our direction, she seemed to float between the tables, her stride so smooth I didn't see a ripple of movement on any part of her body.

She appeared to be in her late-twenties, yet radiated a kind of flawless beauty that transcended age. Her pretty face was framed by copper-tone shades of silky hair flowing soft and light across her bare sun-kissed shoulders. The thigh-high hemline of her sundress revealed shapely, muscular legs, their deep tan contrasting against the light fabric in such a way that questioned her need for clothing at all. I was awestruck, marveling at such rare genetic handiwork.

She was earthy.

Sexy.

Perfect.

The way she greeted Katherine surprised me. Grabbing her in a close hug, Marcie bared her teeth and let out a *grrrrrr*, as if ready to throw Katherine on the table and give her a good tongue-fucking. It wasn't until Katherine began pushing her away that Marcie finally let go, playfully air-pinching at her nipples, leaving no doubt what was on her mind.

Turning to face me, her bangs fell forward over dusty blue eyes as a smile gently parted her full, pink lips. "Hi, I'm Marcie."

I offered my hand. Instead of grasping it in a handshake, she wrapped her fingers around it and pulled me close, her breasts and mine pleasantly jousting for space.

"Welcome to the zoo," she added.

"Jewel will be joining us on the floor tonight," Katherine said. "It's her debut."

Marcie stepped back and swept my body with her eyes. "The guests are gonna go nuts over you."

I didn't know what to say. Remembering Katherine's advice, I smiled, waiting for one of them to speak.

"Jewel came out of a rough situation," Katherine said. "But she's done well in training and is on her way to becoming a valuable department asset."

Marcie softened her eyes, her smile becoming sincere. "That's embassy-speak for giving good head."

"Marcie, others can hear you!" Katherine scolded.

Although her voice didn't carry the tone of a real reprimand, as our superior, she *had* to chastise her. But I had the impression there was a lot of truth in Marcie's street-wise summary.

Marcie released me and reached back for Katherine, planting a quick kiss on her cheek. "Sorry, sweetie."

Katherine was becoming perturbed, but to me, Marcie's disregard for embassy decorum was a breath of fresh air. I knew Katherine didn't want the administrative staff to witness a lack of discipline among the already nebulous intentions of hospitality personnel.

With a hint of frustration in her voice, Katherine said, "I'll leave you two to get better acquainted. Jewel, you can ask Marcie anything you'd like, because God help us, I know she'll tell you anyway. And Marcie, try not to overwhelm. Jewel's a keeper. We don't want to scare her away."

"Will I see you later, before dinner?" Marcie asked.

"I'm swamped, but I'll find a few minutes to go over your assignment." Katherine began backing away from the table. Leveling a stern expression toward Marcie, she motioned toward me and mouthed the words, "Be nice."

Marcie responded with a wide smile, her gorgeous mouth revealing perfect, white teeth. "I missed you, too."

Katherine gave up. Turning her back to us, she appeared to have met her match.

"What was that all about?" I asked.

"It's just flirtatious banter. Katherine does her best to keep up appearances, and she knows I would never intentionally embarrass her in front of a superior. But I've never thought of her as my boss. She's too hot for that."

"So you and Katherine . . . have been together?"

She chuckled. "No, though I've made the offer plenty of times. She keeps playing the same old record, saying it could jeopardize her judgment in determining which assignments to give me. I think there's a concern—and I mean someone else's concern—of Katherine losing her objectivity, becoming protective of her girls rather than using them to best advantage."

Over the next half hour, Marcie and I shared our impressions of the embassy staff, how our jobs were such an alternative from the normal work-a-day-world we grew up in, and how she'd quickly adapted to a sex-positive mindset.

"Sometimes I enjoy it, but mostly it's a job," she said. "Occasionally, I'll have an extremely *challenging* assignment." She grimaced. "That's code for fat and gross," she added. "Then I cue up an old Journey song in my head, crank up the volume as loud as I can, and move my body to the beat. I keep replaying it until the guy is finished."

"And that works?"

"It gets me through it." Her smile vanished, her somber eyes betraying the happy-go-lucky tone of her voice. "Sometimes, that's all we can do. Find a way to get through it."

Marcie set her hand on my arm, lightly stroking my skin. "I'll come to your room a few minutes before the shuttle arrives," she whispered. "We can go together."

I let out a deep breath. "Yeah, I'd like that."

Chapter Eight

Thinking a workout would help lower the stress, I changed clothes and headed for the gym. I figured a couple miles on the treadmill and twenty minutes on the elliptical would either settle my stomach or send me running to the bathroom. Based on the knot building in my gut, I wasn't sure which way it would go.

Adjusting the machine to a slow jog, I thought back to my conversation with Marcie. In many ways she was a living symbol of the embassy's covert "two-faces" policy. With her bubbly, outgoing personality icing a killer face and body, she was as disarming as she was contagious. Her charm drew others to her like a magnet, and yet, I also knew her behavior was carefully orchestrated to accomplish a plotted agenda.

But I wasn't judging her. Criticizing her motives, choices, and actions would only add the word *hypocrite* to the long list of my own faults. More important, I liked her. She was smart, with a vocabulary reeking of advanced degrees in literature and political science. What brought her here, performing the work of a glorified social lubricant, was a question I planned to ask—someday.

After ninety minutes of jogging in place, I needed a shower. I hadn't planned to burn up so much of the afternoon in the gym, but the rush of endorphins had done the trick. I felt better. With three hours left before Marcie's arrival, I wanted plenty of time to get ready and practice my rapport techniques.

Within seconds of opening the door to my room, I knew I'd had a visitor. A black cocktail dress was spread on the bed, next to a pair of four-inch heels. More than a strong suggestion, it left no doubt of my attire for the evening.

The shoes had come from my closet, but the dress was new. Based on the color and fabric, it conveyed simple elegance, allowing me to blend in with the other female guests.

Then I held it up to the mirror. Apparently, blending in was not on the agenda.

The back was open and cut nearly to the butt. Holding it against me, the hem fell just above mid-thigh—barely enough to cover my holster, which I would position to avoid revealing its outline through the fabric. It made me wonder how female agents managed to get through an entire day carrying a loaded automatic next to their pussy. Even with a carbon-polymer frame, the loaded 9MM pocket pistols weighed nearly two pounds. I made a mental note to ask Katherine how she mastered the art of walking with a concealed firearm between her legs. She denied ever carrying a weapon, but I had my suspicions, especially when she left the compound.

I'd intentionally avoided opening the envelope Katherine had given me. Although it contained my duty assignment, seeing it in black-and-white would make it official, removing any doubt how my life had changed, and what I had become. I felt like a nine-year-old with a bad report card, knowing I'd done poorly in arithmetic, and not wanting to see the "F" that would confirm it.

Tearing the seal, I noticed most of the form was blank. Katherine's intention was to familiarize me with the process. I had been designated a "floater," instructed to move from guest to guest, welcoming couples and single men as they left the receiving line. My main job was to introduce them to others, making sure they were actively involved in conversation before repeating the process with someone new. After the last guest had been greeted, I was to revisit everyone I'd met, asking if I could refill their drink and, most important, determine if they appeared comfortable with the people they were with. If I sensed they were ready to move on, I would express the need to introduce them to others, and take them by the arm to another couple or foursome, hoping to find a better social match.

Katherine again reminded me to pay attention to every conversation, and to be especially mindful of discussions involving career advancements, new relationships, changing political ties, and financial involvements. No matter how innocuous it might seem at the time, a year from now, a simple reference to a name, a place, or a past event could prove crucial in "connecting the dots."

It seemed simple.

Easy.

REDEMPTION

Safe.
So why was I shaking?

Chapter Nine

Marcie knocked twice before walking in. "Ready? Katherine doesn't like it when we're late."

I took a last glance in the mirror.

"Screw the mirror, look at me," Marcie commanded.

I turned toward her and curtsied.

She studied me from top to bottom. "Jesus, girl, you're hot. I'd do you right now if we had the time."

Even with her obvious attributes, the thought hadn't crossed my mind. True, Marcie was drop-dead gorgeous, but something was missing. Although I enjoyed being around her, I didn't feel that sexual spark.

The shuttle was already waiting for us in front of the dorm. The uniformed driver—his muscles challenging the seams of his jacket—was immediately on his feet, greeting us with an abbreviated salute and offering his hand as we slid onto the bench seat.

"Crawl speed, Mr. Scott," Marcie said. "And mind what the wind does to our hair."

"Yes, ma'am."

I glanced at Marcie. "I'm nervous about tonight. I don't feel ready for this. What if I get into trouble?"

She slid her arm around my shoulder. "Think of it as prom night. You have the jitters because you don't know what to expect. After you've done a half-dozen of these, you'll be doing mind games to pass the time."

"But Katherine *did* ask you to keep an eye on me, right? So I don't screw up and set off an international crisis?"

"That she did." There was a hint of pride in her voice, as if she'd been elected senior class president. "And she'll ask you to do the same for the next new recruit," she added.

"I feel like a thirteen-year-old whose parents think I still need a babysitter. I'm sorry you have to put up with me. You have your own assignment to worry about."

"You're so sexy when you're vulnerable." Marcie's coy smile was well-practiced. "Want to give Commander Scott here a little show before he drops us off?"

"Marcie! Shush, we're supposed be working. And besides, he shouldn't be hearing this."

She pointed to a tiny console built into the roof of the shuttle. She came close to touching it, but avoided actual contact. "That shiny glass button is a camera. Right now, the boys in surveillance are making odds on whether or not I lay one on you before we arrive at the main hall."

I'd forgotten. The idea of privacy was an alien concept behind the embassy walls, making every aspect of our lives an open book.

Marcie slumped her shoulders, her disappointed sigh purposefully exaggerated. "I was hoping you'd take the hint. Guess I'll have to take my chances."

I was envisioning a group of horny guys, all hunkered over a bank of monitors, when I realized Marcie was leaning in. Cradling my chin in her hand, she pressed her lips against mine.

I didn't resist, but I didn't encourage her, either.

She parted with enough suction to produce a loud *smack*. Grinning directly into the camera, she said, "Okay, guys, pay off the winners." Lowering her voice to a whisper, she added, "Bunch of geeky bozos, probably have to scrape the cum off the computer screens after every shift."

She dabbed at my smeared lipstick—her kiss more than a quick peck, and the evidence was obvious. "You're going to do fine," she whispered. "Katherine gave you the signal asking for help, right?"

A rush of anxiety heightened my voice. "Touch my ear and return my hand to my side."

"Good. Don't hesitate to use it. I'll never be more than a few seconds away."

"Won't it look obvious?" I asked. "Like some guy flapping the hell out of a set of semaphore flags?"

"Not really. You'll be amazed how easily you can work it in without anyone noticing. Most will think it's just another innocuous gesture."

"I know you and Katherine will be there tonight, but in general, who comes to my rescue if both of you are out of town?"

"Katherine's official duty station is the embassy. It's very rare for her to work off-grounds. So ninety-nine percent of the time, she's on the floor during official functions. In fact, some of the staffers call her The Shadow."

I raised my eyebrows. "And that's because . . . ?"

"She blends into the crowd, becoming invisible. Then she appears out of nowhere, as if instantly teleported to where she's needed the most."

In spite of her reference to Katherine as some kind of humanoid alien, I felt better. Marcie and Katherine would be watching over me, ready to jump in if I froze or found myself in an awkward position.

I sat back, letting the breeze tickle my face. I wasn't sure what the rest of the night would bring, but I wouldn't let it worry me. I'd faced far more stressful situations, and compared to the hell I'd endured on the *Kelsey*, this would be a carriage ride in the park.

I covered Marcie's hand with mine, not to encourage her, but to let her know I was glad she was here. Right now, she was the second closest thing I had to a friend. Annie would always come first, regardless of how the future unfolded.

Arriving at the steps of the Fortress, the driver escorted us to the front entrance. The outside guards took a half-step back and the doors opened on cue.

Even though I'd seen the lobby a dozen times, with its comfortable couches, ornate side tables, and elevated reception counter, tonight it gleamed from the extra efforts of the maintenance staff. American and Thai flags hung from the ceiling, and floral bouquets topped any surface larger than a few square feet. Color-coordinated tapestry complemented several large Dhurrie rugs, strategically placed in honor of a large contingent of representatives from India. Even the self-serving display of the State Magazine on several of the tables—usually reserved for employees of the Department—could not distract from the obvious statement of welcome.

Across the lobby, a set of double doors provided access to the main gathering room, a three-thousand-square-foot banquet facility equipped with a portable dance floor, small stage, and a podium. As Marcie and I entered, I noticed the center room divider—used to partition the space for smaller affairs—was compressed against the walls. Tonight the entire room was being utilized.

Sixteen rectangular tables, each accommodating fourteen guests, were set with white linen and official place settings emblazoned with the official seal of the United States. Two matching crystal vases with sprays of roses, lilies, and leafy greenery served as centerpieces. On the far side of the room, near the stage and the permanently struck colors, the traditional round four-top table was set with a bible, a black napkin, a single red rose, and a yellow candle. Although not an official requirement of State Department protocol, the director insisted a table be reserved for prisoners of war and the missing in action at all embassy events.

On both sides of the lobby, bartenders were setting up their stations with bags of ice and a supply of olives, limes, salt, and sugar. Underneath the bars, a stock of premium liquor waited to loosen tongues and calm nerves.

Katherine motioned to us from the other side of the room. With heels clicking in unison, we crossed the dance floor hand-in-hand.

"You're running a little late." Katherine's greeting was short and to the point. "In the future, consider arriving a few minutes early," she added. "I like the floor fully staffed at least half an hour before the arrival of guests."

Marcie squeezed my hand. "It's my fault," she fibbed. "I was late getting to Jewel's room, and I let the girl talk go on too long. It won't happen again."

Maybe it was my imagination, but something was up. Katherine seemed edgy and preoccupied. I wanted to ask if everything was okay. Marcie's intuitive radar must have sensed my concern. She tightened her grip, her way of telling me to keep my questions to myself.

"Any last words of encouragement?" I asked.

"Is that something you need?" Katherine's eyes were unwavering.

I bristled, ready to fire back an insult of equal intensity. Katherine's response seemed especially sharp-tongued. For the last three weeks, I'd been indoctrinated with a team mindset. We were supposed to take care of each other, support each other's efforts, and right now, I wasn't feeling the love.

Again, I felt the press of Marcie's hand. She was signaling me to forget it. I didn't know what the problem was, but there was no point in becoming part of it. Instead of countering her attack with one of my own, I offered an honest assessment of what I was feeling.

"I'm a little nervous. But I can handle it . . . keeps me focused, on my toes."

"Good," Katherine said. "All I expect from you is to be polite and charming. In other words, be yourself."

I swallowed hard. She saw it.

"Jewel, I'm here if you need me. I'll be monitoring your conversations, and I'll never be more than a few seconds away."

There wasn't a hint of challenge in her voice. In her own way, Katherine was giving me her vote of confidence.

"Wearing your holster?" she asked.

"Yep. Right next to my . . . heart."

I hoped to see a smile. But Katherine was suddenly distracted, as if listening to a discussion outside the immediate vicinity. I realized someone was talking in her earbud.

She nodded at me. "You're coming through fine," she said. Security had just confirmed the signal strength of my body wire, a tiny audio transmitter built into my thigh holster. With a range of five-hundred feet, my conversations could be monitored anywhere within the confines of the Fortress.

"Will the mic be on all the time?"

"Yes, and tonight, everything will be recorded," Katherine explained. "For training purposes."

I felt like a novice, required to wear an electronic leash because I was new and too green to be trusted. Marcie must have picked up on my frustration.

She pulled me close. "Big Brother is always listening," she whispered.

"You too?" I asked.

"No one's immune," she said.

"Everyone working the floor wears a wire," Katherine confirmed. "Surveillance is standard procedure for all interactions between personnel and guests."

Standard procedure. Another term meaning *that's the way it is, no exceptions, get used to it.* Still, the idea of someone listening to every word, even the silly, off-handed comments I might make, was a bit unnerving.

Katherine looked toward the room's entrance. "I have an unexpected situation to deal with. Both of you, follow me to the conference room. Marcie, I need to update you on a last minute guest. Jewel, I want you to hear this, too."

We huddled in front of a monitor as Katherine typed in her password. A few clicks of the mouse brought up a picture of a burly, middle-aged man with a receding hair line. The next shot showed him dressed in jeans, a white shirt, and tan corduroy jacket. The caption described him as Charles Weston, 51, widowed for ten years, with one college-age daughter. As the owner of a large machine tool company based in Chicago, he managed over two hundred employees in three locations. Conservative, with a strong work ethic, his financial portfolio was missing the typical extravagant possessions of those with a personal income of over a million dollars a year. The only exception was his five-acre gated estate on Lake Geneva. He was a perfect example of the American success story, and yet, based on his relatively blue-collar status, I wondered why the department had an interest in him.

"He arrived this afternoon," Katherine began. "He was on his way to China to negotiate deals with several large manufacturing companies. He thinks this stopover is a federal requirement to obtain the necessary approval to do business with Asian manufacturers."

"It's not?" I asked.

Katherine's hesitation gave Marcie permission to answer for her. "It's a ploy. We sidetrack business owners, agents, anyone buying and selling, so we can talk to them, find out more about their plans and determine if there's any advantage to influencing their activities."

"We can do that?"

Without answering, Katherine pointed to the monitor, redirecting my attention to Weston's image on the monitor. "He buys electronic controls for automated tooling systems. His customers run the gamut from auto manufacturers to consumer appliance companies, anyone who turns raw steel into a finished product using large-scale mass production. Marcie, this is your assignment for the evening."

Marcie's expression fell serious as she studied the image on the monitor.

Katherine continued with a quick review of Weston's contacts in China, including a few buzz words for Marcie to use in conversation.

I still didn't understand why our government had any interest in the owner of a machine tool business. He didn't strike me as remarkable or as having any political influence. In fact, from Katherine's description, he seemed as far removed from politics as you could get.

My curiosity finally got the best of me. "Is this guy involved with the Soviets?"

"No, dear. We want him involved with us."

"So we can beat the Ruskies to the punch, right? 'Cause he's invented some kind of secret manufacturing equipment and we want it for ourselves?"

Marcie held back a chuckle.

I felt my cheeks flush from embarrassment.

Katherine turned to Marcie. "I realize we're throwing you into the fire without a chance to rest from your trip, but we weren't expecting Weston for several weeks. His visit took us by surprise. We've had previous contact with him, but that was nearly a year ago, and since then, there's been very little progress. We arranged this meeting at the last minute. He thinks he's here to obtain import licensing."

"And none of that is true?" I asked.

"Of course not. But he'll never know that."

"Sounds a little sneaky," I said, "getting him here under false pretenses."

"It's all in how you look at it," Katherine began. "We simply want his attention for a few hours to explain our position and make him an offer. There's real benefit for business owners who decide to work with us."

Marcie jumped in. "Maybe if Jewel understood the overall purpose of the program, at least the basics, it would make more sense to her."

Katherine was pressed for time, and giving me a quick rundown of a complex and confidential program could be more confusing than helpful. She looked at her watch. "Okay, here's the short version. Many of China's largest and best companies are ready to compete for American business. But there are only a few of them designated as *friendly*, meaning they've been granted privileged status. They receive our help in procuring new clients and, in return, they give us an open look at their customer base . . . who's buying what and how much of it. Think of it as industry espionage, without all the cloak-and-dagger."

"So there are only certain companies you want Weston to do business with?"

"Weston's business is an important bargaining chip," Katherine continued. "In return for placing his orders with one of our friendlies, he'll receive tax breaks and a "look the other way" attitude when it comes to certain financial aspects of his company's operation."

She saw the confusion on my face.

"The arrangement may sound a bit unethical at first, but no one is harmed and all parties derive some benefit. For example, when Weston agrees to work with one of our recommended suppliers, he won't have to worry about a tax audit or a call from the Fair Trade Commission." She paused. "All in all, it's a good deal for a man who sees the advantages in cooperating with his country."

There it was, the Foreign Preferred Vendor Program, delivered with a splash of patriotism. The fact that our government offered favors to both sides of the fence in exchange for information wasn't as much a surprise as *where* the activity was being conducted—under the roof of a United States Embassy.

"But what if Weston doesn't agree?" I asked.

"Not an option," Katherine said. "If we encounter reluctance, we up the ante and stay persistent. There's always something we can do to change his mind. A year ago, we offered to help him by structuring his buy-sell agreements with Chinese law."

"What'd he say?"

"He wasn't interested. Said he had lawyers for that sort of thing. Truth of the matter is, he doesn't trust us. So we've decided to take a different approach, present him with another reason to take us seriously." She glanced at Marcie.

"What's the best approach?" Marcie asked. "Family? Hobbies? Or do I go for the honeypot?"

"Honeypot?" I asked.

Katherine smiled. "It's a slang term. It means getting to the bottom line using our obvious skills to persuade and motivate." She paused for a moment, providing instructions to Marcie. "I think he'll be more likely to respond to someone who appears cut from the civilian side of the fence, less trained, less polished. Can you tone it down a bit?"

"Dialing it back as we speak." Marcie tilted her head, as if resetting her personality to a less spirited level.

"And Jewel," Katherine continued, "there's no harm in you shadowing Marcie, at least for the first few minutes."

The prospect of watching Marcie use seduction to elicit a stranger's cooperation brought a wave of nervous excitement. "What do you want me to do?"

"Try influencing the conversation, use body language to reinforce Marcie's dialogue, confirm it as truthful."

Katherine directed her attention to Marcie. "We know he's talking to a couple of electronics manufacturers, obtaining quotes for circuit boards and computer interface modules for his machines. Do you know what those are?"

"Not a clue."

"Hmm." Katherine's lips drew thin. "Maybe this will help. He needs a company to build electronic controls that will allow his machinery to be operated by computer. Can you remember that?"

"Controls that let a computer run his machines. Got it."

Katherine' expression made it clear she was concerned over Marcie's shallow understanding of Weston's industry. But there was no time for a crash course to bring her up to speed.

"This guy's smart, isn't he?" Marcie asked.

"And suspicious," Katherine added. "The only advice I can offer is to treat him as if he's the best in the business. This type of man rarely has an opportunity to receive recognition. Making him feel important might get him to lower his guard, make him more receptive."

Katherine looked at both of us. "Any more questions?"

Neither one of us spoke.

"Good. Let's go to work."

Chapter Ten

I'd hoped the room would fill quickly, making it easier to approach guests before moving to the next group. I should have known better. Like most of the activities under the embassy roof, the rate of arrival was controlled.

At exactly five minutes to seven, the director, ranking members of his staff, and their wives in residence took their place in the receiving line. About twenty strong, it was an expected ritual of every official function.

Outside the room, early arrivals milled around the lobby. A few VIP's had asked to be sequestered in one of the private conference rooms to wait in reserved comfort. Seclusion from the less privileged was an expected courtesy, and associating with the rank and file was only done after being greeted by their equals. In my opinion, those requiring such treatment were pompous, conceited assholes. Of course, Katherine had her own way of explaining it— accommodating pretentious and attention-seeking bureaucrats was an important part of international protocol.

The opening of the doors filled the room with sudden chatter. Marcie slipped her hand around my arm and drew me close. "We'll approach those exiting the receiving line together. After we have a conversation started, I'll leave and go to the next group. You stay behind for a few minutes."

"Why?" I didn't like the idea of being cut loose and forced to function on my own so soon.

"To keep the dialogue going. Ask questions of those who haven't had a chance to talk. Some of these windbags are so used to hearing their own voice, they never let anyone else get a word in edgewise. After you see the group is on a roll, excuse yourself and join me at the next one, then we'll repeat the process."

"What about Weston?"

"Katherine makes first contact, then she'll bring him to us."

As if summoned by the mention of her name, Katherine was suddenly floating across the room, shifting between a trio of military brass and a handful of local dignitaries. I didn't know it at the time, but in addition to her regular duties, she also discretely accepted invitations from high-ranking officials needing a little private time—with or without their wives. Her maturity, intelligence, and obvious physical attributes made her companionship a highly sought-after benefit, especially by representatives from the host country, who felt their status granted them special privileges.

Marcie motioned to several couples exiting the receiving line. "Time to get busy."

I took a deep breath. I should have been nervous, or at least worried about remembering when to offer my hand or simply smile and graciously lower my head in respect. But for some reason, I felt centered, ready. My mind went back to my conversation with the house shrink on the first day of orientation. She'd suggested I was right where I was meant to be.

Maybe she was right.

Marcie was two steps ahead. I picked up the pace, not wanting others to see me trailing behind. I'd taken less than a dozen steps when I felt a tug on my arm. I had to stop. Ignoring it would be rude.

It was Katherine, her smile forced, her shoulders stiff—a very different woman from the one I'd seen working the floor only minutes before.

"Jewel, there's a change in plans," she said.

"How so?" I felt my heart suddenly beating against my chest.

"While the three of us were in the conference room, I mentioned I was waiting for some new intel. I just received it. We have to shuffle things around a bit."

Shuffle things around a bit? That sounded like code for 'You're not going to like this.'

"An Indian official," Katherine continued, "a man named Sekar Joshi, has entered the compound. Previously, he'd sent his regrets, but apparently, he rearranged his schedule."

"Why is that a problem?"

"He's expecting to see Marcie."

"She's right over there." I motioned to where Marcie was now standing with four others, her face lit up like Vegas neon, chatting up a storm.

"No, he doesn't want to see her on the floor. He wants to spend time with her privately. In fact, he expects it."

My victory over an anticipated attack of nerves was short lived. My stomach was flip-flopping, anxious worry chipping away at my confidence. I had no idea what she would say next, but I was sure it would involve me. Marcie and I were the only two girls on the floor, and the demands on Katherine's schedule were already overwhelming. Newbie or not, I was all she had.

I had to show her I could handle it—no matter what she threw at me. "What do you want me to do?"

"I need you to take over Marcie's assignment."

I realized I was chewing my bottom lip, a habit I'd picked up onboard the *Kelsey*. I stopped myself, hoping Katherine had interpreted it as nervous tension and not crippling fear.

"I know it's a lot to ask," she continued, "but we're up against a wall. I can't leave Weston alone, unescorted. He's a priority, and . . ." She glanced toward the double doors. "He's here."

The small amount of resistance keeping my stomach at bay was threatening to surrender. I couldn't let Katherine—or anyone else—see it. "I need to run to the restroom," I managed.

"Make it quick. Then come right back. I'll stay with him until you return."

I nodded and high-tailed it down the hall.

The bathroom was empty. If I did toss my cookies, no one would see it. Bent at the waist, I hovered over the toilet bowl. Too nervous to eat, I'd skipped lunch, leaving my empty gut to produce a few dry belches.

I had to get through this, find a way to bring my confidence back. Maybe a few sips of vodka to take the edge off—

It hit me all at once . . . Annie's face, leaning down to kiss me, her hands, reaching out to take mine. The memory broke me into two distinct pieces—one for me, the other for her. We'd promised to take care of each other, to pull each other through the worst kind of hell, even if we weren't together. But my brand of misery couldn't compare to hers. And the fact that I had let fear and doubt get the best of me was unacceptable.

I was struggling over the prospect of meeting a man—a man who expected me to fuck him. As far as I knew, that's all I would have to do. Annie didn't have that luxury. I seriously doubted she'd been offered the opportunity to dull her senses with alcohol before Gregory wired her up and shattered her heart into a thousand pieces.

I stood in front of the mirror, wiping my eyes. "I swear to God, Annie, I'll find you. And if that monster has hurt you, I'll kill him."

The bathroom was empty, yet I was sure someone was listening. There wasn't a single room in the entire building not populated with microphones. So now they knew.

I wanted Gregory Housing dead.

I drew in a breath and blew it out. I would do exactly what these people asked me to do, and when the time was right, I would expect their help in return.

Chapter Eleven

Our initial meeting was awkward—for both of us.

"Hi, Mr. Weston, my name is Jewel." I heard my voice crack.

"Please, call me Charlie." He slipped a hand into his pocket. He wasn't comfortable.

I began with some benign chit-chat, asking about his flight, the weather back home, if he'd had a chance to see much of Bangkok. It wasn't long before I'd run out of questions, and apparently, he didn't have any.

"Charlie, I've been talking your ear off, and I'm getting the impression you could use a break. Would you like me to get you a drink?"

He thought for a moment, as if not sure how to answer. Finally, he said, "I'm going to be honest with you. I'm not exactly sure what I'm doing here. Some of your people want to meet with me in the morning, but this dinner, all these people . . . this is way out of my league."

I offered a big grin. "Charlie, you'd be surprised to learn how many others here are thinking the same thing."

That did it. He began telling about his business, how he enjoyed the occasional fishing trip to Colorado, and in a surprisingly candid moment, how much he missed his wife.

REDEMPTION

My short but intensive training in international politics and social decorum was completely unnecessary as far as Charlie was concerned. A graduate from the school of hard knocks, he was unsophisticated by society's standards. And while forthright in his speech and actions, I saw a bit of the gentlemen in him. He wasn't grabby, always called me *ma'am*, and told me he'd worn the better of his two suits to attend this "big time government meeting"—the same one he wore to church on Sunday mornings.

I hadn't intended to reveal my newbie status, but with Charlie's matter-of-fact attitude, I was certain I could make it work in my favor.

"Charlie, I need to tell you something. I don't feel right with you not knowing the truth."

He stiffened, immediately on guard. "What do you mean? Has someone been lying to me?"

"No, Charlie, I'm talking about me. I was just hired a few weeks ago as an embassy hostess and I'm brand new at this. Frankly, I'm a little nervous."

There it was. A smile as big as a star-lit sky—the same sky I could easily imagine him sleeping under. "Alright. You came clean with me, so I guess it's only right I return the favor."

I leaned in, suggesting he could confide in me.

"Like I said before, I don't know why I'm here. I was told it has something to do with permits. My lawyer says that's bullshit. A year ago, some government men tried to sell me on a program that would put me in bed with the Feds. I didn't like it then, don't like it now." His smile vanished, his face flushing deep red. "Inviting me to a fancy dinner party won't change my mind. So if your job is to convince me to play ball with these idiots, if that's what they've hired you for, I'm afraid your first performance review isn't going to look too good."

I remembered some of the last advice Katherine had offered Marcie before leaving the conference room: '*Treat him as if he's the best in the business, make him feel important. Reassure him we're on his side. Get him to trust you.*'

It wasn't going to be easy. Charlie had built his business from the ground up, struggling with the day-to-day battles of competition while charting the path of his company's future through a minefield of tight profit margins and aggressive competition. His definition of "trust" was built on experience, not words.

The department's interest in his company had put him on guard. And now, he was outright suspicious. Like any business owner, he didn't like government officials snooping around in his affairs.

I decided to stay low-key. "Charlie, you have a much better handle on this than I do. You know what's best for your company. There's no point trying to convince you to work with the government if it's not right for you, especially if you've already made up your mind. Maybe there are advantages in the government program, maybe not. I know you couldn't have come this far, done as well as you have, without negotiating some tough situations, you know, picking out the good from the bad."

His eyes were steady, taking it all in. "As long as we're on the same page."

I offered a sympathetic expression. I wouldn't polarize our conversation with excuses.

Over the next half hour, Charlie continued to open up. In fact, as the announcement was made to take our seats for dinner, he revealed supposedly "confidential" information involving communications he'd had with a few possible China-based suppliers, not realizing these were the same exchanges that had cued the department to request a personal meeting.

As we approached the table, Charlie pulled out my chair, inviting me to sit. "You know, I was downright dreading this, but after talking, getting it out in the open, I'm ready to eat." His expression became serious. "I haven't made it easy for you, I know that. And I appreciate you listening to me gripe about all this government BS, especially since they're the ones paying your salary."

I was beginning to see how influential I could be in my new capacity as hostess. More important than the unspoken promise of my body, my display of personal interest—and focused attention—had the power to change attitudes and actions.

Chapter Twelve

Charlie and I sat near the middle of the table. I'd hoped Katherine would take the chair next to mine, providing support if and when necessary. She had taken a seat at the next table over. I could see her, but she was too distant to give me immediate feedback or direction.

After a brief welcome from the director—a slight man in his mid-fifties, wearing a tenuous smile like a well-rehearsed façade—the sound of clinking glasses and table conversation filled the room.

"There's a lot more to these table settings than what I'm used to," Charlie grumbled.

I noticed our conversation slowing, Charlie becoming increasingly reserved as other guests took their place at the table. He'd already admitted being uneasy in formal social settings, and now he was surrounded by strangers—except for me. I doubted I could put him at ease, but I would do my best to make the situation as pleasant as possible.

Dinner was predictable. The appetizer was served between benign comments about the local weather, sports, and global economics. I quickly learned that controversial subjects—political corruption, trade embargos, and dictator puppeteering—were reserved until later in the evening, somewhere between dessert and the third after-dinner drink. Through most of the meal, Charlie ate quietly, occasionally acknowledging when someone spoke in his direction. I imagined he wished he was sitting in his favorite booth at Denny's, enjoying the weekend special and a cup of black coffee. Our obvious "coupling" made us a prime target for innuendo and baited insinuation. I carefully responded with a heavy dose of neutrality, gently transitioning the conversation to another subject. However, as the last course was served—a chocolate soufflé—the woman sitting directly across the table, a nasty wench from San Torini, hurled a volley of particularly vicious barbs at Charlie, blaming American capitalism for every war, plague, and planetary catastrophe throughout history. I managed to smile and hold my tongue—until she followed up with a question dripping with spiteful inference.

I jumped in. "Oh, you know, Mr. Weston and I were just discussing that." Leaning toward Charlie, I added, "I remember you mentioning that line of rhetoric being another political move fueled by leftist propaganda, something that would soon burn itself out. I suppose time will tell . . ."

Sensing Charlie's relief, I readied myself with another salvo of generic responses. It wasn't necessary. Apparently the queen bee didn't have much of a sting away from her hive.

Charlie tapped me on the thigh, his touch surprising me. He gave me a slight nod, a signal of thanks. I couldn't let the opportunity slip by. I reached for this hand before he could retrieve it and brought it to rest on my leg.

I was taking a risk. He could've interpreted my boldness for what it was—a manipulated move to encourage a little intimacy. Under the circumstances, I was willing to wager Charlie's need to connect with a confederate was stronger than his sense of restraint. If I was wrong, and he brought it up later, I would explain that I needed his support in an emotionally stressful situation.

Dinner concluded with the director's invitation to enjoy the music and take advantage of the dance floor.

"I'm not much of a dancer, but I would like to stretch my legs." Charlie began to stand.

"Wanna get some air?" I slipped my arm around his.

He seemed surprised and drew back a bit. "Is this okay? You and me, close like this, in public?"

"We're adults. This is a social function. Touching is normal. And besides, you haven't heard me complain, have you?"

He'd been breathing quick and shallow for most of the evening. Now he drew deep, his entire body decompressing. He started to say something, then stopped, distracted by Katherine's approach.

"How's Jewel treating you, Mr. Weston? I hope she's not boring you with endless explanations of what goes on around here."

"No, she's not." Charlie was unmistakably defensive.

It was exactly what she wanted to hear. With her beaming smile matching the twinkle in her eyes, she said, "I'm glad you're enjoying her company. Anything you need, just ask. Jewel will make sure you're taken care of."

"Thank you, ma'am." Charlie's voice was less wary.

Katherine leaned close and set her hand on my shoulder. She spoke softly, yet loud enough for Charlie to hear. "Since this is Mr. Weston's first visit, he might enjoy a tour of the upstairs. I believe B3 is vacant, if you need some privacy."

I'd forgotten the reality of how the night would end. I'd been enjoying the atmosphere, the glitz and glamour, playing dress-up while surrounded by the political elite. But now, all the pretty was about to be left behind, on the other side of a locked door. Katherine was telling me it was time to take this middle-aged man to a bedroom.

To fuck him.

I felt it building, getting stronger—the same kind of fear that took me to my knees when the captain of the *Kelsey* dragged me in front of five men who were waiting for me on the stern of the ship.

But this is different, I told myself. I chose to be here. I had a mission, a purpose. This wasn't just about some guy getting his rocks off.

It sounded good. I wished I believed it.

The truth was cold and raw. I was expected to take off my clothes and let this stranger do anything he wanted to me.

Because it was my job.

The accepted currency for this transaction was sex. It wasn't clear whether I was buying or selling, but it was time to close the deal.

My breathing was suddenly shallow, my chest tight, my stomach turning inside out. I was certain Katherine's radar—with her highly developed sense of acuity—was picking it up. I didn't care. Right now, the only one who counted was Charlie, and I couldn't let him see it.

I faced him. "Want to see the rest of the place? They keep the good furniture upstairs."

"You off the clock?"

"I am if they can't find me."

Apparently satisfied I would pull myself together, Katherine took the hint and excused herself.

Locking arms with Charlie, I led him toward the stairs. I felt his resistance as we approached the bottom step.

"This may not be a good idea," he said, "having everyone see us go up together like this."

"Charlie, I have the run of the place. It's my job to show you around." I quickly scanned the people scattered around the lobby. "Most of the crowd is in the ballroom, and the folks in here are so preoccupied with their own conversations, I doubt anyone will notice."

"Is that part of your official duties, to be a tour guide?"

"It is tonight. It will give us a chance to talk in private, figure out how to get the Feds off your back. I'll tell you what I know, or at least what they've told me. Fair enough?"

Make him believe you're on his side, Katherine had said. I hoped that would do it.

Charlie thought for a moment. "I'd like to hear what you have to say."

I opened the door to the suite and caught the latent flash from the bedside lamps, activated by the room's auto-sensors. The door's movement also triggered several concealed cameras and microphones—everything that happened in this room would be recorded.

"These are used for diplomats and visiting heads of state," I explained.

Charlie glanced around the room. "Bit too fancy for my taste. Not as bad as Vegas though. The way they decorate the hotel rooms with those horrible checkerboard patterns and gaudy colors, it forces you outside and into the casinos. Only time I could relax in that city was when the lights were out."

I couldn't hide my smile. Charlie hadn't been to Vegas in a long time.

"I'll fix you another drink," I offered.

He didn't object.

The bar was stocked with Jim Beam, Charlie's favorite. The ice bucket was full.

Staff must have prepared the room during dinner. I wonder if they also dropped his favorite lube in the nightstand drawer . . .

The idea of bringing Charlie upstairs to seduce him was no longer the most stressful aspect of the evening. Like it or not, he was my first assignment. And I was determined to do it right. Part of me wanted to please Katherine, confirm the department had made the right decision in rescuing me from the auction. More important, doing a good job was the best way to influence the people who could help me find Annie. I had to convince them of my value, and that I was worthy of a special favor.

From the moment we entered the room, the easy give-and-take chatter between Charlie and I had subsided. And now, the tension was rising to the point of being unnerving, like we were tiptoeing around each other. It was time to get the ball rolling.

"Charlie, I need to tell you something."

"Been waiting to hear it. I had the feeling there was more to this than you giving me a tour of the place." He paused, searching my face.

I wasn't expecting that—his subtle accusation I'd been hiding my real agenda. Charlie might be unsophisticated, but he was no dummy. He knew there had to be an explanation for all the attention I was showing him.

"It all goes back to what I told you before," I said. "I'm really new at this, so I've been going with my gut, hoping I was doing the right thing."

Charlie's expression didn't change. He wanted something more substantial than a clumsy attempt at true confession.

I tried again. "Part of my job is to convince you the Feds have your best interests at heart. And Charlie, I'll be right up front with you. I won't pretend I understand all the details of what they want and why they want it. Maybe if I knew your side of the story, what's important to you, I can try to get the information you need to make the right decision."

He stared at me with discerning eyes, no doubt his version of a lie detector. "I'm listening."

"From what I was told, the department wants you to choose your overseas vendors from an approved list of companies."

"Why? What makes them so special?"

"Because they're *friendly*."

"Friendly?" He made it sound like a four-letter word.

"It means they cooperate with our country by supplying information about their other customers so the Feds can keep track of who's buying sophisticated technology, especially if it ends up in the hands of those who shouldn't have it. In exchange, the department promises to bring these companies new American business . . . buyers like yourself."

Charlie frowned. "That's channeling, unfair competition. Might even be illegal."

I felt like I was rationalizing government kickbacks to a Sunday school teacher. "You'd be right, if we were discussing the way things are done in the States. But here, in this part of the world, it's common practice. And if you go along with it, the government will grant you privileged status . . . less red tape, tax breaks, that sort of thing."

I surprised myself. It sounded good, as if I really knew what I was talking about.

But Charlie was watching me with unmistakable suspicion. He was waiting, wanting more.

I threw it out there. "And during all of this process, if we wind up friends . . . well, I think I'd like that."

He was quiet for the longest time. From his expression, he must've been replaying everything I'd said, weighing my words for validity—judging me for sincerity.

I hoped he came to the right conclusion. He might never be sure about this place or the suits downstairs, but I wanted him to be sure about me.

I would fuck him, but I wasn't going to lie to him.

"So what happens now?" he asked.

"As little or as much as you want. We can talk, have a drink, we can lie on the bed and watch your favorite TV show. There's no schedule, no expectations. We can stay here all night if you'd like."

I noticed his cheeks beginning to flush.

He walked to the bar and fingered a couple of ice cubes, dropping them into his glass. "What are you drinking, girl?"

I'd noticed a bottle of chilled Chardonnay. "That bottle of wine, in the biggest glass you can find."

He smiled. I let out the breath I was holding, feeling the pressure lift.

"I need to use the restroom," I said. "Be back in a minute."

I sat on the closed lid of the toilet. *You can do this. Pretend you're an actor, going through the motions.* I put myself on autopilot. No more thinking, just get it over with.

I'd left the bathroom door slightly open, suggesting the need for privacy without actually creating a sense of separation. I'd done it intentionally. 'Never make the client feel like you're closing him off,' Katherine had told me. 'Stay in his world, both physically and mentally.'

Running the water to mask the sound, I opened the full length linen closet and scanned the small hanging space. A sheer white lace negligee shared the rod with a light blue silk robe, its neckline plunging to the waist. I had no idea which one Charlie would like. I decided to wear both, the untied robe over the sheer lace.

The thigh holster had to go. Explaining its presence wouldn't be conducive to setting the mood. And there was no need for the wire; every inch of the room was bugged. I set the holster on the top shelf and checked my leg for compression marks. Fortunately, the straps were lined with soft suede.

What remained of the slight indentation was fading fast.

I remembered Katherine had mentioned there were cameras placed behind the two-way vanity mirror. The boys in security were no doubt enjoying every second. Hell, they'd probably zoomed in for a close-up.

I stuck out my tongue, made a goofy face, and then smiled in vampy seduction as I leaned over the countertop. I was giving some nameless geek an unrestricted view of my boobs. I ended the encounter by flipping off my government-sanctioned voyeur, then bringing my middle finger to my mouth.

If my actions brought a reprimand, I would dismiss them as flirtatious energy, confirming I was centered, confident, and ready. Strangely, my silliness gave me a sense of being in control—and calling the shots.

I hoped I could hold on to it.

As I re-entered the room, I noticed Charlie had moved to the loveseat. He seemed stiff, uneasy, as if waiting for a dentist appointment.

"I was tired of all the clothes," I said. "And I had to get out of those shoes." I curled my toes into the carpet, wanting him to see my bare feet.

Standing there, with my robe open, I was giving him permission to enjoy the sights. I expected him to scan my body—as any man would. I wasn't getting the reaction I'd hoped for. He was definitely looking at me, yet his attention seemed to be on the *larger* sense. Instead of scrutinizing my legs or breasts, readily visible through the fine lace, his eyes were locked on my face, as if searching for something he would only find on the inside.

"You remind me of someone," he said.

"Someone nice, I hope."

He glanced down for a moment, his mind drifting to another time and place. "Yes. Very nice." For the first time since entering the room, Charlie let down his guard. Either he was no longer concerned with business or he'd decided to relax and enjoy the moment. Either way, I took it as a sign we were heading in the right direction.

I jumped on the bed, scooted to the middle, and patted the space next to me. "Come and sit. We can talk."

My robe was spread open. From his vantage point, he could see my breasts and inner thighs, right up to my pussy. I made no effort to cover myself.

Charlie shifted forward in the loveseat, holding his drink with both hands. "Is that what this is about? You have sex with me and in exchange, I agree to use one of the companies the government hot-shots recommend?"

Charlie was no game player. He saw things for what they were. Rather than discretely accept the agency's "hospitality" as a pleasant incentive to doing business on their terms, he wanted everything disclosed, out in the open.

I could have recounted a laundry list of rationalizations, reminding him this was an accepted practice and no one would think less of him for enjoying himself. But in Charlie's world, the sordid nature of the situation wouldn't suddenly become decent and honorable because it was taking place under the roof of an American Embassy.

Honesty . . . that's all Charlie was asking for.

And from what I'd learned about him so far, he seemed to be one of those rare men who deserved nothing less.

"That's the gist of it," I answered. "The agency calls it *conditioning*. They want you to have an enjoyable experience here, so you'll bring a positive mind-set to the negotiating table."

"This goes on all the time?"

I hesitated, not wanting to confirm I'd had an agenda even prior to meeting him. It would be admitting my actions were scripted, my goal to obtain his cooperation with sexual favors making me look like a two-bit whore.

"I'm not sure," I said.

His eyes narrowed. More than skeptical, he didn't believe me.

"Honestly, Charlie, I swear to God. This is my first assignment. I've never done anything like this before. And frankly, I think I've completely screwed it up. But I understand you want the truth, and that's what I'm giving you, as best I know it."

REDEMPTION

By now, Katherine had no doubt learned of my rookie blunder. I'd just taken the last two hours of carefully constructed rapport and shot it straight to hell. She was probably on her way up the stairs, ready to "accidentally" intrude and work her magic to salvage the situation.

Charlie was quiet, the distance between us growing tense and awkward. I wanted to reassure him I was on his side, and that I never intended to mislead or deceive him. But the next words had to come from him. Anything I said would likely be discounted as an excuse.

Another ten seconds of wretched, exhausting silence. I was at the point where I would have welcomed Katherine's intrusion.

Finally, he spoke. "I want you to understand something. I don't think poorly of you personally. And I don't necessarily disapprove of the folks here. But I am disappointed in their methods."

"It was me, Charlie," I countered, taking the responsibility. "I assumed it's what you wanted. It was my mistake, no one else's."

He shook his head. "Jewel, you're the only person who's been honest with me since I set foot in this place. You don't need to take the blame for any of it."

He rose to his feet and set his glass on the bar. He was leaving. Finished.

I hadn't bothered to read the signals—his slight hesitation, his lack of response—indications he wanted a friendly ear rather than a willing sex partner.

I tried to think of a word or two that would break the tension, make it easier for both of us to say goodbye. I decided to come clean and lay it on the line. "Charlie, I don't know what else to say except I'm sorry. I know I've ruined the evening, and I hope you won't let it influence your decision to work with the embassy."

He stared at the fifth of Jim Beam. I was surprised to see him reach for the bottle and refill his glass.

"Booze is a weakness, a vice really," he said. "But it helps me get through the hard parts. My friends tell me I should find a substitute, like golf or smoking." He sighed, his shoulders slumping. "I hate golf."

Without thinking, I automatically agreed. "Me, too."

"Ever play?" he asked.

"I hate it, remember? Not going to spend time doing things I hate."

"Jewel?" He paused, his voice full of concern. "Do you hate this job?"

I felt the pressure of every camera and microphone in the room suddenly focused on me. For a moment, I wondered if Charlie was a plant, an agent playing the part of a reluctant mark. This entire encounter could have been nothing more than a trial run to determine my readiness to be paired with a real guest. As I looked at him, I remembered what he'd said and how he'd rejected the idea of having sex with me. He seemed too real, his reactions too irregular and inconsistently *human*. If the agency wanted to test me, they would have pushed me with kink, with the most twisted shit imaginable, to see how I handled it.

I would bet my life on it—Charlie was the real deal.

"I suppose," I said. "I've never thought about it that way . . . whether I hate it or like it. It's just where I am, at this point in my life."

"So what brought you here, doing this?" he asked.

I had no idea why he was interested, but there was no point in keeping it a secret. "The Feds took me out of a very bad place. The department literally saved my life."

There it was again, that same look of time travel, his mind leaving the present. I imagined him struggling to understand how a twenty-three-year-old girl could have screwed up her life so badly she would welcome the opportunity to provide sexual favors to privileged friends of her employer—and be grateful for the opportunity.

"That invite to sit . . . still good?" he asked.

"It never expired."

Charlie sat back on the bed, leaving a good foot of space between us. This time, I wouldn't second guess his intentions. Whatever he had in mind, I would let him take the lead.

"Remember when I said you reminded me of someone?" He sipped his drink.

"Uh-huh. I hoped it was someone nice, and you said it was."

He was quiet for a moment. "Her name was Marian." His eyes glazed and he added, "She always wanted me to call her by her middle name . . . but I never did."

I wanted to ask why, but stopped myself, not wanting to pry.

"Is there a resemblance? Same color hair? Eyes?"

He shook his head. "It has nothing to do with your physical appearance. It's a sense I have about you, the way you seem to be on your way to somewhere else, and this is only a detour."

I wanted him to explain. I decided to let him talk.

"It was the same for Marian," he continued. "I asked her about it once, why she was always on the move, always searching for something she couldn't quite put into words. She told me she needed to make peace with herself before settling down in a place she could call home."

"Did she ever find what she was looking for?"

"I . . . don't think so. The last time we talked, she was frustrated, unhappy with her job. She decided to travel the world, to see things from a different perspective, hoping a change in scenery would help."

It sounded a little cryptic, but I was curious. "So is that all we have in common, a sense of wanderlust?"

"Oh, there's other things, too. You're about the same age. Mostly, though, I think you and Marian share a lot of the same needs, wanting to believe there's something better out there, both of you seeking a magic potion that will cure the hurt and put everything back together again."

I hadn't expected to hear such insight from Charlie—I would not underestimate him again.

"You and Marian must have been close," I said.

I imagined her as his secretary, or maybe the daughter of a business associate who'd become enamored with the idea of having a tryst with an older man. Charlie certainly wasn't unattractive, and in his financial position, he could afford to bestow a girlfriend with lavish and expensive gifts—plenty of incentive for a younger, attractive woman.

"We were," he admitted. "At least, at first. Then my company began to grow, and it became difficult for me to spend time with her."

"How long has it been since you've seen each other?"

"Almost three years."

"I can tell you miss her."

Charlie took another swallow of Jim Beam, his eyes fixed on the wall.

"Have you thought of tracking her down, to catch up?"

He ignored the question. "Maybe if I'd spent more time with her, made her a priority, things might have turned out different."

I wasn't sure where this was going. He carried the memory of a woman named Marian. There could be a hundred reasons why they were no longer together—all of which were none of my business. And yet, he seemed to want to talk about it.

"Maybe it's not too late," I said, "to let her know how you feel. She could be waiting to hear from you."

Charlie mumbled under his breath.

"I'm sorry, what did you say?"

He cleared his throat. "I wish I could, Jewel."

Never taking his eyes off the wall, he stared as if it contained a magic portal into the past, his detachment so strong, I wondered if he expected Marian to step through it and join us in the present.

"You still have feelings for her," I offered. "There's nothing wrong with that. I think it reminds us to do a better job next time, to learn to appreciate the people who are important to us."

He reached for me, but instead of laying his hand on my bare leg—the natural landing spot for any man in this situation—he touched my arm and gave it a little squeeze. "I know you said these embassy people pulled you out of a bad situation, but I'm gonna go ahead and say it . . . you don't belong here. This place will wear the shine off in a big hurry. It'll turn you skeptical and jaded. And Jewel, your life is worth more than that."

It struck me funny—I knew exactly how much my life was worth, in dollars and cents.

Our conversation had taken a strange turn, and I needed to get it back on track. The only thing I knew was I reminded him of someone he had cared for deeply. And from what I could tell, it was the only part of me he found interesting.

Before I could speak, he scooted toward his side of the bed. "I've enjoyed your company," he said. "You've made the evening tolerable."

"You're leaving?"

"I have a few phone calls to make. And I want to get back to my hotel at a decent hour."

"You're welcome to stay here, in this room. If you want privacy, I'll return to my dorm."

He shook his head. "Too many ears."

He knew the room was bugged. Of course he did.

"I understand," I said. "If you change your mind, call the main embassy number and ask the operator to connect you to my extension."

An idea struck me from out the blue. "You know, if you'd like, I could ask the research department to do a quick search for Marian. It could be done strictly under the radar. No records, nothing on paper."

For the first time, Charlie's expression was transparent, revealing a man who'd finally achieved what he'd worked for all his life but realized he'd paid too great a price.

"Marian's gone," he said. "She was killed in a private plane crash. I was told it went down over water. The wreckage was never recovered. I should have mentioned that in the beginning. I haven't talked to anyone about it since the memorial."

"I'm so sorry. I know what it's like to lose someone you love. I can tell how much you cared about her."

His lip twitched, then trembled in a look of utter despair. "Marian was my daughter."

I felt my stomach drop. I should have put the pieces together sooner—Charlie and Marian growing apart, his work obligations requiring him to spend more time away from home. His daughter had needed his direction and guidance. But at the time, he was busy building his enterprise. Now, with Marian gone, his life was haunted by her memory—her phone call he'd been too busy to take or the birthdays he'd missed because he was out of town. His daughter's death had left him with the kind of regret that comes from too many questions without answers, wounds that never heal. And it would haunt him for the rest of his life.

His memories of Marian, and the similarities he'd seen in me, had kept him on his side of the bed. It was a wonder he hadn't left immediately, repulsed by my behavior.

"I'm sorry," I repeated. "I didn't know." It was so completely inadequate, but it was all I had.

Charlie took a deep breath and shook himself. "Tell your people I'll consider working with them. Between you and me, I don't have a problem with the

Feds looking over my shoulder once in a while. But I won't give up a single ounce of control over the operation of my company." He paused, his expression softening. "If I do decide to get in bed with these bureaucrats, there'll be one condition, and it's not negotiable. Everything goes through you. You'll be my personal representative. Otherwise, no deal."

"I'll tell them, Charlie."

He winked at me as he closed the door behind him, the same way he might have said goodnight to Marian, a lifetime ago.

Chapter Thirteen

"His personal representative?" Katherine was struggling with the idea. "What do you think he meant by that . . . exactly? Did you get a feel for his actual expectations?"

"I didn't get a sense that Charlie, I mean Mr. Weston, expected anything in particular."

She shook her head. "Look at it this way . . . what would Weston need to see, hear, or feel to be satisfied? In other words, how would you know you're meeting his needs as his personal representative?"

I hadn't considered that. In fact, I'd just assumed there was a list of duties in some government manual describing how to perform the function. "Should I have asked him for more details?"

"No, your meeting went well. And prolonging closure might have affected the progress you'd made to that point. I was hoping you'd picked up a few clues along the way."

"Clues?"

"Put yourself in Weston's place. Assume his personality and mindset. What would *you* expect after making a condition like that?"

Katherine and I had met right after breakfast for a debriefing on my first assignment. Sequestered in a small conference room, we were reviewing a quad-video display on a large monitor.

"First, let's look at the video from the time you and Weston entered the upstairs suite."

"What about during dinner? I think I did a pretty good job there." I wanted Katherine to hear my verbal put-down of the bitch from San Torini, to give her an idea what I was capable of.

She shook her head. "Let's start with the bedroom, when the interaction was just between the two of you."

I shrugged. "Because that's where I really screwed up?"

"Because that's where Weston came up with the idea of wanting you involved in the preferred vendor program. Something was said or done to put that notion in his head. We need to know what it was."

"So you haven't seen the video yet?" If she had, she'd be aware of Charlie's guilt-laden association that linked me to his deceased daughter. I was a purgatorial substitute, a way for him to pay homage to her memory.

"I prefer to review recordings *with* my girls. Seems less intrusive that way."

I sighed. "Okay. Let 'er rip."

The first ten minutes were humiliating as hell, watching myself play seductress, trying to convince a man I'd known for less than three hours that I wanted to fuck him.

Katherine began to question me about being so transparent, admitting to Charlie he was my first assignment.

"What was your purpose in that?" she asked.

I felt like an idiot. I didn't have a reason for my erratic behavior. And I couldn't make one up. The only reason my meeting with Charlie had ended well was due to pure circumstance. With another man, it could have easily gone the other way.

"At the time, it was spontaneous," I said. "Maybe if you look at the entire file, you'll have a better idea of what happened."

"No, Jewel," Katherine countered. "I want to know *your* thoughts about what happened, as you watch it being replayed in front of you. The nuances of intention and meaning are important, and it's often difficult to interpret those subtleties from the recordings. I also want to know what the camera may have missed. It might be a glance, a roll of the eyes, a facial expression when the subject's back was to the camera. Those details can change the entire meaning of an exchange. We'll view the tapes, but the most valuable information will come from you."

Apparently, spilling my guts was standard procedure. I would have to describe what I was feeling when Charlie and I were lying on the bed together. Katherine was expecting me to recall my *interpretations* of what happened last night. But from my lack of precision in answering her questions—a jumbled-up mess of *I'm not sure* and *I can't remember*—it was obvious I'd done a lousy job.

"Am I late?"

I didn't hear Mark enter the room. It was bad enough having to review the recordings with

Katherine. I certainly didn't want to share my embarrassing first-time mistakes with anyone else.

"Morning, Mark." I tried to sound cheerful, or at least professional. "Do you and Katherine have a meeting?" My voice rang with expectation—it would give me a chance to slink off and avoid the indignity of Mark's wicked tongue as he watched over my shoulder.

"No," Katherine answered. "I asked Mark to join us."

She must have seen the concern—no, downright terror—on my face. "He's an expert in subliminal communication," she added. "I wanted his input on Weston's body language."

"Doesn't Mark have more important things to do?"

"Well, of course I do," he shot back. His face broke with a huge grin. "Usually, my mornings are dedicated to preventing nuclear holocaust in the mid-east and reversing global warming. But when Katherine asked me to sit in, I rescheduled a conference call with the president and canceled my meeting with the U.N."

"You done?" Katherine's stony stare reflected her limited appreciation of Mark's dry humor.

Mark glared at her, suggesting he was prepared to shoot tiny bolts of electrical energy in her direction. But the gleam in his eyes betrayed him. I wondered if he'd ever fucked her.

"I took a quick peek at the tapes this morning," he said. "I was in early, so I—"

"Damn it, Mark," Katherine interrupted. "I wanted your first impressions, not your vetted opinions, especially after being diluted by time and deliberation."

Mark appeared unfazed by Katherine's outburst. "No worries, my initial observations are intact. I'll exclude any comments resulting from post-evaluation."

Katherine was quietly seething. "You know I want to hear those, too," she growled. "My concern is you've had time to temper your interpretations. And it will naturally prevent you from saying something in front of Jewel that might offend her."

I jumped in. "Should I be listening to this?"

"Professional bantering, my dear, that's all it is," Katherine answered without a hint of apology in her voice.

"We're all family here," Mark added, setting his hand on my shoulder. "We have our everyday squabbles, just like any clan living under the same roof."

"Take your hand off her," Katherine scolded. "You're anchoring again. You know I don't like that in a training atmosphere."

I knew what she was talking about, though I wasn't sure it was Mark's intent. He seemed to be trying to relax me in a tense situation.

Mark gave my shoulder a little squeeze before removing his hand. "So how do you want to do this? A scene at a time or run through the entire file and summarize?"

Katherine's mouth twisted into twin rows of tiny knotted muscles, her expression no different than if she'd bitten into a lemon.

Mark leaned over to make eye contact with me. Lowering his voice, he said, "I think we're in for a little more professional bantering."

Although a stranger might interpret their exchange as combative, I saw a kind of practiced back-and-forth rhetoric, an expected sparring that had become integral to their relationship. Now I was sure they'd spent time in bed together.

Katherine clicked the computer mouse and restarted the video. "The file is pre-marked, so we can fast-forward to the parts with dialogue. That's all Mark needs to see today. Later, he can evaluate how well you paced Weston's physiology. And, Jewel, the entire file is available in your online portfolio, and I'd like you to review it sooner than later."

"Instead of a late night movie," Mark interjected.

"Shush," Katherine said. "I want her to hear this."

As the tape continued, I could see how nervous I'd been. I was much too eager. One moment, my voice rose in a nervous climb, then dropped as I filled a sudden silence with silly chatter.

"Jesus, I sound like an idiot."

"Not true." Again, Mark's hand found my shoulder. Apparently unconcerned with Katherine's warning, he made no effort to break the connection. This time, it was more intentional, supportive. It felt good, like a lover's caress. The thought struck me— how nice it would be to have his other hand on me as well.

Katherine enlarged on Mark's comment. "He's right, Jewel. We tend to be overly critical when we see ourselves in these kinds of situations, focusing on our personal behavior rather than how others react and respond to us.

"So I did good?"

"It was what Weston needed to hear," she said.

"Tell her the rest," Mark said.

"Mark is referring to Weston's changing attitude and manner. In minutes, he begins to follow your lead. It shows you have a natural ability to establish rapport."

Katherine's phone beeped. A glance at the screen changed her entire disposition. "Marcie's back. And she's not happy. Let's finish up."

Short choppy sentences. It was Katherine's trademark style under stress. When things got dicey, she went right to the point, exchanging verbal finesse for clear and precise communication. I wondered if she was some kind of hybrid—part human, part machine, her sprockets and gears finely meshed and well-oiled.

"You want me to stay with Jewel and go through the rest of the video?" Mark asked.

"Jewel and I will complete the session later."

Crap. Some time alone with Mark would've been nice.

"What about Weston's non-negotiable condition?" Mark interjected. "We still need to discuss that."

"Later." Katherine was done. She gathered up her notepad and switched off the monitor. "Jewel, the director wants a meeting this afternoon," she said hurriedly. "So stay available. I'll text you the time."

"A meeting? Do I need to prepare something?"

"This afternoon, dear."

With that, she was out the door.

The sudden silence wasn't uncomfortable, just unexpected. Mark's release of my shoulder coincided perfectly with Katherine's exit. It was probably best. I hadn't realized I was unconsciously tilting my head toward the back of his hand. The side of my face would have soon made contact—an undeniably flirtatious gesture, impossible to misinterpret.

I wasn't embarrassed, just a little self-conscious for being so obvious.

I spoke first. "Now that Katherine's gone, tell me the truth. Is the department happy with me? I mean, there's no chance they might kick me out, right?"

"I think we're stuck with you." He raised his chin slightly, as if inviting a little verbal jousting.

"Seriously," I said. "I want your opinion. I know I screwed up last night. I said too much and forgot a lot of my training. Frankly, I was expecting Katherine to come charging through the door with some made-up excuse to get me out the room so she could salvage the deal with Charlie before I made it even worse."

He locked eyes with me. "Jewel, you got it done. Your methods were a little unorthodox, but you were able to change Weston's mind. And now he's receptive to working with us."

I realized I was holding my breath. I let it out slowly, hoping he didn't notice.

That was stupid. Mark noticed *everything*.

"We'll talk more later," he said. "Got lots of donuts to make."

"To keep the world from blowing up?"

"Too late for that," he said, heading toward the door. "Trying to recover the pieces."

I remembered the meeting with the director.

"Mark, wait! Any chance you could make the meeting this afternoon?"

"Don't worry. Probably nothing more than a formality, some logistics and paperwork."

I didn't hide my disappointment.

He hesitated. "You want me there?"

His question carried both ambiguity and inference—a suggestive invitation laced with plausible denial. He was being careful. The department not only frowned on staff personnel forming relationships with outside agents, official policy prohibited it. My answer—the *correct* answer—should clarify my need for his presence as strictly instructive, to draw on his experience and training.

Fuck that. This wouldn't be the last time I would break the rules. "Yes, it would mean a lot to me if you could be there."

Mark's expression turned serious. "I have a lunch meeting. If I'm back in time, I'll stop in. If I don't make it, go with your gut. Weston wants you as his intermediary, a buffer between him and the shit-storm of bureaucratic nonsense this department is known for. Use it to your advantage. Buy yourself some leverage."

I looked at him with desperate confusion. "I don't know what you mean. I'm worried there'll be questions, and the director may want—"

Mark held up his hand, interrupting. "You'll do fine. Don't anticipate what others want to hear. Not this time. You have someone in your corner. Weston wants you. Fight for him. Fight for yourself."

He smiled, and looked at me the same way a hopeful coach eyeballs a player before sending them to the plate for a turn at bat. "You good to go?"

"Go eat your egg foo young or whatever she's calling herself these days." I grinned, hoping he would interpret the innuendo as an invitation. I waited until he was out the door and a few steps down the hall before adding, "And hurry back."

Chapter Fourteen

"Well, Jewel," the director began. "It appears you've made quite an impression on Mr. Weston. Katherine tells me you were able to reverse a long-standing prejudice and bring him over to our side." His reading glasses were poised on the end of his nose, his eyes fixed on the paper as he reviewed the four-page document—apparently, a report on my conversation with Charlie.

I sat quietly, knowing the compliments were introductory pleasantries. I'd skimmed the video after Katherine and Mark left the conference room. As far as I was concerned, his praise was unjustified. My ass had been saved by two unrelated circumstances—the unprofessional disclosure of my newbie status and my resemblance to his deceased daughter.

Katherine sat quietly on my left. Next to her, at the head of the table, the director—his authority based on a mix of official policy and a nebulous hierarchy that managed the department's more clandestine activities. I had the impression he was more of a figurehead than a leader. While he needed to know what was going on, he didn't actually initiate covert operations. Those directives came from the White House or Langley, and when the objective was especially sticky, from some off-the-books department with arms-length separation from official sources. For the most part, his job consisted of coordinating the department's resources and delegating the day-to-day tasks of representing the interests of the United States in a foreign land.

Across the table, an outside agent specializing in contract negotiations—a mid-thirties, balding man named Paul—sat next to a young data analyst from information services. Appearing every bit the boy wonder, the analyst sat impatiently, his nervous chair-shifting an obvious declaration of more important priorities.

Asshole, I thought. *This guy's your boss. He could fire you. Hell, I'd fire your ass right now, if I could.*

The director focused his attention on a large stack of papers to his left, his fleeting glance at the highlighted sections indicating his need was more to reacquaint himself with the history of the situation rather than finding something specific.

"Seems Mr. Weston has made an unusual request," he continued. "He wants Jewel to act as his personal representative, to be his eyes and ears in our preferred vendor program."

"Actually, Director," Katherine chimed in, "he's made it a non-negotiable condition. I admit it's a bit unusual—"

"It's ridiculous," the young analyst interrupted. "We can't have one of *your girls* directly involved with the data exchange system."

Still in his early twenties, he was outspoken, arrogant, and way too sure of himself. With his comment diluted by his lack of tact and diplomacy, the value of his contribution was better represented by the two raging zits on his forehead.

"Ridiculous?" Katherine shifted forward in her chair, her demeanor immediately defensive. "Would you like to rephrase that?"

"You know what I mean," the analyst countered. "She's not trained. No security clearance. We'd have to give her access to the details of the program. That's only available to level three employees."

Katherine looked at Paul. "Is this chatterbox one of yours?"

Paul shook his head. "A transfer from Langley. They got him from a start-up in Silicon Valley. Supposed to be some kind of computer whiz-kid."

Katherine turned toward the analyst, whose face was now a neon-bright shade of red. "Since you're new, I'll give you some latitude and allow you to stay in the room. For now, I want you to sit there and remain quiet until you're asked a question."

Apparently, he was unaccustomed to being reprimanded. He stiffened in his chair, his eyes widening, nostrils flaring.

He started to speak, but Katherine cut him off. "Uh-uh. Not another word or I'll put a muzzle on you."

I'd been on pins and needles since walking through the door. Hearing Katherine defend me— even though I had no idea what the little twit was saying—meant a lot. I discretely set my hand on Katherine's thigh. I wanted her to know how much I appreciated her support, even if it came in the form of a protective outburst.

She responded immediately, her fingertips brushing over my wrist. Thinking it was a prelude to pushing me away, I was surprised to feel her hand cover mine.

"Let's continue," the director said. He seemed unfazed by Katherine's comments and apparently saw no need to comment or intervene. He simply wanted to get on with the business at hand.

"Here's my take on it," Paul began. "It's a question of how much detail about our operation we want to put at risk. And, if we decide to involve Jewel, how to limit our exposure. We would need new protocols, and she would require training in threat recognition, especially if she'll be continuing with the vendor program in the long-term."

"Aren't you forgetting something?" Mark's voice was unmistakable as he slipped through the door behind me.

Suddenly smiling, I quickly dropped the corners of my mouth, hoping no one else saw it.

He took the chair next to mine. "Has anyone asked Jewel if she wants to take on the assignment? It's a lot more responsibility. No doubt there'll be some travel involved, with possible overnights away from the embassy."

The director spoke to Katherine. "I assumed you had already discussed this with her."

"Not yet. I thought it best to wait," she answered. "This is new territory for us. We don't have an existing job description or employee category to refer to. We'll have to design the parameters as we go, assuming we want to put this one on the books."

Paul shook his head. "We don't have that kind of time. Weston's made it clear he's ready to do business. From what I saw in his correspondence this morning, he wants to put two vendors under contract. I think we should take advantage of the momentum before he changes his mind."

"So run with it off the books," Mark suggested.

"I said it was expedient, not practical." Paul was backpedaling. "Jewel is new, untested. In another year she'll be ready to operate independently. But right now I can't authorize it under my department."

"Then she can do it under mine," Mark countered. "I'll take responsibility. Any immediate training can be handled by Katherine."

Katherine nodded in agreement.

The data analysis had been silent, giving every impression he was no longer interested in the outcome of the meeting. Now he leaned in, anxious to speak.

Paul noticed. "Okay, whiz-kid. What've you got?"

"From what you're saying, you're considering appointing Jewel as a negotiator and vendor representative for Weston's company."

"So?" Mark's challenge was more intellectual than a reminder of an agent's default authority over staffers.

"So," the analyst continued, "once she starts the process, she'll have to stay with it. You know the Chinese. If you change people midstream, they'll get all up in our face about disrespecting their ancestors or some other crap. If for some reason she doesn't work out, they'll start asking a lot of questions, like why we didn't put enough value on the relationship to select the right person in the first place." He glanced quickly at Katherine. "And then there's that other thing . . . the male supremacy shit."

I didn't know what he meant, but apparently, the others did. They fell silent, scrambling for ideas. Even Katherine sat back in her chair, removing her hand from mine, obviously agreeing with the little snot.

I sensed the subtle shift in attention. Everyone was waiting for Mark to respond.

Recognizing his que, he said, "Jewel, how do you feel about all this? Is it something you want to do?"

I remembered to count to two, silently. The technique was intended to convey a more considered response. "Well, first of all, I'm not really clear on what's involved. But if you're asking if I'm willing to work with Mr. Weston as his representative, I'd like the chance to prove myself. I think he trusts me, and from the brief time we spent together, I don't think he'll put up any more roadblocks. So like I said, I'm willing to give it shot."

I expected accolades. I thought my answer was good—hell, it was brilliant. But the table fell silent. Worse, the director seemed disappointed. Either I'd missed the point of Mark's question or—

"Jewel, as I mentioned before," the director said, "I was under the impression you and Katherine had discussed the details of this situation and how it would impact your work here."

Katherine's face reflected a neutral, even pleasant expression, giving no indication of being affected by the subtle reprimand.

I spoke up, covering for her. "We discussed the situation in broad terms. She gave me as many details as I could handle at the time. It sounds like there's a lot to learn, but that doesn't scare me."

The director shifted his eyes around the room, first at Paul, then Mark, then Katherine.

Mark interrupted the awkward hush. "Jewel, there's more to it than that. To begin with, you'd have some of the responsibilities of an outside operative, but limited in scope. Your official job title and duties would remain the same, however, your activities outside the embassy would be unsanctioned and unofficial. These types of arrangements, trading intel for privileged status, have always been handled directly by the company owners, at least that was the impression we wanted to convey. By putting you in the middle, you'd be a government employee working on both sides of the fence. If you get in trouble, if Chinese officials ever discovered the nature of your activities, we'd have to brand you as a rogue employee, involved in industrial espionage for personal gain. We couldn't help you, not officially anyway."

"Not in *any* way," the director added. "Our concern is your lack of experience. The risks are relatively small for someone well-trained and familiar with the surveillance community. But that takes time, and Mr. Weston wants our answer immediately."

I was confused. I'd come to the meeting believing my agreement to serve as Charlie's representative was what they wanted me to do. Now they were suggesting the job came with the possibility of a major ass-kicking—if I screwed up. And no one, including Mark, was giving me a vote of confidence.

Still, I wasn't ready to quit.

"From what I understand," I said, "Charlie Weston's business is an important bargaining chip. And he's willing to work with us as long as we give him what he wants. I've already given you my answer. What's the problem?"

"Mark, you're better equipped to answer that." The director was handing off the question. Later, I would learn he avoided speaking directly about clandestine activities whenever possible. Officially, he was not aware of them, and took every precaution to avoid being implicated.

"What our young intel expert was referring to earlier," Mark nodded toward zit-head, who was now sitting much higher in his chair, "is the level of commitment you'll be expected to make. Under a normal timeline, your dependability would be measured as your training progressed. By taking this kind of short-cut, we're jeopardizing your long-term value to the department by making you more expendable."

"What do you mean . . . expendable?"

"Granting you off-property freedom presents all kinds of temptations. If a question arises concerning your actions or intentions that could jeopardize the department's positon, we'd be forced to go to the bottom line immediately."

There it was. Although couched within the protective jargon of the department's interests, Mark was telling me this new position came with a zero-tolerance policy, including the option of disciplinary action that would be short and swift—and from the sound of it, permanent.

I didn't care. I'd have the advantage of being able to leave the embassy grounds, to have the freedom of working on my own, without someone constantly over my shoulder. It was what I'd been waiting for . . . the chance to find Annie!

I leaned forward and set my hands on the table, allowing my fingertips to touch. Turning toward Mark, I said, "I appreciate your concern, and your candor. And frankly, I expected nothing less."

The director looked up, surprised. Paul curled his upper lip. The kid rolled his eyes.

"And since you've been honest and forthcoming with me," I continued, "I'll extend the same courtesy."

Katherine responded with a subtle nod. It was barely more than a muscle contraction of her brow, but it was definitely there, and it was meant for me.

"I'm going out on a limb here and suggest that you've already made a conditional decision to move forward. And I get the sense you're willing to take a chance on me. So what will I have to do to live up to your expectations?"

Mark spoke first. "I'm assuming Jewel's duties as a business liaison would be in addition to her hosting responsibilities?"

"Yes," Katherine answered. "If there was a scheduling conflict, then the vendor program would take priority. And unless the director has an objection, I don't believe it's premature to consider it an unofficial promotion, with certain benefits that accrue with increased responsibility."

The director placed his glasses on the table. "Mark, from now on, Jewel is funded out of your department. And Katherine, as far as the additional training goes, don't give me some impromptu, thrown-together mess. I want to see an organized program, with periodic progress reports." He turned to the analyst boy-wonder, who had slumped down in his chair so low his chest was nearly under the table. "Have the data center originate new credentials for Jewel, a college degree with a dual major in business and communications. And add an internship at one of our state-side friendlies to give her credibility in the field." He looked at me, adding, "Jewel, you'll continue to report to Katherine. Nothing has changed in that regard. She remains your go-to person for everything."

Katherine patted my arm.

"And Mark," the director continued, "Can I expect you to handle some of the more esoteric training she'll need?"

"Done," he said.

I wasn't sure what the word *esoteric* meant, but if Mark would be the one teaching me, I was ready to learn.

The director was on his feet. The meeting was over.

I'd expected Katherine and Mark to stay behind and give me the "inside" story of what had just happened. But they were busy, pressed for time, and left immediately. Maybe later there would be some chit-chat between comrades, a sense of reassurance I'd made the right decision. For now, I could only speculate on my new opportunity. Hopefully, it would give me unrestricted access to the street, where I could obtain information about Annie and find out where Gregory had taken her. Only when she was no longer a prisoner, no longer suffering at the hands of a madman, would I be able to enjoy my relatively safe and comfortable surroundings. Until then, this job and its new privileges were nothing more than a means to an end.

Chapter Fifteen

"Katherine asked me to drop in and see how you're doing."

Mark's unscheduled arrival surprised me. Thinking it was Marcie, I'd almost answered the door wearing nothing but panties. At the last moment, I'd grabbed a shorty robe and thrown it on, leaving it open and untied.

"That's not like her, sending someone else to do the dirty work."

He seemed taken back. "This a bad time?"

I smiled, trying to lighten the mood. "No, I'm giving you a hard time. Come in."

Wearing a dark gray suit, Mark had stripped off his tie, the open collar revealing hints of muscle rippling just under the surface of the cotton fabric.

An outside agent making an official call on an embassy hostess in her dorm room seemed a bit out-of-place. There was probably some kind of rule against it. Even so, I couldn't help speculating if he'd been thinking the same thing, wondering what it would be like . . . lying close, running our hands over each other, my legs wrapping around him as he sank his swollen cock deep into my pussy. I didn't care if his visit was only a ploy. If he was hoping to use a little innocent conversation as an acceptable prelude to fucking me, I would quickly set his mind at ease.

"I wanted to make sure you were comfortable with everything that happened today," he began. "I know it was a lot to take in. So if you have any questions or need a receptive ear . . ."

"I'm not in the mood to discuss business."

He didn't say anything, the silence suggesting I might have come across too harsh and dismissive. "Can we talk about something else?" I asked.

"Not yet. It's important you know why I said those things in the meeting." His mouth was drawn tight, his lips thin. "The suggestion of having to . . ."

He hesitated, not wanting to finish.

"Put me down like a rabid dog?"

His voice returned calm and steady. "It wasn't personal."

"Katherine said it was standard protocol."

"Yeah, she told me," he said. "I thought you might want to hear it from me, too." He let out a breath. "I guess I needed to vent more than you did. But if you have a handle on everything, I'll let you get some sleep."

I sat back on the bed, making no attempt to close my robe. "Did I say I wanted you to leave?"

Mark made one of those little sounds all men make when they receive an unexpected invitation for sex—a little anxious sigh, barely loud enough to hear.

"Mind if I help myself to a water?" Without waiting for an answer, he opened the mini-fridge and grabbed a bottle.

"Is it what you expected?" he asked.

I gave him a questioning look.

"All of this. The bureaucracy, the bullshit, the attention to detail."

"I didn't come here with any expectations. An old fart named Bobby bought me at an auction and shipped my ass here, remember? There wasn't a lot of time to discuss my future working environment." I took a breath and waited for Mark to smile.

No reaction.

I tried again. "Okay, you want serious? I'll give you serious. Every day, I get a little better handle on what goes on here. Right now, I'm trying to keep up with Katherine and make her happy."

"That's a big job."

"You sound like you know from personal experience."

"I know how she thinks. Just don't tell her I said that."

I noticed his hands, the left wrapped around the open water bottle, the right, poised and ready at his side. He didn't appear anxious, but he wasn't relaxed either.

"Your spring's wound pretty tight. Bad day?"

"No worse than usual."

His stance was beginning to make me nervous. I decided to take a more direct approach. "I don't think you came here to talk. I think there's something else on your mind."

He stared at me, his piercing blue eyes locking on mine. Finally, he said, "No cat-and-mouse. Not tonight. I wanted to see how you were doing, especially after what I'd said today."

Finally it dawned on me! He felt guilty being the one to deliver the department's ultimatum—*screw up and you're dead.*

And now, he was concerned. About me. About my feelings.

"Mark, I don't care what brought you here. I'm just glad you came." I paused. "I'm not sure how this works, you know, when it's real, when I'm not on an assignment. So I'll just say it. I want you to take off your clothes and climb into this bed with me."

He didn't look surprised or pleased.

After a few seconds, I had to fill the big empty completely engulfing the room. "Well hell, don't go getting all emotional on me. I mean, if there's somewhere else you need to be, don't let me keep you." I gave him the best pouty look I could manage, hoping he could read my thoughts.

I'm ready. I'm waiting. Get your ass over here.

"Okay if I use your bathroom?"

"Go ahead."

Mark disappeared in the bath, pulling the door closed behind him.

I said it without thinking. "I suppose you're doing this to test my skills and make sure I can do my job."

Not a sound from the bathroom.

"Mark? If that's what this is about, it's okay. I don't mind."

His continued silence was making me uncomfortable. But it wasn't nearly as disappointing as seeing him suddenly standing in the bathroom doorway, his coat draped over his arm. The look on his face didn't help, either. Without a clear indication of anger or frustration, his expression was miserably neutral, as if he regretted coming to my room in the first place.

He approached the bed and extended his hand, his fingers lightly touching my shoulder. "Good night, Jewel."

His voice contained no possibility of reprieve, nor did his pace allow for one. He pulled the door gently behind him until the latch snapped closed.

I'd completely misread his intentions. There had been no order, no directive to test my prowess in bed. My off-hand comment had been an insult to both of us, tainting the anticipation of the pleasure we could have brought to each other.

I wouldn't make the same mistake again.

I considered calling him, saying I was sorry and, if he was receptive, inviting him back. But that would make me appear to be a self-concerned drama queen—someone better off avoided. My apology would mean more after a day or two, when my stupidity wasn't so fresh in his mind.

Right now, I needed to get some sleep. I had an early morning meeting with Katherine. Yet the thought of Mark lying next to me had left my mind racing. If I wanted to relax, I had to take the edge off.

I reached for the small bottle of lotion in the nightstand drawer. Squeezing a dab on my index finger, I laid back on the bed and spread it between the folds of my pussy. Closing my eyes, it came fast and easy—his warm, soft tongue teasing my clit, his hands massaging my breasts.

Why did I let him leave?

Quickly lacing my fingers through his hair, I drew him close, feeling his cock slide against my thigh as he moved higher to cover my body with his.

Didn't he want to be with me?

My breath turned quick and shallow as he found his way inside me, my pussy turning wet and warm as my juices flowed. My thighs quivered, my body beginning to roll with the building orgasm. I heard a groan—*mine*—as I sensed his cum spurting in spasms, my own release squeezing every last drop from his bursting cock.

I had to change his mind . . . soon.

Chapter Sixteen

My flight had been delayed by weather. The sky over Bangkok was clear, but the plane had originated in Dubai, and an early morning sandstorm had kept it grounded for an hour past the scheduled departure.

The situation was both surprising and a bit humbling. My fantasy of traveling by private jet was quickly dispelled with my discovery of the commercial airline ticket waiting for me in my room.

"First time in Shenzhen?"

My seatmate was an attractive, middle-aged man with a muscular build and full head of auburn hair. His appearance had generated more than a few careful glances from the women passengers as he made his way down the aisle.

"It is," I said reluctantly.

I had no interest in starting a conversation with a stranger. This was my first off-property assignment, and my destination, or the reason for my visit, was not a topic for chit-chat.

"I'm there at least four times a year," he added. "Name's Mike." He offered his hand.

"Jewel," I said, accepting it.

"If you have the time, be a tourist for a couple of days, see the Window of the World and the Splendid Folk Village. Both are real geography lessons. They'll give you a flavor of the place. Of course, the real way to explore Hong Kong is to hire a guide. You're only a few miles north of the city, and there's no other place

like it on earth. Gives you a real sense of perspective .
. . all those people, living and working so close
together."

I nodded, hoping our conversation was over. I
would only be there for a quick in-and-out, my
meeting with Hipong Electronics set for 9:00 AM
tomorrow morning. Then a 3:00 PM flight back to the
embassy. Although it was a short time window, it was
all I needed. Katherine assured me the meeting
wouldn't last more than an hour. And I'd allowed an
extra hour on both sides of the visit to accommodate
the amenities of the culture. If invited to eat, my
acceptance was expected. If offered a tour of the
company facilities, I would graciously agree.

'Always accommodate the host's offer to show
you more,' Katherine had explained. 'It doesn't matter
if it's another part of their working operation or a
glimpse into their personal life. Never refuse. It's an
accepted part of establishing trust and personal
rapport. In China, both are cultural necessities *before*
conducting business.'

This was especially true because of my gender.
The Chinese business community was still slow to
accept a female executive. 'A man will often be invited
to a gentleman's club, a strip bar,' Katherine told me.
'Business is often conducted in that type of
atmosphere. You won't see any briefcases or contracts
strewn across the table, but decisions are being made
on the spot.'

I tried to imagine a CEO explaining the annual report to a group of investors while a stripper flaunted her tits in front of his face—another example of Asian multitasking.

"I'm having a drink. Can I buy you one?" My seatmate again, making nice.

I started to decline, but I was going to be trapped with this guy for the next two-and- a-half hours. "Sure, why not."

I was also nervous about meeting the company representative who would pick me up at the airport and drive me to the Grand Hyatt, my hotel for the night. What if he asked me to dinner or wanted to take me out on the town? Would those be customary gestures? Or would he be hitting on me?

Way too much in my brain. Yeah, a drink would help.

The flight attendant set four tiny bottles of vodka on the tray with a couple bottles of water.

"Thought we'd start with doubles," Mike said, "then go from there."

He'd said 'two and two,' when ordering, but I hadn't paid attention. I looked at the mini-bottles of vodka. I'd missed breakfast and was hoping for a Danish. Instead, my stomach would have to settle for the nutrition found in eighty-proof Smirnoff.

"Cheers." Mike lifted the plastic glass and gulped down half the drink.

"You work for a company I might know of?" he asked.

I'd been waiting for it. I quickly reviewed my back-story, then fell into character.

"Probably not." I took a swallow of vodka. "It's a small firm called Roberts-Hover. Custom circuit design. No hardware. Just paper and debugging." I'd learned the lingo the night before, practicing with Katherine.

I sensed he wanted his turn. "How 'bout you?"

"We're a glass outfit. Make screens for computers, phones, tablets, that sort of thing. It's the touch part of high-tech. Wanted to make that our slogan, but the wife said it was juvenile, a flashback to the nineties." He dropped his eyes, as if remembering the moment. "Crazy bitch. Divorced me three years ago. Took my top chemist with her. At the time, I figured they were just fucking. Turns out, it was a lot more than that. Six months later they opened their doors. Now they're my number one competition. Guess what their company slogan is?"

I smiled. He'd been bought and sold—like me. But I doubted he'd ever been caged, stripped naked, and put on display with a steel butt-plug jammed up his ass before being sold to the highest bidder.

His story struck me in an odd, paradoxical way— his ex-wife had fucked him over and he was making jokes about it. I wondered if I would ever be able to laugh at what Carl had done to me.

"You know," he said, his speech already beginning to exhibit the effects of the alcohol, "I've always thought these planes should be divided into sections. The ones who want to work or read, they sit in the back. That way, everyone knows you want to be left alone. The rest of us would sit in the front, where we could be sociable, friendly, even *more* if folks were agreeable."

"More?" I regretted it as soon as it came out, but the vodka was lowering my defenses.

"Yeah, you know, a little hands-on, to help pass the time." He smiled and took another swallow, emptying the glass. "I'm ordering another double. Want one?"

"No, thanks. I'm good."

The vodka. My empty stomach. I doubted I could walk the aisle in a straight line.

He sighed loudly, a sign we had reached a comfortable lull in the conversation. My senses dulled from the booze, it took a moment to register—his hand had found my thigh. He was testing, seeing if I would object.

I should. I'm working, on assignment.

Hell, I even looked the part . . . a beige blouse buttoned to the neck and conservative-length dark brown skirt.

I could almost hear Katherine in the background. 'In this part of the world, the way a woman dresses conveys their intentions as well as their character. If you're seen wearing sexy clothing, you can easily be branded a whore and lose all credibility.'

Isn't that what I was? I didn't say it out loud, but the thought had crossed my mind.

I should've tactfully lifted his hand, established the boundaries.

Instead, I unfastened three buttons on my blouse, the action completely out of character for the identity I wanted to convey. I was wearing a low-cut bra that was more shelf than enclosure, and I was pretty sure Mike had a great view of my nipples.

The thought excited me.

I felt his palm drifting higher, toward the inside of my leg.

His hand was smooth and warm. He gently stroked my skin, the tips of his fingers circling, caressing.

Even though I was loopy from the drink, I decided right then and there—I wasn't going to fuck him. This was only play—teasing him, letting him touch me, seeing his cock straining against the fabric of his trousers.

I'd missed this . . . the luxury of enjoying myself while having the privilege of saying no. It was nearly as intoxicating as the vodka.

"I'm staying at the Futian Shangri-La," he said. "It's a high-rise, has some great views." He paused. "You never said if you were staying over." He drew a little question mark on my leg with his index finger. It was cute.

"Haven't decided yet." I was enjoying this way too much, and I wanted to hear his pitch.

"I know a hell of restaurant, serves some of the best steaks you've ever tasted."

"A steak? In China? What's wrong with the local cuisine?"

"Believe me, sweetheart. Once you find out what's in the home-grown stuff, you'll stick with the steak." He paused. "Where did you say you were staying?"

"I didn't."

He smiled. "You're cautious. Nothing wrong with that. But be honest, haven't I generated a little interest?"

"Only in the steaks," I answered. "But I'm not sure that's enough to motivate me to change my schedule."

"What else floats your boat? Just name it . . . theatre, museums, any of that tourist crap. 'Course, there's also some pretty decent shows. Like you'd see in Vegas, only toned down a bit, without as much skin."

He fell quiet, as if considering what else to throw into the offer. He was trying so hard. I was beginning to feel a little guilty.

I noticed a small scar on his right hand below his thumb. "Get that in a bar fight?" I joked.

"Oh, yeah," he countered, "that Silicon Valley crowd gets pretty rough at happy hour, especially when a fresh batch of bacon-wrapped mushrooms comes out of the kitchen."

"The Bay area, is that home?" I asked.

"I have a house there, to maintain residency. But I spend a lot of time in Asia. Cuts down on the flying."

The idea of spending the night in my hotel room watching cable was becoming less and less appealing. Although I was certain he would interpret my question as a step in the right direction—moving him closer to his goal of bedding me—all I really wanted were a few suggestions on where a single girl could have a drink and listen to some decent music.

"So tell me more about the night life in Shenzhen."

"Most of the hotel bars are set up for tourists and corporate executives. You know the kind of place, walls covered with chrome and glass, seating areas furnished with couches and overstuffed chairs, and the whole place overrun with potted plants."

"You left out the indirect lighting," I added.

He grinned. "Most of them are full of one-nighters, like us. Some are trying to hook up, others are bored and don't know where else to go. The independent clubs, at least the safe ones, have been taken over by the kids . . . lasers, fog machines, and the most god-awful music you can imagine. And the volume is loud enough to make your ears bleed."

A movie and room service was beginning to sound pretty good.

"So, nothing authentic?" I asked.

He looked at me, puzzled. "You mean a place where you sit on the floor and geisha girls swish their fans back-and-forth acting out the highlights of the second dynasty?"

"Geisha is a Japanese tradition," I said, correcting him. "That sounds like another tourist trap."

"Nope. The Chinese had geisha long before Japan. The Chinese version didn't concentrate so much on the music and dance and polite conversation, but they were well-trained in the stuff that counts. There's a few places in the city advertising that sort of thing. Most are just teasers for high-end strip clubs." He looked toward the aisle, making sure no one could overhear. "Once, one of my vendors took me to a place where you pay a couple hundred bucks to get in the front door, then they bring you anything you want. 'Course, that costs extra." He paused, waiting for me to encourage him to go on.

I decided to placate him. "What happened?"

"Well . . ." He hesitated again, like a kid deciding to tell his mom the school-yard bully had forced him lick the bottom of his shoe. "The place was first class. The girls were pretty, and really young. I was surprised, they all spoke fairly decent English. One of them brought me a menu. Not for food, but for different kinds of sex, kind of an a-la-carte deal. The girls would sit with us as long as we bought them drinks. Eventually, they made their sales pitch. They kept reminding us how the club's policy required men to wear a condom, so we didn't have to worry about catching anything."

He paused, his expression asking if I wanted him to continue.

I nodded, not sure where this was going.

He patted my thigh, apparently satisfied he'd conveyed the proper warning for what came next. "By this time, the girls are getting handsy with us, rubbing our crotches, pressing their boobs against us, really selling it. The one working on me gets real close and whispers in my ear. She says for an extra two hundred I don't have to wear a rubber." He shook his head with a kind of sad disappointment. "'Course, that meant if she'd do it with me, she'd already done it with others," he said, then added, "and life's too short."

I downed the last of my drink, unsure how to respond. I considered complimenting him for making the right decision, but it would be like congratulating him for not jumping into a cesspool. I decided the best I could do was give him credit for his decision to choose logic over pleasure, because after all, he *was* a man.

"Ever go back?" I asked.

He shook his head. "Never paid for it, at least not directly," he bragged. His mouth curved upward in a huge, devious grin. "But that doesn't mean I'm taking those steaks off the table. The offer's still good, and it comes without any strings."

I noticed we'd captured the attention of an elderly Asian woman sitting across the aisle. Cultural bias dictated she should offer a disapproving sneer.

Instead, she was smiling. Maybe she wished she could turn back the clock and join us, or just watch. Either way, I felt uncomfortable.

"I think we have an audience," I said.

"The lady across from us? She's been getting an eyeful since I put my hand on your leg." Mike leaned forward and raised his voice. "Newlyweds."

The woman chuckled and waved us off. She knew better.

The touchdown was rough. The cabin rattled with the sound of computers and shaving kits as carry-ons bounced and shifted.

"Here's my card," Mike offered. "And the hotel where I'm staying." He hurriedly scribbled the name on the back. "Call me. We'll get together."

I heard a slight edge of desperation in his voice.

"We'll see," I said.

"Not even a *maybe*?"

The two-plus hours we'd spent together had been a harmless, flirtatious diversion. I'd actually enjoyed his company, leg-grope and all. But right now, my life was complicated, full of details I couldn't explain. And distractions, even pleasurable ones, would dilute my focus.

I tucked Mike's card into my carry-on and slipped into the aisle, leaving him struggling with a tightly-wedged bag in the overhead bin. Maybe I should've looked back. But that would have given the impression I was interested. And making a dinner date with a civilian seemed counter-intuitive—

something a corporate suit might have done. Maybe after the travel had become routine and I was confident in my ability to get the job done.

But not now.

Chapter Seventeen

"It was wonderful meeting you. Please convey our deepest regards to Mr. Weston. We look forward to a long and prosperous relationship."

He was the international sales director for Hipong Electronics. His patter sounded scripted, as if he'd said it hundreds of times while supervising the exit of a buyer from the building. As he escorted me through the lobby, he continued to babble on about how our time had been well spent, his rhetoric oddly in sync with the snap of our footsteps on the expanse of highly-polished marble.

My meeting had been as boring as it was predictable. After a forty-five minute multi-media presentation explaining how the growing influence of technology had reduced the barriers of cultural bias, I felt like I was viewing a clip copied from a symposium on ethnic tolerance.

Our meeting took place in a glass-walled office, typical of most corporate boardrooms, except this one offered a commanding view of the city from the 24th floor. The three company representatives and I huddled at one end of a long conference table. There were lots of awkward pauses and feigned smiling.

My physical presence had nothing to do with negotiating a contract for circuit boards. The actual agreements had been finalized before my arrival, with details concerning price, payment terms, and delivery pre-approved by Charlie via email. My face-to-face time was a token gesture to confirm the good intentions of the parties. Katherine described it as a kind of wedding ceremony—a traditional and expected formality to kick off a new business relationship. 'In Asia,' she'd said, 'traditions are important. Establishing a personal relationship before writing a check is commonplace. Those who try to do business with Asian suppliers on the internet are at an extreme disadvantage compared to those who take the time to press the flesh.'

And that's exactly what I did—a short courteous bow followed by a quick handshake. It was one of those east-meets-west courtesies, meant to acknowledge both cultures with dignified equality.

Outside, the air on the street was heavy with smog, threatening to choke anyone foolish enough to take a deep breath. A limo was waiting against the curb and a uniformed driver immediately opened the rear door.

"Airport, please."

Leaving the company grounds put us into heavy traffic. It was every bit as congested as the L.A. I-5 at rush hour, yet there seemed to be a sense of symmetry, each driver knowing instinctively when to stop and when to go.

My cell phone chimed, announcing an incoming message. Probably mother hen checking up on me.

Change in plans. Stay one additional day to pick up sample from supplier in AM. Your flight changed to American #1567, departing 10:00 AM tomorrow morning.

Your hotel room extended by one night. More later. Katherine.

It was my first off-property text. Katherine had told me to keep my cell use to a minimum—a precaution to reduce the possibility of monitoring.

"Someone would do that . . . hack into my phone?" I'd asked.

"It's not unheard of. Industrial spying is common here, and your presence at a major electronics firm—not being a known vendor or supplier, and noticeably attractive—could raise the competition's curiosity. There's always someone hiding in the bushes, hoping to pick up sensitive information that can be sold to the highest bidder."

Katherine was describing private hi-tech mercenaries, gray-market entrepreneurs who spent hours on the street outside large firms fishing for anything that could be turned into fast money. Rolex watches and Louis Vuitton handbags were old school. The real bucks were in video games and phone apps.

With Katherine's warning still fresh in my mind, her text surprised me. I would have expected a cryptic message, requiring a codebook or secret decoder ring—neither of which I had.

"Driver, I'm not going to the airport. Can you take me to the Grand Hyatt?"

"Yes, already on the way."

He knows?

I sighed. I was a human drone with tits, waiting for someone to push my buttons and send me running off in a new direction.

I stared at the words on the screen—*More later.*

You're damn right. And this time, send it to me first, before you distribute it to every limo driver in town. That's what I wanted to text back, word for word.

I let it go. I typed in the word *okay* on my phone and pushed *Send*.

The idea of spending another night in my hotel room was depressing. It was comfortable, but as I opened the door, it felt strangely empty and isolated, like a dead zone, void of energy. Last night, I'd ordered room service and watched three back-to-back episodes of the original Star Trek series. It had been my dad's favorite show, and we'd spent hundreds of hours watching it together.

I couldn't do that again. I had to get out and find something else to do.

Chapter Eighteen

"Mike? This is Jewel. We met yesterday, on the plane. You know, when your hand and my thigh became better acquainted?"

"I thought you were long gone, as in *audios amigo and have a nice life.*"

"Alright, so I didn't give you much encouragement. I had a lot on my mind."

"And what's on your mind now?"

"Is that dinner invitation still good?"

"So it's all about the food? What about my enduring charm, my witty personality?"

"You mentioned steak. More specifically, steak with no strings."

"Just my luck . . . a hot woman with a good memory. Okay, steak it is. And then, I have a surprise for you."

"What kind of surprise?"

"I have an invite to a party. Lots of high-rollers."

"A party? I don't know. I was thinking a little dinner, a quick kiss on the cheek, and we call it a night."

"Before you decide, hear me out. The guy throwing the party is rich as hell, puts these shindigs together once a month. There's a regular guest list, and always a few new people, you know, friend-of-a-friend and a few freaks to add a touch of color. It's a real zoo. Wildest shit you've ever seen."

"You mean drugs?" I wouldn't put myself in that environment. Too much risk, especially in China.

"There's always people who show up higher than a kite, but that's not the main event. You go to watch, look at the crazies."

"It doesn't sound like anything I'd enjoy."

"That's because I'm doing a lousy job of explaining it. In fact, I don't think words can do it justice. It's something you gotta see, a peek at how the other half lives."

"That's my only option?"

He was silent for a few seconds. "Alright, I'll be honest with you. It's couples only. I need some arm-candy."

At least he wasn't trying to hide it. "What happens after we get inside?"

"Give it fifteen minutes. If you don't like what you see, we can leave anytime."

"You mean that?"

"Yep. And like the steak, it comes with no strings. You get us in the door and if you see something more interesting, I'll find a couch and park myself. You're in charge."

A party wasn't what I had in mind. I was looking forward to a great meal in a nice, quiet restaurant. And if it came with a little more leg-groping, I wouldn't complain. But a house full of strangers? Sounded like another embassy ball.

"Let's review the terms," I said. "I'm in charge. We leave when I say, even if it's only been five minutes?"

"Fifteen. You gotta give it fifteen. You can't walk through the place in five minutes. And I swear to you, if you don't like it, we're out of there."

I blew out a breathe, then realized it was loud enough to produce a roar in Mike's ear. "Sorry, I'm a little apprehensive. I've lived a sheltered life. Thought about being a nun for a while."

Silence. I'd thrown him.

"Okay, how do you want to do this?" I asked. "Should I meet you at the restaurant?"

"I don't play that way. I'll pick you up."

"And bring me back . . ."

"Whenever you're ready."

I remembered the plain beige blouse and frumpy skirt I'd brought. I didn't have anything sexy. "What do the girls wear to this thing?"

"Everything . . . and nothing. Don't worry, you'll fit right in." He paused. "If you feel overdressed, you can take something off." The upswing in his voice made it sound more like a suggestion than an option.

Chapter Nineteen

"You've already paid the bill?" I asked.

"Yeah, while you were flirting with the wine steward."

"The guy was cute," I teased. "Had nice eyes."

"Get his number?"

I shook my head. "Did *you* want it?"

"Nah, I used up my monthly allotment of wine stewards last week. Two a month, that's my limit."

We'd been nipping at each other all through dinner. Nothing sarcastic, just innuendo and playful flirting. True to his word—at least, so far—Mike was letting me call the shots, from picking the restaurant to ordering the wine, and even setting up the ground rules in advance for leaving the party.

I had to admit it, I was having fun. No schedules, no forced social patter, no boring marks to entertain. For the first time in years, I was on a date—a real date, with a man who was treating me like a real woman.

"Ready for a taste of the high life?"

"Impress me."

As we walked out of the restaurant, the black, four-door Chrysler materialized from the darkness and stopped at the curb. I scooted across the rear bench seat, leaving plenty of room.

Mike followed me in, sitting on his side without crowding me. "You realize everyone in the restaurant was looking at you?"

"Broccoli in my teeth?" I swiped them with my finger.

"I think it had to do with another part of your anatomy . . . somewhere in this area." He waved his hand back-and-forth in front of my boobs.

Unable to talk myself into wearing the only clean outfit I had—a light blue blouse and long gray skirt— I'd visited the hotel boutique and found a deep purple, form-fitting cocktail dress with a scoop neckline. Compared to what I'd worn to the last embassy party, it was conservative. I'd put it on without a second thought.

"Too much?"

He shook his head, smiling. "Nobody asked you cover them up, right?"

We pulled away from the curb and into traffic, the driver seemingly oblivious to our chatter.

"Anything I should know, name of the host or guests?"

"I'll introduce you to the regulars, at least the ones I know. The host usually doesn't make an appearance until late, if at all."

Outside, the city streets were nearly day-bright. Flooded with a thousand halogen suns, the subtle orange glow was accented with faint rainbows of neon, revealing another side of Hong Kong—a city constantly awake, always shifting, changing with a heart-pounding pulse.

The car turned into a parking garage and the driver handed the attendant a small, black plastic card, our host's version of an RSVP.

The attendant peered inside the window. "Hold the card in front of the keypad at the fifth level. Then drive all the way to the top. Park anywhere you can find a space. The card also gives you access to the penthouse level. There's a scanner in the elevator." He spoke perfect English.

Our driver stopped in front of the elevators on the seventh level. This was getting interesting. From what I could tell, we were attending an exclusive party for the ultra-rich—and those who rode in on their coat-tails.

"You do this a lot?"

"Impressed?"

"Hell, no. Just last week, the girls and I were having lunch in St. Tropez, deciding what color marble to order for the vanities in our Lear jets."

His smile diminished slightly, his voice turning serious. "Money buys a lot of things. It also raises the bar on what gets you off. So you have to push the envelope, find something that brings back that high, fires the senses, keeps life interesting."

"Like what?"

"You'll see."

The elevator doors opened to a small alcove, a transitional space for guests to collect themselves before making an entrance. Furnished with nineteenth-century chairs and a set of end tables displaying Asian-inspired ceramics, it might have been a decorator's attempt at post-minimalism. But the cultural influences of flat-weave carpet and glass sculpture were immediately offset by four prominently mounted security cameras, their electric mounts and adjustable lenses in full view.

"Building security. They're running our images through facial-matching software."

I reached for the doorbell.

"No point. It'll open in a second."

Right on cue, two solenoid-operated deadbolts retracted with a loud *snap*.

"Remember, this isn't a convent, so take a deep breath and don't let anything throw you."

I couldn't hold back my smile. It was nice . . . the words of caution, his concern over my assumed innocence.

If you only knew.

Pushing the door open released the drone from a hundred voices. The entry was already overflowing with guests, and behind them, more people were packed shoulder-to-shoulder in the large living room. Standing, talking, drifting from one group to the next, they maintained a constant level of chatter, often reaching out to touch each other without restriction— their hands gently caressing, fingertips brushing over bare skin, lips meeting in a flurry of kisses.

I noticed several women wearing revealing outfits exposing their breasts, not in a brazen, let-it-all-hang-out fashion statement, but as a flowing and integral part of their appearance. Small-chested women were at a definite advantage for making a bare—yet elegant—presentation of their body.

At first no once seemed to notice our entrance. Then a growing wave of turning heads greeted us with varying degrees of interest, curiosity, and invitation—sometimes on the same face.

My embassy training was signaling me to jump right in, approach the nearest group, and introduce myself. The longer I waited, the more out of place I would appear, giving others the idea I didn't belong. But at first glance, this little get-together was far removed from the social constraints of an embassy party. Sexual overtures were obvious, and being expressed and received openly. The scene reflected a reunion of close, sexually-intimate friends, happy to see each other—and eager to express it.

"Mike, you made it. And you've brought someone new."

He was Asian, mid-fifties, and balding, with a slight build and huge smile.

"Jewel, this is Hawg Lee. He's into women's clothing."

"You make them or wear them?"

Lee forced a laugh as he reached for my hand. "I like this one. Perhaps I should introduce her around."

"Not yet, Hawg. I want to break her in slowly."

His face fell. "Then you must promise me some of your time later, after you've had a chance to get a lay of the land. We probably have a lot in common."

"I'm afraid I don't know much about the clothing industry," I said.

Mike shook his head. "I'm pretty sure that's not what Hawg wants to discuss."

Hawg winked at me. "All good things in time." He stepped back and offered a slight bow, his smile spreading to the point his eyes were forced to close. A moment later, he disappeared into the crowd.

"What was that all about?" I asked.

"Hawg is a hyena, a secondary hunter. He waits for other men to get a girl turned on and in the mood, then he tries to join in. The only thing you have in common with Hawg is a compatible anatomy. He's got a dick, you've got a pussy." He paused. "You're okay with me being straight with you, right?"

"I think we're way past the honeymoon stage."

I caught a glimpse of Hawg slipping his tongue into a statuesque blonde's ear, his straining posture—teetering on his tiptoes—as comical as it was sad. With any luck, his dick and my pussy would not cross paths. Maybe fucking *was* part of my job description, but right now, I was off the clock. And I would decide who I wanted between my legs.

I reached down and took Mike's hand. "Mind if I hold on? I'm not quite ready to fly solo."

He interlaced his fingers with mine and gently squeezed. "Remember, you can always say *no*, or just walk away. You won't offend anyone."

From where I stood—the way they were fawning over each other—it didn't look like the word *no* was in their vocabulary.

"So most of what goes on here is about sex?"

He hesitated, as if unsure how to answer. "The things that get these people off is a broad arena, covers a lot of ground. But yeah, sex is usually part of it."

A sudden parting of the crowd provided a glimpse of a portable bar against the far wall, next to the elongated bow of what was certainly a grand piano. It explained the live music, although the volume barely broke through the buzz of the hive.

"Can we get a drink?" I pointed to the bar.

"Double vodka, right?" he asked?

"Mixed with a little water." This time, I wanted the buzz—no way I was doing this sober.

Mike handed me the glass. "Want a quick tour?"

I took a sip. "How do we navigate through this crowd?"

"Hold on and don't let go."

Using the sense of touch to let others know we were passing through, Mike slid his hand around the waists of women or set it briefly on the shoulders of men—a way of communicating without interrupting ongoing conversations. His physical contact was often returned in kind, with both men and women reaching out to gently fondle and stroke, sometimes momentarily pressing their bodies against both of us. Brushing against breasts and semi-erect cocks was unavoidable, yet not altogether unpleasant. It was overt and intentional, and as I would come to learn, a friendly and expected gesture. Realizing the brevity of the exchange, I even caught myself reaching out to return an occasional stray touch of unknown origin.

Mike led me out of the living room and into a small vestibule. I immediately smelled food.

"Let's check out the kitchen," he said.

The kitchen? If the host had hired caterers, they would be busy with food preparation. Loitering guests would surely be in the way.

We ducked inside just as a waiter was pulling hot appetizers from the oven. Next to him, another server arranged fruit garnishes on a large tray of cheese and crackers. I'd been wrong—working in the middle of a dozen guests didn't seem to faze them. In fact, they happily hand-fed anyone with an open mouth, paying especially close attention to a beautiful bare-bottomed Latina sitting spread-eagle on the opposite counter. Another woman with long blonde hair and naked to the waist, knelt in front of her, exploring the Latina's pussy with her tongue.

The sight of the two women—their contrasting light and dark skin joined in pleasure—was as out of place as it was intoxicating. Yet, in this kitchen full of food and guests and happy chatter, nothing was inappropriate. Instead of casting a critical eye— judging them for their choice of time and place—the other guests were appreciating the display, relishing in the women's abandon and unabashed enjoyment of each other, vicariously sharing the experience.

"The dining room is around the corner. Might be able to find a chair so you can get off your feet."

Mike had no idea how much engineering had gone into the design of my stiletto heels. I could stand in them all night if necessary. His gesture was well intended, and I needed to show my appreciation.

I took a last look at the two women, hoping the image would retain its detail later, when I recalled it from memory. "Let's check it out."

By now, I'd grown accustomed to the constant press of arms and torsos, the sensation of disconnected hands sliding around my waist, under my breasts, and across my bottom. Never lingering, they stayed long enough to acknowledge me, inviting my response.

I had to admit, if only to myself . . . this was fun.

The distance to the dining room was only ten feet, but the trip took several minutes, our progress interrupted by those who recognized Mike and wanted to say hello and catch up. Finally squeezing through the arched entrance, Mike looked around and shrugged. The only furniture in the room was an immense table. Divided into three serving sections by the caterer, the center portion was occupied by a small, naked brunette, her body covered with strawberries, chunks of pineapple, and strands of grapes. Guests were encouraged to eat directly off her skin, using their mouth to pluck a piece of fruit, then top it off with a lick of whipped crème from her nipples. A living centerpiece, she laid perfectly still, her eyes open and expressive, her smile responsive to the movement of the guests.

Even though I had no interest in the fruit, I couldn't stop myself. Reaching out, I placed my hand on hers. Immediately, she wrapped her fingers around mine, as if grateful for human contact.

She whispered a few words. Unable to hear, I leaned closer.

"You're pretty. Touch me, if you want."

"I am touching you."

"I mean you can put your hands on me, anywhere you want."

It wasn't so much an invitation as a request. Maybe she was tired of being treated as an object, unappreciated as a living, breathing woman. I skimmed my other hand across her thigh. Her chest rose, her breathing becoming short and rapid.

She was excited, and had no reservations about showing it.

"Quite a serving tray, huh?" Mike was suddenly next to me, sampling one of the carrot sticks wedged between her toes.

"You think she's well paid?"

He looked confused. "Like a doctor?"

"I mean, when the party's over, will she collect a paycheck and go home?"

"I guess so. Where else would she go?"

Either he'd never heard the stories of young girls sold into sex slavery or didn't want to consider the possibility. But I wanted to know.

I bent down, pretending to nuzzle her face. "Are you being forced to do this?"

Her breathing halted. "No one forces me," she whispered, with a touch of defiance. "I do this for Gary. He pays me to serve at his parties."

I gently squeezed her hand. This time she opened her fingers, releasing me. She was upset with my question, not only for the unintended offense my suggestion carried, but also for breaking the mood. She'd been enjoying my attention, reveling in the feel of my hands on her body while the other guests hovered over her, watching.

Mike noticed the change in her demeanor. "Trouble in paradise?" he asked.

"We were done."

"Yeah, no point in filling up on strange when there's plenty of familiar waiting for you." He raised his eyebrows, making it obvious who he was referring to.

"Is there more to see on the tour?"

He motioned toward the opposite archway. "Stairs are around the corner. Second floor . . . gateway to perversions and deviant fantasies."

"Sounds like you've spent a bit of time up there."

His upper lip twitched as he pulled me toward him. The kiss was simple and quick—the kind you'd give a neighbor for bringing over a batch of freshly baked cookies. It was the first time he'd shown affection and he was keeping it light. He was either a real gentleman, letting me decide when and where, or he was playing it coy, planning to take me by surprise when the time was right.

The second floor wasn't as crowded. People congregated in the hallway, some talking, others groping each other in every combination of gender. Although newcomers were never rejected, most occupied themselves with their immediate group, having retreated upstairs for an imagined sense of privacy.

"Mike? That you?"

In his sixties, the man was slender and attractive, with a full head of silver hair. Impeccably dressed in a suit and tie, he looked as if he'd just attended a board meeting and had come to the party to shake off the corporate noose.

"Hi, Larson. How's business?"

"Oh, you know, still trying to keep the sweat-shops from organizing. Once they get a taste of American money, they start asking for air conditioning, coffee breaks, and health insurance . . . like they see in the movies. Can you believe it? They make two-fifty a day and they want health benefits."

"Larson, this is Jewel."

He scanned me from head-to-toe. "You're quite a lovely woman. Can't imagine what you're doing with this guy." He motioned toward Mike. "His reputation alone should've scared you off."

"He has a reputation?" I asked. "You mean in plastics?"

"Is that what he told you?"

I softened my eyes. "He also said I should be wary of older, distinguished gentlemen who have an unusual appetite for young women." I almost added, *and like to walk around with a banana up their ass*, but decided to hold off until I had a better idea what direction the conversation would take.

"Owww," he said. "I like this one . . . quick tongue and all."

Mike started to speak, then stopped as he noticed a younger man—early thirties and well groomed—headed directly for Larson.

Larson acknowledged him immediately. "Tommy, meet an old friend of mine. This is Mike, and his date, Jewel."

Tommy offered his hand, first to Mike, then to me.

"What do you do, Tommy?" Mike asked.

Larson answered for him. "Tommy's in shipping. At least that's what he tells everyone. His real job is damage control." He turned toward Tommy. "Looking for that wayward bother of yours again?"

Tommy's jaw tightened, his expression strained.

"Oops, I've said something I shouldn't have. I'll shut-up now and let you speak for yourself."

It was obvious Larson suffered from a bad case of foot-in-mouth disease. And the fact that he loved to hear himself talk made it impossible to cure.

Tommy broke the awkward silence. "Like Larson said, I'm in shipping." It almost sounded like an apology.

"That term, *damage control,*" Mike said. "Are you a trouble-shooter, you know, the guy people call when they unload a shipping container and find a dozen Chinese immigrants inside?"

"No, not exactly." Tommy was growing noticeably uneasy.

Even though he'd promised, Larson couldn't contain himself. "Tommy here works for the family." He lowered his voice, as if offering Tommy a little sympathy. "It's a damn shame. Really is. It's gotta be hard on you and the old man."

Tommy shifted from one foot to the other. "We deal with it as best we can," he said, then added, "If you'll excuse me, I'm going downstairs and grab a bite to eat." He looked at Mike. "Nice to meet both of you."

Seeming as embarrassed as he was frustrated, Tommy stepped back and disappeared down the hall.

"What was that?" Mike asked.

"It's not exactly a secret," Larson said. "Not like it used to be, especially after what that idiot brother of his keeps doing. Why that bastard hasn't been shipped off to some shit-hole prison and left to die is beyond me. Just goes to show what money can buy."

He could've been talking about anything—or anyone. It was all supposition at this point, but he'd set my mind racing. Circumstance or coincidence, I had to know for sure.

"I didn't catch Tommy's last name."

Larson's expression was guarded. "I shouldn't say. He comes here to get away from the questions, you know, blow off a little steam. He's a good man."

I leaned closer, my boobs almost touching his chest. "And his brother isn't? A good man, I mean."

Larson didn't like the pressure. "Let's not bring down the mood with all this serious talk," he said. "This is a party. Let's have some fun."

Bullshit. He'd spent the last five minutes shooting off his mouth. Just because he'd opened up a Pandora's Box and now wanted to slam it shut, I wasn't letting him off the hook. I slid my arm around his waist, skimming my cheek against his face. "You want a party? I'll give you one. All you have to do is tell me Tommy's last name."

His eyes widened. "It's that important to you?"

You have no idea.

I almost said it. Catching myself in time, I tried a more subtle approach. "If Tommy's brother is as bad as you say, you wouldn't want me accidently getting mixed up with him, would you?"

I felt the quick rise and fall of his chest as his hand found my back, pulling me in tight. "It's a house rule," he whispered. "No personal questions. If someone volunteers their real name, that's fine. Pressing for information is liable to get you thrown out."

I brought my fingers to the back of his neck, feeling the heat. "You've never broken a rule?" I flicked my tongue at his earlobe. "Especially to get what you want?"

He swallowed hard. "His name is . . . Housing. He comes from money. Big money. But he's clean, nothing under the table. Like I said, he's a nice guy."

Housing.

I realized my right arm was quivering, my eyes blinking against the gray fog pressing on my brain. Fighting the nausea, I laid my head on his shoulder.

Not now. Push it away. Do it for Annie.

Interpreting my physical surrender as an offer of submission, Larson dropped his hands to my butt. Leaning back, he nearly lifted me off the floor. I didn't care. It was what I needed—a moment to recover.

I felt his lips on my ear. "None of what I told you about Tommy came from me, understand?"

I managed a shallow nod.

"There's a bedroom behind us," he said. "Let's see what's going on inside."

I needed a few more seconds. I brought my legs up and wrapped them around his waist. "Carry me."

Mike's face was etched in surprise. I would explain later. Right now, I had to recover my stamina, shake myself free of Larson and find Tommy before he left the party.

Attempting to cover his struggle with the additional weight, Larson baby-stepped into the nearest bedroom.

"The bed is right behind you." He began lowering me into a pile of writhing bodies, their collective consciousness knowingly making room for one more.

My head was clearing. Bringing my hand to his face, I said, "Sweetie, I have to take a break." I kissed him on the nose and started unwrapping myself from the sudden web of anonymous arms and legs.

"Wait! Where you going?"

"Need to visit the bathroom. Don't worry. I'll be right back."

His disappointment was obvious. "I'll be waiting."

Chapter Twenty

I should have felt guilty abandoning Larson. But I didn't—even though I'd set him up, using the promise of sex to convince him to reveal Tommy's last name.

I'd just met Gregory Housing's brother. While I had no idea of the kind of man he was—Larson had said he was a *good man*—if I told him the truth, he might be willing to help me find Annie, or at least point me in the right direction. Even though Tommy was estranged from his brother, he no doubt knew where Gregory lived, his hangouts, his habits. And with that kind of information, I'd have a place to start.

After excusing myself with a ploy of using the restroom, I'd made a beeline downstairs. Tommy had said he was hungry. It might've been a convenient pretext to break free from the awkward conversation, using food as a diversion to distance himself from a stressful situation.

I had to be careful. Nothing too forward. There weren't any obvious signs of security, but that was the mark of real pros. They did their job from the shadows, without being visible. Only low-budget rent-a-cops made a big splash of being seen, believing an intimidating presence was key to preventing problems—an assumption that only worked in the absence of power and money.

Getting down the stairs was easy. Those using the steps as seating had uniformly shifted to one side. As I stepped into the small alcove, I reached an impasse. Jammed between a cigar-smoking Russian and a beautiful Thai woman, I lingered long enough to be polite, then smiled and pointed toward the dining room. With me sandwiched between, they shuffled a quarter-turn, patted me on the bottom and released me into the crowd. Another half-dozen steps and I saw him, pressed against the wall by two women who were working him like a couple of seasoned strippers selling lap dances.

"Tommy! There you are. I've been looking all over for you. Mom called. She's at Heathrow and her flight's been canceled. She needs your help getting rebooked, said she's waiting for you to call her back."

His confusion lasted for only a second before he feigned a look of total concern. "Sorry girls, you'll have to excuse me. Gotta give mom a call."

Like two snakes reluctant to release their prey, they uncoiled from him slowly, skimming their fingertips along his arms and chest before retracting their fangs.

"You'll hurry right back, won't you Tommy?"

"Don't forget us. We'll be waiting for you."

Tommy guided me out of earshot. "That was balls-y."

"They were setting you up."

"I got the same impression. Not sure what they were going for, but they were really putting their hearts into it."

I stared at him with the stern scrutiny of a Catholic school nun. "It's the money, Tommy. It's always about the money. You have it, they want it."

"And you, Jewel? What do you want?" His eyes narrowed. "Are you planning on taking over where those two left off?"

I raised my clenched fist to his face, raised my middle finger and wiggled it under his nose. "I rescue your ass and you thank me with accusations? Maybe I should have left you with the vultures."

Tommy play-nipped at my finger with his teeth. "Hmmm . . . I suppose time will tell if I made the right choice." He paused. "Really, Jewel, what *do* you want from me?"

Instead of answering, I pressed my finger against his mouth until he opened up. Laying my fingertip on his tongue, he closed his lips and began to suck.

"Right to the point, huh?" I said. "I'd hoped there'd be a few minutes of pitter-patter, me saying how handsome you are, and you trying to impress me with your usual line of bullshit. You know, both of us whitewashing what we're really thinking."

Seeing the huge question mark forming on his face, I slowly pulled my finger from his mouth.

"Just so I'm clear and don't screw this up, what *are* we thinking about?" Tommy's eyes grew large.

I had one shot at making this work. I could play coy and take my chances, or I could go for broke. I couldn't see any advantage in holding back.

"Same as it's always been with people like us. I want to spend your money, you want to fuck me." I waited a few seconds, letting it sink in. "Here's a suggestion. Let's have an unforgettable night splitting a few bottles of Merlot in a hotel room with a view of the city."

He cocked his head to one side, as if replaying my words a second time. "You don't beat around the bush, do you?"

"Life is short. And besides, when Larson introduced us, you took off before we could chat. I wondered if it was something I *didn't* say."

He smiled. It was a bit placating, but I would take it.

"I didn't mean to be rude," he said. "I just wasn't in the mood to party. I guess I'm still not. Got a lot on my mind."

I reached for his hand. "I'm a good listener."

"Uh-uh. It would bore the hell out of you. Not a good first impression."

"You don't need to impress me." I leaned in, bringing my hand higher on his arm. "You seem distracted . . ." I stopped, letting the suggestion hang.

"You're perceptive, and pretty. That's a rare combination, especially in this crowd."

I could have said something clever or sarcastic—responses that would have provided a transition to more superficial subjects. Instead, I offered a look of concern and put my arms around him in a consoling hug. I intentionally kept it therapeutic, hoping it would bring the walls down.

I waited for it—his hands on my waist or an arm around my shoulder. If he moved, even a few inches in an attempt to put more of his body against mine, I had him.

I felt his palm cradle my neck, his face brushing against mine. He drew deep, taking in the smell of my hair.

"You need anything?" I asked. "Another drink?"

"Maybe some privacy. It's getting a little claustrophobic."

I felt his cock stiffen against my belly.

Bingo.

"Is there a place upstairs?"

We can use the bedrooms, but the doors have to be left open. House rules. The only place offering any kind of privacy is the laundry room. And it doesn't offer much in the way of atmosphere."

I thought he was kidding. He wasn't.

I waited long enough to avoid sounding overanxious, then shrugged my shoulders. "If we turned off the lights, we could use our imaginations, make it into anything we want."

"You sure?"

He was asking if I was really serious about accompanying him to the laundry room —*to fuck him.*

I kept my voice flat, without a hint of emotion. "Yeah, I'm sure." I could've been talking to a soda-jerk at Haagen-Dazs, confirming my preference for strawberry over vanilla.

We made our way past the food table—I couldn't help taking another look at the naked brunette centerpiece—and started up the stairs.

I had two immediate concerns. I didn't want to run into Mike. He'd said I was free to spend time with others, but he seemed like a nice guy and I didn't want to flaunt it in his face. Larson was also waiting for me. He *didn't* seem so nice—even more reason to avoid him. I could easily imagine him playing the drama card by unleashing a sudden barrage of accusations.

Arriving at the top of the stairs, I scanned for third-wheels—single men obviously waiting on a woman. I'd caught a huge break. I didn't see Mike or Larson.

"See that pocket door at the end of the hall?" Tommy asked. "That's it." His tone carried the unmistakable underpinnings of an apology, like an embarrassed high-school kid walking his prom date to a '58 Nash Rambler.

"Probably no way to lock it," I said.

"Don't know. Never needed to use it before," he grinned.

He was beginning to enjoy himself. I wanted him to open up, but first I had to gain his trust. And if that meant spending twenty minutes on my back, I wouldn't hesitate.

"It's best if no one sees us go in. We'll have to hang out in the hall until it's empty," he added.

Nervous over the possibility of being spotted by Larson or Mike, I stayed as close to Tommy as possible. Stroking his crotch, nuzzling against him, I hoped we blended into the dimly-lit atmosphere—just another couple waiting for a vacant spot on a bed. My view of the master bedroom's interior, with its king-size mattress and pillow-strewn floor, confirmed it as ground-zero for anonymous hook-ups. More orgy than coupled sex, it was packed with people, most of them naked and physically connected with at least two others. By comparison, a simple pairing was passé, a waste of the senses. With most craving the rush of sensory stimulation that accompanies multiple partners, mouths were filled with eager cocks, while extended tongues explored freshly-fucked pussies. Without regard to gender, one connection was replaced with another in a constantly changing, always rotating motion of bodies. An equal opportunity fuck-fest, the only requirement to participate was a set of genitals.

There was a constant stream of people coming and going. Bringing my lips to Tommy's ear, I whispered, "Screw this, we're going in."

I didn't give him a chance to argue. Seeing an opportunity, I pulled him inside the laundry and closed the door behind us.

"Look, there's a lock." I fumbled with the knob, twisting it both directions until I heard the latch click.

"Meant to be," Tommy added.

The size of the room was no more than six-by-ten. With a full-size washer and dryer, wall-mounted ironing board and upper storage cabinets, there was no place to sit—or lie down. Except for the ceramic tile floor.

"I wonder . . ." I opened the dryer and glanced inside. Scooping out a load of clean towels, I dropped them to the floor. "It's all we have to work with." I looked at the machines and grimaced. "Turn off the lights, before the image sinks in."

"It's a dimmer. Okay if I bring it to low?"

"Mood lighting in a laundry room. Yeah, why not?" I said.

Tommy slid the switch down, bathing us in mock twilight. "This is a first for me. Reminds me of high school."

"It's kinda cozy." I wanted him to relax, but I had to know how much time we had. "I didn't see your other half. Will she come looking for you?"

"I'm here by myself."

"I thought it was couples only."

"It is. You're supposed to bring a spouse, or friend. It keeps the ratio between men and women about equal. The host knows I don't have a steady girl, and I don't do a lot of dating, so he cuts me some slack."

"That seems odd. You clean up nice. Got a steady income. I'd think you'd be a real catch." I paused for second, then added, "Are you one of those guys who's too picky for your own good?"

"I don't have time for all the games, the back-and-forth nonsense. My work requires a lot of travel, so it's hard to make plans."

"Shipping, right?"

He was quiet for the longest time, and in the dim light, I couldn't evaluate his expression. Finally, he said, "It's a family business. My father started it from scratch." He hesitated. "Wish he could enjoy what he's built."

"Your brother again?"

It took him another moment to answer. "You heard about my brother?"

I had to be careful. I was approaching the subject head-on, and that could easily turn him off or make him suspicious of my motives.

"I'm a computer hardware consultant," I said, lying. "A few of my clients use your company to ship their products. The subject's come up."

He blew out a breath laced with frustration. "Gregory's cut a pretty wide swath, most of it right through our company's reputation."

Hearing the name made me cringe. I realized my fingers had balled into fists, my teeth clenched.

Control it, back it down.

"Is that what's bothering you? Family issues?" I half-whispered.

"I spend over half my time cleaning up Gregory's messes. At first, I could take care of things with a few phone calls or write a check to pay for the damages. But this last fiasco forced me to make a personal visit, with a briefcase full of cash. I know he's family, but there's a limit. And I reached mine a long time ago. My father says we can't abandon him and leave him to the wolves."

"So what happened? What's different *this time*?"

I could hear him breathing, wondering if he could trust me. "It's not something I usually talk about . . . with anyone."

The polite thing for me to do was change the subject. But strapping Annie to a table and attaching a set of high voltage electrodes was as far from polite as you could get.

"I know we just met, and you don't have any reason to believe me, but it seems like you need someone to talk to, and I promise whatever you tell me will stay between us." I reached out, touching his arm with my fingers. "If that's not good enough, I understand."

"Honestly," he said, "I could give a shit about Gregory. What concerns me is the stress he puts on my father. Gregory's a liability, to the business, the family, to my father's health. Every time I hear the phone ring at three in the morning, I know it's another problem with my brother."

"You mean with drugs?" I was leading him, trying not to push.

"Drugs would be a blessing."

He slid to the floor and leaned against the wall. I joined him, scooting between his legs, my back against him, inviting him to hold me. He immediately drew me in.

"Gregory is sick," he continued. "We've tried to get him help, move him to a facility where he can receive therapy or medication, at least be monitored. But he won't stand for it. Once we had the local authorities commit him for observation. He became so violent they had to lock him up. That was fine, as far as I was concerned. But my father wouldn't allow it. So now, we try to keep him under the radar, pay off the damage before it becomes public, and buy him protection from the police."

"And that works?"

"It did, for a while. But in the last year or so, he's gone over the edge, gotten himself into some really serious shit. I've been able to keep most of it from my father, but I can't let it go on. Gregory's behavior has reached the breaking point. He needs to be put away where he can't hurt anyone."

I wanted to tell him it was too late. Instead, I asked, "That's what he does? He hurts people?"

Tommy slid a hand to my cheek and gently brought my face to his. I had the sense he wasn't being forward as much as seeking comfort.

Then it dawned on me . . . the silence, the gentle closeness. *He was done talking!*

But I wasn't.

"So where is your brother now?"

I'd shattered the moment. My question was as ill-timed and as out of place as if I'd asked what interest rate he was getting on T-bills.

"You mean, where does he live?"

Careful . . .

"You mentioned being here to straighten out a problem. So I'm guessing Gregory must live in Hong Kong." I held my breath.

"He has a place here."

My hands began to quiver, my throat clamping shut. I couldn't think—or speak.

Hold it in. Don't let him know.

I casually brought my fingers to my face, feigning the need to brush away a stray hair, hoping I could swipe the single tear before he noticed.

"It must be hard on you," I managed.

I felt the muscles in his face tense—an involuntary sign of resignation.

"I wouldn't mind so much," he said, "if there was an indication he was getting himself under control. But it's getting worse. A lot worse."

I was ready to leave, to call Mark and have him contact the Hong Kong police. But something Tommy had said stuck in my mind . . . he brought a briefcase full of cash. Tommy was here to deliver a bribe, hush-money to keep Gregory out of trouble, and more than likely, from being charged with a crime. But Hong Kong wasn't known for its "dirty" cops. The money had to be for someone else—

someone in authority, a corrupt political official with enough power to make the police look the other way.

I needed more, enough to be able to act on my own . . . if it came to that.

"When was last time you talked with him? Your bother, I mean." An address was too much to hope for. But a general location, a direction from the city center—it would be a place to start.

"It's been over two years. He knows how much I disapprove of his behavior and what he's doing to our family. He thinks of me as an errand boy, a necessary nuisance that allows him to perpetuate his lifestyle. I gave up on having any kind of relationship with him a long time ago."

He seemed sincere as hell. And as far as I knew, he had no reason to lie to me. I decided to back off. There was a lot more information Tommy could share, but I couldn't take the chance of alienating him with more prodding about an extremely personal situation.

I felt his hands sliding lower, sweeping my legs, then working his fingers under my dress to the inside of my thighs.

I wouldn't resist his advances. This was what he needed . . . to satisfy him now, to make him want me in the future.

He brushed the lips of my pussy. "Hmmm, we need to fix that."

Retracting his hand, he brought his middle finger to his mouth and coated it with saliva. "This should help."

I opened my legs, waiting for it.

This time, he slipped inside without resistance. Finding my clit, his touch was gentle. Even so, I knew he was re-establishing his role as the dominant male, and penetrating my pussy was a quick way of putting the last few minutes of vulnerability behind him.

I would do whatever it took.

"I need to get rid of this dress."

Rising to my knees, I pulled it over my head and tossed it to the corner. Bunching the towels into a make-shift bed, I laid back. It was far from comfortable, but I'd been fucked on more unpleasant surfaces.

I reached out for him. "Come, lay down."

In a few minutes, he would be done with me. But if I could make an impression beyond the simple pleasure an orgasm would provide, I might become a priority in his life. He would take my future phone calls. He would drop whatever he was doing to meet me, wondering if I would service him in exactly the same way.

I expected him to settle between my legs. Instead, he straddled my chest, his ass brushing against my nipples. Bringing his swollen dick to my mouth, he ran the tip back and forth over my lips.

I didn't hesitate. Relaxing my jaw, I opened wide as he laid his cock on my tongue. Licking the head in short strokes, I tasted a trickle of pre-cum. Reaching behind my neck, he lifted me closer as he slid deep into my throat. With my right hand, I gently cradled his balls, moving my middle finger toward his asshole. His thighs began to quiver, a low growl escaping from his lips.

I wanted him to explode.

I wanted him to remember.

Chapter Twenty-One

"Get a better offer?"

Mike was grinning, wondering where I'd been.

I didn't want to lie to him. He'd been the perfect escort all evening, buying me dinner, introducing me to his friends, and never once putting the hard press on me. As far as I could tell, he had few if any expectations—and if he did, he was keeping them well hidden.

"I was in the laundry room, fucking that guy Larson introduced us to."

"Uh-huh. You know, I get that same urge once in a while. I gotta admit, there's nothing like getting my rocks off while sitting spread eagle on a front-load Kenmore."

He didn't believe me! Perfect. Now I had to come up with a story he *would* believe. "I'm sorry, I'm afraid I haven't been very good company this evening. I've been making regular visits to every bathroom in the house, fighting a queasy stomach. Might've been the hollandaise sauce. I know, you warned me. And now, I'm paying for it."

His good-natured teasing turned to concern. "Do want me to take you to your hotel?"

"Yeah, probably best. I think I'd feel better if I could lie down."

Taking my arm, he plowed a path through the living room, toward the front door.

I felt a little guilty, using him. But I had what I needed. I'd exchanged cell numbers with Tommy, extracting his promise that he would call me when he made his next visit to Hong Kong. 'Let's stay in touch,' I'd suggested. 'No strings, just talk and some fun, if you want.'

From the gleam in his eyes, he wanted it plenty.

As the car left the parking garage and drove onto the main street, I was struck by the intense glow from multiple layers of blazing neon. Although I'd noticed them on the ride over, we'd arrived in the hazy twilight of a late setting sun, preventing me from seeing the floating panels of red, yellow, blue, and green in all their gaudy and garish glory.

"I thought the Vegas strip owned the title for tacky, but this is surreal."

"Lots of people think it's an art form, something to be preserved. And there are just as many who complain about light pollution and the waste of energy." Mike paused. "Feeling better?"

"I really am. Thanks for not insisting we stay."

"I was ready. I usually leave after an hour or so, about the time it takes to say hello and do a little catching up with people I know."

"Ever meet anyone new?"

"All the time. But after we cover the basics, there's not much to say. Tonight, it was all about you."

"What do you mean?"

"It gave me a chance to show you off, get credit for bringing some premium eye-candy. And from the looks you were getting, I'm pretty sure my stock rose a few points."

"You fucker!" I poked at his ribs with an imaginary sword. "I still don't know when you're being serious and when you're screwing with me."

He reached around my shoulder and drew me close. It was the first real move he'd made all night. And yet, it was so spontaneous, so innocent, I never considered rejecting it.

It suddenly dawned on me. I was in the back seat of a limo with an attractive, successful, intelligent guy who apparently liked me. He had just taken me to a party filled with the wealthy and powerful. And now, we were driving through the streets of Hong Kong at one o'clock in the morning.

It was the fantasy of any young woman. But I'd been so absorbed in thinking back about my conversation with Tommy, I was missing out on the present moment.

It was time to take a break. For the rest of the ride I would open my senses to the here and now, experience my surroundings from the perspective of a single gal having a night on the town with a handsome bachelor.

I brought my hand to Mike's cheek. From the slight lurch of his head, it surprised him.

"Leftover canapé on my face?"

"Don't know. I'll check." I brought my lips to his. Nibbling at this mouth, I teased him with my tongue, offering it, then pulling it back. There was no agenda, just a desire to feel the rush of a sweet kiss, the press of his body against mine, the sensation of his cock sliding deep inside me.

And I wanted it now.

Here. In the backseat of this limo.

I swung my leg over his lap, straddling him. "You think the driver will mind?"

Realizing I was lifting any previous restrictions, Mike's hands were immediately on my breasts, his fingers scooping from underneath, freeing them from the dress.

"Do you care?" he asked.

I shook my head. "Not at all, 'cause I know how hard he's gonna get watching us fuck in his rear-view mirror."

I leaned in, placing my right nipple between his lips. "Here, nibble on this."

"Mmmmmm."

"Shhhh, it's impolite to talk with your mouth full."

Needing more room to free his dick, I rose slightly, my fingers unzipping his trousers. In moments, I began stroking his cock, bringing it to full size.

"Let me change positions," I whispered. "I want to suck you."

REDEMPTION

Pulling off the dress and heels, I laid my head in his lap and stretched out across the seat. I wanted him to see me naked, touch me, play with my ass if he wanted to. Grasping the base of his cock, I skimmed it with my tongue. Even in the subdued light from the overhead billboards and passing street lamps, I could see his penis was absolute perfection. Standing straight, tall, and firm, the shaft was smooth and hairless without a hint of a twist or bend. I ran my tongue over the circumcised head, its ridged bulb inviting me to form a tight bond with my lips. It was exactly the way I'd imagined a cock would look when I was a young teen, before Jeremy Sandal had shown me his excuse for a penis at a drive-in movie and then asked me to jack him off during the cartoon.

As I took his dick deep into my mouth, I felt his hand on the back of my head. Keeping me close, he arched his torso with each stroke.

It would have been easy to tell myself I was doing it was for his pleasure. But I loved feeling his shaft deep in my throat, then pulling back so I could suck on the head. It made me light-headed, knowing he was building his load, his cum only moments from flooding my cheeks.

But that wasn't the way I would take him.

Fucking my mouth was only an appetizer, a foretaste of what was to come. My pussy was wet, my clit screaming for attention. And when he came, I wanted his cock buried inside me, his cum filling me until it overflowed onto the fine leather seats inside this limo, with its driver pretending not to notice as he raced through the neon-soaked streets of Hong Kong.

Chapter Twenty-Two

"Did you enjoy yourself?"

They were the first words out of Katherine's mouth. She sounded accusatory, as if I'd played hooky instead of doing my job. I wondered if she'd found out about the party.

There was another reason her odd way of greeting me was disappointing. I'd been looking forward to seeing her. Personally, I wanted to throw my arms around her. I considered her as family.

I wondered if I would ever be able to tell her that.

"I don't think *enjoy* is the right word," I began. "Look, if this has to do with the mini-bar charge I put on the hotel bill, I'll reimburse the—"

"No, Jewel," she interrupted, a smile breaking the tension in her face. "I'm asking because I really want to know. Did you enjoy yourself?"

I had no idea where she was going. I hoped she wouldn't take what I said next as a confrontation. "I don't want to play this game. Not with you. I can do cat-and-mouse with the others, but when it's just you and me, I want to talk openly and say anything I think needs to be said."

Katherine was still smiling. "And?"

"And . . ." I drew it out for emphasis. "I need you to say what's really on your mind."

Katherine tilted her head slightly to the side. "Okay. You had lunch?"

It was 10:30. "Not yet," I said, ignoring the time. "I slept late and missed breakfast."

"That's another thing they need around here . . . brunch. Let's go raise hell with that twit who runs the cafeteria."

Katherine mirrored my stride. "So what's foremost on your mind, what did you learn from your trip?" she asked. "I need to write a report. Anything you can tell me will make it that much easier."

I started to answer, but she cut me off. "You know, I can't remember anyone mentioning they actually read those off-ground reports. Unfortunately, we still have to write and file them, back 'em up on some remote server."

"Because they might prevent an international meltdown?"

She smiled. "If paperwork is what it takes to stop future wars, then we've definitely done our part."

There was no one else in the short hallway. I reached for Katherine's arm. "So anything happen while I was gone?"

"Plenty. First of all, you tried to call Mark from Hong Kong. Then you texted him, asking him to call you back."

I couldn't deny it. I waited for her to continue.

"What did you want from Mark?" she asked.

"Just some details about picking up the sample from Hipong Electronics."

Her expression turned skeptical. "You called from a private residence."

They'd tracked me!

"Is that a concern?" I tried to suppress the challenge in my voice, but it was impossible to hide.

"I wasn't aware you knew anyone in Hong Kong." Katherine's tone was curt.

"I don't. I met someone on the plane and he asked me out."

"Anything I need to know?"

"You mean did he ask me to marry him?"

"No, Jewel. I'm asking from a professional standpoint. I need to know you maintained your cover. I don't want a bunch of horny playboys showing up at the gate asking to see you." Katherine paused. "Look, I don't mind when my girls engage in a little recreation. But I need to know where you're going, who you're with, and for how long."

"I have to ask for permission to go on a date?"

"Our girls don't *date*. At least, not in the conventional sense. In your position, you can't form personal relationships that have the potential to become romantic entanglements."

"No worries, mom. The man took me out for burgers and fries. And later, I gave him a quickie in the back-seat."

Katherine frowned. "That's not what I mean and you know it." Katherine seemed a little peeved at my arrogance. I hoped most of it was contrived, because right now, I needed a friend, not a handler.

"I'll give you the official version," Katherine added. "Then we can discuss it."

"Shoot."

"Anything that takes you outside the department's direct oversight and supervision has to be authorized. At least for the present. Later on, after you've gained more experience, you'll be given more latitude with your time."

It was like hearing the cage door slam shut behind me. I'd forgotten—although no longer forced to live in a cell, I was still a captive.

"Okay," I said. "Let's say I *had* called and told you where I was going. Would you have given me permission?"

"On your first off-property assignment?" Katherine grimaced. "Accepting a date from a stranger was a bold move on your part." She slowed her pace to look at me. "Actually, Jewel, it was on the edge of stupid. You were in Hong Kong. The guy could have turned hostile, tried to hurt you, or worse."

"You were worried about me?" I wanted to hear her say it.

"The department has made a sizeable investment in you, and we don't want you putting yourself in situations that could expose you to unnecessary risk."

I'd wanted to ask before, and had waited to hear what Katherine had to say. Now I had to know. "How did you know where I was?"

"Your phone. It has a GPS locator chip in it."

"I suppose I should have switched it off."

Katherine shook her head. "You can't disable it. And I can't imagine a situation when you'd want to.

If you miss a meeting or don't show up for an appointment, we can back-track your route. It gives us a place to start."

The department's leash was a long one. I wondered how far I would have to run before they would lose their ability to yank me back.

"So now what? You want me to stand in the corner or are you gonna ground me for a week?"

Her smile returned.

"Like I told you, we were worried. That's all. I'm not going to clip your wings. You completed the assignment. The department's happy. Mr. Weston's happy. So it's time to move on to new business."

She pointed to a table in the corner of the cafeteria. As we sat down, a server with two cups of coffee appeared out of nowhere. She must have seen us enter, and being familiar with Katherine's expectations, responded automatically.

"You were starting to tell me about new business," I began.

"Tomorrow night's reception. We have a full house. You'll have an assigned guest as well as a secondary priority."

"I don't understand. What's a secondary priority?" I realized what she meant before she could answer. "Sounds like I have two guests. How does that work?"

"It can be tricky, but in this case, it's a natural combination. The two know each other and have been entertained at the embassy before . . . together."

"Sounds like a threesome."

"Most likely, but you can't always count on it," she said. "Either one could have different expectations. You'll have to test the water, let the primary guest make the first move . . . if she makes one at all."

"She?"

The question on Katherine's face was obvious. "Problem?"

"No, just surprised."

Honestly, I felt relieved. Not that the idea of accommodating a man was unpleasant—it was my job and I would perform it without question. But another woman could be a welcome change, and might even make for an interesting evening.

"Good," Katherine said. "Because your secondary guest is *also* a woman."

"Two women." I let out a deep breath. "Okay."

I'd never imagined it, much less considered the physical logistics.

"Remember to avoid showing any kind of favoritism to the secondary priority," Katherine continued. "If she's the first to suggest some sort of play, drop a hint that it would be fun to include the other woman, too."

I was struggling with the proper decorum of consensual group sex—if there was any. My experiences on the *Kelsey* had been dictated by testosterone and rank, the pecking order of the crew determining who fucked me first, second, and last.

The men had offered no give-and-take, and never asked if I was willing or receptive. I accommodated them out of necessity. I did it to survive. This was different. My participation was still mandatory, but I was part of a team, working to produce a result, and there was no reason for me not to enjoy the process.

I shifted in my seat. "Question . . ."

Katherine set down her coffee cup and looked at me with eyes that could cut glass.

"Let's assume they want to play. Anything in the manual about who goes first?"

"There's no real protocol. Just follow their lead. And if they choose to play as a group, remember to accommodate them both. Leave a smile on their faces."

"I understand . . . smiles, all around."

Katherine was telling me—in her own slightly obscure way—to treat both women equally, even though there was a definite priority in their importance to the department. If I gave one of them an orgasm, I was not to let the other one leave the room without the same experience.

"And Marcie, is she available to help?"

"She'll have her own assignment . . . a high level business contact. He likes to keep a low profile, so I doubt you'll see much of her on the floor. Don't worry," she continued. "You'll be fine. Use that charm and intelligence of yours and the evening should go well."

"Not to mention these," I added, bringing both hands under my boobs and giving them a squeeze.

"Goes without saying, my dear."

Katherine was on her feet, pushing the empty coffee cup toward the middle of the table. "It doesn't sound like you had much sleep last night. You should take the rest of the afternoon to re-center yourself. Walk around the grounds, clear your head. Tomorrow will be a busy day."

I reached out, touching her arm.

"Was there something else?" she asked.

I frowned. "Jesus, do you ever let your guard down?"

"Not here. Not now."

I assumed she was referring to the cameras—always on, always recording.

"Let 'em watch," I suggested. "I bet we could drop a few jaws, maybe even start a rumor flying that would get us called into the director's office."

There was a hint of a smile, but it never materialized.

Chapter Twenty-Three

Katherine's suggestion of taking the day off was a welcome break. I threw on a pair of shorts and a T-shirt and headed out for a long walk around the grounds—barefoot.

I'd taken a few steps down the hall when Marcie burst out of her room.

"You're back!" she squealed, breaking into a run.

In moments she was on me, smothering me in her arms before whirling me around in a circle.

"I missed you," she said. "That Italian prick kept me off-grounds for four days."

I'd never developed a real affection for Marcie, and yet, with her cheek next to mine, our bodies tightly connected—it felt good.

"I missed you, too," I said, knowing she needed to hear it. "How was the assignment?"

"A long weekend in hell."

The obvious entered my mind. "Did he hurt you?"

The corners of her lips turned down. "Nothing broken or bruised. Except my ego."

Without releasing me, she pushed me inside my room. "Katherine said you had an assignment in Hong Kong. What happened? Who did you meet? Tell me everything."

Katherine hadn't cautioned me against sharing the details from my trip, and Marcie was one of the family. I saw no reason not to confide in her.

"It was a vendor meeting, everything by the book, very proper, strictly pinkies up."

Her face fell. She wanted dirt.

"I did meet someone on the plane, though."

She perked up, her eyes beginning to sparkle. "Really? Was he cute? American? How old was he? Did he ask you out?"

I sat back on the bed. "Yes, yes, late thirties, maybe early forties, and yes."

"Oh my God! First time off-grounds and you score. Where did he take you?"

"We went to dinner. It was nice, a low-key place with good food in a decent part of town. Nothing fancy."

"So did he make his move? Did he fuck you? Was he any good?"

I broke out laughing.

I couldn't believe it. Not because of how excited Marcie was, but because it was the first time I'd laughed in over a month.

"We had a moment," I said.

Her eyes widened, begging for more.

"Nothing over the top," I added, "just a little affection between fellow nomads." I realized I'd used similar words in high school to describe a good-night kiss. Now that simple adolescent peck on the lips seemed so innocent, a preliminary exchange to whet the appetite for a more satisfying experience.

Marcie was quiet for a moment. "You know what made it nice?"

His gorgeous cock? It was the first thing that came to mind, but I wasn't sure what she meant, so I shook my head.

"You didn't *have* to fuck him," she said. "You did it because you wanted to. It was *your* decision, not another assignment to serve the department's greater agenda."

I wondered if the room mics were on. I pointed to my ear and brought my finger to my lips, suggesting the possibility.

"I could give a shit," she said. "It's time somebody told the truth around here. We're nothing more than government whores, paid to work on our backs and take cock in every hole we have. Just because we do in the name of ol' Glory, doesn't make it respectable."

I'd only known Marcie a couple of weeks, but her attitude was a complete one-eighty from what I'd seen and heard before. Something had made her angry, and she didn't care who knew it.

"Marcie?"

She lifted her head, focusing on me with huge blue eyes.

"What did you mean when you said your assignment was like spending four days in hell?"

She hesitated. "It was a long stretch with someone I didn't care for. I need to put it behind me." She'd been sitting at the foot of the bed. Sliding close, she put her arms around me. "I'm glad you're here," she whispered.

She was dismissing my question. She didn't want to talk. But if I had returned upset from an assignment, she would press me until I told her what happened. "You're sure this guy didn't hurt you?"

I felt her quiver, her breathing fall shallow. "There was more than one."

My mind flashed back to the deck of the *Kelsey*, when five men had surrounded me in a circle, each one waiting to take his turn.

"How many?" I asked.

"I lost count. They just kept coming. Then they started the second round. Including the slime-ball ambassador, there were nine."

"You're kidding, right? Did Katherine know this upfront?"

"I . . . I don't think so. It's not like her to throw any of us into that kind of situation without some warning. I found out the ambassador had been planning this party for months, to entertain some of his business contacts as a way to show his gratitude for political favors."

"And you were the only . . . entertainment?"

"Yeah. Sometimes they took turns. Mostly, they came at me three at a time, a dick for each hole. Then a couple of them got creative and tried to squeeze two cocks into my pussy." She drew a deep breath. "If it had only been a day or two, I could have handled it. But four days . . ."

I pulled her tight. "You're home now. That's all that matters."

She wiped at her eyes. "Would you do something for me?"

"Of course."

"Would you take off your clothes and lie next to me, stay with me until I fall asleep?"

I began pulling off my top. "My bed okay?"

Chapter Twenty-Four

"Will Marcie be on the floor tonight?" I asked.

Katherine and I were having breakfast together, an activity quickly becoming a Friday morning ritual. Reviewing my assignment for the weekend—the two women she'd previously told me about—she added a few specifics describing their political affiliations and personal details to confirm what subjects to avoid and which ones to work into the conversation.

"You won't see Marcie," she answered. "Her assignment likes to keep a low profile. He may spend a few minutes mingling with the other guests. Then again, he may not."

"And Marcie is his favorite?"

Katherine smiled. "They get along. He visits the embassy three or four times a year. While he's here, he enjoys her company."

"And speaking of Marcie, where is she? I thought she was coming to the meeting."

"Not today. I gave her some last minute errands to take care of, off campus."

"So I won't see her until tonight at the party."

"Like I said, Jewel, you probably won't see her at all."

I was getting the strange sense Katherine was intentionally keeping Marcie and I apart. Her reserved, even cryptic manner when discussing Marcie's duties wasn't suspicious on the face of it. But it was unusual, since the more Marcie and I knew each about other's assignments, the more we could work together, especially during the cocktail hour and dinner. In this case, Katherine was making it clear our respective guests wouldn't appreciate a double date. They wanted their activities to remain private, and that meant the less people who overheard any kind of flirtatious chatter and innuendo, the better.

She should have known better than to try and keep Marcie and I apart. Three hours later, we were sitting together in my room.

"It was strange not having you at the meeting," I said. "It felt sterile, stiff."

Marcie took a sip of coffee.

"Katherine seemed worried about something," I continued. "If I didn't know her better, I'd think she was trying to keep us from talking to each other before tonight's party."

"Did she say anything?"

"Not really. I asked where you were and said you already had your assignment. Then she went over a few details for mine and said she had to leave."

Marcie blinked.

Was it my imagination or was she also being a bit reluctant to talk about tonight?

There was one way to find out.

"So, is your assignment anyone interesting?" I asked.

"Some guy whose family is a preferred vendor."

"What industry?"

"Shipping, transporting blacklist stuff."

"Like what?"

"Anything. People, technology, weapons, whatever the government wants delivered to friendlies without public knowledge. They keep it off the manifest or disguise it as something else."

I was already jumping to conclusions. I had to slow down, stop all the assumptions. I could ask her outright, but too many questions might result in having to explain my curiosity, and I wasn't sure how Marcie would react—especially if she'd been cautioned by Katherine to keep the details to herself.

"Sounds boring," I said. "You met this guy before?"

"First-timer. At least for me. Katherine said he used to visit every quarter, but it's been a while."

That didn't jive with what Katherine had told me. Supposedly, the man was a regular, someone who preferred Marcie's company.

"Old, fat, and hairy . . . right?" I was fishing.

Marcie grinned. "Not according to the picture in his file. Just the opposite. He's on the young side of forty, good-looking, and in fairly decent shape. Might turn out to be a fun evening."

I kept prodding. "Maybe he's here to negotiate a new contract or make arrangements for a special shipment, you know, *a box full of monkeys*."

That was the term used for restricted technology, the kind of stuff that couldn't be legally sold or shipped to the third world, and yet, the state department had decided to make an exception, citing extenuating circumstances that served our county's long-term interests.

Marcie cocked her head. "Katherine gave me the impression it was a PR visit. You know, fuck 'n go."

I was ready to ask her to break the rules, to open the seal of confidentially Katherine may have imposed on her. I could only hope her loyalty to me would supersede her allegiance to the department.

"Did Katherine explain why the assignment was so under the radar?"

Marcie paused, perhaps weighing the risk—and the penalty—of disregarding Katherine's warning.

"Not really. She told me to meet him at the gate, pour him a drink, and take a walk around the grounds. Then straight to my room. And whatever we do, I'm supposed to keep him away from the main hall."

"Won't he think that's a little strange, being an embassy guest and not attending the party?"

"Katherine said he prefers it that way. He doesn't like the formality, or the bullshit. He'd rather get right down to business."

I'd waited long enough. I had to ask. "What's his name? So if I see him, I can say hello."

She didn't hesitate. "Thomas. Can you believe it? I think it's religious, from the Bible. Apparently he prefers Tommy."

My mouth went dry, a huge lump in my throat forcing me to whisper. "Marcie, I need to ask you something."

"Sure."

"The last name . . . is it Housing?"

Marcie's face twitched in surprise. "You know this guy?"

I felt my muscles straining, my body becoming as rigid as an Easter Island statue. For a moment I considered disguising it. But Marcie had always been upfront with me, and right now, I needed her honesty—and trust.

"Remember the other girl I told you about, the one with me at the auction?"

"You mean Annie, the girl who was bought by some torture freak?"

I nodded, trying to control the fear—the hatred—rising inside me as I remembered the two men pulling Annie and I apart, her screams filling my brain as the drugs turned my legs to rubber.

"I'm pretty sure . . ." I stopped. There was no point in beating around the bush. "I *know* Tommy is the freak's brother. He's also the guy I met two nights ago at the party in Hong Kong."

Marcie grew quiet, her expression an equal mix of surprise and concern. "So that's why Katherine acted the way she did."

"How so?"

"She wanted me to keep the details to myself. She told me the less I said about this assignment, the better. You know, real cloak-and-dagger stuff."

"Has she ever done that before?" I asked.

"Not with me. I can't remember a single time when she's asked me to keep the identity of a guest from another girl. She knows we talk with each other. It's how we process things, get it out of our system."

"Marcie, I need to talk to Tommy. I have to spend some time with him."

She shook her head. "You might as well ask for a one-way ticket to Paris."

I gritted my teeth, ready to argue my point, but she cut me off.

"I know you want to find out about Annie," Marcie said. "But this isn't the way to do it. Katherine will be watching us like a hawk. You and I won't even be in the same room together. And if I deviate from the planned route, one of her security goons will be all over me."

Maybe I was asking for the impossible. But tonight, Tommy Housing would be inside the compound. If I could find a way to let him know I worked here and was anxious to see him, he could tell the suits to back off and force them to give us an hour or two together. Hopefully this time, he would be more receptive to talking about his brother—revealing some clue as to where the scumbag might have taken Annie.

First, I had to convince Marcie that, even though the chances of pulling it off were small, I had to try—and I needed her help.

"Humor me for a minute," I said. "Let's say we decide to give this a shot. How would we do it?"

Her face contorted with doubt.

"You're more familiar with the buildings," I said. "And the layout of the grounds. Is there a way we could *accidentally* bump into each other?"

She thought for a moment. "Maybe. If we could manage to get you two together, how much time would you need?"

"A few minutes to get re-acquainted, maybe another ten to move us in the right direction."

"Hmmm . . . you might be looking at this all wrong. How did you leave it with this guy the last time you last saw him?"

It was an open question, but I knew exactly what she meant.

"I fucked him."

"Don't you think he'll want a repeat performance?"

"That's what I'm hoping."

"So come right out with it. Tell him."

I looked at her, the question planted on my face.

"Look," she said, "you and I can decide where to meet, maybe someplace outside the main hall. We'll make it look like a coincidence. Then you tell this Tommy character how much you enjoyed the last time, and how nice it would be to spend more time together." She paused. "Don't forget to use your hands, touch his face, his neck. Don't leave any doubt what you have in mind."

Neither of us had mentioned the most challenging part of the plan. "How do we handle Katherine?" I asked. "She'll have a fit."

"She'll get over it. What's more important? You being able to talk to this guy or keeping Katherine happy?"

Maintaining Katherine's happiness was the least of my worries. Her wrath was another matter. Marcie was purposely ignoring the possible repercussions our little plan could have. We were considering intentionally disobeying Katherine's instructions, abandoning our respective assignments—unpardonable offenses. It could get us kicked out of the department—or worse.

Marcie had nothing to gain from taking that kind of risk, and yet she was suggesting she would do it—for me.

As far as I was concerned, I *wanted* Katherine to confront me. I had plenty of justification to turn the tables. From the day I'd arrived at the embassy, she'd lied to me. She knew who Tommy and Gregory Housing were. She'd also known one of them was a psychotic killer, a sadistic freak who had taken Annie as his prisoner. With the relationship between the Housing family and the state department based on mutual deception and international deceit, a simple phone call was all it would have taken to determine Annie's whereabouts. Apparently, the suits had decided political protocol was more important than Annie's life—her location and well-being an unpleasant subject to discuss across the negotiating table of the high and mighty.

Fuck Katherine and her two-faced brand of loyalty. I had tried to be her friend, but my trust had become another method in which she could manipulate me. It was time to push back and, tonight, the bitch would find out how far I was willing to go to save my friend.

Chapter Twenty-Five

Dinner had been the usual bland piece of chicken and rice pilaf, the creamy mushroom sauce decorating my plate appearing every bit as tasty as that of the guests, yet completely devoid of flavor—something I still had to get used to.

The place-cards had seated me next to my assignment, Sabine Garrard, a representative in the lower house of the French Parliament. Celebrating our introduction over a continuous volley of champagne—my glass refilled with an alcohol-free look-alike—we'd bonded immediately.

A lovely woman in her late forties, Sabine had pretty, sensual hands, her long, slender fingers often touching my shoulder to emphasize a point or brush a stray hair from my eyes. A single ring adorned her right third finger, its large center stone—at least two carats—radiating enough fire to project a geometric rainbow on the table linens. Flanked by two smaller diamonds and set in platinum, the ring was a statement of simple elegance. I'd never really liked the pretentious message a large diamond ring implied, but in this case, I'd commented on it, not out of placating her expectations, but because it impressed me as a symbol of independence, a sign of liberation and self-reliance.

As the booze reduced Sabine's reservations, she abandoned the customary dinner conversation and spent the majority of the meal chatting up her love of

American rock-and- roll, the French countryside, and Chanel perfume, the sampling of which had given me the opportunity to hold her wrist to my nose for much too long, then leave a kiss on the back of her hand—a well-received gesture that resulted in her lingering touch on my cheek, until stares from our tablemates became too obvious to ignore.

It didn't matter. The message was clear. We were going to fuck.

Her friend and my secondary assignment, Yvette, eyed us from across the table, occasionally play-biting on the end of her index finger, a less-than-subtle indication she wanted to join in.

More than once, I realized this could have been enjoyable. Sabine had a nice figure, attractive face, and had come to the party to have fun. My concerns over how to approach her had vanished in the first five minutes of our introduction.

But I was far too distracted to anticipate spending time with her. My thoughts were completely focused on Tommy. Marcie and I had concocted a plan to "run into each other" at precisely 9:30 PM. Our rendezvous point was a memorial stone bench, located fifty feet behind the rear entrance to the Fortress. Marcie would be walking the grounds with Tommy, and I would just happen to step outside for a breath of fresh air.

Timing was critical. Infrared cameras would be monitoring Marcie's route through the compound. Her detour to bring Tommy closer to the Fortress would arouse immediate suspicion. And stopping or even lingering at the bench for more than a few seconds would initiate a shit-storm of radio crackle—instructions for security to intercept and redirect. At the most, I might have thirty seconds—my window of opportunity—to convert Tommy Housing's surprise into sexual arousal. Once he understood what I had in mind, I would suggest he ask the suits to allow Marcie and I to exchange places. If I were lucky, all of this would take place before two sharply-dressed gorillas strong-armed me back to my room to face Katherine.

"The music is nice. Think anyone would object to us dancing together?" Sabine had interlocked her arm with mine and was taking the lead into the ballroom.

"It might draw some attention, but I don't mind," I said.

Without another word, she led me to the dance floor. "We'll keep a respectable distance for a while, until these stodgy old farts have had a few more drinks."

It was 9:05. I didn't have a while. I had twenty minutes.

I leaned in, my chest touching hers. "We don't have to stay here," I said. "There are private suites upstairs."

Her eyes dropped to the floor. Before my training, I would have worried that I'd said the wrong thing and possibly turned her off. But I knew she was processing her feelings.

She looked up. "You remember my friend, Yvette? I'm afraid she wasn't the least bit discreet during dinner. I was wondering . . ." She hesitated, leaving the thought dangling.

"Would you like her to join us?"

Her eyes grew large, her pixie smile saying it all.

Sabine motioned to Yvette, who'd been standing on the edge of the dance floor. Suddenly we were a threesome, holding onto each other while surprisingly able to maintain a rhythmic pace to the music. Sabine whispered to Yvette, then gazed at me with eyes that anticipated the opportunity for more.

"Yvette wants us to go up first. She'll join us in a few minutes. She wants to give us a chance to get . . . settled."

From the corner of the room, I saw Katherine offer a nod, an approval for initiating the party early, not caring that our behavior on the dance floor suggested it was a prelude to greater indiscretions.

Three minutes later, Sabine and I were upstairs, opening the door to the suite.

I had fourteen minutes before I had to leave and meet Marcie.

"Is this your room?" Sabine asked. Before I could answer, she added, "No, it couldn't be. It lacks character, personality. I imagine your room as one full of grace . . . and fire."

She was a master at offering the spontaneous compliment. And more important, there was no question of her sincerity or intent.

"This is a guestroom," I said. "If you'd like to spend the night here, it's available."

"I suppose it depends," she said, a sly undertone in her voice, "on the level of service." Her eyes swept my body, not in the same way a man does, but in an appreciating and grateful manner.

"More champagne?" I offered.

"No, thank you. I want my senses to clear a bit so I can take in every touch, smell, taste."

She spoke as if preparing for a decathlon, removing any distraction that might reduce her performance or diminish the rush of the moment. Normally, her matter-of-fact attitude would have bounced off me, but it left me feeling a little intimidated, no doubt a by-product of her strong personality.

It was 9:18.

At best, it would take three minutes to make my way down the stairs, through the hallway, and out the rear doors. Then another thirty seconds to the bench, or at least close enough for Tommy to recognize me.

A gentle knocking caught me off guard. I cracked the door and saw a vertical slice of Yvette's face pressing against the jamb.

"I couldn't wait," she confessed, offering a toothy grin. "I know I promised to give you a few minutes, and . . . well, I didn't want you to start without me."

I reached out and took her hand, bringing her inside. "I just offered Sabine a drink, but she turned me down. Can I get you something?"

She glanced at Sabine, then at me, her expression soft and inviting. "Yes, please. I'm afraid I don't possess Sabine's strength of character."

As I handed her a vodka on ice, she extended her hand to Sabine. "Join us."

The press of our bodies brought a sensual rush, a joining of three independent spirts and willing flesh.

Tommy!

I snuck a look at the time . . . 9:24. I had three, maybe four minutes to figure a way out of this.

Sabine broke from the hug first. "I have to get these shoes off. If men knew the torture these heels put us through, I wonder if they would still insist we wear them."

"But it's not just for them," Yvette said.

Sabine threw her a puzzled glance.

"You know how I like you in heels," Yvette continued. "The way it makes your legs . . ." She paused as I handed her a second drink—she'd already gulped the first one down. She took a sip and set the glass down.

Sabine took advantage of the interruption. "There you go again, Yvette, thinking like a man. Sometimes I wonder if you have a set of balls tucked inside your vagina."

Yvette threw her a mischievous grin. "Did you want to take a look?" She lifted her dress, inviting Sabine to examine her pussy.

Sabine shook her head. "Slow down, Yvette. We just met Jewel. We don't want to give her the wrong impression."

Yvette wrapped her arm around my waist and pulled me close. "I'm sorry," she whispered. "Do you forgive me?" She kissed my cheek repeatedly, moving closer to my lips with each peck.

Knowing she would expect it, I brought my arm around her shoulder and began stroking her back.

"Mmmmm, your breasts are so soft," she said, running her fingers over my chest.

Bringing my hand to her forehead, I gently brushed the hair from her eyes, then saturated her face with kisses. To Yvette, I was extending a lover's touch. In reality, I was stealing a glimpse at my watch.

It was 9:28.

I had to go—now!

"Could you both excuse me for a moment? I need to check in downstairs. Just have to let security know the room is occupied and we're not to be disturbed."

Sabine pointed to the phone. "You could call."

"It's policy. I have to do it in person."

She shook her head. "American bureaucratic nonsense."

I stepped backward, toward the door. Yvette held on, needing more.

"Let Jewel do her job," Sabine chided. "You and I can jump in the shower."

Reluctantly, Yvette released me. "She's a clean freak, but I love her."

I had ninety seconds to get downstairs, make my way through the crowded lobby and dash down the hall toward the rear entrance. If I had more time, I could cover the distance at a normal pace, pausing to acknowledge guests who noticed me. Now I didn't have the luxury. I had to move quickly, no matter how much attention I called to myself.

I avoided the temptation to pull off my shoes. If Katherine saw me racing through the building in bare feet, she'd have security stop and hold me until she arrived.

The milling crowd of bodies filling the lobby was now a living wall of human flesh, slowing me down, forcing me to stop and change directions. Even the music and droning conversation pulled at me, dragging me down like thick, gooey molasses.

What the fuck are all these people doing here? Why aren't they in the ballroom?

"Jewel?"

It was a man's voice, familiar, but I couldn't place it. I pretended not to hear. I had to get through the lobby, past the reception area, down the hall, then through the double doors leading outside, where the memorial bench waited some fifty feet away.

"Jewel, is something wrong?"

The same voice, calling to me again. It faded as I entered the dimly lit hallway—the lighting reduced by the automated energy management system.

Finally out of the guest's line of sight, I broke into a run, the soft, padded drumming of heel and sole against the marble floor a welcome replacement to the usual hard clatter of production fashion shoes.

I noticed the overhead cameras. Too late to worry about that now.

The doors . . . thirty feet.

Twenty.

The guards began reacting to my approach by opening one of the doors. They usually opened both for approaching guests and employees. Reducing access by half was a security measure, to maintain a greater degree of control over suspicious traffic. My frantic approach had cued them to use caution, and they'd initiated a minor security protocol.

I slowed down, nodding at them.

One of them stepped in front of me, blocking the exit. "Everything okay?" the guard asked. His arms were at his side, his eyes searching, his stance spring-tight. He was assessing the level of threat.

"I'm fine. I left something in the room. I need to retrieve it for a guest." It was all I could think of, and I'd delivered it on a series of short breaths and a flushed face—less than convincing.

He yanked on the radio clipped to his belt.

He didn't believe me.

"Excuse me," I raised my voice. "I have two guests upstairs waiting on me."

At least that part was true.

The guard had no specific reason to stop me. At this point, I was nothing more than an embassy employee, exiting the building in a hurry. Nevertheless, he was talking to security, asking for instructions from his superior.

I knew the drill. Until he received authorization to detain me, he would use verbal commands and intimidation, hoping it would be enough to keep me right where I was. Without observing a direct threat, he would not physically restrain me or attempt to use force to prevent me from leaving.

"Excuse me," I repeated. I slipped to one side and brushed past him.

Dropping down the steps two at a time, I met the sidewalk hard, my right ankle burning from the impact. Hiding the pain, I kept moving. If the guards had any reason to believe I'd hurt myself, they would be obligated to come to my aid.

Scanning the lighted path, I saw my target—the General Christianson memorial bench, its white granite surfaces reflecting the glow from several inconspicuous LED fixtures. Even at this distance, I could see it was empty. Marcie and Tommy were nowhere in sight.

Knowing the outside guards were fixated on my every move, I continued my quick pace, favoring my ankle as best I could.

Approaching the bench was like drawing near a gravestone, the cold, vacant slab confirming a complete absence of life. Skimming the connecting ribbons of faux cobblestone, I searched for silhouettes and shadowed outlines—some indication Marcie and Tommy were within shouting distance. But the illusion of space and light produced an eerie picture of an empty courtyard, the narrow pathways of stamped concrete seeming to go on forever, until devoured by the darkness.

I'd missed them.

It couldn't have been by much.

9:32—two fucking minutes late.

I wondered if security had ushered them away. It would have been a normal response after realizing Marcie had deviated from the pre-established route, her stop at the bench unplanned and much too close to the rear entrance of the Fortress.

I wanted to kick myself for not keeping track of the time more closely, and not giving myself enough of a head-start. I imagined Marcie would have a few choice words for me as well.

With the night holding no possibility of seeing Tommy, I had to get back to my assignment. Confirming the outside guards were watching, I pulled up the hem of my dress and pretended to adjust my thigh holster. I held the dress up a few extra seconds, giving them a show of my bare butt cheek. A little distraction might help my story.

"Find what you needed?" Again, the guards had opened a single door.

"Yes, and I have to return to my guests." I was back in character, conveying not only my cooperation, but the urgency of my duties—in other words, business as usual.

"Thanks," I added as I walked inside. "I have two lovely ladies who are no doubt wondering where I am. I don't want to keep them waiting."

"Good night, ma'am."

I'd pulled it off, managed to slide back into the standard of decorum expected of me. Now I had to get my ass upstairs. My chance to talk with Tommy would come another time.

"Jewel? What the hell is going on?"

The voice came from the shadowed corner at the end of the hallway, and even from that distance, it struck me as no less commanding than a battlefield commander confronting one of his troops for committing a major fuck-up.

As the dimly lit figure stepped into the center of the hall, a sudden eruption of harsh fluorescent light filled in behind.

Even with her features obscured by the glaring backlight, I immediately recognized Katherine.

The guard's radio dispatch had set off a security alert, initiating a barrage of questions that had been transmitted directly to Katherine's earpiece.

I began creating an excuse. I would tell her I was responding to a personal request from Sabine to check the outside temperature and determine if our threesome might be more enjoyable under the stars.

It sounded ridiculous.

What if Katherine had already talked to Sabine and Yvette? Maybe they'd asked her to track me down, find out where I was and why I hadn't returned to them. Worse, what if she suspected me of intentionally leaving the women upstairs to pursue a clandestine operation of my own—trying to intercept Tommy Housing?

My heart was beating a mile a minute, the adrenaline driving my muscles to twitch spontaneously. Katherine was ready to confront me, chastise my slip of protocol, and perhaps even punish me for my actions.

The idea made me furious.

I was tired of being lied to. And the overlording bitch responsible for deceiving me was standing ten feet away.

"Jesus, Katherine, I don't know. Why don't *you* tell me what's going on?"

I could see it building in her face—she was a micro-second away from reaching critical mass.

"You had a job to do and you ran out," she began. "You left your assignment. I asked you upfront if you had any qualms being with a woman, and you told me you were okay with it. And from the way the three of you were flirting during dinner, I had the impression you were having fun. So I need to know what happened. Right now!"

Maybe she could continue with the charade, but I couldn't. I was tired of keeping her secrets, of suggesting I was okay with her game of pretend.

"I know Tommy Housing is on the grounds. And so do you. You've done everything possible to keep it from me. I thought you were my friend, on my side. But I'm nothing more to you than another stable-bitch. You trained me well, Katherine, getting me ready to turn tricks for the embassy. And now you want to treat me like the whore you've created. Good job, well done. Oh, and by the way . . . go fuck yourself."

My legs were shaking, threatening to buckle. I locked my knees, refusing to give her the satisfaction. Unfortunately, there was nothing I could do about the tears.

Katherine was silent for the longest time. She shook her head, slightly at first, as if unable—or unwilling – to engage me. I had the impression she considered my outburst immature and irresponsible—and disappointing.

Finally, she spoke. "Do you know Tommy Housing?"

"I've met him. At that party I went to in Hong Kong."

"I see."

She stared at me, waiting for more. Realizing I was done, she continued. "Tommy Housing isn't here. He called and canceled an hour ago. I planned on briefing you in the morning . . ." She paused.

"You're in no shape to service those two women. Come with me."

"But you knew he was coming," I argued, "and you intentionally kept it from me. You know he can give us the location of his brother, and that could lead me to Annie."

"Come with me," she repeated sternly.

My feet were numb, my knees locked and rigid.

Katherine reached out and took my hand. "Take a step."

I could have resisted, laid into her with a hard right, but I was done. I couldn't fight Katherine or the department, at least not with any chance of winning. And what I did from this point on could impact my future—and my life.

Katherine began pulling me toward the nearest restroom. "I kept the details of Marcie's assignment from you because I felt it was the right thing to do. I wanted to keep you focused, prevent you from becoming distracted. Does that make any sense to you?"

"Not yet," I mumbled. I wanted to scream, *no fucking way*.

She was hoping I would yield to her logic, maybe even apologize. Right now, I wouldn't even entertain the possibility we were *both* right.

"For what it's worth," she continued, "Mark is trying to get more information about your friend."

Guiding me inside the bathroom, she led me to the vanity and handed me a tissue. "Here, blow your nose."

Turning one of the cotton towels into a damp washcloth, she dabbed at my face, her expression no different than a concerned mother scrutinizing a daughter who'd stayed out past her curfew, wondering how much to ask while being mad as hell over making her worry.

"I want you to return to your room. No detours. I'll take care of Sabine and Yvette."

"You'll . . . service them?" I managed.

"No, I'll make up an excuse. Sabine will be disappointed, but she'll get over it. I'll have to promise them something special, maybe a private excursion for just the three of you. You okay with that?"

I nodded in agreement.

"Good. Now, one final thing," she continued. "I want you to wear this." She held out a large-face fashion watch. Even though the dial was at least 35mm—the size of a man's sports model—the style was plainly feminine. I flipped it over and noticed two gold contacts on the bottom of the case. It was more than a timepiece. A variation on Pavlovian conditioning, it could be remotely activated to send a trickle of electric current to the wrist, interrupting the nervous system. I'd worn one during training exercises to keep a nervous stomach at bay. My tutors had also used it to send a message when the topic of discussion had wandered into a sensitive area, and should be changed immediately.

"Why do I need this? Are you concerned I'll wander off again?"

"Something like that. Just put it on and forget it."

I did as she asked, feeling the gooey conductive gel coating the two gold contacts as they sealed the bottom of the watch case against my skin.

"Promise me you'll leave the Fortress and go directly to your room. Or do I need to assign an escort?"

I shook my head. "I want to walk to the dorm by myself."

"Good. I'll let Sabine and Yvette know you're unable to return. Then I have to get back to the main floor and help Marcie handle the guests. There are lots of unescorted men who need a pretty girl to smile at them and listen to their bullshit."

I swallowed, trying to find my voice. "That's what it's all about, isn't it?"

"Since the dawn of time, my little angel. Since the dawn of time."

Chapter Twenty-Six

The shortest route to my dorm was down the hall and out the rear exit. But I wanted to walk through the lobby one more time. I was hoping to see Marcie and ask her what happened to Tommy Housing.

The lobby was absorbing the overflow from the ballroom. Mostly men chatting in large groups, it could've been an impromptu meeting of the clan, where the subject matter was general in nature, opinions were non-committal, and unwavering eye contact was an expected part of the exchange.

"Jewel?"

That voice again! The same one that called to me as I dashed through the lobby earlier.

I turned to see a man headed toward me, his face obscured by the crowd. There was something familiar about him, stirring me with an obscure feeling of liberation. I wasn't ready to trust my intuition. The last fifteen minutes had dragged me through a gauntlet of emotions and my guard was up. And for now, that's where it would stay.

The man advanced through the crowd like a tractor plowing a field of corn stalks. As he emerged from a maze of Italian Ravazzollo's and dark Brioni silks, I recognized him immediately. It was like laying eyes on a ghost from my past. It made no sense, and yet, I savored the sense of relief surging through me.

"Charlie!"

I closed the last few feet between us with a jump. I couldn't help myself. Forgetting protocol and decorum, I threw my arms around him and held on, feeling something I hadn't felt in a long time from any man—safety, security, and trust.

"How've you been, Jewel?" His arm found my shoulder.

"I'm fine, busy as always."

I let out a deep breath, stopping myself from taking another. *Hold it back. He's a client. Don't let him see it.*

Charlie's face softened in concern. "What's wrong, Jewel?"

A single tear had streaked down my face, giving me away. "Dammit, you weren't supposed to see that." I quickly brushed at my cheek.

"Can you tell me about it?" The expression on his face shook me to the bone. I felt vulnerable and protected at the same time, something I'd experienced from only one other man—my father.

My throat was closing, my voice gone. I was seconds away from losing it. I shook my head.

Realizing I couldn't answer, he said, "I want you to promise . . . if I can help, you call me. I don't care how deep the water is, you call and I'll see what I can do."

I forced a slight grin.

"I'm meeting with a couple of the department's *yes-boys* in the morning," he said. "Might be good to have you there."

I swallowed hard. "I wasn't told anything about a meeting, but if you want me there, I'll see if I can get it cleared with the suits."

"Not necessary. I'll tell the director it's not optional." He offered his version of a smile, his mouth lifting up more on one side than the other. "Yeah, the more I think about it," he added, "it's a good idea to have you with me, to make sure my interests are properly represented."

I blinked at the tears. "You get it approved, I'll be there."

I pulled away and wiped at my face. "Do I look okay?"

"Like a champion."

It was impossible to pretend, to re-assume my role as a swallow with Charlie standing next to me. And that meant I had to get away from him. Now I really needed to find Marcie. Not only to find out what had happened to Tommy Housing, but to avoid having to return to an empty dorm room. I didn't want to be alone. I hoped rejoining the party would flip my switch, shut off my feelings and make me hard as nails—the veneer I needed to get me through the rest of the evening.

"I'm expected to work the party," I said, lying. "I guess I should go."

"I understand. You're on the clock." He took my hand in an awkward attempt at closure. "You turn in early and we'll give 'em hell in the morning."

I squeezed his fingers and let go, making a beeline for the ballroom. Seeing Charlie again had brought mixed emotions. He'd reminded me there were decent men out there, and maybe someday, I'd meet one. But right now, my circumstances made it unlikely—in this place, there was little promise of a future.

Crossing the ballroom threshold, I stepped to one side. I needed a moment to get my bearings.

"Well, this night has been a quick ride down the crapper, hasn't it?" Hearing Marcie's voice behind me immediately lifted my spirts.

Turning to face her, I gave her a quick hug. "Yeah, another fucking day in paradise."

"I guess you know Tommy Housing didn't show," she said. "Anyone say what happened to him?"

"Not exactly. Katherine mentioned his name when she was chewing on me, but she didn't tell me much."

Marcie glanced around to see if anyone could overhear—even though we both knew our conversation was being monitored. "I waited at the gate, but the guy in the car wasn't Tommy. Didn't look anything like the picture. The driver dropped us at the training center. I waited in a separate office while a couple of suits talked to the guy." She paused. "One of the suits was Mark."

"Ever seen him before?" I asked.

"No. He was older, wore an expensive suit, gold Rolex, big diamond ring. Custom shit. Not understated, but it fit him, you know? It wasn't like he needed to convince anyone he was loaded. It was a fact, part of who he was."

"Jesus, in this crowd, that could be anybody."

Marcie's mouth drew tight. "I kept thinking about you standing around outside, waiting for us to show up. I tried a text, but they'd blanketed the grounds with radio dampening. It's the procedure during these parties."

"It doesn't matter. I had a late start and ended up running through the lobby. I capped it off with a fifty-yard dash down the hall."

"Does Katherine know?"

"Oh, hell, yes. It's all on camera in fucking technicolor. Security notified her. She was waiting for me when I re-entered the building."

Marcie grimaced. "Not happy?"

"She went nuclear. Then I gave her a round of return fire. I don't which one of us was worse. The guys in monitoring will be laughing for days."

"I'm sure by now she knows all about our little plan. We can expect her to be swooping down on her broom any time."

"I don't know *what* Katherine knows, but it's a lot more than she's letting on."

Marcie's eyes swept my body, her expression turning playful. Placing her lips on my ear, she whispered, "I would really like to . . ." She flicked her tongue, then smiled. "Fucking inappropriate, huh?" she said, then chuckled at her own unintended innuendo.

I would like that. I almost said it, then decided to keep it inside. Although I wasn't attracted to her in that way, tonight I desperately needed to bond with another soul, someone who wouldn't suck the life out of me. I knew if I asked, Marcie would let me wander over her body like a lost child reconnecting with her mother. Being together would give us both what we wanted, even though our needs were very different.

Her hand lingered at my wrist, her expression quizzical. As her fingers traced the face of the watch, she looked down.

"Oh, shit! Did Katherine put this on you?"

"Yeah, right after she confronted me for leaving my assignment."

The play in her voice vanished. "We need to mix in with a group, start chatting, laugh at the jokes, act like you're having a good time."

"Why? What's going on?"

"Katherine's concerned about something you might do, and it's some serious shit. Otherwise, she wouldn't have strapped that thing on you."

"The watch is no big deal. I wore one in training. I think Katherine wanted me to use the *test* button to clear my head. You know, a little electro-shock therapy," I joked.

"Jewel, at full power, that thing can fry your nervous system. It's their version of a shock collar. If

Katherine pushes the crash button, you won't know what hit you. You'll drop to the floor like a sack of wet cement."

I froze, terrified to think I could be seconds away from a state of temporary paralysis. I started to dig at the band, unfastening the clasp.

"NO, don't touch it. You can bet security has eyes on you. If they see you trying to take it off, they'll nail you. Right now, you have to play along. Just get through the party. Then we'll find that bitch and make her tell us what's going on."

I felt a sudden pinch of pain. But it didn't come from the watch. I'd bitten down on my lower lip.

Chapter Twenty-Seven

It didn't really matter which group I approached, I needed to look involved and busy, engaging with the guests.

I surveyed the four men closest to me. Circled in a tight huddle, their shoulders were nearly touching, their eyes down, their expressions serious. Normally, four men would make an excellent social target, but in this case, I realized their conversation was just above a whisper, to keep their voices from carrying. Whatever they were discussing, they wanted it to remain private. Since my approach might be a rude intrusion, I decided to keep looking.

I looked behind me, waiting for someone to make eye contact, followed by a sudden and spontaneous upturn of the mouth—a sure sign they would like some company.

Ten feet away, I noticed a loosely knit threesome that appeared to be politely tolerating each other. I took a few steps in their direction, close enough to hear one of them discussing the proliferation of poverty in third world countries and how very little was being done to change it.

The other two were nodding in unison like bobble-headed dolls.

The man doing all the talking was another bureaucrat attempting to convince someone he had a conscience. The only thing worse was an ass-grabbing geriatric trying to squeeze my tits.

Certain at least two of the men would welcome me, I started my approach. I was a few feet away, ready to interrupt the constant flow of chatter, when I noticed Marcie waving from the other side of the room. I took it as a sign from God and changed course.

"What's up?" I asked. "You meet someone interesting?"

She shook her head. "Remember the older man I told you about, the one who was in the limo instead of Tommy Housing?"

"Yes, the unexpected switch."

"He's right over there." She brought her hand to her chest and covertly pointed to the left.

I shifted in the general direction. "Tall guy, over six-foot, balding with a dark blue suit. Has his back to us?"

Marcie tipped her head. "Behind him."

I could make out a pair of shoulders swaying back-and-forth, the man shifting his weight from one foot to the other. The four men were paired off like two couples, effectively blocking their faces—and ours—as long as we remained directly behind them.

"Let's move in," I said. "I want to hear what they're saying."

"Not too close," Marcie warned. "He might recognize me."

"So?"

"The guy was definitely wary of his surroundings, like a Baptist minister in a whore house. I had the impression he'd been forced to come, and he wasn't happy about it. After the driver dropped him at the personnel building, I was told my assignment was canceled, and the guest would be in private meetings the rest of the evening. I was also told to forget my interchange with him, and not to acknowledge him if I saw him in the future. Guess that's why he wasn't at dinner."

For some reason, the man or his situation was politically sensitive. It wasn't unusual—the private meetings, the seclusion from other guests.

"Okay," I said. "We'll stay under the radar, try not to call any attention to ourselves."

"Oh, yeah, that's gonna work." Marcie flexed her chest muscles, her boobs jumping in response.

"Stop that," I said. "Come on, let's flit from group to group until we're behind the tall guy and his wide friend. We'll use them as a buffer."

Marcie and I began slipping through the crowd, smiling, saying hello to anyone who noticed. The idea was not to disclose our destination, yet not allow anyone to interrupt our progress either. A few minutes later, we were finally close enough to overhear bits and pieces of conversation.

". . . Those contracts will be more difficult to complete. The port authority usually puts inspectors on the ship to take a physical inventory. Sometimes it's military personnel. They like to cut the locks on containers, snoop around until they find something they can confiscate."

"So we should plan to lose a percentage of everything we put onboard?" It sounded like the director's voice.

"You should count on it. Overfill the orders by twenty percent. I'll try to keep the seizures to a minimum."

A pause . . .

"I'm sorry you had the make the trip in person. Of course, it's always nice to see you, though I know it's a hardship to leave your family."

Yes, definitely the director's voice.

"It couldn't be helped," the older man said. "The boy's got himself into a real situation. I knew a phone call wouldn't take care of it this time. As I mentioned earlier, I'll likely need your help on this one."

"Of course. You know we'll do everything possible."

It was an odd conversation, especially to be taking place in the relative public setting of a packed ballroom.

Another man suddenly approached the group from the opposite side. Dark and mid-thirties with a slight build, he obviously knew the director and wanted to press the flesh. I assumed he was a local envoy making the rounds, leaving no ass un-kissed.

"Nice to see you again, Director," he said, extending his hand.

"Mr. Meesang! What a pleasure. I wasn't expecting to see you. Your office indicated you had a scheduling conflict."

"It was resolved," he said, offering a short bow.

"Gentlemen, Mr. Meesang is the head of Thailand's Office of Tourism," the director announced.

The older, mystery man leaned forward, indicating he expected top billing.

The director complied. "Say hello to a long-time friend of the Embassy . . . *Gregory Housing.*"

The name entered my ears like a profane curse, ripping into my skull, ricocheting off bone and memory. My body refused to respond, the shock of hearing his name rendering me catatonic. I felt faint. The introduction of the other two men was lost in the roar of blood draining from my brain.

I reached out for Marcie. "I feel dizzy. Put your arm around me."

Her hand found my waist, pulling me tight against her shoulder.

The possibility others would see me half-staggering against my embassy counterpart didn't cross my mind. It should have.

"Jewel, is everything alright?"

The director's voice carried more than simple concern—I felt the shift in attention. I had no choice. I had to answer him.

Still shaky, I shifted to the side, uncoiling from Marcie's arm. As I did, I felt my wrist tingle. Little more than a pin-prick, it quickly became more intense, like a bee sting. The worst of it lasted only a second, nothing more than an intermittent slap on the wrist. Whoever was monitoring me had activated the shock-watch, interrupting my autonomic nervous system to prevent me from fainting. As much as I didn't like it, it may have prevented me from hitting the floor.

The five men were eyeing me with uncompromising expectation.

I scanned their faces, settling on the man who'd been introduced as Gregory Housing.

I took a moment to assure myself this guy wasn't the same Gregory I remembered—a minion of Satan with all-American looks and a penchant for killing innocent women, the man who had bound Annie and carried her off screaming. The man I had sworn to kill on sight.

I considered the odds of another person having the same name, but the unmistakable resemblance and the obvious age difference suggested another explanation: This man could easily be . . . Gregory's *father.*

If I was right, he had come to the embassy out of necessity, to smooth over some new mess his degenerate son had gotten himself into. And it sounded like he needed the director's help in getting it done.

I noticed the deep furrows beginning to line the director's forehead. He knew! And now he was more than nervous, terrified of how I would react to meeting the father of the madman who had likely killed Annie.

It explained why Katherine had instructed me to leave the Fortress and go directly to my room. She knew if I stayed, there was the possibility of running into Housing and discovering his identity. It also explained the shock-watch. It was an insurance policy, an option of last resort in the unlikely event Housing and I found ourselves face-to-face . . . *like now.*

I heard myself panting.

Bullshit. I won't let him have that much control over me.

"The champagne must have gone right to my head. But I'm feeling much better." I did my best to smile.

Housing was eyeing Marcie and I from top to bottom. Turning to the director, he asked," Aren't you going to introduce me to these young ladies?"

The director forced a tight-lipped smile. "Of course. Marcie, Jewel, this is Gregory Housing."

"I'm sorry, what was the name?" I pretended not to have heard.

"Gregory," he said. "Gregory Housing. Please, call me Greg."

I left my hands at my sides, relieved he didn't offer his. The thought of touching him was revolting. I tipped my head slightly, keeping my expression neutral.

Sensing the silence becoming awkward, the director jumped in. "Mr. Housing is here representing his family's shipping company. It's usually his son, Tommy, who attends these little get-togethers. But we always enjoy Greg's visits."

Greg Housing took a moment to reflect on the director's comments, then added, "Tommy had planned to join me on this trip. Unfortunately, a last minute scheduling conflict prevented him from leaving the country."

The director continued. "Well, someday I hope we'll be treated to another father and son visit."

"I know we'd all enjoy that," Marcie chimed in.

I saw Katherine approaching from the corner of my eye. She looked frantic.

Sliding between myself and Housing, she offered a relaxed smile. "Greg, so very nice to have you with us again. I see you've met everyone."

"Just getting to know each other, especially these two lovely ladies, Jewel and Marcie."

Katherine's deadpan expression dripped with apprehension. "Jewel, you look a little pale. Everything okay?"

"Just fine. I'm afraid it was a case of too much champagne and not enough dinner. But it's passed."

Apparently satisfied I would maintain control, she continued. "I'm afraid I must excuse myself for a moment. There's a phone call I need to make, a bit of a juggling act between six time zones."

Greg Housing nodded. "I understand. Hopefully, we'll have a chance to chat over a nightcap." He leaned forward and planted a kiss on her cheek. The idea of him showing Katherine affection, only a few inches away, made me want to puke. Although he

242

wasn't the architect of his son's actions, he was more than an accomplice. Not only did he overlook Gregory's atrocities and forgive his barbaric forays, he continued to enable his son's passion for torture and murder with money and protection. In my eyes, he was no better than a mob boss giving the orders to make a hit on an innocent, unsuspecting victim.

I wanted to kill him. Right here. Right now.

But the slightest hostility on my part would no doubt bring another, even stronger shock—one that could leave me physically incapacitated, and put my future with the agency in a questionable, if not dangerous, gray area.

I would wait until I could focus my rage on Gregory Housing Junior, where it would do the most good. But that didn't mean I had to hold my tongue.

"How about your other son, your namesake? Have you heard from him lately?"

The director's face dropped. Apparently, my question took him by surprise. He turned to Housing, not knowing what to say.

Greg Housing's breathing was suddenly labored and heavily audible. "You know my youngest son?"

"We've met."

His demeanor turned serious, not in a show of fear, but guarded, as if he'd just been confronted by the authorities about his son's latest vile exploits. "I haven't spoken with Gregory in several days," he said. "I hope to see him before I leave the country."

I felt another tingle from the watch. I might have

only a few seconds to get it out before someone cranked up the power and sent me to the floor.

"Well, of course, you need to see your son," I said. "That's why you're here, isn't it? To keep him out of jail, pay off the authorities and bribe them so they'll look the other way. It must be really serious this time, to bring the family patriarch into the public eye."

The gloves were off and I was picking a fight with one of the most important vendors of the department. And I was doing it in full view of several hundred politicians and international businessmen.

In the true fashion of an experienced statesman, Greg Housing refused to honor my comment with a response.

Turning toward the director, he said, "It was nice to see you again. Please extend my apologies to Katherine, since I won't be able to stay for that nightcap."

His intentional snub infuriated me. "What's the hurry?" I asked. "Hope it wasn't something I said."

The director finally jumped in. "I must apologize for Jewel's behavior. I'm afraid it's my fault. She hasn't been feeling well and I pressed her back into service too soon. She's been taking medication that makes it difficult for her to sleep, and I can see it's catching up with her. I assure you, she's normally a delightful girl and . . ." His voice trailed off in the distance as he guided Greg Housing toward the main doors.

I was shaking, too angry to cry, too scared to run. I saw Katherine coming at me. Not in her usual determined gait, but with a full head of steam, her eyes locked on me, ready to hold me to the fire.

She'd heard what I'd said.

"Follow me," Katherine commanded.

I trailed behind her as we left the ballroom and walked to an unoccupied corner of the lobby. Finally out of earshot of the guests, she went ballistic. "You've really gone out of your way to piss off a lot of people. The director is ready to pull your credentials and ship you off to the worst hell-hole he can find. What the fuck were you thinking?"

I thought of saying I was sorry, but I wasn't feeling very apologetic. I'd been holding it in for too long, and now it was my turn to unleash some anger. This time, I wouldn't hold anything back.

"You've lied to me from the very start," I growled. "You've kept me in the dark because the Housing family is a preferred vendor. Gregory is a fucking lunatic, a serial killer, and you're protecting him. You even let him take Annie from the auction, even though you knew what he'd do to her. And when I asked if you could help her, you gave me the impression the embassy had no influence over the Housing family."

Katherine's face was frozen with fury. Fifty people were standing less than thirty feet away. She had to stay in control, no matter what the situation. She turned her back to me and began talking to her chest. It was a whisper, yet loud enough for me to hear.

"I need security to the lobby. I want Jewel off the floor. If she resists, drop her."

I felt another prickling on my wrist. They'd re-activated the watch, and if I didn't remain absolutely still, they'd hit me with a full discharge, inducing temporary paralysis. As far as any of the guests were concerned, my collapse would appear to be a faint, easily explained as a result from not eating all day.

"Does our girl need a time out?" I recognized Mark's voice.

"Get her out of here!" Katherine was seething.

"Mark's grip on my arm was supportive yet firm.

"Let's take a walk, princess."

I took a few steps, then pulled back. "You're no better than the rest of these assholes."

Mark started to answer, but I was in no mood to hear it. "Go fuck yourself."

Twisting free, I high-tailed it down the hall toward the closest bathroom. It wasn't a real escape, but it was the only place I could think of that might slow Mark's pursuit.

The first jolt wasn't bad. My wrist tingled, my fingers involuntarily cramping backward. It didn't stop there. As the intensity quickly rose above the initial stinger irritation, my wrist began to spasm, the muscles contracting with the cycling current. Rather than completely incapacitate me, they were trying to slow me down.

I tore at the band. If I could rip it free—

Wrenching pain tore at my elbow. More current, jabbing into my shoulder like a hot needle. As it spread into my chest, I clutched at my neck, as if I could prevent the voltage from reaching my brain. I slammed my body against the bathroom door, sending the flat panel of oak crashing against the door stop with a loud bang.

"You see where I am now, fuckers? I'm in the bathroom, away from the rest of the guests. Nobody will know what you do to me in here. So go ahead, crank it up. Lay me flat out on the floor. 'Cause that's what you want, isn't it? So hit it, cocksuckers! Turn up the voltage until I'm shaking like a rag dog and squirming in a puddle of my own piss!"

I waited for it—dreading it—knowing I was seconds away from a traumatizing jolt of stinging, burning current. Instead, the voltage began to decrease, the stabbing ache slowly retreating from my chest. My arm relaxed, and although my hand was still shaking—from either residual muscle contractions or a small amount of juice flowing from the watch—the searing pain was gone.

My rant had changed someone's mind.

I retreated into a stall. I had to sit, figure out what to do next. As I flipped the lock, I heard the pneumatic closer on the main door hissing up a storm.

"Jewel? Are we done playing hide-and-seek?" I immediately recognized Mark's smooth baritone.

"You shouldn't be in here," I said.

"There are a lot of places I shouldn't be. Remind me to add this one to the list." He paused. "You okay?"

I put a finger in my mouth and bit down. Hard. I was determined not to lose it. All the tears in the world wouldn't change the fact that Gregory's father was out there, a few feet down the hall, ready to use his wealth and influence to allow his psycho-bastard son to continue torturing young girls . . . like Annie.

"Hell, no, I'm not okay. Housing is no better than his son, and you know it. When I see both of them lying on the ground with their heads blown to shreds, then I'll be fine."

"You going to open up or are we having this conversation through the door?"

I wasn't ready to face him. "Give me a minute."

"I don't have a minute. Someone will notice we're both missing from the floor and begin to speculate what we're up to. My job comes with a lot of autonomy, but I'm not bulletproof."

"Bullshit. They sent you in here to retrieve me."

I was regaining control and feeling a little defensive—no, angry. The embassy was treating Housing like an honored guest while his serial-killer son was free to torture and kill.

The more I thought about it, the more pissed I became.

"Putting me in the same room with Gregory's father was fucking cruel."

"You weren't supposed to run into him," Mark countered. "Katherine told you to go to your room. If you'd followed her instructions, none of this would have happened."

"That doesn't change the fact that Housing is being wined and dined like he was some kind of celebrity."

"His company serves an important purpose. Housing is a preferred vendor. He carries partnership status with the department."

"His son is a fucking lunatic."

Mark didn't hesitate to agree. "You're right. He's a psychopath, with no sense of right or wrong. He's been known to kill on a whim, just to have something to brag about."

"Then why is he still free? How does he continue to get away with murder?"

"That part is complicated."

"No, Mark. It's simple. And it's wrong. And the department allowing it to go on makes them just as guilty."

"No argument there. The politics are dirty . . . on both sides. But there's a system here, and you're not going to change it."

I sensed the caution in his voice. "You're keeping something from me. What do you know?"

"Jewel . . . I know what happened to Annie."

He couldn't hide it—the drop in register, the words coming more slowly. He was preparing me. Maybe Gregory had told his father how he'd killed her, describing what he'd done in graphic, gory detail, and how much pleasure he'd taken as he'd watched her writhe in agony. Or perhaps the police had found her body and they needed someone to identify her. My heart was pounding, the sweat beading on my face. Fighting the sudden wave of nausea, I cradled my head in my hands, waiting for it.

"Are you listening?" he said.

I couldn't speak. I hit the door with my fist, the sound reverberating in the still, antiseptic air.

Mark took it as my answer. "Gregory didn't kill Annie. She escaped the same day he took her from the auction. She's on the run."

His words seemed jumbled, not making sense. "You mean she's alive?"

"There's a good chance."

"Mark, don't play games. I'll never forgive you if you're lying to me."

"I talked to Housing earlier, right after he arrived. He was explaining why he was here, and what he needs from the department."

"You mean the private meeting Marcie told me about?"

"Yeah. Housing has everyone on the street looking for her. And he's put out a reward, so—"

The rest of his words became a dull roar, my own thoughts overpowering every sense, everything, around me. Annie had escaped from that piece of shit and now she was running, fighting for her life.

I unlatched the door and pushed it open. "I have

to find her."

"That's exactly what you're *not* going to do. So take a minute to calm down. I need you to listen, not threaten to go AWOL. Otherwise, we're done."

I waited long enough to be convincing. I would promise him anything in exchange for more information. Making good on my promise was another thing entirely. "Okay, I'm listening."

"I've put out a few feelers with my contacts, mostly dealers, pimps, guys working the street who will trade what they know for cash. One of them may have heard something."

I had a thousand questions—how she escaped, where to start—but right now, I wanted to know if Gregory had put his hands on her. "Did he hurt her?"

"Doesn't sound like he had the chance. Gregory had just come from the auction. He had her locked in the trunk of his car, drugged and unconscious. At least that's what he thought. Gregory left one of his bodyguards outside with the car while he went in the house to prepare her cell. Sounds like the guard took a personal interest in Gregory's newest acquisition. Apparently, he opened the trunk and moved her to the backset."

"So he could fuck her," I added. My stomach twisted into a knot.

"Gregory came out of the house and saw it. He went ballistic. Shot the guy five times in the ass. Maybe Annie woke up from the sound of gunshot or was only pretending to be unconscious. Either way, she figured out what was happening. As Gregory pulled the guard off her, she landed a foot to Housing's throat. Slammed it hard enough to take him off his feet. She was handcuffed, but she managed to put enough distance between herself and Housing to disappear into the city."

"She's been running all this time?"

"As far as we know. There's been no word from the street."

Annie had escaped on the day of the auction. That was over a month ago—nearly a lifetime on the streets of Bangkok. She could be anywhere, sleeping in trash dumpsters, hiding in alleys, or working the backrooms of the Cowboy Sol, all the time hoping she wouldn't be recognized from pictures Housing had surely circulated to slavers in the area.

"How long have you known this?"

"I told you, I met with Housing before dinner. He's here asking for the department's help. Wants us to intercede on his behalf, smooth everything over with the authorities to prevent any repercussions, even after paying off the bodyguard's family."

"I don't understand. Why is this time different?"

"The bodyguard was the nephew of the Chief of Police."

There was a strangely perverse humor in all of it. "So the Chief has a personal stake in this?"

"He wants Gregory's ass on a skewer. That's why the old man had to fly in personally, to make the payoff and deliver an apology to the Chief . . . and of course, make sure the blame is placed on Annie."

That fucker. He was bribing the police to move the responsibility for the shooting from his son to Annie, eliminating any possibility of Annie receiving help from local law enforcement. As far as I was concerned, the Housings had sealed their fate—both father and son needed to die.

"You have any idea where to begin?" I asked.

"Nothing concrete. As soon as the cops agree to pin the shooting on Annie, they'll issue a warrant for her arrest. That means she can't get out of the country on public carrier. But there's always the underground."

"You mean the network?"

"No. These people aren't slavers. They provide services for a fee, and look the other way for the right price."

Mark knew our conversation was being monitored. Either he didn't care, or he had something else up his sleeve. In addition to revealing outright collusion between the department and street criminals, he was also telling me Annie's survival depended on how much money she could generate in the short-term. And that meant she was probably spending plenty of time on her back.

"So when can we get out of this bathroom and start looking for her?" I asked. "I can be out of this dress and in a pair of jeans in ten minutes."

Mark cocked his head. "You still don't get it. Right now, we have nothing to go on. If I receive any feedback from my street contacts, I'll check it out. The department doesn't have an official position in situations like this, but off the record, they'll support Housing. The best thing you can do, at least right now, is to get back on the floor and occupy yourself with the guests. As far as I know, Housing's left the property, so you don't have to worry about running into him again." His expression seemed a mixture of compassion and disappointment. "You have a lot of fences to mend and a long way to go before you're back in Katherine's good graces. Throwing your little fit in front of Housing has the director steaming. You definitely made an impression tonight, but it was the wrong kind. And it's likely to get you shipped off to some third world snake pit."

I blew out a breath in frustration. "Well, before you go and get all high and mighty on me, explain why I'm expected to be okay with all this? Katherine's done nothing to help me find Annie. She promised she'd keep an eye out for her whereabouts, let me know if she heard anything. She knew Housing would be here, at least Tommy, and she hid it from me. All she's done is use and manipulate me into believing she was my friend. She's a two-faced bitch, working me the same way she works any assignment . . . for the good of the department."

Mark nodded in surprising agreement. "The only thing I can say is she would have told you eventually. We had no idea you'd already met Tommy Housing. If you hadn't kept it a secret, if you'd gone to

Katherine or talked to me first, you would've had a lot more leverage. But you tried to pull this off on your own, and it paints you as a troublemaker."

"Uh-huh." It came out with disparaging rejection—exactly the way I wanted. "Dammit, Mark, I've always liked you because I thought you were being straight with me. But this time, I'm not buying your line of shit. You let me down and as far as I'm concerned, you can go fuck yourself."

His expression changed—not a sudden shift or obvious downturn, but more subtle, as if I'd reached inside and unplugged the light in his eyes. Seeing it, knowing I'd touched him in such a negative way, made me realize I'd gone too far. As far as I could tell, he was being honest with me. More important, he'd given me my first shred of hope that Annie was still alive.

Part of me wanted to apologize.

But I couldn't. Not right now.

Chapter Twenty-Eight

Before we left the bathroom, I'd asked Mark to remove the shock-watch.

Without saying a word, he'd reached for my wrist and methodically unsnapped the double clasp. As he dropped it in his coat pocket, I glanced at the time.

10:30.

It was early, but I was exhausted. My altercations with Katherine and Mark had left me drained.

Ignoring Mark's instructions to resume my duties on the floor, I returned to the upstairs suite where I'd left Sabine and Yvette. I wasn't expecting them to be there. In fact, I hoped they'd left. Right now, I wanted some privacy, a chance to compose myself and digest what Mark had told me. If Katherine questioned me, I would tell her I went back to the suite to confirm the girls were no longer in the room. Sabine was my primary assignment, and keeping her as my first priority was something Katherine would understand—if and when she started speaking to me again.

I knocked out of courtesy.

"Come!" It was followed by suppressed laughter.

Surprised by the response, I opened the door and found Sabine and Yvette snuggling in the bed, their satiated, dreamy expressions a revealing indication of the post-orgasm endorphins flooding their systems.

"You're back!" Yvette squealed. "Katherine told us you weren't feeling well."

I managed a coy smile. "I couldn't stay away."

"We missed you. You were gone for over an hour." Sabine's voice was soft and tempting, not really asking for an explanation.

"I hope I didn't miss all the fun," I purred.

Sabine flipped off the covers. "Take off your clothes and get in here."

It sounded like an invitation to cuddle. She had expectations and I needed to meet them. Part of me wanted to resist, to explain I'd only returned to say goodnight. But if I walked out now, I was done. I'd have no reason to justify my continued employment with the embassy. And I could easily find myself on the street in the morning—or worse. Regardless of how empty I felt, in spite of having no interest or motivation in having sex with either of these women, I had to perform. I reached back and unzipped my dress, letting it fall to the floor.

Sabine's demeanor grew strong, definite. "I suppose we can forgive you, because I know you plan to make it up to us in so many ways."

I climbed into bed and nestled against her, face-to-face. "I've been looking forward to it," I said, a softly whispered lie. "Just tell me what you want."

Her hand brushed the side of my cheek, then pulled my mouth to hers. As we separated, she said, "I had a feeling you would be back. I waited . . . for you."

I reached over her to sweep Yvette's chest, confirming she would be included.

Sabine intervened, drawing my arm close and tucking it between her breasts. "That will come later." Bringing my hand to her lips, she kissed it and directed it lower, between her legs. "It's time to initiate you into the tribe."

"Yes, the tribe. Of course." I had no idea what she was referring to, but refusing her, even hesitating, was not an option.

"Not everyone can pass the test," Sabine continued.

"I'll do everything I can to please you," I assured her.

Yvette began tracing my butt crack with her fingers. "Mmmm, I like this one. I hope we can keep her."

"We'll see," Sabine said.

Yvette began giggling with anticipation "I know you'll become part of the tribe. I just know it!"

Her enthusiasm was supportive, if not a bit worrisome. I put it out of my mind. I wanted to get this over with. "I'm ready. What do you want me to do?"

"You don't have a gag reflex, do you?"

I felt the smile leave my face, my cheek muscles tensing. "I don't think so."

"Are you afraid?"

I'd hoped the low lighting had prevented her from seeing my reaction. It hadn't.

"You won't hurt me," I said. "That's not who you are." I hoped she believed me—because I didn't.

"The ceremony has nothing to do with pain. It's a ritual to take my very essence inside you, so I can become a part of you. Literally."

Now I was getting nervous. I'd been through a lot on the *Kelsey*, forced to submit to despicable sexual acts, but none of them were remotely related to any kind of ceremony. I wondered if Sabine was a Wiccan or claimed herself a descendent of the Druids. Alleging kinship with an ancient society was often used to rationalize subjecting others to the weirdest shit imaginable.

I did my best to appear interested. "Sounds fascinating."

"Lie back on the bed. You won't need the pillow."

I did as she asked. As I settled, she climbed on top of me and sat on my stomach, facing me.

Yvette was squirming with excitement. "Tell her the best part."

"I'm going to straddle your face."

"You want me to tongue-fuck you?" I asked.

"That's part of it."

"Tell her the rest!" Yvette was on the verge of exploding.

"When I come, I will provide you with my essence," Sabine said proudly.

"You mean you're going to squirt?" I asked.

"I don't like that term. As I said, I will deliver my *essence* to you."

I'd seen girls squirt in porn videos, not certain if it was real or simulated for the camera. And while my girlfriends and I had debated the possibility, I'd never known anyone personally who could do it. Admittedly, I was curious.

"I'm game," I said. "What should I expect?"

"We'll build it slowly, and when it's time, you will take it all."

Yvette's grin was so wide, I thought her face would split in two.

"*Take it all?*"

"When I'm finished, you will rise from the bed, so I can examine the sheets. If I find a single drop of my essence has touched the fabric, I will punish you."

Yvette was at my feet, the sudden constriction of leather around my ankles surprising me.

"What's she doing?"

"I don't want you squirming out from under me. Once we begin, there's no changing your mind." Her face reflected harsh determination.

I tried to wriggle my legs, but Yvette was now happily sitting on them. I was beginning to feel uncomfortable with the entire situation, and I had no idea what kind of punishment she had in mind—if I disappointed her.

Sabine noticed the concern in my face.

"You're willing to participant in the ceremony, aren't you?"

"I . . . suppose. I didn't know you planned to restrain me. I don't like being tied down."

"You won't submit?"

"It brings back bad memories. Men used to tie me up, bind me with rope and chains. They did it to hurt me, to break my spirit as well as my body."

"MEN! The fucking pigs! We give and give, and they still want more. They would take our souls if they could."

Now I understood. Sabine was a man-hater. And she used this strange ceremony to create an artificial separation, not only between genders, but to isolate and identity those women who were worthy of bonding with her.

"Yvette, remove the bindings."

I felt a tug at my ankles, the leather restraints slipping away.

"I knew it from the moment we met," Sabine said. "You *are* one of us. You *must* take my essence, become my sister, and allow our spirits to mingle as one."

I was relieved to have my feet unfettered, though I was beginning to wonder if Sabine had taken some type of psychotropic when I was gone.

I did my best to sound convincing. "You know I want it, too."

She bent down and brought her lips to mine, her tongue gently exploring my mouth. I gave her access, wanting to convey my submission and willingness to join with her.

Sitting up, she scooted higher, bringing her legs over my shoulders until her vagina was directly over my face. "Seal your lips against mine . . . and breathe. Always breathe. I'll let you know when I'm ready."

Working her middle finger between the lips of her pussy and my mouth, she began to massage her clit.

Apparently, my job was to wait.

I wasn't sure what to expect. In adult videos, I'd seen everything from a small, short burst of fluid that wouldn't fill a shot glass to a huge gush of liquid, enough to overflow a ten-ounce water bottle. The smaller amount I could handle. The larger possibility had me concerned. Maybe she would cut me some slack and lower her expectations as a benefit of our sudden and newly-formed sisterhood.

Looking up at her, I realized it was too much to ask. Her eyes were closed, her senses focused on Yvette and I in the hope of joining the three of us through her invented ritual. To her, this was more than simply sex. It was a test to determine if I was qualified to be a member of a very exclusive girls' club. And while I had no desire to be inducted into her coven, my job was to convince her otherwise.

It wasn't long before Sabine's breath began coming in quick draws. Even on the edge of orgasm, she kept her hips still, maintaining our connection to make the transfer of her liquid as precise and complete as possible.

Yvette slid in behind her, straddling my chest as she massaged Sabine's breasts. "Jewel is ready," Yvette assured her. "She wants to be one with us."

I tried to become lost in the moment, to find a sense of abandon in our coupling. But I was nervous as hell, overwhelmed with anticipating her orgasm. How much would I have to swallow? Could I get it all down?

Sabine's head fell back against Yvette, her raven hair spreading over both of them, her full lips displaying a wicked smile. "Almost . . . there," she said, her voice a fevered whisper.

She began moaning, the muscles in her thighs tensing, contracting. She was close.

Keep your throat open, pass it quickly. And for god's sake, don't choke or gag.

I knew spilling it would disappoint, but spitting it up would be sacrilege.

Chapter Twenty-Nine

I'd been awakened by Mark's phone call. As Charlie promised, he'd requested my presence at the vendor meeting. I had twenty minutes to shower and comb my hair. Throwing on the standard knee-length gray skirt and ivory silk blouse, I headed for the door.

Outside, the campus shuttle was waiting. "Coffee?" The driver handed me an insulated cup with a lid. "Powdered creamer with Stevia, correct?"

"Have we met before?"

"I don't think so."

"Then the coffee . . . how did you know?"

"Katherine told me."

"Did she tell you anything else, like maybe to rough me up a bit on the way in?"

"No, ma'am, not that I recall."

Of course not. She was saving the privilege of payback for herself. And knowing Katherine, I'd never see it coming. She would attack when I least expected it. Whether she took her revenge now or later, I was certain of one thing—our relationship had changed. Unless the director transferred me to another location, Katherine would continue as my immediate supervisor. But I'd never be able to count on her to cut me a break when I really needed it. Maybe my faith in her had always been a displaced fantasy, her efforts at honest concern the same as she extended to any of the department's assets. In her eyes, I was nothing more than a sacrificial tool to be manipulated for the greater good.

"Good morning, Jewel. Please turn your badge over so the picture faces out."

In my haste, I'd clipped my name-badge on backward. The door guard noticed it immediately.

"Thanks, got it," I said, flipping it over.

I walked through the metal detector and caught the eye of the receptionist. She held up three fingers—meeting room C.

Seeing the closed door, I glanced at my watch. I wasn't late, but through the shuttered blinds, the changing shadows indicated the meeting had already started. Knowing Charlie, he'd shown up fifteen minutes early, anxious to get it over with.

"Come in, Jewel. I think you know everyone here. Of course, you remember Mr. Weston." The director displayed his usual formal yet friendly demeanor, even though we both knew I wouldn't be here without Charlie's insistence.

"Morning, Charlie!" I threw my arms around him, feeling the director's disapproving glare bounce off my back. "We didn't have much of a chance to talk last night. I hope we'll have some time today to catch up."

Embassy protocol dictated I address all guests by title and last name, regardless of the level of intimacy we'd shared. I hadn't expected Charlie to respond. He surprised me with a single arm around my shoulder.

"Everything okay?" he whispered.

"It will be. Just working through a rough patch."

He leaned in and whispered, "Like I said last night, if there's anything you need, anything I can do, you call me. Understand?"

I felt his fingers digging at the front of my skirt, pushing something under the waistband. I didn't flinch, not wanting to give him away. I hoped no one else saw it.

The director's voice interrupted. "Jewel, Mr. Weston is on a tight schedule and we don't want him to miss his flight. So if you'll take a seat, we'll get started."

I took a quick inventory—the director was in his usual place at the head of the table. To his left, Katherine had her eyes locked on a set of notes. Sitting opposite, Mark offered a silent greeting, the smallest hint of a smile breaking through.

Part of my training had taught me the advantage of maintaining a proper seating arrangement during business meetings to avoid the inference of polarizing the conversation. Again, in a subtle protest of the director's decision to withhold the truth about Annie, I pulled a chair to the other end of the table next to Charlie, making it clear I was aligning myself with his interests.

The director's expression confirmed he was less than pleased.

Katherine took a deep breath and silently exhaled, the way she might when watching a wayward child continue to irritate a parent with unacceptable behavior.

Mark winked at me.

"Jewel, there's been some concern expressed by Mr. Weston regarding the economic stability of the Chinese vendor we recommended."

I turned toward Charlie. "I'm not familiar with the dollars and cents of the transaction. Is there an issue?"

"I'm not sure. Some of their recent correspondence raised a few questions. During the evaluation period, they indicated they had enough inventory to fill ten times the volume of orders I've sent them. Now they're suggesting many of the critical components they need are back-ordered. They're also requesting cash releases against my letter of credit."

I knotted my brow. "And that means . . . ?"

The director jumped in. "Jewel, is there anything you might have seen during your factory visit, anything unusual?"

"In what way? Without a comparison, I'm—"

Mark interrupted. "Maybe if you told us about the tour you received, including as many details as you can remember."

I paused for a moment. "High-end offices, polished marble on the floors. In some ways, it reminded me of this place."

Katherine finally spoke. "In your report, you indicated you toured the manufacturing facilities and the equipment used to make the circuit boards."

"That's correct."

"Was the machinery running?" Mark asked. "Do you remember the noise level in that part of the building?"

I faced Charlie, wanting my answers directed at him. "I don't think the equipment was on. Our conversation was at normal levels. I didn't need to raise my voice."

"Do you remember how many workers were on the floor?" Charlie asked.

"I wondered at the time if it was some sort of Chinese holiday. The place didn't seem very busy."

Charlie nodded, as if confirming his suspicions.

Mark leaned forward. "Did anyone offer you a hardhat or safety glasses?"

"No. Should they have?"

"If the plant was operational, it's standard practice," he said.

I still didn't understand, but from the expressions on everyone's faces, my answers weren't making them happy. "Does all of this mean something?"

"It means," Katherine said, her tone full of accusation, "Those details should have been in your report. They are normal environmental observations."

I looked at Charlie. "Did I screw up?"

His large hand wrapped over mine. "No, dear." He stared directly at Katherine, his voice steady and uncompromising. "I won't have anyone pointing the finger at Jewel, regardless of how this turns out. I want that understood. Are we all on the same page here?"

Charlie's posture made it clear his request wasn't negotiable. In true diplomatic fashion, the director immediately diffused Katherine's comment. "Katherine didn't mean to suggest any wrongdoing on Jewel's part, and I apologize for any unintentional inference. I assure you we were on the verge of checking into this, and if there's any possibility the factory tour offered to Jewel was a ruse or this company has used the preferred vendor program as a smokescreen to pirate your technology, we'll take immediate steps with the Chinese government."

"Take whatever steps you need. But if I find out the company you recommended was nothing more than a front, a set-up to convince me to hand over my engineering diagrams, you just bought yourself a three-year contract at thirty-five million a year. That's what the business is worth."

The director didn't flinch. "We'll put our best people on it immediately. They'll be able to—"

Charlie began shaking his head. "I don't know anything about your so-called best people," he said, interrupting. "But I do know Jewel. Give her what she needs, and she'll get the job done. She's already established herself with these people as my company representative. You replace her with someone new and the vendor will get suspicious. If this contact turns out to be rogue, I want to catch them from the inside, determine how far they've gone in distributing my technology. I want Jewel in charge."

The director's jaw muscles began to twitch, his eyes glazing. Finally, he spoke. "I'm not convinced Jewel is the right person. You see, this assignment will take someone with extensive field experience, and she hasn't—"

"You know, Director," Mark interrupted. "Mr. Weston has a point. Jewel's continuing role as the main contact will keep the Chinese at status quo. And after a few repeat visits explained as strictly procedural, to satisfy an OSHA requirement, they might lower their defenses, allowing her to take a closer look at their buy-sell agreements."

Katherine remained silent, giving no indication of her agreement or dissent.

The meeting was adding another set of wrinkles to the director's already tired appearance. He was quiet for a moment, then said, "If that's the way you want to proceed." Unable to hide his reluctance, he added. "I suppose Jewel could continue to monitor the vendor's activities. And unless we find something requiring us to make an immediate protest to the Chinese government, she can work toward verifying their legitimacy."

"Good," Charlie said. "And now I have a plane to catch." He scooted his chair back and stood. "If I could have a moment of privacy, I'll like to say goodbye to Jewel."

Unaccustomed to being excused in favor of a subordinate, the director glanced at Katherine, then Mark. His ego bruised, he shook himself off as he rose, offering Charlie a placating mix of gratitude and wishes for a safe trip home.

Charlie shifted impatiently, waiting for the room to empty.

Finally, he said, "I didn't know if I'd have a chance to give you my number, so I—"

I pressed a finger to his lips, stopping him. I pointed to my ear, then at the ceiling. "Always listening," I whispered.

I flipped down the front edge of my skirt, confirming his card was still there. Bringing my lips close to his ear, I said, "Don't be surprised if I give you a call one of these days."

He squeezed my arm. "Anytime, for any reason. Especially if these yahoos start giving you a hard time," he added, raising his voice to make sure he was heard.

He gave me a quick kiss on the forehead. "I gotta go."

I wanted to thank him. Not for insisting the director keep me as his vendor representative or, even more important, for giving me back some of the leverage I'd lost last night. I felt indebted to him because he wasn't asking for anything in return. He was proving himself to be my friend. And that kind of gratitude was beyond words.

Chapter Thirty

I found Mark waiting in the lobby. That was odd. I'd never seen him waiting on anyone before. He always seemed to be on the move, places to go, people to see.

He motioned me over. "We're not done."

I started to speak, but he cut me off. "Not here." He pointed to the hallway. "Let's find an empty one."

I rolled my eyes. "I'm really tired, and if this is about what happened last night, I'm not in the mood. So if it's all right with you, I'd—"

Mark slipped his hand under my arm. Without another word, he led me past several empty conference rooms until opening the door to a small, windowless space containing a table, four chairs, and an easel holding a white-board.

"Is this the time-out room?" My voice rang with sarcasm.

He pointed to one of the chairs. "No ears in here, unless they're activated. Never repeat that."

"Okay. So what's up?"

"Charlie Weston wasn't the only person the director met with this morning."

I shrugged my shoulders. "So? What's that have to do with me?"

Mark hesitated. "Everything. And it's not good."

I searched for humor in his face. He was dead serious.

"The director also met with Housing," he continued.

"That piece of slime is still here?"

"Not anymore. He left a few hours ago. He's staying in Bangkok for a couple days until he gets things worked out with the local officials."

"You mean he's haggling with the cops until they come to an agreement on what it'll cost to keep his son out of jail."

"Something like that."

I wondered if Mark was about to give me another lecture on department policy and being a team player.

"Before you start reading to me from the operations manual, what I said last night still goes. Put me in the same room with either one of them, give me a gun, and I'll empty the clip." It sounded harsh, angry, but I didn't care. I meant every word.

"Jewel, there's a problem. Housing asked us to find Annie."

My mouth went dry. The idea of bringing the department's resources—official and otherwise—to the task of locating Annie seemed like a dream come true. But if Housing was behind it, Mark was right—there was a problem.

"Wait a minute," I barked. "I've asked Katherine several times to help me find Annie. Now Housing comes along and wants the department to jump, and everyone's ready to stand on their head. Don't misunderstand me, I think it's great the director agreed to help track her down, but why the sudden change of heart?"

Mark was quiet for a moment, then said, "This won't be easy to hear." He paused, scrutinizing my face. "And before I go any further, I want you to promise you'll listen to everything I have to say. I don't want you going Rambo on me, storming out the door and kicking everybody in the balls."

This didn't sound good. In fact, it sounded like another government shit-storm, with Annie caught in the middle.

"Tell me."

"Housing wants to keep Annie from telling her story. He wants our street contacts to find her . . . and eliminate her."

I felt my stomach turn. "And someone will authorize this?"

"It's a rubber stamp."

All the anger I'd felt toward Katherine, Mark, the director, was suddenly replaced by the shock of realizing the very people I was counting on to help me save Annie were now going to hunt her down and kill her. It didn't matter that my fight to find and set her free had been launched from the moral high ground. My logic had been based on fairy tales and fantasy— on the way the world was *supposed* to work. From the department's perspective, I was naive and inexperienced, and compared to real-world influences of money and politics, my arguments had been completely ineffective.

REDEMPTION

My words came slowly, reluctantly. "How . . . does it work?"

"The department puts out a reward. It's disguised as a missing person's bulletin, broadcast to the network as well as independent contractors. Everyone on the street will be looking for her."

"Will they find her?"

"There'll be no place for her to hide. Usually we get a call within forty-eight hours."

I glanced at my watch. "Starting when?"

"The order won't be processed until tonight. It'll take a few hours to circulate."

It was Annie's death sentence, and it would be carried out in the next two days.

"Does Katherine know?"

As if on cue, Katherine suddenly walked into the room in another demonstration of perfect timing. Without a word of greeting, she shut the door and pressed the handle until it responded with a solid snap, confirming the room was sealed from sound leaks.

Ignoring me, she turned to Mark. "You told her what Housing has asked the department to do?"

He replied with a nod.

I couldn't hold it in any longer. "I don't know why you're here, but as far as I'm concerned, if the department goes after Annie, they'll have to take me out, too."

Katherine shook her head. "Does she have an off button?"

"If she does, I haven't been able to find it."

"Jewel," Katherine said, "if you'll stop your posturing and switch off the bravado, we'll get started."

I began to object, but she cut me off. "Every minute you continue to bitch and moan is one less minute we have to help Annie."

Surprised, I asked, "Say that again?"

Mark walked to the far corner of the room. "You're sure everything's off?" He gestured toward the ceiling.

Katherine nodded. "I have a friend in monitoring. He likes my blow jobs."

Mark smiled. "Don't we all?"

Katherine pulled out a chair and sat. Reaching into her bra, she retrieved a tightly-folded piece of paper that opened to reveal a map of the city. With its overlapping color codes and unusual grid overlays, it no doubt originated from a clandestine satellite feed.

"This is two hours old," she said. "The pink areas are high priority search zones. It's where our outside contractors will begin."

I'd wanted to ask before, when Mark had first used the term. Now I had to know. "When you say *outside contractors*, you mean killers, right?"

She didn't answer, her silence confirming the horrible truth.

Mark stepped toward the door. "Bring her up to speed, then text me. Have her ready to leave in twenty minutes." He turned the handle then paused to look back at me. "We're not making any promises, but we'll do what we can to help."

Katherine waited for Mark to close the door. "At best, we have twelve hours to find her before word goes out."

Before word goes out . . .

The department's order was an unofficial endorsement of Housing's open contract on Annie's life. It sanctioned the illegal actions of street thugs and network killers, freeing them to carry out the operation without risk of criminal charges. No effort would be made to investigate her disappearance, and if questions were asked, they would be quickly swept under the rug.

I could barely breathe, my throat closing. I brought a hand to my neck and pushed out the words. "You know I can't stand by and let this happen. I have to do *something*." I hoped she understood: I was going to leave the compound and look for Annie—whether she gave me permission or not.

She stared at me, the strain falling from her face. "I know," she said softly. Her expression reminded me of the first day we met, when she'd introduced herself from the foot of my bed. Back then, it had said, *trust me*. Now, I couldn't be sure of anything.

"Remember, Jewel, we have to work under the table. If the director suspects either Mark or I are attempting to subvert the efforts of the department, we'll be out of business by the end of the day. Understand?"

I answered quickly. "I get it."

I couldn't second-guess Mark, but I wondered why Katherine was willing to put herself and her career in jeopardy. It didn't surprise me when she seemed to read my mind.

"I can't stomach any more of Housing's demands," she said. "Especially when it means losing another innocent. He's crossed the line too many times, and Mark agrees it's time to throw a monkey wrench into the system." She paused, then locked eyes with me. "I can't give you any assurance we'll find Annie. I can't even give you a sense of hope. But if you're willing to do it our way, with the three of us working together as a team, it'll give us the best chance of finding her while she's still alive."

I nodded.

"That's not good enough. No heroics, nothing stupid. I need your promise."

"I promise." I hoped it was one I could keep.

"Oh, before I forget . . ." Katherine reached into the pocket of her jacket. "Hold out your hand. Sabine wanted me to give you this." She dropped Sabine's diamond ring into my open palm, the same ring I'd admired the night before. "You did a good job with those girls. It was all they talked about this morning."

Surprised, I stumbled with a reply. "It was just another assignment. I'm glad they had a nice time."

"There's no need to brush it off. I know all about their version of playtime. As far as I'm concerned, you should wear that thing like a combat medal."

I knew why she was giving me the diamond. Normally, government employees were prohibited from receiving gifts beyond the value conveyed by a simple card, bottle of wine, or spray of flowers. Giving me the jewelry was a huge infraction of the rules. But Katherine understood the street value of a forty-thousand-dollar ring might come in handy if I had to buy Annie's way out of Bangkok.

"How do I get off embassy grounds?" I asked.

"I'll make it a requirement of your training." She hesitated. "And this is the part I don't like. If anything goes wrong, there'll be an inquiry, lots of questions."

Participating in a rogue assignment and lying to embassy personnel was the least of my concerns. My future with the department wasn't the priority. If Annie was out there, I had to find her.

"What do you want me to do?"

The furrows in Katherine's forehead deepened. "I'll authorize an off-grounds day pass. If it were an overnight, I'd be required to originate a file, then complete it with the details of where you went, what you did, and who you talked to. And that's something I'd prefer not to do."

I took a shaky breath. "Seems like you'd be able to create some sort of alibi, especially with all the contacts you have outside the wall."

"I'll advise the director I started you on your next phase of training. It's called Field Situational Analysis, FSA for short. You spend time on the street with an agent—in this case, Mark—watching people involved in everyday exchanges. The premise is to pay attention to facial clues and body language, determine who's buying and who's selling, which party is desperate and which one isn't. Then you make a determination of what's happening, if the transaction is legal or illicit."

"Won't that seem a little suspicious since it coincides with the department's orders to eliminate Annie?"

"I'll advise the director it was already on the schedule. And I won't tell him about the exercise until you've left the compound so he doesn't red-light your pass. If he gives me any flack or questions the timing, I'll explain the paperwork was initiated days ago and he must have overlooked it."

Even as she spoke, Katherine was considering the options, struggling with regulations and policy.

I pointed to the color-coded map spread on the table. "How do I use this?"

"The red zones are known to harbor the greatest concentration of runaways and non-documented aliens. It's where the network will begin their search." She looked at her cell phone, apparently reading a coded text. "Mark's already checked with his contacts on the street," she said. "So far, no one's seen her."

"And that's good, right?"

"Maybe," she said, giving me the same reluctant expression that haunts the face of anyone who has to tell a loved one to expect the worst. "There are a lot of places she could be hiding, back alleys, flop houses, brothels. You'll have to depend on Mark's contacts for leads."

Katherine began folding up the map. "If Mark spots her, he'll have to keep his distance. That's where you come in. You'll have to approach Annie first, convince her Mark is there to help."

"And then we get her out of the city, right?"

Katherine remained silent, as if unsure how to answer.

"I know, I know," I added. "I'm jumping the gun. First, we have to find her. And when we do, our problem's solved."

Katherine raised her eyes, her expression full of caution. "Jewel, *if* we find Annie, our problems will just be starting."

Chapter Thirty-One

It was called *the street* for a reason. Overhead, a dense web of telephone and power lines blocked most of the sky, preventing the sun—but not the heat—from touching the endless ribbons of steaming asphalt. Hundreds of side streets and alleys fed the main thoroughfares in seemingly mindless design, creating a bustling frenzy of cars, motorized trikes, and motorcycles constantly challenging each other for the right-of-way. With push-carts and hand-drawn wagons adding to the congestion, the city was a living labyrinth of confusion and chaos.

Both drivers and pedestrians seemed to pay no attention to those around them. Staring straight ahead, their eyes remained fixed in hypnotic drudgery—not in an indication of trust, but of trance-like boredom and indifference.

Between each short block, dark narrow alleys hinted at unknown danger, in spite of the constant stream of people disappearing and emerging from the shadows.

To know the city was impossible. More than an amalgamation of bricks, shingles, and siding, it was a raw and constantly changing jumble of money and power, greed and survival, with most of the inhabitants asking an absent god to give them one more day, to find a way out.

Here, survival of the fittest was more than a Darwinian concept. The younger, stronger, and smarter took advantage of the weak, old, and infirmed. Those with legitimate businesses took every precaution to keep the undesirables away. The majority of storefronts were framed by rolling iron grates. At night, owners pulled them shut and secured them with a row of padlocks, hoping to deter the honest and challenge the determined.

During the day, the fine line between integrity and misconduct was less obvious. On both sides of the street, groups of young men loitered under make-shift canopies. Seemingly engaged in serious business, they negotiated with exaggerated hand gestures and head movements, their cigarettes twitching up and down in their mouths as they talked.

"What are they selling?"

"Everything," Mark said. "The big three are videos, cigarettes, and alcohol."

"Illegal?"

"Most is bootlegged or stolen."

"What about drugs?"

"Seldom sold in the open. The dealers won't take the risk. If they're caught with the stuff and don't have someone on the inside to reduce the charges, they're gone for good."

I didn't ask for an explanation. Death sentences for dealing drugs were common in third world countries. Even so, stiff penalties hadn't stopped the trade, just pushed its operations further underground.

"And sex? Is that sold on the street too?"

"Why? Are you looking for a second job?"

"Fuck you."

"I'm sorry," he shot back. "It was a bad joke. To answer your question, yes, there's plenty of traffic outside the clubs." He paused. "Strange though . . . if it has to be arranged on the street, it usually has something to do with BDSM. Some of it is so bizarre the girls won't consider doing it for any price."

I was tempted to ask for specifics, but decided I was depressed enough.

We stopped at an intersection, waiting for the light. A vendor's food cart crossed in front of us, then turned into traffic, barely squeezing by Mark's side of the car.

"And I thought rush hour on the 405 was bad. At least we were all driving in the same direction."

"That guy will move up and down this street until he's out of food. Then tomorrow, he'll do it all over again. As long as he has something to sell, he'll push that cart until he's either too old to handle it or he gets run over."

"The things we do for money." I hadn't intended to say it out loud.

I motioned toward the shifting group of young men across the street. "Any chance those guys might know something about Annie?"

"I doubt it. Unless someone's standing in front of them flashing a roll of twenties, they'll conveniently claim a loss of memory."

"Did you bring cash?"

"Some. Keep in mind there's a downside to offering money to strangers, especially if we're trying to motivate them to report a sighting. Most will invent what we want hear. It's a common ploy, so we need similar stories from multiple informants before we can give the details any credibility."

"You have better sources?"

He nodded. "It's a small group, but if they see or hear anything about an American girl on the street, they'll call."

"But they won't hurt her . . ."

"Unless a contract goes out, they won't touch her. We don't have a lot of time, and this is a process."

"What do you mean, *process*? Your people call, tell us where Annie is, and we go get her. Right?"

"I wish it was that easy. First, I have to meet with the contact and pay upfront. Then he tells me what he knows. Hopefully, that gives us another piece of the puzzle. A real-time sighting seldom happens. In most cases, the information is days, even weeks old. Sometimes the best we can do is establish her direction and guess where she's headed."

Mark's system for finding Annie was far short of the scientific methods I'd hoped we'd use. Where was the satellite imagery, the facial recognition software, the high-tech tracking technology I'd seen in spy movies?

"Jesus, Mark, you mean all you're relying on is the memory of a bunch of eighty-year-old men pushing food carts who might've seen Annie crossing the street a week ago? If that's the best we can do, Annie's fucked."

"It's not quite that bad," he countered. "If she's on the run, it increases the chances of someone seeing her, which also decreases the time between sightings." He hesitated. "But if she's found a place to hide, this could take a while."

"We don't have a while," I mumbled.

Mark was quiet, apparently agreeing with me.

"What about the actual order to track Annie down?" I asked. "Can it be revoked?"

Mark paused to dodge a Moped cutting in front of us, then slowed to put a little more distance between our car and the cycle.

"Once the order goes out," he began, "the department will immediately distance itself from the situation. They'll claim no knowledge of Annie and will dismiss any inquiries regarding her presence in Thailand. If they tried to cancel a contract or change it in any way, it would leave a communications trail, which could easily become evidence of their involvement."

Mark was telling me there was no Plan B. If we weren't able to find Annie before the deadline expired, there would be no judge to listen to mitigating circumstances, no jury to consider a plea for mercy.

I felt my anger coming back. "So that's the way it is? In twelve hours, some asshole sitting behind a desk picks up the phone and Annie becomes a target?"

"Bitching won't help," he said. "We live with the facts. That's why we have to find her first."

"And if we find her before the order goes out, we can bring her back to the embassy, right? She's entitled to asylum as an American citizen."

Mark shook his head. "She would have to come in on her own, walk through the front gate, and demand protection. And before she could receive it, she'd have to prove who she is. She'd need a passport or a relative to authenticate her identity."

"Surely someone in research could pull up her birth records and confirm her citizenship."

"So security can arrest her? She's wanted for shooting Gregory's bodyguard, remember?"

"That's a pile of shit and you know it," I growled. "She's a scapegoat, and the department is writing her off to stay on the good side of Housing so he can keep his kid out of jail."

Mark's voice took on a frustrated edge. "I don't make the rules, but that doesn't mean we can't stretch them a little. If we can get to her in time, Katherine will run interference, send out a directive that Annie's been seen in another part of the country. But that's only if we find her in the next few hours. After that, Annie's on her own."

Mark's comment made me wonder if this last minute scramble to find Annie might already be doomed—pointless from the start.

"Mark, I need the truth. Are we wasting our time? Is this just some token effort before calling in the executioner?"

He broke his concentration on traffic to glance at his watch. "We have eleven hours left." His voice was flat, without emotion.

I closed my eyes and covered my face with shaking hands. I couldn't hold it in any longer. In all probability, Annie was living the very last hours of her life. I had no idea if she was hurt, hungry, or scared. I just wanted to be with her, to share another sunrise . . . together.

Mark reached for my shoulder. "I'll do everything I can to get a lead on her, break down a few doors if I have to."

Mark's only knowledge of Annie came from a two-by-three picture and computer print-out of her physical description. Yet, he was risking his career— putting himself between the department and a group of network killers—to find her in time. And if I was reading him correctly, he wouldn't hold anything back. It should've made me feel better. But I was living in a broken world, a place of reckless ambition, betrayal, and deceit.

I wondered if I would *ever* feel better.

Chapter Thirty-Two

"Look over there, by the fish market." Mark pointed to the right side of the street. "That big Swede standing out front, he's one of my contacts. Calls himself Alvin."

"Nobody calls himself Alvin."

"He thinks the name evokes star power, like Elvis. He's fascinated with American culture, especially from the fifties."

"Yeah, but Alvin?"

"You know, Alvin from the Chipmunks. An old Christmas song? The three singing chipmunks? Okay, before your time . . ."

Seeing a space open up, Mark quickly changed lanes and edged close to the curb.

The Swede stood a good foot above the crowd, his blonde hair and broad shoulders making him an oddity in the swarming throng of smaller Thai's.

Mark rolled down his window and hit the horn, the abrasive noise forced to compete with the constant roar from diesel trucks and buses.

In spite of the traffic, the sound reached Alvin's ears. Turning in our direction, he recognized Mark and offered a quick wave, shaking his head.

"You believe him?" I asked.

"We don't have a choice. If we start second guessing our contacts, we'll have nothing to go on."

"We've got nothing to go on now," I reminded him.

After another ten minutes of driving, I noticed the traffic was beginning to thin out. "Where are we headed? I thought we were concentrating on the city center."

"There's a brothel up ahead, right off the main road. I know the owner. She has a big house, puts up girls on the run. 'Course, while they're there, she expects them to work for their room and board."

"Of course she does," I muttered. "The bitch."

"Yeah, she can be, but she doesn't use muscle to force the girls onto their backs. If they don't want to work, she gives them a meal and a place to sleep for the night, then tells them they have to move on. Even if she hasn't seen Annie, she might have heard a rumor about an American white girl on the street."

It was a long shot, but Mark seemed to be following some sort of plan, collecting information from known sources rather than driving the city aimlessly, hoping to catch a glimpse of Annie—a runaway who didn't want to be found.

Mark slowed the car and turned onto a narrow, dirt road. There was no sign or marker, nothing to give an indication of the *xingle gongdian*—pleasure palace—located a quarter mile off the highway.

As we drove through a large grove of kokko trees, an old, ramshackle house appeared at the end of the drive.

"You wait in the car."

"Yeah, right," I said, opening the door. "You can tell the head bitch I'm Annie's sister, and I'm here to take her home. Maybe a little tug on the heartstrings will loosen her tongue."

Mark sneered, obviously unhappy with my insistence to accompany him. "It won't be pretty. You sure you want to see this?"

"We're wasting time."

I began walking toward the house, letting Mark catch up. I wasn't afraid, but I wanted him to take the lead.

The front of the place was in drastic need of paint. A few stray chips of faded color clung to the water-stained wood as a reminder of the original sky-blue tint. Climbing two steps to the porch, I noticed the split planks under our feet, many of them loose from missing and rusted nails.

I wondered why I hadn't smelled it before—the stench of rotting vegetation. At least, that's what I hoped it was.

"It's the middle of the day," I said. "You think anyone's home?"

"They're open twenty-four-seven."

Mark rang the bell, stepped back, and lifted his head.

"You looking for something?"

"I want to make sure Mama Sarai recognizes me. She's not crazy about Americans."

I followed his line of sight to an old video camera. Bolted to an exposed roof joist, the rusty housing and dirt-covered lens could've been retrieved from a trash pile. A glowing red pilot light gave the only indication it was working, although I doubted it produced much of an image.

The sudden *buzz* from a solenoid lock made me jump.

"You sure you don't want to wait out here?"

I shook my head. "Let's go."

Mark entered, took three steps and stopped. The contrast between the dark interior and outside light made it impossible to see what was holding him just inside the door. I followed him in.

As my eyes adjusted to the dim light, I saw Mark standing in front of a make-shift counter. It was a stopping point, where clients could be screened, services negotiated, and prices established. Behind the counter, the home's original living room stood in gloomy shadow. Sparsely furnished with an old couch and two straight-back chairs, I wondered if it doubled as a display area for the available inventory of girls during busier times.

"Ma-ko boy! You not come here for long time. You still work for gover-men? You know, like James Bond?"

He'd emerged from the dark hallway, displaying a wide smile and several missing teeth. Appearing to be mid-thirties, he was around five-foot-six and balding, his wide frame augmented with steroid-fed arms that burst from his shirt sleeves like telephone poles.

Mark returned his greeting immediately. "Chaow! You look good. Still working hard?"

"Always work. Always make money. Lots of kids to feed." He gestured to his mouth.

"I was out this way on an errand," Mark said. "Wanted to stop in and say hello. Is Mama Sarai here?"

The man narrowed his eyes. "Why? You want to fuck her?"

"Not today. I was hoping to talk to her. I wanted to find out if she had a new girl, an American, young, early twenties with—"

"You not need new girl," he interrupted. "You bring pussy with you . . . fine pussy." He stared at me, his eyes raking up and down my body.

Mark tried again. "The girl I mentioned, the one we're looking for, she might be sick. We need to find her and take her to the doctor."

The man's friendly demeanor immediately turned suspicious. "Ma-ko, Ma-ko, why you lie to me? I think this girl you look for, she is not sick. No, I think she done something bad and you want to find her to bring her to gover-man, put her in prison." He smiled. "This true, Ma-ko?"

Mark didn't flinch. "You're too smart for me. I can't hide anything from you, can I, Chaow?"

The man beamed with arrogant pride. "Yeah, you try to pull spy job on me, but I know what's going on."

Mark mirrored the man's smile.

Chaow glared at my chest in approval. "Big titties. Good for sucking, eh, Ma-ko?"

Mark ignored the question. "What about you, Chaow? You heard anything?"

His eyes glued to my breasts, Chaow appeared to be deliberating, composing an answer. "I tell you something. Other men come here. They look for American girl, too. Maybe they already find her. Maybe not." He pursed his lips and tipped his head sideways. "I think this girl better off if you find her first. Prison much better place for her than what other men got planned, eh?"

Mark's jaw stiffened. "These other men, you've seen them before?"

"Some yes. Some no. They all come asking. Everybody want to find pretty American white girl. They say will pay big dollars if I help find her. So I thinking this girl important. Maybe I should be looking, too."

Mark understood. Reaching into his pocket, he pulled out a roll of hundreds, peeled off two, and laid them on the counter. Rubbing the roll of bills with his thumb, he said, "The rest of this is yours if you tell us where we can find her."

Chaow's eyes shifted from my chest to the hundreds. "You wait," he said, pocketing the two bills. "I come back."

"Bullshit," I said. I'd had it with his coy game of cat-and-mouse. "You either know something or you don't. Quit jerking us around and tell us the truth. Is she here or not?" The anger in my voice pushed the last few words an octave higher, on the verge of screeching.

I felt Mark tapping my arm, warning me to calm down.

Chaow shook his head. "Ma-Ko, your girl got big mouth on her. Not like Thai girl." He studied my face for a moment. "Hope she know how to use it to give good suck. Otherwise, she not good for nothing."

"She's new," Mark said. "Have to make allowances . . . you know how that works." He winked.

Chaow nodded, then stepped back and disappeared down the hall. A few moments later, the hollow *thudding* of his fist against a door echoed from the rear of the house. "Kanda! You come now. Customer for you."

The silence grew like an ominous plague, the dreary light seeming to retreat even further into the murky shadows.

"Kanda! You hear me? You come out NOW! Mama Sarai kick your ass out if you not come now!"

I assumed the reluctant girl knew something. Otherwise, why was Chaow insisting she make an appearance?

I turned to Mark. "Maybe if I told her we only want to talk."

He shook his head and brought a finger to his lips, warning me to remain quiet.

"But if she understood we just want to ask her a few questions," I argued, "she might not be so reluctant to see us."

"No," Mark whispered. "We wait here. It's the protocol. We have to respect the gatekeeper, do as he says."

Respect. That was an odd word to use in a brothel.

"But what if she won't leave her room?"

"He won't let it go much longer. She's challenging his authority, making him look bad. If he has to, he'll break the door down and drag her out."

Shit. I hated this place . . . this house, these people who enslaved others as a method of making a living.

The girl's lack of response was making me nervous. Mark picked up on my rapid breathing. He put his hand on my shoulder, attempting to calm me down.

"You think there's a chance it might be Annie behind that door?" I asked.

He shook his head. "I know you want it to be. But if Annie was that easy to find, the network would already have her."

"But there's a possibility, right? She could've found her way here, asking to work until she saved enough money to get out of the country."

He shrugged. "You're setting yourself up for disappointment."

The metallic snap from a heavy door latch penetrated every inch of the dark house. Followed by the drawn-out squeak of hinges, I realized the girl had finally decided to open her door.

My head was pounding, my heartbeat playing soccer with my brain. I tried to take a deep breath. The air caught in my chest. If it *did* turn out to be Annie, I couldn't let her see the concern—or pity—in my face.

Shuffling footsteps.

Chaow emerged first. "I have fine girl for you. Best in house, very good price. Make much fun for you."

I turned to Mark. "What the hell is he talking about? We're not here for sex."

"Shush. This is how it works. Let me handle it." Mark offered a broad smile. "Yes, she'll be fine. But first, my friend would like to talk to her. The girl is for her."

"Talk or fuck, same money. Make no difference to me."

I wanted to rip his eyes out. And only because they were easier to get to than his balls. "Listen Chaow, you piece of—"

"Yes, of course. Business first." Mark raised his voice, cutting me off. "I like that about you, Chaow. You're always professional, always looking out for Mama Sarai."

Chaow puffed out his chest, pleased with the compliment. He glance toward me and scowled. "You sure you want to waste good piece of ass on this bitch?"

"Very sure. She'll give me what I need later."

"Oh, I see. You give her lady-candy now and she pay you back with good suck."

"That's right." Mark continued to offer a wide grin.

I whispered to Mark, "I am so kicking your ass when we get outside."

Mark pulled me close, as if to nibble on my ear. "Stay on track. Find out everything you can. And remember your training. Gain her trust first before you start asking questions." His tone was serious, and while it left no doubt he was my superior, it was also well-timed advice.

The girl was hiding in the shadowed hallway.

"Do we get to look at her before we pay?" I asked.

"Kanda, you come out here," Chaow ordered. "I set price now."

She stepped out of the darkness, her head bowed. Small in stature—barely five-feet—she wore a black bra and tiny boy-shorts to show off her small waist and muscled thighs. She took a few more steps and stopped several feet from the counter.

I knew from the moment she walked into the light—it wasn't Annie.

"You see? She fine!" Chaow's voice turned smooth and syrupy. "Worth top dollar. How long you want her?"

"How much for an hour?" Mark asked.

As the men continued negotiating price, I kept my eyes on the girl, hoping she would look up. Finally, I said, "I want Kanda to come closer. I want to hold her hand."

Chaow glared at me, then at Mark. "She want to hold hands? Like little kids in school?"

"It's her way. She wants the fantasy." Mark paused for a second. "You know what it means . . . fantasy?"

"Don't care what it mean. You pay now. This make me crazy."

"Then tell your girl to come closer," Mark said.

Chaow blew out a deep breath. "Kanda, do as he say. Get your ass to counter."

Her head still bowed, she shuffled forward.

I extended my hand. "Hi, Kanda. Is there somewhere we could go to talk?"

Tired of letting my hand hang in the air, I dropped it and smiled. "I just want to talk with you. That's all."

Chaow said something in Thai, then lifted the moveable portion of the hinged countertop, giving me permission to enter his side of the house.

"Don't wander too far," Mark warned.

"Go to room," Chaow instructed. "Only to room. Nowhere else."

I felt Kanda's small fingers suddenly wrap around mine. She took a step, pulling me toward the hall. As the darkness swallowed us, I heard Chaow continue to haggle with Mark, "Two hours minimum. I give you discount."

His callous, bottom line demeanor reminded of the captain of the *Kelsey*, the man who had dragged me from my house kicking and screaming. I made a mental note . . .

I would add Chaow to *the list*.

Chapter Thirty-Three

"No, Kanda, you don't need to do that. I only want to talk."

She was lying on the bed, slipping her shorts down over her hips. I immediately softened my voice. "Let's sit together, side-by-side."

The room was devastatingly bleak, the dirty wood floor tracked with wear marks. In the far corner, a single dresser with most of the knobs missing reflected a lifetime of use. On top, an incense burner overflowed with ashes. A small nightstand held a half-melted candle, a lighter, an open box of baking soda, and a deeply tarnished spoon.

Kanda hadn't spoken a word. The realization she might not understand what I was saying sent me into a panic.

"You speak English?"

She lifted her head, nodding.

"How long have you worked here?"

"Three months."

"Does your family live close by?"

I saw the lump in her throat. She swallowed hard. "No family," she whispered.

Without thinking, I reached for her shoulder. Surprised, she jumped and scooted back. Realizing she could be punished for not being receptive to a "customer," she immediately slid against me, setting her hand on my right breast. It was completely mechanical, a pitiful substitute for the intimate touch of a lover.

I laid her hand back in her lap. "Kanda, you can touch me, but only if you want to. Understand?"

She forced a little smile.

"I want to ask you something that's very important to me," I said.

Our shoulders touching, I could feel her rapid breathing, no doubt anxious about what I would say next.

"You see, I've lost a close friend," I continued. "Someone I care for very much. If I describe her, can you tell me if you've seen her or heard anyone talking about her?"

For the longest time, Kanda was quiet. I waited, hoping she wasn't fabricating a story. Finally, she said, "This girl . . . you love her?"

"Yes, very much."

"Then how you lose her? Maybe you don't love her as much as you say?"

It was a damn good question. And I didn't have a good answer.

It was a risk, but I decided to tell her the truth. "Some bad men took her. She escaped from them and ran way. They're looking for her. If I can find her first, I'll take her to a place where she will be safe. A place where they can't find her."

"A place that is safe?" She looked up me, her eyes growing large. "There is no place like that."

"Yes, there is," I argued. "A place where men can't buy and sell our bodies. A place where we're protected."

Kanda brought her small hand to her crotch. "No more this?"

"Only when you want."

She was quiet for a minute. "Will you take me to this place?"

Shit. I'd blown it. I'd let Kanda take control of the conversation and now she was negotiating for what she wanted.

I couldn't blame her. I'd do the same thing in her situation, try every way possible to get out of this hell-hole. In spite of what Mark had told me about Mama Sarai's policies, the reality was on Kanda's face, in her tear-filled eyes and broken, halted breathing. She could no more walk out of this house than if she were a condemned prisoner serving a life sentence.

She might be twenty—or fifteen. This kind of life accelerated the aging process, robbing girls of their youth . . . and their future.

"*I will take you to the place.*"

I knew the instant it left my lips I should have kept it inside. But leaving Kanda in this rat-infested building was no longer an option.

Hoping my promise would give me some leverage, I tried again. "And you'll help me find my friend?"

She blinked, then nodded. "A girl *was* here. Two weeks ago. Pretty face. Sad eyes. No cry."

"Was she American?"

"American. Yes."

I held my breath. "Her name . . . what was her name?"

Kanda hesitated. "I don't think she be the one you love."

"Why? What makes you say that?"

She ignored my question.

"Mama Sarai tell her to stay, make much money. But they fight. Mama Sarai lock her in storage room. After two nights, she get out, run away."

"Her name, Kanda. Did she tell you her name?"

I could sense her reluctance. She'd no doubt promised to keep the girl's identity a secret. But if she really believed me, she would realize breaking that trust could save the girl's life.

She took a deep breath. "Her name Khel Si. She said name is special, means where she from."

It was more than disappointing. The girl she described had a native Thai name. I was ready to leave, get on the road and continue searching for Annie. But there was something Kanda said that bothered me.

"You said the girl was American. Did she say she was from the United States?" I'd seen plenty of Thai girls who didn't reflect their cultural heritage, their universally attractive appearance easily suggesting an American birthright.

"She *look* American. Talk American."

Kanda had assumed the girl's nationality. And it sounded like she was wrong.

"What else did Khel Si say?"

"Same as you. She lose someone she love . . . Chatmanee. She look for Chatmanee."

Any remaining hope I was holding vanished into the thick, stale air. I was no closer to finding Annie than I was an hour ago. All I could see was a huge clock looming over my head, counting down the minutes while Annie dangled at the end of fraying rope. And if I didn't find her in time, she would die.

"Kanda, I need to go."

Her expression brightened. "We go look for Khel Si?"

"No, not today. The girl I'm looking for must be found this afternoon."

"When you look for your friend, you look for mine, too?"

"I wouldn't know where to start."

"She hiding in city. Maybe on Wat grounds. We find her easy."

"I can't. I have to leave. But I'll come back for you, as soon as I figure out how to get you out of here."

Her face began to contort with fear, her eyes filling with tears. "NO! You take me with you *now*. You promise."

I didn't have time to argue. "Do you have anything you want to bring with you?"

She shook her head.

"Alright. Let's go."

With Kanda in tow, I walked toward the front of the house. I wasn't looking forward to telling Mark what I'd done. Getting her out of here would be completely dependent upon money. And buying Kanda's freedom wasn't part of the anticipated expenses.

Chapter Thirty-Four

We drove the first few miles to the city in silence. Kanda sat in the backseat, seemingly fascinated with the passing countryside . . . and her newfound freedom.

Convincing Chaow to release Kanda on the premise I wanted an overnight playmate had cost Mark his entire bankroll—money originally intended to pay "friendlies" for information on Annie's whereabouts.

The added pressure from Mark's silent treatment was putting me over the edge.

"Are you ready to talk?" I asked.

"You've done enough talking for both us."

"I couldn't leave her."

"What the hell were you thinking? She's a Thai national. This is her home. We can't expatriate every poor bitch who gets caught up in the sex trade."

"Her name is Kanda," I snapped. "Don't call her a *bitch*. Understand?"

I was shaking, not from anger, but from my own stupidity. I'd done everything wrong—taking Kanda with us, blowing our financial reserves, and now I was fighting with Mark. Not only was I pissing all over his manhood, I was attacking the only one who could help me.

"I'm sorry," I said quickly. I put my hand on his shoulder. "I'm worried sick we won't find Annie in time. The day's half gone, and we still don't know where to look."

Whatever anger Mark was holding for me, he let it go. "I have to stop at a bank. We need more cash to keep the information channels open."

"I owe you."

"Fucking right you do."

I looked at Kanda, concerned the heated exchange between Mark and I might have upset her. She seemed oblivious to our conversation, completely absorbed with the passing scenery.

Noticing my attention, she asked, "We go to Wat now, to find my friend?"

I turned to Mark. "She's talking about another runaway, a friend of hers from the brothel. Kanda said girls sometimes hide on the grounds of the temples until it's safe to move around the city. Do you know what she's talking about?"

Mark's eyes shifted to the rearview mirror. "Kanda, do you mean Golden Mountain?"

She smiled. "We go there, find my friend."

Mark shook his head, directing his conversation to me. "It's a large Buddhist temple right in the middle of the city. The grounds are surrounded by a jungle thick enough to get lost in. At least that's what a lot of runaways believe. It's closed at night and there's a high fence surrounding the place, so they get a false sense of security. They think they can disappear into the foliage in the afternoon and spend the night without being found. I've heard some go in with a backpack full of food and water, planning to hide out for a week or more.

"And?"

"It's the first place the network looks. They even pay the monks to keep a close eye on visitors, especially young girls traveling by themselves."

"So if Annie tried to hide there, they might already have her?"

He didn't answer my question directly. Instead, he said, "Based on how much time we have, the Wat is a low priority."

I felt an overwhelming sense of helplessness. "So where do we look?"

"We have to expand our eyes and ears. I need to visit another half-dozen street operators. They know the club owners. They hear the rumors. A hundred bucks will motivate them to make a few phone calls. If they hear anything, they'll let me know."

"How long will that take?"

"Couple of hours, maybe three."

"But it's already two o'clock! By the time we hear anything it'll be getting dark."

"We can't keep driving the streets, hoping to get lucky. We need a lead from someone who's seen her or knows someone who has. Otherwise, we're on a wild goose chase."

I hadn't been watching the passing landscape and suddenly noticed the vastly improved neighborhood. Mark had driven us to an upscale area of downtown Bangkok. He activated the turn signal and shifted into the center lane. His destination appeared to be a parking garage.

"Okay spy-man. Now what?"

"We're checking into a hotel. I need to drop you and Kanda off so I can get back on the street. I can't approach my contacts with you two in the background."

"I won't get in the way, and Kanda can stay in the car. Don't make me wait in some hotel room while Annie is living out the last hours of her life."

"Not an option. The best way you can help Annie is to let me do my job. Either one of you would be a constant distraction. I want these men concentrating on the money, not on negotiating a blow job."

I wanted to scream. But I knew he was right.

Chapter Thirty-Five

Mark handed the clerk his credit card.

"*Two* ladies this time. Very pretty. You want suite, big room?"

"No, two standard rooms are fine. One with doubles."

"Bellman for your luggage?"

"We're leaving the luggage in the car," Mark said. "I'm going to need a few things. I'll phone down a list later."

I'd calmed down, slowly realizing Mark's suggestion we stay overnight in the city made sense, but not for the reasons that first came to mine. I'd initially thought he wanted to stay close to his base of informants, to hit the street running when a call came in. But his concern centered on my extended absence from the embassy. Once Mark returned me to the compound, I was done. And I wouldn't be allowed to leave again without answering a lot of difficult questions. Questions that I—or Katherine—might not be able to deflect.

On the drive in, I'd off-handedly asked Mark how the order to find and eliminate Annie would be disbursed. He'd been reluctant to answer—at first. Finally, he'd explained. A coded fugitive alert would go out to the department's independent contractors—some of the most barbaric and heartless scum on the face of the earth. A few hours later, emails and faxes—disguised as a public service announcement for a missing American—would be dispersed to the public. Displaying Annie's picture and description, it would offer a "reward for any information leading to the return of this U.S. citizen to any American Embassy." On the surface, it sounded like a humanitarian effort to locate a lost patriate. In reality, those sixteen words were operating instructions directed exclusively to the network—*a kill order*. Anyone familiar with American policy knew the state department was prohibited from offering a reward to locate and recover missing nationals. Considered an offer of ransom, it would only become an incentive for kidnappers, perpetuating the problem. The oddly spaced phone number listed at the end of the message served two purposes. A recorded line to report the location of the body and, more important, the price on Annie's head. Later, Mark would show me the number: 011-66-852-5000. He told me the operatives would read it right to left, discerning that Annie was a high priority target, worth $25,000 upon the recovery of her remains. His personal copy would also assign him the duty of confirming her death.

Listening to him describe the prospect of identifying and disposing of the body made me sick.

I barely got it out. "Sounds like you've done this before."

Mark turned solemn. "Once." He hesitated. "I wasn't aware the girl had left the embassy until after the fact. I got a call telling me she had taken off the night before, trying to leave the country. A few hours later, I received orders to *clean* a hotel room. That's when I found her."

"Did you know her, before she ran?"

He nodded. I waited for more, but from the sudden set of lines crossing his brow, I knew he didn't want to talk about it. The silence that followed was more frustrating than uncomfortable. I'd wanted to reach across the seats, rest my hand on his shoulder and assure him I understood—even though I didn't. While I was becoming increasingly aware of the subjective moral code integral to embassy politics, I still couldn't imagine the kind of ruthless animal that would kill a young girl simply because she wanted her freedom.

I let the thought dissolve into the silence.

"This room has double beds." Mark handed me the room key-card.

Kanda was trailing behind us, completely overwhelmed by a degree of luxury she'd never seen before. I reached back and took her arm. "This is our room. Go inside and choose the bed you want. I'll be there in a few minutes. Understand?"

"Her eyes lit up. Is there television?"

"Watch whatever you like." I ushered her inside. "Keep the door closed and don't open it for anyone. I'll use my key to come in."

I wanted some time alone with Mark. I didn't have anything specific to talk about, but I was hoping he did.

His room was nicely furnished, with a king-size bed, mini-bar, two overstuffed chairs, and a flat-screen television. A small desk held a telephone and room service menu.

I noticed two interior doors. Opening the first revealed a large closet, the second provided access to the adjoining room.

I looked at the solid flat slab separating our rooms then turned to Mark. "Is this going to be enough to keep you on your side? I mean, with you being a master spy and all, I don't want this to be a constant source of temptation for you."

He was flipping through the hotel's guest services book. Apparently in no mood for jokes, he ignored my poor attempt at humor. "What do you and Kanda want for dinner? There's a restaurant on the top floor. Nice view. Food is fair." He pushed the book away. "There's also room service. It's the usual . . . burgers and fries, salads, sandwiches, that sort of thing. You in the mood for anything specific?"

I could tell he didn't want to go out.

"I just want to get out of these clothes and take a shower," I said. "If it's okay with you, I'm fine with staying in. Kanda won't care what we do. She's occupied with the TV."

"Room service will take the better part of an hour. I'll get it ordered. You want something healthy or should we eat crap?"

"Surprise me."

He smiled, just a little. It made me feel better.

"I'll also have a few things sent up," he added. "Tooth brush, comb—" He paused. "What else do you need? Lipstick, hairspray?"

"Whatever they have is fine."

He made the calls, then walked to the door between the two rooms.

"You should check on Kanda. I need to call the department, let them know I'm keeping you out overnight. We'll decide on a cover story later."

He took something out of his pocket about the size of a credit card. Made from tightly woven spun steel, the gray metallic surface was inlaid with what appeared to be strips of black plastic. Holding it at an angle against the door, he slid it sideways until half of it disappeared into the jamb. The door opened with a push.

Kanda barely noticed me enter the room. Engrossed in an old science-fiction movie, she turned away from a giant, helicopter-eating lizard just long enough to confirm it was me.

"You need anything?" I asked.

"All good," she said, then resumed her connection with the television.

She'd found a way to escape from reality for an hour or two. I wouldn't interrupt her again.

I could hear Mark talking with someone at the embassy. "That's right, we're picking him up tonight. I've gone over the assignment with Jewel. No problem. She'll handle it."

I walked back into his room and waited for him to finish the call. "Sounds like you were volunteering my services. Should I be concerned?"

"It's our cover story. We'll go over the details later. I got another eighteen hours clearance for you."

Chapter Thirty-Six

After meticulously removing every shred of meat, I placed the chef salad in front of Kanda. I didn't think she'd care what Mark ordered for her, but as I laid the grilled chicken breast and baked potato in front of her, she'd immediately pushed it away, disgusted with the prospect of eating animal flesh.

We'd started dinner together, with Mark joining Kanda and I in our room. After sitting through ten minutes of a Three Stooges marathon, he'd pointed to the adjoining door, suggesting we take our plates to a quieter location.

Before we left, I'd turned to Kanda and said, "We'll be in Mark's room. I'll leave the door open."

She made a slight movement with her head, completely engrossed in the screen.

Mark surveyed the furnishings, looking for a place to put down his plate.

"We can sit on the bed," I offered. "And don't be bashful about meeting me in the middle."

I wasn't trying to be funny. I needed to re-establish my bond with him. It had been a long and difficult day, and I'd said things I regretted. He was doing everything he could to help find Annie, even risking his reputation—and maybe his career—with the department.

In short, I was feeling guilty as hell.

"You want some of this?" He tapped the filet mignon with his knife.

"Yeah, maybe a bite."

He cut off a third from the large piece of meat and dropped it on my plate.

"I'd hoped by now we'd have heard from your contacts," I said.

Mark took a bite before answering. "Sometimes you get a lead right away. Sometimes not. If we don't get a call by midnight, I'll send out a few texts. I don't want to raise the importance of the information . . . it'll push the price up. I've taken as much cash as I can from my working account. Asking for more will raise questions."

I'd asked. He'd answered. And we'd both carefully avoided the obvious. It was nearly seven. In a few minutes, the order would go out. Some nameless son-of-a-bitch would pick up a phone and speak a dozen words that would make no sense to anyone outside the network. Three seconds later, he would repeat it and hang up. That would put the devil's machine in motion.

After showering and putting on a robe, I'd turned the bathroom over to Kanda. Prying her away from the TV had been harder than I'd imagined. I had to promise her another two hours of watching anything she wanted before we called it a night.

Walking into Mark's room, I caught him in a towel, searching through the closet.

"Where'd you find that damn robe?" he asked.

"In the bathroom, under the cabinet next to the sink."

"Well, are you gonna get it for me or do I have to traipse around in front of you?"

I didn't answer right away. Instead, I kept looking at him, oogling his chest, smiling. Finally I said, "Is this good for you, too?"

"Okay, I get it. You're giving me a taste of what it's like. Lesson's over." He walked by me and into the bath. My eyes followed him, taking in his ripped torso and broad shoulders. A few moments later, he emerged wearing the cinched-up white robe.

I said it matter-of-fact, without a trace of tease in my voice. "You have a nice body."

He threw me a slightly confused expression that's exclusively male. Shrugging his shoulders, he sat on the bed. "How's Kanda doing?"

"Still watching some over-dubbed sci-fi flick."

Mark glanced at his phone, then at me. "No matter how it goes down, it'll be a long night. You should try to get some sleep. I'll wake you if there's any news."

He walked to the doorway between the rooms. "You want this left open or closed?"

I felt hurried, rushed. The question was his way of telling me it was time to leave and join Kanda.

"Leave it open." I paused. "Mark, I really don't want to—"

Why did I stop myself?

Mark wasn't stupid. And neither of us was interested in playing games. "If it's okay," I added,

"I'd really like to stay here . . . *with you.*"

Chapter Thirty-Seven

I was suffering the effects of time-drift. We'd started with a drink, then two. Lying on the bed, my head had found Mark's shoulder while an old Andy Williams album played on the cable music channel. Thinking back, I figured we'd been enjoying each other for a couple of hours.

"It's three in the morning," Mark had said.

That meant six hours, not two.

For me, time had ceased to exist inside this hotel room, on this bed. I'd left it only once to pee. Then quickly scampering back, I'd jumped under the covers, my hands gliding over Mark's muscled chest and stomach, reacquainting myself with the terrain. Without hesitating, I'd drifted lower, my fingers grasping an erection that never seemed to quit.

The first time, he took me from the back. Crossing my legs at the ankles, he'd tucked me underneath him, in a position where I could please him the most. I'd asked if he wanted to use the robe's belt to tie my feet together, to insure I stayed just as he wanted me.

"Not unless you want me to," he'd said as he brought his rock hard penis between my hips, anxious for a connection.

Pressing himself tight against my bottom, he plunged into me, his balls resting momentarily against my ass, then pulling away in delicious rhythm. More than once I considered uncrossing my ankles to rise up and join with him, meeting his stroking with my own.

I didn't dare. I wouldn't risk interrupting his slow, hungry thrusts into my pussy.

Between rounds, I rested in happy exhaustion, reveling in the feel of his warm skin against mine, the wet, close connection reminding me of how much I'd missed a man who shared instead of demanded.

Gently rolling me onto my back, he stretched me out spread-eagle, firmly holding my wrists against the bed as he covered me with his body. Able to give me the entire length of his cock, he sank deep, staying close against me, keeping the pressure against my clit with short, rapid strokes until I couldn't hold back. As I came, my contractions pulled him in deeper, tighter.

Seconds later, his hot liquid exploded into my pussy, his semen overflowing onto the sheets.

Even after four years of sex with my husband, I couldn't remember being so completely satisfied, so consumed by a single experience with a man.

And now, I couldn't shake it—the returning thoughts of Annie, the guilt of having enjoyed myself while she . . .

A loud *click-click* broke the silence.

"What's that?"

"Sounds like Kanda moving around," Mark said. "Maybe she pushed her side of the adjoining door closed. You did make some noise on that last one."

"Yeah, she may have heard us."

I'd left the doors between the rooms open a crack, so she didn't feel like we were locking her out.

"You should get some sleep," Mark suggested.

"You, too."

"Don't need it. I'm a bionic hybrid, constructed from war surplus. I think I used to be a Jeep."

I scooted out of bed. "I'm gonna check on Kanda."

"Are you coming back or is this a permanent change in sleeping partners?"

"The alone time will do you good, give you a chance to bring down the pressure."

Mark's phone stopped me in my tracks.

"Hello?"

"Yeah, I remember."

"You sure?"

"How long ago?"

"I understand. I'll bring the money with me."

Mark laid the phone on the nightstand.

"Someone saw Annie?" I asked.

Even in the darkened room, I could see the concern on his face. "Pretty sure the guy is telling the truth." He paused. "And it isn't good."

What the hell does that mean? Had someone already grabbed her?

I sat next to him on the bed. Holding my breath, hoping my voice wouldn't break, I whispered, "Tell me."

"The guy thinks she's camped out at some old ruins south of here."

"He saw her?"

"No, it was one of the boys who works for him. The kid sells untaxed cigarettes on the street. Said he took her there two days ago."

"Is it far? Can you find the place?"

"A forty-minute drive will get us close. It's a hike in."

I jumped off the bed and started for the other room to grab my clothes.

"Hold on!" Mark said. "There's a problem. Last night, the same kid also disclosed her location to two men flashing a wad of cash. They were canvasing the clubs and strip joints."

I felt my stomach twist. "The network?"

Mark shook his head. "I don't think so. From the way he described them, how they were dressed, it's more likely they were IC's . . . independent contractors."

"Is that good or bad?"

"They typically pass the information along to the network, for a price."

"So they can take care of the dirty work?"

Mark was quiet for a moment, then said, "Yeah."

"So if we know where Annie is, why don't we go get her?"

"Jewel, this is going to be difficult, but you need to know it going in. If we run into bounty hunters, I'll have to pull you out. There's no Plan B, and no negotiating with these guys. If we're challenged, I'll have to back off."

I was ready to explode. There were a hundred good reasons to stop the network from finding and killing Annie. Foremost, it was wrong. It broke every law, every moral code on the books. And yet, Mark was telling me his allegiance was sworn to a different authority . . . one originating from the pit of hell.

I wanted to tell him how Annie didn't deserve any of this. The sad part was I knew he would agree with me. His job was forcing him to subordinate the most basic tenets of decency to the political priorities of bureaucrats. To them, Annie was an inconvenience, a thorn in their side. And the sooner she was gone, the better.

"I understand what you're saying," I began slowly. "But I won't abandon her. When I was a captive on the slave ship, Annie kept me alive. After the storm hit, when the boat was sinking, she was willing to sacrifice her life to save mine. And now I'm expected to turn my back on her and just walk away?"

He looked at me a long time, then shook his head, frustrated, not only because he didn't have an argument, but because he knew I was right. Finally, he broke the silence. "Get your clothes on. Our best chance is to arrive before sunrise. If we can get there first, we might be able to pull this off."

"I'll wake Kanda," I offered.

"No, let her sleep. We'll leave her a note telling her to stay in the room. As long as she has a television to watch, she'll be fine. I'll ask the front desk to bring her breakfast."

"You sure?"

"It's too risky to take her with us."

"I just want to see if she's okay," I said.

I opened the connecting door wide enough to peek inside. The television was still on, lighting the room with flickering artifacts of Katharine Hepburn and Humphrey Bogart rigging the African Queen with explosives as they prepared to attack an enemy warship.

The bed was empty.

"Kanda, it's me. Are you in the bathroom?"

Not a sound.

I switched on the light. The bath was unlocked, the separate potty room empty. I checked the room's main door to the hall. I'd made sure to set the dead-bolt before heading to Mark's room.

It was open.

"Mark, Kanda's not here! Can you call downstairs and ask if anyone has seen her? Maybe she's in the lobby."

He appeared in the doorway. "No point." He held up a small piece of paper, torn from the note pad on the desk. "Kanda pushed this under our door. That was probably the sound you heard earlier, the dead-bolt snapping open and the door closing behind her."

"Where the hell did she go?"

Mark handed me the note. "Read this."

The script looked like a third-grader's scrawl. *I go Wat. Find friend.*

"What do we do now?"

"The sooner we get to the ruins, the better chance we have of finding Annie alive. It's your call."

It wasn't much of a choice. Taking the time to track down Kanda could cost Annie her life. Maybe Kanda would blend into the crowd on the temple grounds. Maybe the monks would take pity on her instead of turning her in to the network.

I pulled my clothes from the closet and began to dress.

Chapter Thirty-Eight

Even at four in the morning, the streets were nearly as crowded as they'd been in the middle of the afternoon.

"Who *are* these people?" I asked.

"A lot of 'em are tourists. Some are bar-hopping, partying, others are negotiating for a hooker or black market watch. The rest are locals, ready to give them what they want."

I wondered if Annie had spent any time here, needing some quick cash. "Are the prostitutes expensive?"

"It's all relative, I suppose. Fifty bucks will get you laid. Prices go up from there. A hundred will go a long way."

We were talking about sex as if it was an openly-traded commodity, and apparently the level of competition had made skin a real value.

Mark turned down an open alley. "I need to make a quick stop."

"What for?"

"To pick up a few things, some clothes, a wig to disguise Annie, make her look more like a local in case we find her."

"She's been on the run for over a month. I doubt she'll be mistaken for a tourist."

"Can't take the chance." He opened the door. "I'll be right back, and for god's sake, stay in the car."

He pressed the electronic key and the locks snapped shut.

I was fuming. Annie was hiding somewhere on the outskirts of town, being stalked by Bangkok's nastiest thugs, and Mark had decided it was a perfect time to go shopping.

Tapping on the rear glass. Startled, I twisted around.

Out of the shadows, two people were walking up on my side of the car.

Where the fuck was Mark?

I was relieved to see my visitors were women, both of them young and dressed in slut-wear.

The smaller one motioned with her hand, signaling me to roll down the window. I showed her my palms and shrugged. "I don't have the keys, nothing works from inside."

The other girl pointed to the door lock. "Open up, we come in with you."

I shook my head. "The man I'm with, he's coming right back. If I open the door, he'll beat me." It was all I could think of—convince them I was also a prostitute.

The smaller girl pressed her nose against the glass. "How much you get, pretty girl?"

They were working the street, hoping to pick up a late-night john. Their usual rate might be fifty dollars, half of which went to their pimp. I couldn't let them think I was doing any better. Otherwise, they might decide to break the window and take a look inside my wallet.

I raised my voice, making sure they could hear me. "I'm trying to get forty bucks out of this guy, but he's really driving my price down. I'm hoping to make thirty."

The smaller girl nodded knowingly. "Cheap dicks, always want to fuck us, then don't want to pay up. You let us in, we work him good, split the money." Her tone was serious, just short of a demand.

I smiled and shook my head. "I have to wait 'til he gets back. Then I'll ask."

That seemed to satisfy the larger of the two, but the small one wasn't buying it. "Damn, bitch, you always do it in the car?"

"Got to, if I want to eat," I said.

"You got rubbers?"

"Always."

"You give us some, you share with us."

I figured I was less than thirty seconds away from having to shield my face from a shower of broken glass. I began shifting my hand toward my cell phone.

The taller one saw the light spill from the face of the phone. "Who you call?"

"The man I'm with. I want him to buy more rubbers."

Both of them glared at me with building suspicion. "I don't think so," the smaller girl said. "I think you scared. I think you fucking with us."

The larger girl reached for the other's shoulder, pulling her away from the car.

"Leave me alone, bitch. Stop messin' with me!"

"Her man's coming."

Both girls backed away from the window.

It *was* Mark. I watched him approach in the rearview mirror.

They started right in on him. "Hey, busy man, you buy what you need?"

"Your lady friend say you need good fucking. How about two more for half price? What you say?"

Mark fingered the remote. I froze as I imagined both girls jumping into the car. I relaxed as only the lock-plunger on the driver's side opened, leaving the other doors locked.

"Getting acquainted with the natives?" Mark slid into the seat.

"Get us out of here."

He handed me a brown paper bag. "They didn't have everything, but if we find her, these may help."

. . . *if we find her.* I knew he didn't want to raise my hopes.

It was too late for that. As far as I was concerned, we were bringing Annie back safe and sound. And I wanted Mark to believe it, too.

The bag contained a black wig, tan face makeup, and a long wrap skirt called a Sampot, the traditional Thai garb for women.

Mark handed me a wad of American currency. "Here, separate this into twenties and hundreds. Put a thousand inside the bag, in case we have to drop her."

"Drop her? I don't understand."

"If we pick up a tail, we may have to drop her off. The money will help."

"Put her back on the street? That's not happening."

"If we're followed, we'll have no place to take her."

"Bullshit. We can take her to the embassy, right through the front gate. I'll give her political asylum, or sanctuary, or whatever it's called. It's my right as an American citizen."

"Not anymore," Mark corrected. "As employees of the government, we're prohibited from offering protection to Americans who've broken foreign law."

"Annie hasn't broken any laws."

He pressed his lips together as if reminding me we'd had this discussion before. "The police issued their warrant," he said. "Attempted murder."

"When did that happen? We were supposed to have more time."

"Right after the department released the fugitive-in-flight alert."

"Jesus, Mark, you work for these fuckers."

"So do you. All we can do is work around it . . . *carefully*. We're on our own, now. There won't be any help from the embassy."

REDEMPTION

"As long as we get Annie to safety. That's all I care about. The rest of them can go to hell."

Chapter Thirty-Nine

We'd driven for thirty minutes. During the last five, Mark had checked his GPS several times, determining the best way to approach the site.

"The place is an old Buddhist temple. It was abandoned at the turn of the twentieth century."

"I thought the temples were sacred, like national monuments or something."

"This one is too far off the main road for any tourist traffic, and the structures aren't considered significant enough to spend the kind of money it would take to restore them."

"So it's been empty all this time?"

"Except for history scholars and students. The site's still protected, but there are no guards or fencing. The local police used to send a man out once a month to shoo away the homeless and runaways. I doubt they even do that anymore."

Mark glanced at the blinking dot on the GPS. "This is as close as we're going to get, at least from the highway."

The headlights revealed a gravel turn-around coming up fast on the right. "That might work," he said, braking the car and stopping in a spray of dirt and stones.

"I'd like to hide the car in the foliage," he said, "but I can't see beyond the line of vegetation." He pushed the shift lever into Park. "I'm taking a walk. Do you want to come or stay here?"

Stumbling through the bushes didn't appeal to me. "Leave me the keys?"

He'd been gone less than a minute before I regretted not going with him. Sitting alone in the dark, the empty stillness made every creak of the seat, every sudden, wind-gusted rustle from the trees a ravaging assault on my nerves.

My breath seized in my chest as the beam of Mark's flashlight swept across the window.

"Find anything?"

"Maybe. Looks like an old maintenance road. It's overgrown and pretty narrow, but it's worth a shot."

"Any chance it'll take us to the site?"

"Hard to know. We'll see how far we can go before it becomes impassable. At least we'll be able to hide the car."

The four-door sedan dropped six inches, nearly to the skid-pan, as we drove off the edge of the concrete apron.

"You sure this is a good idea?" I asked.

"It was never a *good* idea. Just the only one I could come up with."

As Mark eased us down the abandoned road, dense undergrowth crunched beneath the car, while fender-high foliage scraped against the doors. With the only indication of the forgotten roadbed an obvious absence of trees, he was forced to back up several times as he realized he'd strayed off the center portion of the flatter ground.

We'd gone a little over a mile when I saw the faint beginnings of light on the horizon.

"How much farther?" I asked.

Before he could answer, Mark stomped on the brake pedal. The opening in the trees had come to an abrupt end.

"This is as far as we go."

"How close are we?"

Mark eyed the GPS. "If this thing is accurate, we're a half mile from the temple. We need more light to walk it. We'll wait ten minutes, then go."

I opened my door. "You can wait if you want. Just point me in the right direction."

Mark gave me one of his frustrated, you're-being-a-pain-in-the-ass looks. "I'd rather you weren't thrashing around in the dark and stepping on a pit viper."

"Snakes?"

"Yeah, the cobras usually rise up and do a little dance, let you know they're pissed off before lunging at you. But the vipers lie there until you get close enough, then . . ."

"Fuck it." I jumped out and slammed the door.

I figured there was less risk of snake bite than the possibility of Annie being found by the network, especially if we didn't get moving. Our early start was the only advantage we had, and that would rapidly diminish as the sun began to rise.

Mark growled under his breath. "Stay behind me, and walk in my footprints."

Chapter Forty

"You sure this is the right direction?" I asked.

We'd been stumbling through the brush for ten minutes. Mark hadn't said much, letting me curse at the jungle for both of us.

"We're halfway," he whispered. "And keep your voice down. It carries."

"You think someone's already out here?"

"If there is, I want to give them a wide berth."

"What if we run into some locals, you know, out for a morning stroll?" I asked.

"Not likely. Not out here."

"But you said the site is occasionally visited by students. So how do you tell the bad guys from the natives?"

Mark's expression told me he wasn't in the mood for an explanation. But he didn't blow me off. Instead, he gave me the short version. "The network has an unofficial uniform. They all tend to wear some version of a gray vinyl jacket and blue baseball cap to identify themselves, and intimidate others."

"Doesn't sound very original."

"It isn't. But you won't find anyone wearing it unless they're in the business of trading flesh for dollars."

As the orange-red dawn began to add form and shadow to the jungle, I picked up the pace. I welcomed the light, but the rising sun was the equivalent of a solar hourglass, ticking away the seconds before we would likely run into unwanted company.

"What's that?" I was certain I'd heard a noise.

Mark cocked his head, then raised his hands . . . nothing.

Must've been my imagination.

I'd walked another twenty feet when I heard it again. This time I was sure—the rise and fall of inflection, the characteristic edge of an Asian accent. It was a voice, a broken word or two carried on the breeze.

I froze. Others—*probably bounty hunters*—were here!

I waved at Mark. "Don't move," I whispered. "Sounds like voices."

He nodded, listening, waiting.

Piercing rays of sunlight suddenly spanned the openings between the trees, the slivers of light exposing pockets of lifting fog. Drops of moisture glistened around us as a sunbeam fell on the very spot where I stood. I felt exposed, vulnerable. Anyone within a hundred feet could see me.

Mark offered an exaggerated nod, his expression turning stone hard. He'd heard it too. And not just one voice, but a mixture of pitch and tempo. It could have come from a mile away or as close as a hundred yards.

He brought his finger to his lips. We would keep our voices low, if we spoke at all.

With one hand, he motioned for me to join him. With the other, he pushed toward the ground, a signal to move slowly. Directing me behind a large swamp pine, he waited until I was close enough to bring his lips to my ear.

"We have to determine their location," he whispered.

I nodded, instinctively sliding my arms around his waist. His right hand met mine, but instead of offering protection, he brushed it away.

More than once I'd been an outright bitch since we'd left the hotel, but this wasn't the time to push me away. My frustration turned to apprehension as I realized I'd misinterpreted his actions. He was drawing his gun from the holster. As he brought it to waist level, his other hand slowly pulled back on the bolt and chambered the first shell. The noise was barely perceptible.

Now I was scared.

During the drive, Mark had repeatedly told me the situation was risky. He'd made it clear if we encountered men sent from the network, they would be the very worst of the lot, capable of killing without hesitation.

But the reality of a gunfight seemed far-fetched. In my imagination, I'd seen our rescue mission as a perfectly-timed maneuver, our early start giving us at least a two-hour advantage—plenty of time to find Annie and take her to safety. Now the danger was all too real. Using the large tree for cover, Mark was training his gun in the direction we'd last heard the voices, ready to drop anyone who presented a threat.

"You told me you couldn't shoot anyone," I whispered.

"Things have changed. We don't have a clear path of retreat. Those men out there are searching for an American white girl. The fact that you have blonde hair won't make a bit of difference to them. As far as they're concerned, you could've dyed it to hide your identity. For twenty-five grand, you're close enough to meet the description."

"Close enough?" I hadn't considered myself as a target.

"Shhhh. They're nearly on top of us."

"I don't hear anything."

Mark mouthed the words. *That's the point. The birds . . . they're quiet.*

He was right. It was dead still. The constant calls of the jacana and egrets, easily carrying for a quarter-mile, were silent.

I was glad I'd refused Mark's offer to grab a snack from the hotel to take with us. An empty stomach was a lot easier to control.

"Over here. This way." English, spoken with a heavy Thai accent.

My breath caught in my chest.

Thrashing noises. More than one person, moving at a fast clip. There was no question—*they were coming toward us.*

I looked at Mark. His training had kicked in. Seemingly unaware of my presence, he had gone into a kind of trance, his senses focused on the approaching strangers. Completely absorbed with every sound, every motion, he was making split-second evaluations of what was happening some twenty yards in front of us.

Another rustling of foliage, followed by the same heavily-accented voice. *"Come, this way. Hurry."*

They would be visible in seconds.

Mark's hands moved with expert precision, his right resting the butt of his .40 caliber Glock on his fisted left. I heard him exhaust two short breaths through his nose . . . then nothing. His eyes fixed and unblinking, he wrapped his index finger around the trigger. His instincts sharpened by sheer repetition and conditioning, he had become a killing machine. No longer influenced by emotion, his calculating resolve eliminated any reluctance in maintaining his advantage over the opposition.

I didn't like seeing this part of him. But if it came down to who would fire first, who would walk away alive and unharmed, I couldn't be in better hands.

I considered lowering myself to the ground, shutting my eyes, and covering my ears. I didn't want to see or hear it—the muzzle blast, the impact of the bullet as it ripped into flesh and bone, the pitiful cries from the men as they took their last breath.

But my movements might break Mark's focus and concentration. And as bad as an outright execution of slave traders might be, the other option—letting them put a bullet in my brain after leaving Mark's body in the jungle to rot—was not an acceptable alternative.

Motion on the edge of the clearing. They're breaking through.

The first man came into view, his arms swishing from side-to-side, thrashing at the giant elephant ears rising up through the waist-high salt-grass. "Only ten minutes more to old road," he said. "Then we go faster."

I gritted my teeth. He was wearing a gray jacket, soaked and shiny wet from the rain-heavy foliage. A light blue baseball cap—it seemed unnatural and out of place—sat on his head in garish contrast against his dark Thai complexion. He was young, maybe mid-twenties.

It was a clear shot, but I knew Mark was waiting until he could include all of them in his firing pattern. I looked at the extended clip protruding from the Glock's handgrip. Fifteen rounds—a prescription for an ambush, not a firefight.

The second man entered the clearing. He was smaller and struggled to walk against the vegetation. He wore a khaki shirt and medium-brimmed straw hat, the kind the locals sold to tourists. It blocked his face. I couldn't see how old he was, but his actions, his energy, suggested he was also young.

Mark lowered his head, the movement so slight I almost missed it. He'd fire four shots—two into each target—taking out the smaller man first, because he was the farthest away.

Mark had dropped the manual off in my room. Even though it was against regulations, I'd insisted he let me read it. At the time, the instructions had seemed academic, a theoretical how-to guide in preparing for an unlikely event, like a nuclear attack or an extinction event from a meteor strike. The final paragraph had made me realize it was more than a conceptual model of combat—*You may not be ready to kill, but your enemy is ready to die, if his death also results in yours.*

"Keep going. Must hurry." The lead man was chatty, his voice low and strangely encouraging, as if trying to motivate his companion.

"Only a little more to go, Khel Si. Then much easier."

That name . . . it's familiar.

The second man cleared the shoulder-high bush. Mark's target field was complete. The men had only a few seconds left to live.

I couldn't take my eyes off the smaller man. Something wasn't right, my instincts telling me I had to—

Dear God, it's not a man!

I almost touched Mark on the shoulder, then stopped myself in time. Instead, I managed a whisper. "Mark, that's not a man. Look at her chest. She has tits!"

I looked back at her, hoping I could direct Mark's eyes to see the same thing. Her wet shirt clung to her chest, revealing feminine breasts.

My mind spun back to yesterday, sitting on the bed with Kanda when she'd told me about the girl who escaped from the brothel—*Khel Si!*

This girl was not a network killer. She was a runner. And based on the one-sided encouragement from her companion, he wasn't a bounty hunter. The man was attempting to guide her out of the forest.

But Mark wasn't lowering his gun. He remained ready to dispatch them both. His training would not allow him to compromise the advantage of surprise.

I had no choice. Backing away, I took two steps from the tree to avoid revealing Mark's position. I needed to put some distance between us before I revealed myself to Khel Si and her companion.

Another step or two, that's all I needed . . .

Too late. The man saw me and turned in my direction. I had to speak. "Khel Si? Don't be afraid. Kanda sent me."

The next few seconds were an exploding blur of confusion as both Khel Si and her guide immediately dropped to the ground, disappearing from view. A sudden rush of motion intruded from my left, followed by the crashing impact of two-hundred pounds of charging human steel slamming me to the ground.

Stunned, unable to think or move, it took several seconds to realize Mark's body covered mine in a suffocating shield of muscle, bone, and determination.

I struggled to draw a breath. "What the fuck?"

"Shut up! There could be *others,* close behind."

I hadn't considered that. And the *others* would think nothing of killing four instead of two.

"Okay," I whispered, "I screwed up. So what do we do now?"

"Who the hell is Khel Si?" he asked.

Kanda's friend. I told you about her in the car . . . a runner from Sarai's brother."

Mark's voice was sharp. "Jewel, are you sure about the name?"

"Yeah, that's what Kanda called her."

"Jewel, listen to me. Khel Si is Thai for *Kelsey*." He paused, thinking, recalling conversations, files, reports—about me. "Wasn't that the name of the ship you were on?"

Again, my mind raced back to yesterday, sitting on the bed with Kanda.

'Her name is Khel Si. She say it's special, means where she from.'

'What else did Khel Si say?'

'Same as you. She lose someone, someone she love . . . Chatmanee. She look for Chatmanee.'

"Mark, do you know what *Chatmanee* means? How it translates into English?"

He looked at me with confused concern. "It means . . . Jewel."

My throat was closing, my eyes filling, blurring my vision.

"Get off of me!" I pushed against his chest, trying to squirm out from under him.

"Hold on," Mark countered. "Calm down and listen to me. We'll do this slowly, a step at a time. And nothing stupid. You understand?"

"Yeah, right. Just get the fuck off me."

There was a good chance that twenty feet away, Annie was lying on the ground, scared, and ready to bolt. As long as Mark had me pinned there was nothing I could do.

He shifted his weight, removing some of the pressure. "I'll move ten feet to the right, into the tall grass. You stay low and to my left. Never cross in front of me. Understand?"

"Just don't shoot me. And for god's sake, don't shoot Annie."

Mark rolled off and crawled a few feet into the salt-grass. Fully hidden, he lifted his head and scanned the clearing, his gun pointed in the direction of where Khel Si—Annie, I hoped—and her companion were lying on the ground. Without taking his eyes off the open glade, he said, "What are you waiting for? Go get her."

Chapter Forty-One

In spite of Mark's warning to stay low, I'd approached the area standing on my feet. If it was Annie, I wanted her to recognize me, without her vision corrupted by fear and suspicion.

I was nearly on top of them when her head popped above the grass.

My first real look at her face tore at my gut. Her left eye was swollen and bloodshot, and her cheek carried the fading bruise of a cruel and vicious blow to the head. The fear and sadness in her face made her look ten years older than I remembered. But beneath the grit and grime of living on the street for over a month, she was still my Annie.

At first, she just stared at me, her eyes searching mine, not believing it was really me. Even after closing the last few feet between us and wrapping my arms around her, I had to keep whispering my name.

Mark's insistence in maintaining his defensive posture—crouched in the grass with his gun leveled at Annie's companion—didn't help to calm her nerves. Although I continued to reassure her Mark was there to help, Annie was still anxious as hell, constantly glancing behind her, ready to jump.

Needing privacy from Mark's line of sight, we slowly dropped to our knees. Keeping my arms around her quivering frame, I tried to estimate how much weight she'd lost. The tight, supple muscle that had defined her shape had yielded to the abuse of irregular meals and lack of sleep. And yet, as she pressed herself against me, I felt that indescribable strength and passion that had always made us stronger together than we could ever be apart.

She pulled back, enough to look at me. "Are you okay?" she whispered.

In spite of the marks on her face—obvious evidence of the brutal treatment she'd endured—her thoughts were only of me.

"I'm good. And you will be too, as soon as we get you out of here."

I heard Mark's voice in the background, challenging Annie's companion with pointed questions.

"Where were you taking the girl?"

"Who paid you to find her?"

"If you don't work for the network, why do wear the jacket and hat?"

I heard the man's answers, but I wasn't really listening, my senses completely focused on Annie.

Suddenly, her hands raced over me, sweeping across my breasts, caressing my bottom. I gently kissed her cheeks and forehead, returning her touch in the same way a sweetheart reacquaints herself with an absent lover.

The sound of parting foliage announced Mark's approach. "You two can reminisce later. We need to go."

"He's right," I whispered. "The network is looking for you."

Annie stiffened and bared her teeth. "I know. Gamon told me there's a contract out on me. And the preferred method of delivery is by body-bag."

"Gamon . . . that's the guy you're with?"

"He came to the ruins early this morning to warn me. He was leading me out of the forest."

I started to tell her there was a good chance he was also the one who'd sold her out, revealing her location in exchange for a hundred dollar bill. But Mark spoke first.

"I'm not going to say it again. We have to go. NOW!"

Helping Annie rise from the ground, I asked Mark, "You believed Gamon's story? What about his jacket and cap?"

"I'll explain on the way. Let's go."

With Gamon taking the lead—where Mark could keep an eye on him—Annie and I stayed a few steps behind. Holding hands, we walked side-by side, helping each other through the thick foliage.

After a few minutes of walking in silence, Mark motioned for Annie and I to join him, close enough to hear a whispered exchange.

Mark explained Gamon's decision to wear the network's colors was a deceptive ruse, in the event he and Annie ran into real bounty hunters. Hoping they would be hesitant to shoot one of their own, he believed exploiting the commonality would give him the chance to talk his way out of a confrontation. He would say Annie was his prisoner and he was taking her to his boss, a ruthless, cold-blooded flesh-peddling kingpin who would think nothing of killing anyone who interfered with one of his lieutenants.

Gamon grinned as he heard Mark relate the story, beaming at his own ingenuity.

Mark saw it. "It nearly got both of you killed," Mark said.

"And yet, you have not told me to take off the jacket, have you?" Gamon countered.

Mark didn't answer, apparently thinking his plan might have some merit, especially since there was still the possibility of encountering network operatives on the way to the car.

We'd traveled a hundred yards when Mark pulled out a cheap, throw-away cell phone. With a quick call to the hotel, he extended our checkout to late afternoon.

His plan was simple. Annie would return with us to the hotel while Mark made arrangements to get her out of the country. As long as no one saw her moving between the car and the room, she was relatively safe—at least for a few hours.

Chapter Forty-Two

After dropping Gamon on the outskirts of the city, Annie and I had stayed in the rear seat, my arm around her shoulder as she cuddled tight against me. With her head low and eyes closed, I'd hoped she was finally getting some rest, if only for the short ride.

Using the wide-brimmed hat to cover her face, we moved through the lobby of the hotel one at a time. I went first, waiting for Annie at the elevator entrance. Mark followed three minutes later.

Once inside the room, Mark continued to check the hallway, to confirm no one had followed us. After ten minutes, he appeared satisfied.

While he situated himself at the desk to make phone calls, I brought Annie into the bathroom. I could tell she was exhausted, but she didn't object.

"Let's clean you up. You'll feel better after a shower." Her matted hair and patches of dirt on her skin suggested she hadn't had such a luxury in weeks.

As I unbuttoned her shirt, her hands found my waist. "I didn't think I would ever see you again," she said. "I didn't even know if you were still in Thailand. There was no one to ask, no one I could trust."

"I didn't know where to start looking for you, either," I said. "I got lucky, ran into the right people."

She managed a smile, not needing an explanation.

The story of Annie's month on the run was visible on her thin frame. A large green and yellow bruise colored her left thigh, its size making the smaller purple marks on her arms and back seem less serious prominent.

She caught me looking.

"I know," she said. "I must look like shit."

"Not to me." I gave her a quick peck on the lips then turned to reach for the shower handle. I kept my back to her intentionally, pretending to test the water, waiting for it to warm. Seeing the evidence of what she'd endured was tearing me apart. But I would not let it show.

She'd seen enough.

Growing impatient, Annie nestled against me. "Let's get in."

Quickly slipping out of my jeans and top, I stepped into the stream and reached for her. "Careful, it's slippery."

For a moment, we stood there facing each other, naked, silent, as if both of us needed to make sure this was real, and not some fragment of a misplaced dream.

Stepping in behind me, she slid her hand across my shoulders, slowly working her way down my back, then under my bottom, reacquainting herself with my body. Placing my hands on the shower wall, I leaned forward, giving her access. Closing my eyes, I stood there, feeling Annie touching me, connecting with me, as the water sprayed against my face, washing away the vision of her injuries.

Finally turning to face her, I wrapped my arms around her in a moist embrace. Sealing our lips together, we shared the taste of our reunion.

"You came for me," she whispered. "When I'd given up hope of ever seeing you again, you found me."

I wanted to tell her she was safe, that her ordeal was over. But I'd never lied to Annie, and I wouldn't start now. I hoped she didn't notice the lump in my throat as I managed, "It's all going to work out. I promise."

Picking up the soap, I lathered my hands. "It's my turn now. Be a good girl and let me have my way with you."

For the first time since bringing her out of the jungle, I saw it—the hint of a twinkle in her eyes.

Chapter Forty-Three

After checking on Mark—still making phone calls, trying to track down a *friendly* who constantly changed his number to confuse government officials—I led Annie to the bed.

We climbed in together, both of us looking forward to getting an hour or two of sleep. But she was too excited to close her eyes.

She started with how she'd escaped from Gregory, and then taken shelter in the backrooms of some of the more charitable store owners. I knew she was leaving out a lot of unpleasant details—the daily grind of avoiding street thugs, con men, and slavers, human vermin who were constantly combing the city looking for runaways.

Eventually, with fatigue taking over, she closed her eyes and drifted off.

It didn't last long.

As Mark entered the room, I could tell he had plenty on his mind. But he was hesitating, and that wasn't like him. I figured he wanted to give Annie more time to recuperate before hitting her with a plan that was less than foolproof.

Stopping at the foot of the bed, he glanced at his watch and pressed his lips together. He couldn't wait any longer. "Wake her up."

Annie jolted at the sound of his voice.

"Are you two ready to go over the details?"

Annie managed a sleepy, "Yeah."

"This isn't going to be a Sunday picnic," Mark began. "The people I've hired are trustworthy, but there's always a chance of being seen by an informant. I'm assuming someone will be watching the docks, so stay alert. Once we're on the pier, Jewel, I want you to pretend to take pictures with your phone. Annie, keep your hat pulled low. The more you can block your faces, the better."

Annie's lips were trembling. "I don't understand. Why can't I come back with you to the embassy?"

Mark stared at me. "Tell her."

"We have to get you out of Thailand. Mark is calling in a few favors."

"But you work for the government. If you explain what happened, they'll protect me, right? They can grant me immunity or asylum . . . something like that."

I couldn't tell her the very people she thought of as her protectors were the same ones who had ordered her death. The truth would rob her of all hope of ever returning home.

"The embassy can't help us, at least not right now," I said.

The look on her face was like a fist closing around my heart. She was begging for my protection, my promise that I wouldn't let anything happen to her.

Biting her lower lip, she asked, "You're not taking me with you?"

I wanted to put my arms around her and say it . . . *let's go home*. But I had to face reality. My employer had put out a contract on her life.

"Right now, it's better to keep you hidden until we can get someone to listen to your side of the story."

With Annie brushing back an occasional tear, Mark explained the best option was to get her off the mainland. By sending her to a small island—one without advanced communication technology or locally-generated media broadcasting—there would be less chance of her being recognized. His main concern was Thailand law enforcement classifying her as a dangerous fugitive-in-flight, and possibly drawing the attention of police on nearby islands. Fortunately, small island-based police forces were typically understaffed and overworked, keeping them far too busy with their own problems to be concerned with the possibility of escaped felons living quietly among their population.

Mark's phone rang. In the background, I heard bits and pieces of conversation that were easy to put together. A price had been set. There was agreement on the meeting time. The call ended with Mark instructing the other party not to make any more calls to the throw-away cell.

Annie's red-streaked eyes grew wide with fear. "He's setting up a deal with the network, isn't he?"

I started to scold her for thinking such a thing, especially after I'd told her Mark was a trusted friend.

But she needed sanctuary, not a reprimand. At this point, my assurances of Mark's good intentions would mean nothing. And why should they? I wasn't offering her liberty or even the promise of her future freedom.

Still, I had to try.

"Annie, I swear to you, we can trust Mark. He's putting his career at risk to help you. And these people he's talking to, he's used them before."

I'd hoped to keep her calm. Judging from the frantic expression on her face, I was doing a rotten job.

She rolled away from me and jumped off the bed. "I think I'm better off on my own." Reaching for the small gym bag I'd picked up to hold her makeshift wardrobe, she added, "With the money you've given me and these clothes, I can make it out of the city. I need to find a place to hide for a few weeks. Then we can try again, after they've stopped looking for me."

I'd blown it. She was ready to leave, to risk it on her own. I couldn't blame her. The only thing she knew about Mark was what I'd told her—not enough to trust him.

I followed her off the bed and put a heavy hand on her shoulder. "Listen to me. I will not let you disappear into some shit-hole knowing I'm never going to see you again. Give Mark five more minutes to explain. If you don't like it, you can cut us loose and try it your way. He's not here to take you in. He wants to help. Hear what he has to say. Then decide."

She collapsed against me. "I don't know who to trust," she whimpered. "The network is out there, waiting. And if they catch me . . ." She buried her face in my neck, too exhausted to cry.

"I swear I won't let anything happen to you." My words rang hollow, not because I didn't mean it, but because we both knew there were too many details outside my control.

She nestled closer. "I still don't understand what's going on, but I'll stay long enough to listen to Mark." She brought her lips to my ear. "When this is over," she whispered, "when we're finally together again, can I stay with you, sleep with you at night?"

"Of course you can," I said. "When we're home, together."

I would have promised her anything.

Chapter Forty-Four

Mark had changed into a beige sports shirt and khaki pants, courtesy of the hotel concierge. I picked out faded baggy jeans and a loose-fitting top from the lost-and-found. With Annie wearing the wig, Sampot, and wide-brimmed hat, we hoped to give the appearance of two American tourists and a native Thai guide taking a tour of the docks and fishing pier. With any luck, we would blend into the crowd without anyone questioning our real identities.

Mark's plan was simple—and dangerous as hell.

He'd arranged a small day-charter fishing boat to pick us up at the end of the main service pier. As far as the boat's crew was concerned, they believed we were no different than any other group of vacationers ready for a day on the water—with one exception. Instead of filling the boat with a dozen beer-swilling, cigar-smoking, Hemingway-wannabes, we would be the only passengers. Of course, that was based on our making it onboard without the countless eyes of the trafficking network or local law enforcement noticing us.

Mark had assured me of the crew's loyalty. The boat's owner was an expatriate, having worked for the agency before his retirement five years ago. He was still active as an independent contractor, now choosing his jobs with a sense of conscience rather than blind allegiance. Mark said the guy had been lucky. Most company-trained agents who came out of retirement to freelance usually found themselves prone to fatal accidents.

"It's a good cover," Mark explained. "The dock is full of tourists, and boats are always coming and going. There should be no reason for anyone to challenge us."

He sounded like a high school football coach pumping up his players at half-time.

"Once we're outside the harbor," he continued, "Annie will transfer to a ship capable of making an open sea passage. Her destination is Samui, an island about 250 miles south of Bangkok. It has reasonable access, an airport, and generates its own electricity and clean drinking water."

"Another fucking piece of paradise," Annie mumbled.

Mark continued to explain that deep in the interior of the island, a charity-supported orphanage provided the cover for a private safe-house. With money the only criteria for admittance, those taking refuge there ranged from political refugees to fugitives from justice. Since the orphanage was always in need of contributions, "paying guests" were housed in a separate building two hundred yards from the eyes and ears of the children. It was considered a reasonable, albeit questionably safe tradeoff.

"How long do I have to stay there?" Annie asked.

"That's what we're going to work on," I said, "as soon as Mark and I get back to the embassy." I knew my answer would continue to haunt me, and just as certain it would never leave Annie's mind.

I wondered if she was weighing the alternatives, determining her chances of survival if she returned to the street.

"Annie, if you try it our way, at least I'll know where you are," I said. "And I can keep working on bringing you home. But if you run, I'm afraid I'll lose you forever."

Angry, frustrated, and mostly afraid, she shook her head. "I don't know what to do." She hesitated, then asked, "Will we be able to talk, you and me?"

"Not by phone," Mark answered. "You'll have a coded form of email."

She was quiet for a moment.

"It's only for a few weeks?" She searched my face, pleading for the truth. "And then you'll bring me home?"

"As fast as I can." It was nebulous and vague— the best I could do without lying.

Her eyes fell to the floor. "Okay," she said softly.

I waited for more. But there was nothing left to say.

Chapter Forty-Five

The ride back to the department was its own form of torture. Mark seemed unsettled, no doubt thinking about what he'd done, maybe even second-guessing some of his actions.

The boat trip from the dock to the larger vessel had only taken twenty minutes. I'd spent most of the ride cradling Annie as she lay against me, letting the sea air wash over us.

As the small freighter came into view, we both felt the pangs of separation.

"I don't think we're ever going to see each other again," she said. Her voice was strangely neutral, as if she'd decided all of this—moving her offshore, hiding her from bounty hunters as well as the law—was only delaying the inevitable, leaving her to face a future without hope or reprieve.

"You know that's not true," I argued. "You and I are connected. We'll always have a bond between us." I felt something on my forearm. Glancing down I saw the first of Annie's tears tracking across my wrist. "And now that I know you're in a safe place," I added, "I can start working on the legal process to get you home."

"I don't want to go home," she murmured. "I want to be with you."

The ocean-going ship was the *Ratana*, a small cargo transport anchored around the point and outside the view of other boats moored in the harbor.

At first, its profile sent a shiver down my spine, reminding me of the *Kochi Mar*, the slave ship that had offered rescue during the storm that sunk the *Kelsey*.

That seemed like a lifetime ago.

Mark had directed the crew of the fishing boat to pull up along the blind side of the ship, facing the sea. "Fewer eyes on us," he'd said.

Then much too soon, it was time to move Annie aboard. I kept searching for a reason to delay the process, to give us a few more minutes together. But our position next to the freighter was precarious, our small boat bobbing against the hull as both crews worked to maintain the space between the two vessels.

Suddenly, I was putting the handles of the gym bag in her palm, shuffling her to the side of the boat, holding her, touching her arms, her shoulders, trying to stay close enough to inhale the scent of her hair— desperate to remember . . .

Mark hit the brakes, barely avoiding a wildly darting scooter. The jolt brought me back to the here and now.

"We should have waited," I said. "We should have gone onboard with her, made sure she was safe."

"Too risky," Mark countered. "The only reason a fishing boat pulls up alongside a ship anchored outside the harbor is to transfer illegal cargo. Anyone seeing us would know what was going on. They might have reported us."

He was right, but I couldn't shake the feeling of helplessness as I continued to replay those last moments with Annie.

Before stepping aboard, she'd paused and turned around, the tears streaming down her face. Seeing how scared she was, I'd put my arms around her one last time, giving her a quick hug. But it seemed so rushed, inadequate, and empty. All I could remember is feeling her uncontrollable shaking, then Mark pulling us apart, taking her by the shoulders and directing her across the few inches of space between the two boats.

We were abandoning her.

As Annie disappeared through the sea-level access hatch, the freighter's captain stepped forward. It was far more than a token appearance. Mark handed him the ring I'd received as a gift from Sabine. The captain turned it over in his hand a few times, then slipped it on his little finger, officially accepting it as payment for Annie's safe passage.

I hated it—the men, the money that drove them to destroy innocent lives. And right now, I even hated Mark.

"What happens next?" I asked, swiping at the single tear streaking down my cheek.

"Tomorrow, I'll set up a website. The address is a string of random letters and numbers to make it appear like a place-holder, temporary and not worth tracing. I'll pass along the instructions to Annie through the orphanage's email. She'll use it like a blog, posting on it through a couple of shadow servers. It should give us a way to keep track of her, at least for a while."

"How long is a while?"

He blew out a breath, my challenge adding to the strangling cloud of frustration that had settled over both of us.

"We bought her some time. Right now, it's all we can do.

Chapter Forty-Six

Even in the advancing twilight, I spotted the white perimeter walls of the embassy from a block away. As Mark navigated the car through the front gates, I watched the surveillance cameras pan the vehicle, their rotating zoom lenses scanning for scratches on the paint, punctures in the metal, and cracks in the glass—evidence of a possible confrontation.

Mark rolled down the windows to allow the guards to check the interior.

"You two must be involved in something really hot. I have orders to report your arrival the minute you're on property."

"Who's asking?" Mark challenged.

"The director. Called personally. Got a real hard-on about you two. Don't know what you've been up to, but there's lots of interest."

Mark grimaced. "Can you give me a minute before you call it in? I want to get Jewel inside. I don't want her shanghaied for a three-hour debriefing until she's had a chance to change clothes."

The guard bent down and took another look at me through the window.

Mark added, "I'll put in a good word with personnel, do my best to get you off night duty."

"I can give you sixty seconds, and then I gotta make the call."

"I owe you one." Mark touched the rocker-switch and rolled up the windows as we drove onto the grounds. "The guys watching the monitors probably have the same orders. We don't have much time. We need to review our story, get the details straight."

Mark had brought it up before. I'd put him off more than once. Unable to get my mind off Annie, I couldn't think about our cover story. Now we were out of time—I didn't have a choice.

"Just tell me what to say."

"A little white lie isn't going to work. To keep them off track, we need to invent a full assignment, complete with details."

"In other words, lie through our teeth."

"You good with that?"

What other option did we have? "Like you said, we're running out of time."

As Mark navigated the rotary leading to the rear of the complex, timers and photo cells began activating the low level landscape lighting, creating a false sense of refuge.

"I have a friend, he's a vendor client. He sent me a text earlier this week, letting me know he would be in town. He's agreed to cover for us. Here's what you need to remember. His name is Daniel Lockard. He has citizenship with three countries, none of which are Thailand. It automatically puts him on their watch-list. I usually meet him at the airport to make sure he gets through immigration without the third degree." He stopped, then added, "Now listen carefully."

I nodded, giving him my full attention.

"Last night, Danny took us out to dinner. The two of you hit it off and, after dinner, he asked us to have a drink with him. Because he's a vendor, we don't say no."

"What's this guy look like?"

"Six-foot even. Two-hundred-and-twenty pounds. He shaves his head. Always wears tinted glasses, no prescription. He's educated, and will throw in a two-dollar word without blinking. Remember to refer to him as Danny. He hates Dan. Oh, and his business is modems, high speed data transfer devices."

"What did we talk about over dinner?"

"His kid, Jason. He's into sports, plays baseball at Colorado State."

"And the wife?"

"Divorced. Doesn't mention her. It was nasty."

I had to ask because I knew I it would come up. "Did I spend any time with him . . . you know, later, after the drink?"

"I think it makes a tighter story to say you did. Tell them it happened late, after the three of us spent a couple of hours in one of the clubs, uh . . . the *Route 66*. Since Danny wanted some private time with you, it was my decision to get the room."

It was a lot to remember. And when the questions came, I couldn't hesitate with the answers. After supposedly spending the night with a guy named Danny, I would normally have the information on the tip of my tongue.

"If I can talk to Katherine first," Mark continued, "she'll be able to cut the bullshit in half. If I can't, remember that everything, the dinner, the show, staying overnight, was either Danny's idea or mine. You did what you were told. Never start any of your answers with the words, *I thought . . .*"

Mark was willing to take the blame—if there was any to take. I didn't like pointing the finger at the same man who had just helped me rescue Annie, but I understood his logic. He would report his activities as a part of normal procedure. And with my involvement an expected response to a superior's request, my actions would be considered innocent.

I reached across the center console and laid my hand over his. "Last night—"

"Yeah, we need to talk about that," he interrupted. He paused, switching mental gears before putting his next thought into words. "Katherine will know our story is a cover. When you're alone with her, tell her anything she wants to know, except that we slept together."

"We didn't," I smiled. "I don't remember either one of us getting much sleep."

"Well, in case it comes up in the conversation, don't take the risk of alienating her. You need to keep her on your side."

"You mean if she knew we'd had sex, it would be a problem for her?"

"Relationships between the staff and agents are messy. You can develop feelings, grow close."

"And that's a bad thing?"

"It can take you off your game, lower your objectivity."

Mark's explanation was too textbook. I had the feeling it was a lot more complicated than that. "So you and Katherine, huh?"

Mark was quiet for a moment. "It happened a long time ago. There's been the occasional repeat performance, but it's not something we talk about. Understand?"

"So I have to share you with Katherine?" I'd occasionally considered her as a possible playmate, and although my question didn't directly imply a threesome, the idea was suddenly interesting.

He glanced at me with an unhappy look. "With our responsibilities and the expectations of the people we work for, does that question even make sense?"

I wasn't sure what he meant. He could've been trying to tell me it was a one-time thing, and I shouldn't expect any future liaisons with him. Or maybe he was suggesting if the opportunity presented itself, we'd go for it. All I knew was that I'd really enjoyed our night together, and I was looking forward to a repeat performance.

"Seems odd, you quoting me official policy," I said. "You've never struck me as the *official* type."

His jaw tightened. "I'm giving you some advice. Stay on Katherine's good side. Regardless of how you feel about her politics, you need her."

His concern seemed sincere.

I could live with that—for now.

Chapter Forty-Seven

The debriefing—if you could call it that—was cryptic and uncomfortable. With only four of us in the room—myself, the director, Katherine, and a senior analyst from the intel department—I wondered if Mark had been intentionally excluded to prevent him from influencing my responses. A few minutes before the meeting, I'd received a text from him, saying I'd done a good job with "Danny," and the client had commented on how much he'd enjoyed my company.

Mark had sent the text to add credibility to our cover story. It was an expected courtesy for agents to compliment the staff—especially the hostesses—when we made an extra effort or if a client was especially pleased with our attention to detail. In addition to boosting our ego, it helped justify the legitimacy of our actions, including the often unorthodox and unconventional aspects of our job.

The intel guy introduced himself as Richie. Although I'd never seen him before, his name said it all. Richie was short for Richard, and the resulting nick-name of Dick. And that was something intel guys had in common—they all acted like dicks.

The meeting started without fan-fare or small-talk. The director took the lead with a few open-ended statements about how Mark and I picked up Danny at the airport, took him to dinner, and then . . . silence. I assumed that was my cue, to offer comments or observations.

I'd talked in vague terms, describing my conversation with Danny, throwing in a few details about his son, his unpleasant divorce, and how proud he was of his company's product line, hoping it added authenticity to my story.

The director glanced at Katherine, then back at me. "You're aware these spontaneous off-campus assignments are very unusual, especially when an overnight is required?"

"Yes, Katherine told me it was unusual." I repeated his words, not certain what he was implying or where he was going with it.

"Did you feel your time with the client was well spent? Productive?"

He was digging. I could have answered with a simple *yes*, but that would have been too predictable. Glossing over my activities with short, easy answers might eliminate the need for invented details, but the director might also recognize it as a pattern, inferring my need to cover something up.

"I think it was a good learning experience for me," I began. "I found myself reacting instinctively, while keeping in mind the importance of the client's relationship with the department. Mark had given me a brief run-down on Danny's background, but nothing about his personality, or his expectations. I only knew he was a preferred vendor and it was my responsibility to keep him happy."

"And did you . . . keep him happy?" The director wasn't pulling any punches.

"He didn't have any complaints." I hoped the innuendo was enough.

For most of the fifteen-minute session, Katherine sat quietly, occasionally nodding in agreement. I assumed her simulated focus was for the director's benefit, to indicate her solidarity. Once, she leaned toward me, as if emphasizing the importance of the question. It seemed odd, since the subject struck me as benign—the director asking my opinion of the heavy street traffic and aggressive driving habits of the locals. Later, I would learn he was using a technique called a trans-derivational search, to determine if I was describing an actual experience or an imagined mental construction—his version of a lie detector.

Finally, the director turned to the dick from intel. "Any waves?"

He shook his head. "No complications on our end. Apparently, they didn't raise an eyebrow."

I looked at Katherine, confused. "What's he mean?"

"Our policy prohibits government employees from visiting the sort of places you were in last night. We know certain clients expect to be entertained in those environments, so whenever our personnel spends time in the private sector, we listen to the rumor mill to determine if an agent was recognized or if one of our people accidentally disclosed they work for the government. But it's not an issue here. Apparently, the three of you were very well-behaved."

"Yep, it's as if you were invisible," the dick added.

The director smiled. "Zero gossip on the street, huh?" It was a rare and cringe-worthy attempt at using generic slang, the director attempting to be more like one of the guys.

"Well, not exactly," the dick countered. "Actually, there's plenty of buzz out there, but it has nothing to do with them."

"Anything to be concerned about?" The director had resumed his usual serious demeanor.

"Typical chatter about a new runaway. Slavers looking for a white girl." He paused. "Except this one seems unusual. I keep hearing the same thing over and over again . . . the girl was seen with two Americans, a man and a woman."

I froze. Someone had spotted us. More important, they'd reported it to the network.

"And it doesn't stop there," the dick continued. "Marine radio was all lit up last night with a story about a girl being picked up outside *Krung Thep* harbor. The message originated from a radio operator on a small freighter. He kept saying how pretty she was, and get this, *how he's sure she's an American.*"

I felt my gut tighten, my face draining.

"Something we need to check out, from the standpoint of missing persons?" the director asked.

What the fuck? The director acted like he didn't know what was going on. Had he been taken out of the loop intentionally to insure plausible deniability?

"Don't know yet," the dick said. "I'm not even sure the two occurrences are related. All I have is some intercepted cell calls and marine chatter. Kind of unusual though . . . two Americans seen with a runaway, then a radio operator running off at the mouth about picking up an American girl without papers. The circumstances seem a little strange."

Katherine jumped in. "Director, is there anything else you need from Jewel?"

She was trying to get me out of there, before changes in my physiology gave me away or, worse, I began asking the wrong questions.

He shook his head. "We're done."

Chapter Forty-Eight

Katherine leaned against the dresser. "Jewel, I know this isn't what you want to hear, but I'm not going to lie to you. Annie's in a bad situation and there may not be anything we can do." She paused, letting it sink in. "Things like this are part of the job, and I know it's hard to understand. But after you've been here a while, you'll have a better handle on knowing when we can help, and when we have to walk away."

I'd been fidgeting with the bedspread, unable to look her in the eyes. I cleared my throat. "Is that what you're telling me, that this is one of those times when I'm supposed to walk away?" I lifted my head. She was watching me intently, gauging my reaction. I didn't turn away, and I didn't give her a chance to answer. "Annie trusted me," I continued. "She was ready to go back on the street to survive on her own, and I talked her out of it. I'm the reason she's on that ship. We both know she's headed into an ambush. Maybe you can turn your back on her, but I can't."

Katherine had accompanied me to my room. Sitting side-by-side in the shuttle, we'd remained silent. It'd been the longest two minutes of my life, silencing my questions, holding back the tears.

"It's too soon to start making assumptions," she said. "I'm going over to intel from here to find out what else they've picked up."

"It won't matter," I argued, my voice nearly breaking. "The transmission from the freighter's radio operator was heard by dozens of people. And some of them were bounty hunters and slavers. When that ship docks, they'll be waiting for her. She's walking into a trap . . . and I set it."

"You can't blame yourself. You did what you thought was best. That's all anyone could—"

"I have to find a way to warn her," I interrupted. "Where's Mark? Does he know what's going on?"

"He's getting ready for another assignment. In fact, he may have already left. There wasn't time to debrief him."

My heart sank. Mark was my ace in the hole. He had the privilege of coming and going, he was connected to the street. If anyone could get a message to the captain of the freighter in spite of the ship's radio operator, it was Mark. Annie's only chance of survival was to find a way off the *Ratana* before it reached the dock.

Katherine's voice was stern. "I need you to promise you'll wait here until I get back. No ideas about wandering around the Fortress trying to talk someone into breaking policy. Maybe there's still something I can do. But you have to understand, I can't take any action that could put the department in a bad light. They don't have an official position in this. And unofficially, they've—"

"Turned their back?"

REDEMPTION

Katherine pressed her lips together in a forced frown, but it wasn't directed at me. It was the only way she could acknowledge the truth—and this time, the truth was dirty.

Chapter Forty-Nine

I'd kept Charlie's card under the bath vanity, taped to the underside of the sink. Keeping a vendor's personal information in my cell phone was forbidden, which was okay with me since I didn't want anyone to know he'd given it to me.

My call had immediately gone to voicemail, bringing on a wave of panic.

Do I tell him the truth?

The message I left was frantic and a bit over the top. In the sixty seconds before the beep cut me off, I did my best to tell him about Annie, how she'd escaped from a psychotic killer, and that the department had put a contract on her life. Then I told him I was leaving the compound to do whatever I could to save her.

I had no idea when he'd get the message or what he would do—if anything—when he heard it. The more I thought about it, the more stupid I felt. I was asking a respectable American businessman to help me battle the seamy Asian underworld. I hadn't even asked him for anything specific, thinking he would somehow know what to do.

The quick knock on the door surprised me. It opened immediately.

Normally, I would've been glad to see Mark. Right now, I wasn't so sure.

"I was told you'd left the compound," I said.

Mark's expression was serious. "I was on my way out, then I overhead something in communications. You've been making phone calls."

Someone had intercepted my call to Charlie. That was less than ten minutes ago. I shrugged my shoulders. "So?"

"The director's upset. He's asked Katherine to escort you back to his office. He wants to know why you made a personal call to a vendor without prior approval."

"If they're monitoring my phone calls, he already knows why."

"Dammit, Jewel, if you want to have a private conversation, you can't use a department-issued phone." He paused. "What are you planning?"

"Well, it sounds like I need to get out of here in the next five minutes, before Katherine slaps me in irons."

"And go where?"

I hesitated, even though I was fairly certain Mark wouldn't turn me in. "I'm going to meet the freighter. If I can get there before it docks, Annie might have a chance."

He said it under his breath, but I heard it as plain as if he'd shouted in my face. *"Jewel, you haven't learned a damn thing."*

"I've learned plenty," I said, my voice rising. "I've learned I can't trust anyone. And that most of what I'm told around here is nothing more than well-constructed lies. It's all just a front to justify the personal agendas of a bunch of suits whose ethics are based on a balance sheet."

Mark didn't flinch. "You knew that going in. This entire operation is a sewage pit of double-talk and politics. There's no black-and-white here."

I was arguing morality in a place where concepts like integrity and decency didn't exist. And I was wasting time. None of this was putting me into a better position to help Annie.

"Did Katherine tell you what's happened to Annie? The ship's radio operator sold her out."

Mark answered with a nod.

"And you're okay with that?"

He glared at me. I couldn't tell if he was disappointed or angry—or both. Finally, he said, "You think you're the only one who's ever lost someone?"

I wasn't in the mood for a pissing contest. "I'm only sure of one thing. I talked her into getting on that ship. And now, the network is waiting for her. Because of me, she doesn't have a chance of coming out of this alive."

For several seconds, he was quiet. Noticing my bare feet, he said, "If you're planning on getting out of here before Katherine arrives, you better put on some shoes. She's probably leaving her office right about now."

Mark *was* going to help me.

I scanned the room, wondering if there was anything I should take with me. No time. I had to move. "Can you get me past the guards?"

"Don't know. They may have received a stop order on you." Mark checked the time. "Meet me at the front gate in four minutes. And don't call for a shuttle. Just get your ass to the gate. Four minutes. Understand?"

I nodded. Scared. Determined. And ready.

Chapter Fifty

Katherine was right on time.

I crouched on all fours and held my breath as she passed through the dorm's reception area, hoping she wouldn't see me hiding behind the large sofa closest to the doors. Waiting until she was down the hall, I tip-toed toward the entry.

My hand had barely touched the door handle when I heard it. "Be careful."

Her warning split the air like a well-placed bullet. I turned and saw her standing on the other side of the room, her face etched in worry.

"I'll wait five minutes before reporting you missing," she added. "After that, I won't be able to help you."

There was so much I could have said, knowing it might be the last time I would ever see her.

With my lips trembling, I tried to smile as I closed the door behind me.

Chapter Fifty-One

"You need to hand over your badge." The guard extended his palm, reminding me to surrender my government ID before leaving the compound.

He punched a few keys on his computer and began scrolling down the screen. "Hmmm . . . I'm not finding your exit order."

"Must be a last minute transfer of assignment, not on the roster yet." Mark's voice surprised me. Walking up from behind, he followed his interruption with a quick apology for being late, inferring to the guard we were leaving together. "Probably the boys in scheduling taking an extra-long lunch," he added.

I held my breath. Mark's lie sounded sincere as hell, but was it enough to convince the no-nonsense, military mindset residing under that starched blue cap?

The guard scanned us head-to-toe, looked at the phone, then nodded as he tapped on the computer, activating the gate.

"Let's go, Jewel. We don't want to keep our clients waiting." Mark ushered me outside the wall, then dropping his voice to a whisper, added, "Keep walking at a normal pace. We need some distance between us and the embassy before we can really talk." He pointed at his ear, signaling the perimeter cameras and mics were recording everything.

For the next few minutes, we kept our conversation neutral, chatting about the weather, the new faces in the research department, and the addition of non-slip edging on the entry steps of the Fortress.

Finally away from the eyes and ears of embassy security, Mark reached into his coat pocket and pulled out a cell phone. "Use this instead of the one in your holster. It's not traceable until you make your second call to the same number. It will buy you time, and hopefully some distance."

"You're not coming with me?" I'd assumed we were going after Annie *together*. The idea of doing this on my own was suddenly overwhelming.

"It won't be long before the director has security looking for you. I need to be here, to confuse the issue. Then I can volunteer to bring you back."

He was hoping to throw the hounds off the scent.

"You don't think anyone will suspect you of helping me?"

Mark hesitated. He knew I was referring to a level of authority far above that of the director's. "We'll know soon enough."

Even though he didn't say it, Mark could be in deep shit. After returning to the compound, he had to convince the director he knew nothing of my intentions to help Annie, and as far as he knew, my leaving the grounds was under authorized orders. As an outside agent, he was given a great deal of flexibility in performing his duties, but attempting to circumvent a kill order from the department would label him a rogue agent—and an expendable asset.

He pulled out a roll of cash and tucked it into my hand. "Take a taxi to the Sathorn Central Pier and get on the hydrofoil. Samui is not a usual stop on today's run, but—"

"You know a guy and he owes you a favor," I said, finishing his sentence.

He smiled. "Something like that."

"There's a good chance you'll get there before the freighter docks," he continued. "Go directly to the harbor master. Tell him you suspect someone onboard the *Ratana* has been kidnapped. That should bring plenty of police."

"But she's wanted by the police."

"Make up a name. Say she's French, has relatives who are worried about her. It will take the officials a day or two to check out her story. In the meantime, they might escort her to another part of the island. Even if they take her in, she'll be a lot safer in police custody than on the street." He paused. "But, Jewel, if you're late, if you arrive after the ship docks, get your ass back here as fast as you can. I'll try to cover for you, but the longer you're gone, the harder it'll be to convince the department you're worth keeping."

"What if you called the harbor master right now?" I asked. "Wouldn't it carry more authority coming from you?"

"That's the problem. I can't reveal my identity as a government employee. It would trigger an official request for verification from the department, and then we'd have a real mess on our hands. It has to be done face-to-face. If you're convincing, you'll create enough of a disturbance to discourage the network from trying anything."

I realized he was about to cut me loose. This was becoming all too real, and the fear was twisting my gut, distorting my face.

"Jewel, are you sure this is what you want to do?"

"She would do it for me," I said, desperate to hide the quiver in my voice.

I stood there for a few more seconds, watching as he crossed the street and headed toward the embassy gate. There were no goodbyes, no quick hugs, not even a wink for good luck.

Chapter Fifty-Two

The first call I made with the new cell phone was to Charlie. This time he picked up. "It's Jewel," I said. "I'm using a new phone. Capture the number and save it."

"Jewel, I've been calling you . . . your phone goes right to voicemail. Are you alright?"

The department had already rerouted my calls, making it impossible for anyone to contact me on the embassy-issued cell.

"Charlie, I didn't know who else to call. And if you want to hang up on me, I'll understand. I was hoping that, well, maybe you could give me some advice."

"I'm in Hong Kong, but I'll do what I can. Your friend, her name is Annie?"

"Yes, and the situation I was telling you about has gotten worse. She's going to die unless I help her." I paused. "And Charlie, I've left the embassy. They're looking for me."

"I understand," he said. An anxious edge had crept into Charlie's voice. "What do you need?"

"I'm on my way to Samui, an island 250 miles south of Bangkok. I should be there a little after five."

"How are you getting there?"

"By hydrofoil. Cuts the trip down a few hours."

The phone was silent for so long I was concerned I'd lost the call. "Charlie, are you there?"

"I'm here. Are you on the boat yet?"

"No, I'm on my way to the dock."

"Hold on."

I heard conversation in the background. Muted voices, questions about when *it* would be ready, how long it would take.

"Jewel, you still with me?"

"Right here."

"I want you to go to the airport. The private side. Tell the clerk behind the flight desk you're looking for a pilot named Sumack. He'll fly you to Samui. His plane is small, but it's a lot faster than the boat. And there'll be fewer people seeing you make the trip."

"Charlie, I don't know how to thank you. I—"

"We need to hang up," he interrupted. "The longer we talk, the more likely they'll get a trace. I'll check in with you later."

The line went silent.

Leaning over the front seat, I told the driver our new destination. Charlie had bought me a couple extra hours, insuring I would arrive on the island in time to meet the freighter at the dock.

Now I needed one more item.

"Driver, I need to make a stop on the way." I waved a hundred dollar bill over the seat. "Do you know where I can buy a gun?"

Chapter Fifty-Three

"I'm Sumack," the man said, introducing himself. "It might be bumpy this time of day, but so far, the weather is clear, so should be a good flight."

He had approached me as I walked through the doors of the private terminal. I figured Charlie must have given him a description.

Since I was the only passenger, he offered to let me sit in the co-pilot's seat—as long as I didn't touch anything. I was a little hesitant in accepting, preferring not to engage in conversation for two hours.

I needn't have worried. When Sumack wasn't keeping his eyes on the large instrument cluster, he busied himself with weather updates. He only broke once from his radio to explain that he usually flew down the coast at a much higher elevation. But a quickly developing squall-line was building over the mountains and he'd made a wide swing to the east and out into the gulf to avoid the clouds.

After enduring nearly two hours of roller-coaster turbulence, I saw the island of Samui on the horizon. I scanned the surrounding water for a sign of the approaching freighter, but at 7500 feet, it was impossible to see any detail.

The airport received two commercial flights a day. The rest of the traffic was private. Although a small facility, it was fenced for security and had on-site service bays and a fueling station.

As Sumack taxied the Beechcraft King Air toward the tie-downs, I checked my watch. It was a little after two. Unless I ran into a problem, I would be at the port in plenty of time.

"I need to get to the commercial dock," I said. "Where do I get a taxi?"

"No need. Easy walk, less than a quarter-mile. I show you."

Once inside the terminal, Sumack pointed toward the exit and the two-lane street out front. "Go left. Not far."

I nodded. "And Charlie's taken care of your payment?"

"Yes, everything is taken care of."

I was curious. "Do you and Charlie see each other often?" I asked.

"No."

I waited for more, an explanation of how they knew each other. Apparently, it wasn't a subject for discussion. A short, abbreviated bow from the native Thai pilot ended our conversation.

Outside, the hot, damp air was stifling. I'd first felt it on the runway as I left the plane, and had attributed it to the over-heated asphalt and recently churning engines of the closely-spaced planes parked in the rows of tie-downs. But now, even the constant breeze did little to camouflage the heat and humidity. I ignored it. I had to keep moving.

Less than a quarter-mile, Sumack had said.

Admittedly, I didn't have much of a plan. My attempt to buy a gun had been a complete failure. Guns were banned in Thailand, and the only illicit firearms dealer the taxi driver knew was a pistol maker living up in the hills, hammering out rough, home-brewed versions of a single-shot .38 caliber pistol. With their smooth bore and flimsy construction, the hand-machined weapons were inferior to even the most basic—and dangerous—Saturday night special. While the gun might have provided a psychological advantage, the dealer wouldn't confirm his inventory over the phone. Knowing we would have to make the forty-five minute round trip just to find out if the guy had something to sell, I decided I couldn't waste time on what could easily turn out to be a wild goose chase.

Without the threat of force to protect Annie, I had to find another way to keep her from walking off the ship and into the hands of bounty hunters.

Mark's suggestion of contacting the harbor master made sense, but it would expose Annie to possible arrest. I wanted to explore the option of contacting the *Ratana* before it docked. A quick call to the mobile operator wasn't encouraging. Cell phone coverage off the island was practically non-existent, and like many commercial vessels without automated cell-satellite relay equipment, the process was dependent upon an operator-originated sat-com connection, and subject to the ship's pre-established contract for voice service. The operator suggested I try the commercial agent's office inside the Port Authority. She told me the agent could communicate with the ship by radio and, with any luck, I'd be able to talk directly to Annie. If the radio operator refused, I would ask for the captain, prefacing my request as a life or death emergency.

Plan B was to hire a small power boat to intercept the freighter as it entered the port. If I could board the ship and remove Annie before anyone realized what I was doing, she would never have to set foot on the dock. While approaching the ship during a docking maneuver would certainly get the captain's attention, it would also be seen by the harbor master. And if a pilot boat wasn't already heading toward the ship, one would be immediately dispatched to prevent me from interfering with incoming traffic.

My last resort was Mark's suggestion—contacting the authorities. Annie could end up behind bars, but a police presence might prevent network operatives from grabbing her in front of local law enforcement.

The area surrounding the airport was typical of a small island community—a rural infrastructure with too much traffic and little adherence to zoning. Small pockets of tropical foliage defiantly broke the scruffy landscape—stubborn reminders of a pre-development paradise.

As I approached the road, I realized the absence of sidewalks would force me to walk very close to a constant stream of cars and trucks with drivers who had no concept of speed limits. As I stood there watching the traffic, I couldn't help but wonder if the small sedan with darkened windows held network thugs on their way to meet the freighter, or if the van that veered far enough off the asphalt apron to kick gravel on me was loaded with rope and chain, the men inside planning to take Annie to a deserted part of the island before killing her and collecting the reward.

Deciding it might be safer to walk against oncoming traffic, I crossed to the opposite side of the street.

At first, I didn't think anything of it—a man seemingly materializing from the parking lot and following me across the road. Maybe the airport lot was a more convenient place to leave his car, especially if he was picking up the daily fresh catch from the small market up ahead.

My mild apprehension erupted into sinking panic as he called out to me.

"Jewel, is that you? Could you wait a moment? I'd like to talk with you."

His voice was deep, his British accent ringing with precise diction. Glancing back, I saw he was not of local descent. A white man with salt-and-pepper hair, he appeared mid-forties, a little under six-feet with a muscular build. Dressed in dark slacks, a light-blue dress shirt, and dark aviator sunglasses, he looked like a contradiction between a generic corporate employee and a private body-guard.

Seeing he had my attention, he tried again. "Your name is Jewel, correct?"

He picked up his pace, trying to catch up.

Who was this guy? And how did he know my name? No one on the island could possibility know my identity.

Unless he was an independent contractor, working for the department. He certainly dressed the part, his build reflecting quintessential agency muscle.

I started to jog, to see if he would follow me.

He did.

There was no doubt. He'd been waiting for me.

Somehow they'd tracked me. Maybe Charlie and I had spent too much time on the phone. Like he'd said, the longer the line was open, the greater likelihood of a trace. A stray thought crossed my mind—what if Mark had turned me in, supplying the department with the phone's GPS marker? It would have been a good-intentioned double-cross, a negotiated compromise to retrieve me before I got hurt.

Or worse.

But how the department had found me wasn't important. I had to lose this guy. Otherwise, Annie was dead.

I broke into a full run. While the Brit looked strong, he might not be fast. If his muscle was acquired at the cost of aerobic deficiency, my constant five-mile-an-hour pace would quickly wind him.

I glanced back. He was gaining on me.

Shit! Don't break stride to see where he is. Just run!

I saw a small building ahead. A restaurant. If I made it inside, it might make him think twice before trying to take me in front of witnesses.

I slowed enough to grab the door handle. My body's momentum nearly tore it off the hinges. Inside, the place was dark. My eyes needed a moment to adjust.

Damn, it's nearly empty.

A woman behind the breakfast counter was cleaning the coffee maker. A young girl—another employee—was setting tables with silverware. She looked up, startled by my noisy entrance.

"Not open," she said. "One hour."

I looked at the door behind her. It might lead to a rear exit. I bolted for it.

The swinging two-way flew backward, banging hard against the wall. I'd found the kitchen—a small ramshackle collection of wooden shelves, peeling Formica counters, and two old residential-style ranges. Off to the side, a young man wearing a dirty white apron leaned over a sink full of dishes. Surprised, he glared at me with a combination of suspicion and defensive posturing.

I heard the hollow *crash* of the front door echo through the building.

The Brit was right behind me. "Police!" he yelled. "Where is she?" His deep voice resonated throughout the restaurant.

Police, my ass. Declaring his intrusion was based on official authority might convince the three employees, but I knew better.

I scanned the kitchen for a way out. On the other side of a dairy case, a small alcove revealed the edge of a door.

"Hey, will that take me outside?"

The dishwasher stared at me, his face full of arrogance and smug superiority. Assuming my activities to be criminal, he refused to speak.

If that was the way he wanted it . . .

I picked up a large butcher knife from the counter and pointed it at him. My words left my throat on a desperate growl. "Listen to me, asshole. Is that the way out or not?"

He reluctantly nodded and pointed to the alcove.

Dropping the knife, I streaked through the door and began kicking a path through empty cardboard boxes, sidestepping a food-spill of noodles and gravy. I'd hoped to find an alley, some kind of access to the rear entrance of another building. Instead, I was facing an eight-foot-high chain-link fence topped with barbed wire—common security for most mom-and-pop retail businesses on the island. The only exit was through a single swinging gate—*chained and padlocked.*

I was fucked.

The rear door burst open, releasing a blur of barrel-chested, testosterone-charged human terminator.

My breath came in quick, shallow draws, my muscles wound spring-tight. More pissed than afraid, I was determined to defend myself.

I should've kept the knife.

I braced for it, resolved to withstand the impact of his first strike.

Seeing my raised fists, the Brit held up his hands "Stop! This isn't necessary."

I swallowed hard. "If you're here to bring me back, you might as well kill me now. Because no matter how long it takes, I'll hunt you down and shoot your balls off one at a time."

He shook his head. "Charlie said you might be a handful. Hold on a sec."

"What did you say?"

The Brit reached behind his back. Instead of a blue-steel revolver or matt-black small caliber automatic, he produced a cell phone. Pushing a couple buttons, he brought it to his ear. "I've got her. No, no damage." He paused, listening. "I understand."

He took a step toward me. I drew back, ready to land the first punch.

"Calm down. It's for you." He held out the phone.

Cautiously, I took the cell. "Who is this?"

"Jewel, this is Charlie. The man with you, he's a friend."

"Whose friend? He looks like a hit man."

"He's more of a private investigator. Leon was the man I hired to look for my daughter."

"Charlie, I don't understand. Why are you doing this? What does this man have to do with me?"

"He's there to help you. He can be very useful in a situation like this."

Charlie had no idea what the *situation* really was.

"Jewel, listen carefully," Charlie continued. "I'm on my way to Samui. We're less than an hour from the island."

"You're coming here?" My protective instincts immediately kicked in. "As much as I appreciate everything you're doing, this is about to get dangerous. Both the network and the police are searching for Annie, and there's no telling what kind of trash the department is sending out about me. Once they figure out where I am, I wouldn't be surprised if they decide to shut me up, too. It's not something you want to get involved in."

Charlie ignored my warning and pressed me with questions "How much do you know about your friend, Annie? Her background?"

"We were on a slave ship together. She kept me sane, taught me how to survive."

A long silence.

"Charlie, are you there?"

"Yeah." Another pause.

"What about before then . . . she tell you anything about herself?"

"She mentioned being a dancer, working in a nightclub in Bangkok. Charlie, I don't have time for this. I have to go."

"Bangkok?"

"What difference does it make?" I was running out of patience.

Charlie didn't answer. Someone else was speaking, conversation in the background.

"What's the airspeed?"

"Three-sixty."

"I want us on the ground in forty minutes."

"It'll stretch the engines. They'll have to be replaced before we can fly again."

Two people talking at once. I couldn't make out what they were saying.

A high-pitched whine rose in the background. "Jewel, stay with Leon. He's very good at his job. I'll be there soon."

"Does Leon carry a gun?"

"Ask him yourself. Ears . . . remember?"

The phone went dead.

Chapter Fifty-Four

After flagging a taxi to take us the short distance to the port, Leon flashed a fake government ID to get us through security. He'd suggested I put my hair up and hide it under a baseball cap I'd "borrowed" from one of the restaurant employees. Even so, the security guy gave me the once-over.

My concerns over Leon's role as a protector—preventing me from confronting dangerous network operatives—were quickly dispelled. He explained he was there to back me up, to compensate for my shortage of muscle and help balance my lack of firepower.

It took less than ten minutes to formulate a battle plan with my new ally.

He quickly talked me out of hiring a local boat to intercept the freighter. He knew an experienced captain would ignore my attempt to stop the ship, since allowing a stranger to board under such unusual circumstances would carry undetermined—and unacceptable—risks.

"You carry a gun?" I asked.

He nodded.

I had no idea about his background, but if he was ex-agency, he might be in the habit of carrying a backup.

"How about a reserve?"

"A nine short."

I held out my hand. "Give."

He didn't flinch, pulling it from an ankle holster.

"Ever used a small caliber?" he asked.

"Yep," I lied.

"Has the normal amount of bounce, but it's a bit more accurate than most. Use both hands and you'll get a fairly tight spread at twenty feet."

In his opinion, the small .380 auto was a high quality firearm—for its size. He was also confirming I'd have to be within twenty feet of my target before having a reasonable chance of hitting what I was aiming at. It also meant Annie could not be anywhere near my line of fire.

We went directly to the commercial agent's office.

Attempting to contact the ship before it entered the harbor turned out to be an exercise in futility. The agent wasn't in, and his assistant spent most of his time scrounging for coffee filters. My request for a radio link produced a shoulder shrug and a promise that the agent would be back in the morning. Leon immediately pulled out his bogus government badge and reminded the twenty-something assistant that the ship's manifest and dock reservation must be available for immediate inspection by authorized personnel. And if the assistant didn't know where it was, he would have to allow us to look for it. In less than a minute, the freighter's paperwork emerged from beneath a pile of newspapers and magazines.

Now that we knew the *Ratana*'s docking berth, we could determine its approach and choose the best defensive position. Then it was a matter of waiting.

Leon picked up an empty clipboard and stared at the kid. "Where's your ten-seventy forms?" It was a description as bogus as his badge. After giving the assistant a few seconds to scan the office for the fictional form, Leon shook his head in mock professional disappointment, grabbed several copies of an official-looking checklist and stuck them in the clipboard. "Never mind. I'll use these. In the future, I'll expect you to have your ten-seventies ready and accessible." He pitched a five dollar bill on the desk as we were leaving. "I trust you can replace the clipboard for me?"

The young man answered quickly. "Yessir."

Outside, the constant breeze did little to mask the thick smell of oil and diesel fuel permeating the dock. Workers and maintenance men scurried around us like ants, and while they didn't break their methodical pace, their obvious stares made it clear they viewed us as intruders, our presence a suspicious anomaly.

"That's it," Leon said. "Berth 9."

I walked to the very edge of the dock and peered down at the patches of floating seaweed and dead jellyfish drifting with the current. "How long before we see the ship?"

"Could be fifteen minutes if it's early. Might be two hours. They still have to hang the dock bumpers, so I'm guessing we have some waiting to do."

Earlier, I was worried I would arrive late. Now there was plenty of time. I should have been relieved.

I wasn't.

I wanted this over with. I wanted to see Annie walking down the gangway. I wanted to run to her, grab her by the hand, and pull her to safety. I planned to draw the small pistol and use it to intimidate the foot-traffic, opening a path to the entrance gate. I'd noticed dock security didn't carry weapons, so I didn't anticipate much resistance. But I had no idea who might be waiting on the street.

Trying to plan and strategize was impractical. Network operatives could come from anywhere, at any time. Annie's rescue would have to play out spontaneously, from moment to moment.

I saw the outline of a ship break the horizon. A lump rose in my throat. "Leon, any chance that's the *Ratana*?"

He pulled out a miniature set of binoculars. "Too far out. Moving in the wrong direction. Probably just passing by the island."

Concerned my obvious pacing a few feet from the first tie-down was arousing suspicion, Leon suggested I find a less conspicuous place to wait. "How about you park yourself over there by that stack of pallets?"

"I can't sit. I'm too keyed up."

"Then take this." He handed me the clipboard. "If you insist on staying out in the open, you need an official appearance, like you're supposed to be here.

Try walking from one end of the berth to the other, pretend you're inspecting the condition of the pier and the shoring underneath."

Hoping the appropriated clipboard would lend an air of authority, I slowly covered the length of the berth, repeatedly glancing down at the water, then at the printed form, as if comparing the state of deterioration against minimum standards. I also kept my eye on the long line of vans and cargo trucks parked down the centerline of the dock. Any one of them could be loaded with vicious killers, waiting to grab Annie as she walked off the boat.

I'd turned to back-track my steps when I saw Leon motioning to me from behind a stack of small shipping containers, a position that kept him out of sight, but provided a view of the dock's foot traffic.

"I don't see anything on the horizon," he said. "I'm going back to the agent's office. They might have an update on the ship's location."

"The kid won't know anything."

"I know. I'll ask him to call the harbor master. He'll be able to give me an exact location."

"Okay, but hurry."

The minute hand of my watch ticked off the time. It was grueling. Ten minutes. Twenty. Now forty. Where was that fucking ship?

A rush of activity on the adjacent pier caught my attention. A fuel tanker and a large forklift were pulling up in front of an empty berth. Several dock hands were busy hanging inflated bumpers between the huge, permanently-mounted tractor tires to provide extra cushion against docking shock, the usual procedure when a ship lacked bow and mid-ship thrusters.

I didn't give it much thought. It couldn't be the *Ratana*. Not only was it a different berth, it was a different pier.

Maybe a small cruise ship, I thought. Seems odd though, making preparations this early. There's not a boat anywhere in sight.

I was wrong.

A ship *had* entered the harbor—*from the opposite side.* With its approach hidden from view by a football-length building used for freight storage and shipping, it had advanced toward the dock in near silence, and now, the bow was just clearing the huge facility.

I scanned the hull for a name. Nothing. Probably on the stern. If it was, I would never see it—the rear of the vessel faced away from me.

I told myself it was nothing more than a distraction, and yet there *were* similarities . . . the ship was a small freighter, with a mid-ship pilot house, and an unusual twin-boom configuration. The color was a non-descript gray-black, with plenty of rust and scratched paint from harbor tugs. Those last details I didn't remember, but at the time, I'd been distracted, my mind focused on Annie, not the ship.

I looked behind me, at the single dock hand working to clean a small diesel spill a hundred feet away. He'd been taking his time, brushing the stain, adding detergent, brushing it again. More than once, I'd caught him staring, not in the same way his co-workers had—with suspicion and disdain—but with sexual interest.

Would he know the name of the ship?

I started walking toward him, as if I were still inspecting the dock, moving in that direction out of necessity.

He looked up.

I gave him the biggest smile I could muster, waiting to see it returned.

Responding to his flash of teeth, I waved and walked over.

"You worked here long?"

"Two years."

His eyes dropped to my breasts, my waist, my crotch.

"I bet you know the names of most of the ships that dock here, the ones that come and go on a regular basis."

"Yes, yes. Some of them."

He was young, eager, wanting to talk.

"I've been watching that freighter." I pointed to the other pier, then pretended to re-fasten the top button of my blouse. In truth, I was *unbuttoning* it. Simulating frustration with my inability to close it, I gave up, letting it fall open. "Does it make regular runs to the island?"

If the kid didn't swallow soon, he'd have a line of drool running down his chin.

"Once a week," he panted. "Delivers fruit and vegetables to the markets."

I scratched my shoulder, letting my arm rest momentarily under my boobs, pushing them up.

"I don't see the ship's arrival on my roster. Do you know its name?"

He nodded, his mind—and eyes—focused on my tits. Finally, his spoke. "It's the *Ratana.*"

NO! It couldn't be.

Maybe there were two ships with the same name, registered under different flags. Even so, the odds of two identically-named ships docking in the same port at the same time were astronomical.

I felt the anxiety build as I realized the truth: *The Ratana's berth assignment had been changed.*

I had to move.

I glanced down at my clipboard. "I'm supposed to meet that ship. What's the fastest way to get there?"

The kid pointed toward the far end of the dock. "The connector. That's where the two piers are joined."

Nearly the width of a single-lane road, the connector provided a short cut for fork-lifts and light vendor trucks. Using it would save me from having to back-track to the dock entrance. Even so, I estimated I had a thousand feet to cover—and I had to do it before the freighter's gangway hit the concrete.

"Thanks." I turned away from the young man and started jogging.

Leon had returned from the agent's office twenty minutes ago, and from a distance, had lifted his hands and shrugged his shoulders. He'd learned nothing new. Having resumed his position behind the stack of crates, he was nowhere to be seen. I didn't have time to run back and explain what was happening. It would take me in the opposite direction. And that extra minute could make the difference in reaching Annie in time. All I could do was point at the adjacent pier, hoping he was watching.

I reached behind, under my blouse, feeling for the pistol. I couldn't risk having it work its way out of my pants and fall to the ground. The sight of someone carrying a firearm would initiate a flood of calls to port security, who would alert customs officials—and they *did* carry guns. I snugged it tight under a belt loop and picked up my pace. In less than thirty seconds, it was obvious I wasn't moving fast enough. The mooring crew had secured the freighter's lines and the ship's winches were bringing them tight. Several uniformed officials were gathering next to the ship, talking, nodding their heads, offering each other cigarettes. I assumed they were immigration officials, ready to check the ship's manifest. Before anyone could disembark the freighter, they would board the ship first to confirm its passenger complement. If there were no irregularities, the crew and passengers would be allowed to disembark. The formal process could take fifteen minutes, but if there was an established relationship between the captain and the officials—meaning the ship always carried a couple bottles of liquor for the immigration staff—it could be accomplished with a simple nod of the head.

I hoped the men gathered at the dock were honest and accountable. I needed those fifteen minutes to find a defensible position to wait for Annie.

In a dead run, I raced across the oil-stained concrete surface of the connector. Several dock workers turned as I passed. They said nothing, but I didn't have to be a mind reader to know what they were thinking—*Why are you running? You must be in trouble—or about to cause some.*

A large stack of crates loomed ahead on the left—hundreds of wooden boxes bound with metal strapping. It didn't matter. I had plenty of room on the right, at least six feet of clearance.

The guttural roar of a diesel engine hammered the air, a plume of black smoke erupting from behind the mountain of boxes.

Run faster.

Beat it.

Steel blades emerged from behind the stack. Skimming six inches off the surface of the concrete, they looked like twin scythes headed directly into my path.

The forklift came into full view.

Shit! I can't get around it! I have to get the driver's attention.

Without slowing, I waved my arms. "I need to get through," I screamed. "You have to let me through!"

He didn't hear me. And he was determined not to look in my direction.

My heart was throbbing. I needed to catch my breath, so I could sound half-way coherent.

Not sure if the man spoke English, I pointed to the other dock, my finger poking the air like a woodpecker's beak, my way of asking him to keep the forklift in place long enough for me to work my way around it.

What the fuck? He was also pointing, but at the stack of crates. No, that's wrong—he was pointing at something *behind* them. He motioned me forward, giving me permission to walk in front of the lift.

I didn't hesitate.

As I hopped over the extended forks, the driver killed the engine, the sudden silence calling attention to my interruption of his work. I thought it odd when he jumped off the seat and high-tailed it down the pier.

"Jewel! What's your hurry? Aren't you going to say hello?"

The voice was familiar, sending a surge of pure hatred through my spine.

I twisted left and saw him—the man who'd dragged me from Morrison's house kicking and screaming, tortured me with a syringe needle, then choked me until I nearly passed out. It was R.J., staring at me like an apparition from Satan's lair.

Any other day, the sight would've sent me to my knees. But not now. I no longer feared him. Not because I had a gun tucked against the small of my back, but because I knew the truth—*he was here for Annie.*

I looked behind him, scanning the dock for the captain or other crew members from the *Kelsey*. Either they were well-hidden or, more likely, R.J. was here on his own—the way he liked to work. It gave him the autonomy he craved to inflict his own twisted form of cruelty on the girls he retrieved.

In the distance, I could see the freighter's crew lowering the gangway. The port officials were preparing to board.

"Damn you, R.J. I don't have time for this."

His shitty grin widened. "It's okay, Jewel. You don't need to worry about Annie. I've got a special reception waiting for her. Yeah, I'm gonna take real good care of our girl."

It wasn't hard to put together. The captain of the *Kelsey II* had heard the freighter's radio call describing the new runaway—an American girl. From the department's clandestine broadcast of her description and offer of a reward, he knew it was Annie. She'd spent two-and-a-half years on the *Kelsey*. As far as the captain was concerned, she was easy pickings. He'd sent his number one henchman, R.J., to bring her in.

A suffocating sensation tightened my throat. *This bastard is going to end Annie's future right here, right now on this sweltering, filthy dock.*

If that's the way it was, if there was nothing else I could do to prevent R.J. from taking her, I had nothing more to lose—except my life.

I yelled at him. "Hey, asshole! I didn't know they'd let a piece of shit like you walk the streets here."

I saw it building in his face—his need to hurt me, tie me up and watch my face turn blue, to feel my throat vibrate from my silent screams as he crushed my windpipe with his fingers.

There was ten feet between us. He took a step toward me.

Still, I felt no fear. And this time, it *was* because of the gun. In this part of the world, it was rare that anyone carried a firearm. Only those with money and power could buy that privilege. As far as he was concerned, I was as defenseless as I'd ever been.

I kept my stance as casual as possible. Setting my hands on my hips, I hoped to convey an attitude of defiance. I wanted him to make his play, to give me the excuse I needed . . . to kill him.

He took another step, his nostrils flaring with excitement, a rush of saliva spilling over his lips. Below his waist, his cock strained against the fabric of his trousers.

The polymer handle of the 380 Sig Sauer was beefy for such a small caliber—plenty of room for 12 rounds of 9mm short ammo. Still, I'd have to slide it out smooth and quick. And I'd need an extra second to pull back the bolt and chamber the first shell.

R.J. took another step, savoring the anticipation, aching to put his hands on me.

Six feet between us.

I could smell his rancid breath—fumes of brimstone belching from his panting chest.

That's close enough!

I grabbed for the piece.

Something's wrong, resistance from the gun. It's not sliding out clean, the front sight is caught on the waistband of my pants.

Realizing I was reaching for a weapon, R.J.'s eyes erupted with rage. "You bitch," he hissed. "Now I can finish the job."

He lunged at me.

I pulled harder, twisting the barrel, finally dislodging it from the fabric.

It was too late. R.J. grabbed my right wrist and pinned it behind my back. "Drop it," he snarled.

I felt his teeth clamp down on my ear. I was certain he'd bite it off if I didn't obey.

"Fuck you!" I screamed.

Stabbing pain followed the gritty sound of crushing cartilage and splitting skin. I cringed, fighting the instinct to yank my head in the opposite direction, hoping to prevent my ear from being torn away.

R.J. dug his thumb into my wrist, forcing my muscles to involuntarily release the gun. I heard the clatter of precisely machined metal hitting the concrete.

Demanding my complete submission, he forced my arms higher, taking me to my knees. Wrenching my joints, pushing my shoulders nearly to the point of dislocation, he began to cackle with delight.

"How's that, bitch? Now you've got something to scream about."

Through the searing pain I felt his crotch bouncing off the back of my head.

I caught a blur of motion, someone approaching from the freighter's berth. Probably one of R.J.'s minions wanting to share in the fun.

I tried to turn, to see who it was. But I couldn't hold up my head, my entire upper body burning in agony.

I felt R.J.'s spit on my neck. "You and me," he said. "We're gonna have us a reunion party."

"Let her go." The words thundered across the dock with no-nonsense authority.

It took a moment to sink in . . . someone was ordering R.J. to release me.

R.J. opened my arms wide, then slammed my hands together, sending a bolt of searing pain deep into my back. Wrapping his fingers around my wrists, he held them with a single hand. In a different position, I would've been able to break his grip. But I had no leverage, no strength at all.

Grabbing a handful of my hair, he yanked me tight against his crotch. Sliding his fingers over my forehead, he searched for my eye sockets.

"Drop it or I'll rip her eyes out," R.J. barked.

There was nothing empty in his threat. He would blind me for the sheer joy it would bring him.

Suddenly I felt the pressure on my shoulders letting up, his grip on my wrists easing. As his fingers withdrew from my eyes, I felt his body shifting, moving backward.

R.J. was changing position, taking a different stance. But he was also giving up his leverage. That made no sense.

Releasing the pressure on my shoulders allowed me to raise my head and glance in the direction of the voice.

It took me a moment to recognize him. Standing thirty feet away, Mark's expression was stone-hard, his body statue-still, every muscle straining against the light blue fabric of his shirt. With his gun still trained on R.J., he could've taken on a charging rhino—and won.

I thought of saying something clever, like how he'd shown up in the nick of time or that he really knew how to make an entrance. But I wasn't feeling very witty.

A heavy groan from behind broke my attention. I turned to see R.J.'s legs collapsing, his knees cracking on the concrete, his body slumping to the pavement. For a split second, we were eye-to-eye, his pupils receding to black pinholes, the white sclera floating in blood. In the center of his forehead, a small red dot pulsed with a heavy flow of blood, the crimson stream dividing his head into equally defined left and right sides.

I hadn't heard the bullet. I doubted R.J. did either. He might have seen the blow-back from the gun's bolt ejecting the spent shell, but by that time, the bullet had already exploded deep into his brain. The forty caliber slug had left Mark's weapon silently, and now, only the sun's glint off the spent shell served as testament to a well-deserved death. As Mark picked up the brass casing and tossed it into the ocean, only R.J.'s crumpled body remained as evidence.

Mark's voice broke my death stare. "First rule of the game. Always clear the weapon from your pants before giving an ultimatum." He was scanning the dock, unconcerned with the attention his drawn gun might raise.

I tried to get up. I couldn't feel my arms. "Can you give me a hand?"

Chapter Fifty-Five

"That ear looks nasty." Mark reached into a coat pocket and pulled out a handkerchief. "Here, wipe the blood off your face."

I swiped at my cheek. "We have to get to Annie before R.J.'s people can grab her." I thought for a moment. "There's three of us now. Charlie sent help, some guy named Leon."

"I know. By now, he should be onboard the freighter talking to the captain."

"You know Leon?"

"We've run into each other." Mark's answer was matter-of-fact.

As the feeling returned to my arms and shoulders, I picked up the Sig and tucked it into my pants. "Let's go. We have to get Annie off the dock."

"Jewel, listen to me. The situation has changed. The dock is secure. The network can't touch her."

"See that pile of shit lying on the concrete?" I pointed to R.J.'s body. "You can bet there's others just like him waiting on the pier ready to grab her." I reached around my waist, testing my access, slipping the Sig in and out.

He shook his head. "The threat's been neutralized. A lot has changed since this morning—"

"We can talk later," I interrupted. "Right now, we need to move."

I could tell there was a lot more on Mark's mind, but taking time to chat about the situation was out of the question. I turned away from him, ready to race toward the freighter.

"Jewel, wait! The deal is just going down. You need to give it a few more minutes."

I froze. "What the hell are you talking about?"

Mark motioned toward the *Ratana*. "Look at the crowd at the bottom of the gangway. Recognize anyone?"

The boat was a hundred yards away—too far to make out a face, but there *was* something familiar about one of the men. Standing off to the side, he was talking to the port officials, handing them a briefcase.

"Is that Charlie?"

"It is. He arrived about the same time I did."

It hit me . . . what if Charlie was working for Housing? He might even be Housing's friend, here to do him a favor. That's why he'd been in such a hurry to get to the island, so he could get to Annie first and keep her from talking to the authorities.

I raised my voice. "Is he trying to double-cross us?"

"No, he's here to—"

"Is this more of the department's bullshit, letting Charlie buy Annie right off the boat so he can deliver her to Housing?" On the verge of exploding, I jumped all over him. "If that's true," I said, gritting my teeth, "I'll kill all you fuckers."

I took a step back. I wasn't fast enough. Mark surrounded me with both arms, enclosing me in a forced bear hug.

"Jewel, calm down and listen to me."

"Let go of me!" I yelled.

I had to get to Annie. Determined to break free, I landed a foot against Mark's shin.

"Dammit, Jewel!" He pushed me away with enough force to take me off balance, sending me to one knee.

I pulled out the nine-short and pointed it at him. Immediately, I knew it was the wrong thing to do.

He shook his head. "Really? You're gonna shoot me?"

I lowered the gun and dropped my head. "I can't just wait here and let them take her." I swallowed hard. "Please, Mark, I need your help."

He started to speak, and I cut him off, my voice breaking. "If you care anything about me, you'll pull out that piece you carry and back me up. I can't do this alone."

He tipped his head toward the freighter. "What does that look like to you?"

The port officials had opened the briefcase, their eyes scanning the contents. They quickly closed it, as if to prevent anyone else from seeing the contents.

"Looks like a payoff."

Mark nodded. "That part you've got right. Are you ready to hear the rest?"

I'd run out of options. The chances of grabbing Annie and blasting my way out of the port seemed as remote as surviving a cage match with a dozen of the network's nastiest thugs.

Angry as hell, I glared at Mark's. "Tell me."

"The payoff has nothing to do with Housing. In fact, Weston and Housing are on the verge of becoming sworn enemies."

"I . . . I don't understand."

"Charlie is buying Annie's freedom. The department can't formally rescind the criminal charges and arrest warrant until tomorrow, so to get Annie off the island tonight and eliminate any delays with foreign protocol or legalities, Charlie's paying them for their *cooperation*." He paused. "Jewel, there's a lot you don't know about Annie. But I want it to come from her."

I clenched my teeth. I was still upset. He wasn't giving me the full story.

Mark reached out his hand. "Give me the gun and get your ass down there. You have friends waiting to see you."

Reluctantly, I handed him the Sig. "Can't you just explain?"

He motioned toward the freighter. "The answers are waiting for you at the bottom of that gangway. Now go."

Chapter Fifty-Six

Mark's cryptic manner had left me with the feeling that the urgency surrounding Annie's rescue was no longer a priority. He'd also made it clear I needed to be there, waiting in the mix of immigration officials and dock hands.

The *why* was making me very uncomfortable.

As I jogged the remaining distance, the crowd at the base of the gangway began to disperse. The port officials left first, one of them carrying the briefcase. Sailors from the freighter began to stream onto the dock. Heading toward the harbor exit, they were anxious to spend a night on the town.

With his eyes fixed on the ship's open hatchway, Charlie hadn't noticed my approach. His expression worried me. More than apprehensive, he was sweating bullets. If I didn't know him better, I would have sworn he was scared.

My struggle with R.J. and the hundred-yard jog forced me to use short sentences with quick draws of breath in-between. "Charlie, what are you doing here?"

It took a few seconds for my question to break through. "Jewel!" He reached out for me. "Jesus, what happened to your head? Are you alright?"

I was still unsure of his motives, but seeing him again in person was helping to restore my trust. "I'm fine. Mark rode in on his white horse and saved my ass."

Deep furrows lined Charlie's brow. "I know. I saw it from here." He paused, then added, "I want you to know that's the last time you'll ever be in a situation like that."

His words threw me.

"Jewel," he continued, "I've talked to the embassy officials about your job there. Whatever arrangement you had with them is over. You work for me now."

"I . . . what?"

"I don't want you mixed up with these people anymore. It's dangerous. You need to be back in the States, close to your family."

I pressed my lips together, as if the absence of kinfolk was something to be embarrassed about. "I don't have any family."

"You do now. You're coming home with me." He glanced up at the ship's hatchway. Confirming it was still empty—except for the captain—he continued. "You can work for my company, go to school, or whatever you want. But first, I want you to take some time off, put some distance between you and this part of the world, time to forget what you've been through."

I started to object, but he wasn't finished.

"And don't get the wrong idea. This isn't charity. I need you. There's a lot you can do to help me put my life back together. It's been on hold for a long time, and I don't think there's anyone who could do a better job."

424

Again, Charlie glanced up at the hatchway. This time his eyes widened, his mouth falling slightly open.

Without any fanfare or notice from the captain, Annie had appeared at the top of the gangway. She'd abandoned the wig Mark bought to disguise her appearance and was wearing the flowing Sampot. She looked tired, but the fear and worry that had etched her face yesterday as she'd boarded the *Ratana* were gone.

Our eyes met simultaneously. For a moment, she blinked, as if clearing her vision. Even from twenty feet away, I could see her lower lip beginning to tremble. She reached out for the railing to steady herself.

I was across the metal ramp in seconds. I wouldn't let Annie walk down the gangway alone. Wrapping my arms around her, I felt her entire body vibrating in uneasy release. But this time, it was alright. We were together, and no one was going to harm her without going through me first.

The freighter's captain nodded, then disappeared into the shadows. Apparently, his job was done.

"Your ear," Annie managed. "You're bleeding."

"Don't worry. I'm going to have the other one done the same way, so they match."

She grimaced and shook her head, knowing it had to hurt.

"Do you know what's going on?" she asked. "The captain told me the network isn't looking for me anymore. This new job you have with the embassy, do you have that kind of power?"

I shook my head. "I've got the lowest job on the totem pole."

She pulled back to look at me. "Then how?"

I shrugged my shoulders. "I don't know the details, but apparently, it has something to do with a friend of mine." I brushed the hair from her eyes. "He's waiting for us on the dock. I want you to meet him."

I brought my arm around Annie's waist and nudged her down the ramp. "That man standing to the right of the gangway, he's made a payoff to the port officials. It means you're safe. You can go home."

She scanned the dock, her eyes finally locking on Charlie. Suddenly, her body was rigid, her muscles refusing to cooperate. Her voice breaking, she asked, "Jewel, what's the man's name?"

"Weston. I call him Charlie."

Annie gasped, her legs threatening to buckle.

Something was wrong. More than nervous apprehension, Annie was in a state of shock. Seeing her face turn pale, I pulled her tight, concerned she would faint.

I tried to reassure her. "It's okay, Annie, he's a friend. We met at the embassy. He's got money, the kind that can buy influence and protection."

She took a step forward. Then another.

"Annie?"

I was certain she heard me, but she seemed to have shut me out. As she dropped her arm from my waist, she began to mumble.

"They told me . . . you were dead." Then louder, directly at Charlie. "*They told me you were dead!*"

Confused, I looked at Charlie.

His face was distorted in pain, happiness, grief, and joy—a mix of emotions all coming out at once, and seemingly focused on Annie.

I called after at her. "You know Charlie?"

She glanced back, her face streaming with tears. She nodded quickly, then breaking into a run, Annie raced over the last few feet of the ramp, flying into Charlie's arms.

In that moment . . . *I knew.*

Chapter Fifty-Seven

I felt a hand on my shoulder. Leon was standing next to me. "The odds of finding her alive were less than one in ten," he said. "That's what I told Charlie over two years ago. But he refused to give up. Somehow, he knew she was still out there."

"He kept me on retainer," he continued. "Kept paying me to check out rumors about a young American girl who'd been kidnapped and sold into slavery. In fact, it was one of those rumors that led me to the auction in Bangkok. But I got there too late. I was able to find out what happened to you, but nobody wanted to talk about the other girl, until Housing's name came up." He shook his head. "I decided not to tell Charlie. He'd been through enough."

I looked down at Annie. Still holding on to her father, I realized this was not a normal reunion. As far as Charlie was concerned, his daughter had returned from the grave.

"Leon, I'm confused. Charlie said his daughter's name was Marian."

"That's her given name. But Annie never liked it. Made everyone call her by her middle name."

I remembered . . . Charlie had mentioned it, but hadn't gone into detail, thinking it unimportant or not wanting to relive the memory.

It was time to move the party to a more neutral setting. While Mark's assurance that Charlie's payoff had eliminated any potential issues with the local law, I was still nervous.

"Will we be able to get off the island without any problems?" I asked.

"See those suits scattered around the dock?" Leon motioned toward the half-dozen G-men clones milling around the pier. "They're your people, mostly from the department. There's a few agency guys, too. They're easy to spot . . . they leave a smell."

The fact the embassy had sent a small army of reinforcements was both assuring and infuriating.

"Leon, you know how this shit works. Why now? Why did the department put out a contract on Annie's life to appease Housing, then change their mind and decide to save her?"

He shook his head in frustration. "I've been in this business more years than you've been alive, and I still have no clue how these fuckers make decisions. Just be glad it worked out the way it did."

"It was because of Charlie, wasn't it?"

"Most likely. They may have realized if he ever found out the department was complicit in having his daughter killed, there'd be holy hell to pay."

The final piece of the puzzle dropped into place. "That would've meant the department would've had to get rid of him, too," I said.

Leon smiled at me, a look of sympathetic compassion that could only come from someone much older and far more experienced.

Finally, I knew the truth. The suits had chosen to help Charlie save his daughter because it was the lesser of two evils. For now—for Annie's sake—I would keep it to myself.

Chapter Fifty-Eight

Charlie had been serious about wanting me to live with his family. Concerned I would feel like an intruder, he promised me the run of the guesthouse. He also added the incentives of a car and a little spending money. In effect, he wanted to "adopt" me as his second daughter.

His offer was tempting. It would give me the chance to return to a normal life without the immediate pressures of finding a job and the need to support myself. It would also make my sisterhood with Annie official—although it was difficult to think of her that way, especially with all the bed-swapping I anticipated if we were both living under the same roof.

"Try it for a year," Charlie encouraged. "If that's too much of a commitment, give it six months. Then decide if you want to stay longer. As far as I'm concerned, you're family now."

The more I considered it, the more I realized it would never work. Not after what I'd been through. Returning to an eight-to-five world—where conversations revolved around football, beer, and bar-b-ques—would be nothing short of domestic punishment. By comparison, my job at the embassy was exciting. There was always new people to meet and new situations to explore. To top it off, I was living in Bangkok, one of most exotic places on earth. And with my new status, offered as an incentive to stay with the department, I now had the privilege of choosing my assignments. No longer required to accommodate the sexual demands of strangers, I could decide when and where to use my body as a negotiating tool. My new position also came with greater freedom, including the authority to leave the embassy without the approval of a superior.

On the downside, staying with the department would mean Annie and I would be half a world apart, our time together restricted to an occasional three-day weekend and annual vacations. While I loved Annie, I knew she was ready to share a life together, with me.

I was not.

My decision would disappoint her, but I felt the separation would make our time together even more special.

Admittedly, there was another consideration in deciding to stay with the embassy. I wanted to spend more time with Mark. I liked him. And the idea of clandestine overnight dates sounded exciting and sexy . . . as long as the department didn't find out.

For the first time in my life, I saw a real future for myself. One full of adventure and promise.

I'd decided to stay not because I had to, but because it was the best place for me.

At least for now.

Chapter Fifty-Nine

Charlie insisted I spend a month with Annie before returning to work. The director had reluctantly authorized the time, classifying it as a special diplomatic assignment, especially after Charlie explained it was one of his non-negotiable terms in coming to an "understanding" about the department's role in the treatment of his daughter.

For me, it was a vacation away from the political world of smoke-and-mirrors. I also knew Charlie wanted me to help Annie with her transition to a more "normal" life, one filled with shopping malls, cable television, and cell phones.

Unsure of how she would handle the post-traumatic stress of returning to the relatively benign and safe environment of the suburbs, I let Annie decide how we spent our time together.

Seldom wanting to be alone, she filled our days with shopping, going out to lunch, and afternoon trips to the movies. We often took advantage of the five-acre park-like estate of Charlie's home, sitting for hours in an old chair-swing wide enough to hold us both. Sometimes we talked, other times we sat together in silence, watching the sun slip below the horizon, waiting for the first stars to appear. We drew from each other's strength, thankful we had been together during our ordeal, and trying to forget our time served in hell.

Annie's reunion with her father was a slow and often painful process. During our month together, I watched both of them cycle through the highs and lows of joy, relief, regret, and guilt.

It was especially difficult for Charlie. Forced to accept what had happed to his daughter was hard enough, but the thought of his little girl having returned to him as a world-weary woman, her optimism destroyed by exposure to the most cruel and barbaric conditions imaginable, became a constant source of pain, anger, and frustration.

One night, when he was sure Annie wouldn't overhear, he confided in me the worst part was knowing Annie was dealing with the same demons—tormenting memories that would continue to haunt her for the rest of her life—and there was nothing he could do to change it.

By the end of my second week in their home, Charlie's usual straight-to-the-point attitude quickly gave way to careful questions, wanting to know every detail of his daughter's capture and enslavement. He especially wanted to know about the auction in Bangkok, the names of those who had offered Annie for sale, and the man who'd bought her. He seemed to take a special interest in Gregory.

"Can you describe them?" he'd asked. "Do you think you would recognize any of the men if you saw them again?"

Once, Annie overheard him giving me the third degree. "Why are you asking Jewel all these questions? It's over. There's nothing we can do about it."

Charlie pulled back, not wanting to upset her. "I know, I know. I just want to make sure I have all the facts. If we can keep someone else from falling into the same trap, then we need to make the effort."

But prevention wasn't the motivation behind Charlie's questions. I discovered his real intentions months later, when the network's rumor mill was buzzing with one story after another of slave traders falling prey to a sudden epidemic of tragic accidents.

Although it cost him tens of thousands of dollars to accomplish, Charlie quickly extended his eyes and ears deep into the Asian slave markets. After gathering reams of information—confirming and re-confirming the identity of every man who'd been responsible for abducting his daughter and eventually placing her on the auction block—he began to take action. Approaching the task no differently than his other business activities, Charlie was methodical in his work—and very thorough.

First, he hired Leon to approach the marine broker who sold the captain of the *Kelsey* his new boat. Posing as an Interpol detective, Leon obtained the broker's records of sale for the transaction, which included the name of the engine manufacturer and the serial number of the *Kelsey II*'s power-plant. Using a mock-up of the manufacturer's letterhead, Charlie created an "official" engine recall based on safety concerns associated with the fuel system. Scheduling an authorized technician to meet the boat at the next port, an exchange of parts was accomplished in a few hours, and to compensate the captain for the inconvenience, the company left him a case of new oil filters.

Realizing the technician would have to work under the watchful eye of the boat's mechanic, Charlie knew direct sabotage of the engine's fuel system wasn't an option. Instead, he packaged his revenge within the box of oil filters. Identical in appearance, the majority of each filter's interior was replaced with C-4 explosive wired to a tiny receiver. With eleven of the twelve units prepared in this manner, the "technician" was able to store a total of fourteen pounds of fiery hell next to the *Kelsey II*'s fuel tanks. The twelfth filter unit contained a sophisticated GPS transponder, including a detonation transmitter to set off all eleven bottles simultaneously. Far from a basic stick of dynamite with a countdown timer, the GPS device was state-of-the-art. Providing real-time updates of the ship's location, it allowed Charlie's operative to choose the time and place of detonation.

The captain's final and fateful trip occurred during a run to deliver a private shipment of contraband. After confirming there were no innocent passengers onboard and the ship was far out to sea, the detonation code was sent.

I first learned about the *Kelsey II*'s demise from Annie, who overhead a phone conversation between her father and Leon. A few days later, Mark confirmed the explosion. "At 2:00 AM," he'd said. "The scorching burst of erupting plasma was so bright, it had registered on the infrared sensors of the Terra EOS satellite as an unusual heat anomaly."

"Any chance of someone surviving the blast?" I'd asked.

Mark had shaken his head, then added, "The captain, his men . . . they're out of business. Permanently."

I remember feeling a twinge of pity, not for the captain, but for the others who, for whatever reason or circumstance, found themselves working for an hourly wage onboard a slave ship. But then the memory of that first day on deck—when five of the crew had bent me over and penetrated me from both ends—returned with raging intensity. Stripping away more than my clothes, those men tried to take away my identity, attempting to change me into something less than human—all in the name of profit.

I would not waste my pity on the likes of them.

The most interesting news came from Tommy Housing. During a lengthy text, he mentioned he was in town on family business, a not-so-secretive code for *I'm here to straighten out another problem with Gregory and the law*. My first thought was Gregory had killed another young girl. Thankfully, the news was different. Seems Gregory was missing, his family not having seen or heard from him in weeks. Tommy confessed it might be a blessing in disguise. But his father was worried sick and wanted to know what had happened to his wayward son.

A week later, the officials found Gregory. Turned out, he wasn't doing well at all. Stripped naked and tied to a metal table in his "playroom," his body was stiff from the effects of rigor mortis.

The police might not have checked the secret room if it hadn't been for the power company's investigation of an electrical outage in the neighborhood. Eventually tracing the issue to a burned out transformer on Gregory Housing's suspiciously unguarded property, they found the unit had failed due to some kind of overload originating within the house. Inside, they found the source of the problem was Gregory's flash-fired body, the high-voltage electrodes still strapped to his wrists and ankles.

The police report hypothesized Gregory's demise came at the hands of skilled thieves who broke into his home, took several valuable works of art, then restrained Gregory to the metal sparking table. After applying the wrist and ankle electrodes, they'd set the current controls to produce a series of pulsating shocks at a relatively low voltage, followed by a four-second burst at the system's maximum 12,000 volt capacity. Set to continuously repeat, the coroner estimated Gregory had endured his own favorite kind of torture for twelve to fourteen hours before his strong, healthy heart had finally burst.

Over the next year, I continued to hear new reports of slavers falling victim to foul play, and with every new rumor and story, I listened for the name of one man in particular . . . Morrison. Not that I was anxiously waiting to hear confirmation of his death. In fact, just the opposite. I hoped he would escape Charlie's private campaign of retribution.

My hatred of Morrison hadn't mellowed, but I couldn't stomach the thought of subjecting Maria to the heartbreak of losing her husband. To her, Morrison had been a protective and loving partner. While taking vengeance on him might balance the scales of justice, it would destroy Maria's life. And I would not—could not—subject her to that kind of pain.

And then there was Carl, my bastard of a husband. I still thought about him, wondering what kind of life he was living, if he missed me, and if he ever regretted the night he gambled away his wife in a poker game.

Mostly, I wanted the satisfaction of one final conversation, to tell him what I'd been through, and how much I'd suffered because of him.

I mentioned it to Mark one night, asking if the department could do some fishing and find out what he was up to. Two days later, Mark handed me a month's worth of Carl's phone records and transcripts of his emails and text messages. From those, I learned he'd applied for and received a divorce, with me in absentia, claiming I'd abandoned him. He'd also struck up a new relationship with the twenty-year-old daughter of an influential politician and, if he played his cards right—no pun intended—it would put him in line for a well-paying if not cushy position managing Sri Lanka's rolling stock.

I got over the hurt in a week. The anger would take much longer. In fact, I might have carried the seed of vengeance for years if Mark hadn't made the suggestion.

"You should screw with his head," he said. "Put *him* in hell for a while."

I didn't know exactly what he meant until he told me about an obscure federal law authorizing the recall of ex-military personnel to active duty. The more I thought about it, the more the idea began to crystalize into a perfect plan of retaliation.

After giving him the thumbs-up, Mark made a call to a friend stationed at Langley, who originated a request to the Secretary of Defense. Six weeks later, my ex-husband Carl, the original beach bum who enjoyed the sun and sand more than stroking his own cock, was on his way to spending the next two years of his life on the bleak and frozen landscape of Thule Air Base in Greenland, the northernmost U.S. military base in the world.

I had my revenge, but I wanted redemption. It came six months later, when Carl sent a letter addressed to me, care of the U.S. Embassy in Bangkok. He'd learned what happened to me, that I'd survived being sold into slavery, and was now a government employee, working in a gray-area of politics and influence.

In three pages of hand-written script, he emphasized how sorry he was, how he had learned from his mistake, and how he hoped I would forgive him. It wasn't until the very end of his letter that I realized the real reason he'd written to me.

He was afraid of what I might do next. He'd realized I was making friends—powerful friends, who could pick up a phone and turn someone's world upside down.

I hoped he thought about that every day.

Because life can be a lot like a poker game, and you just never know who's holding the winning hand.

If you enjoyed this book, I hope you'll tell your friends and leave a review on Amazon

RedemptionBookThree.com

About the Author

Jaye Frances is the author of seven books including *The New Girl in Town* and the suspense thriller trilogy, *World Without Love*. Her other published works include *The Beach*, *The Kure*, and *Love Travels Forever*. Storyteller, truth-seeker, and optimist, Jaye explores relationships, philosophy, and the complexities of life—a day at a time.

For more info, visit:

JayeFrances.com
JayeFrancesBooks.com
JayeFrancesYouTube.com
JayeFrances.Substack.com
LinkedIn.com/in/JayeFrances
Facebook.com/JayeFrancesAuthor
Twitter.com/JayeFrancesNews

Books by Jaye Frances
World Without Love Series

Betrayed
Book One - World Without Love

Reunion
Book Two - World Without Love

Redemption
Book Three - World Without Love

The New Girl in Town
And Other Journeys Above and Below the Belt

The Beach
Including the Novella, Short Time

The Kure

Love Travels Forever

Jaye Frances Books are Available in eBook and Paperback at JayeFrancesBooks.com

World Without Love - The Series
Betrayed – Reunion - Redemption

Betrayed
Book One - *World Without Love*

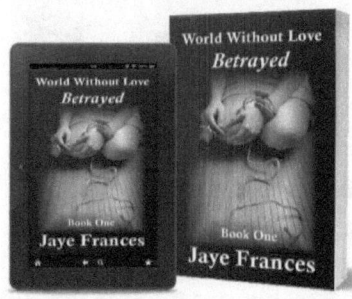

Jewel has everything going for her—a handsome husband, a promising future, and lots of time to explore an island paradise she now calls home. But when a group of strangers accompanies her husband home for a friendly game of poker, her life quickly becomes a hellish nightmare of deceit and betrayal.

Now her very survival depends on entering a world where sex, domination, and money are inseparable, where women must obey all masters, and where every desire has its price.

World Without Love contains mature content
and is intended for an 18+ audience

Betrayed is available in eBook and paperback at

BetrayedBookOne.com

Reunion
Book Two - *World Without Love*

In **Reunion**, Jewel's story continues as she finds herself stranded in a far-flung corner of the world. Struggling to elude her captors and a network of bounty hunters, she meets her would-be savior, a man who promises to provide protection and comfort. Believing her nightmare has finally come to an end, Jewel begins making plans to return home, where she can start her life over again.

But greed raises its ugly head, and the terrifying future she thought she'd evaded becomes a reality. Deceived by the only one she believed she could trust, Jewel is left defenseless against the sadistic abusers who take pleasure in teaching her their own form of discipline. With the dream of rescue and returning home to San Diego even further from her reach, she begins planning her revenge on the men who have stolen her life—and her future.

World Without Love contains mature content and is intended for an 18+ audience.

Reunion is available eBook and paperback at
ReunionBookTwo.com

Redemption
Book Three - *World Without Love*

Rescued from Bangkok's evil flesh markets, Jewel's victory over her captors is bittersweet. Haunted by her last memories of Annie, Jewel vows to do whatever it takes to find her friend—hopefully in time to save her from a sadistic killer. Using her new position as an embassy hostess, Jewel begins to form alliances with the constant stream of visiting political attaches and power brokers, hoping one of them can help find Annie—still alive.

Quick to recognize Jewel's special assets, her supervisors offer her more responsibility, and with it, the benefits of unsupervised travel and the latitude to call her own shots in the completion of her duties. No longer under the scrutiny of the all-seeing covert government network, Jewel realizes she has been given another special privilege, one that her superiors could not have anticipated—the freedom to extract revenge on all those who attempted to destroy her life.

But again, the hand fate touches Jewel's heart. And before she can stop herself, a professional relationship becomes very personal, forcing her to choose between the man she loves and the one who helped her escape a dismal world of enslavement and cruel domination.

World Without Love contains mature content
and is intended for an 18+ audience

Redemption is available in eBook and paperback at
RedemptionBookThree.com

World Without Love – The Complete Series
Includes *Betrayed, Reunion, and Redemption*

In *Betrayed*, Jewel has everything going for her—a handsome husband, a promising future, and lots of time to explore an island paradise she now calls home. But when a group of strangers accompanies her husband home for a friendly game of poker, her life quickly becomes a hellish nightmare of deceit and betrayal. Now her very survival depends on entering a world where sex, domination, and money are inseparable, where women must obey all masters, and where every desire has its price.

Jewel's story continues in *Reunion*, as she finds herself alone and stranded in a far-flung corner of the world. Struggling to elude her captors and the network of bounty hunters, she meets her would be savior, a man who promises to provide protection and comfort. Jewel believes her nightmare has finally come to an end. But greed raises its ugly head, and the terrifying future she thought she'd evaded becomes a reality—one that seems impossible to escape.

In the final chapter, **Redemption**, Jewel is rescued from Bangkok's evil flesh markets by a covert government agency. Haunted by her last memories of Annie, Jewel vows to do whatever it takes to find her friend—hopefully in time to save her from Gregory's sadistic and murderous intentions. In her new position as an embassy hostess, Jewel forms alliances with political attaches and power brokers, hoping one of them can help her find Annie—still alive.

World Without Love contains mature content
and is intended for an 18+ audience

World Without Love–**The Complete Series** is available
in eBook at **WorldWithoutLove.com**

The New Girl in Town
And Other Journeys Above and Below the Belt

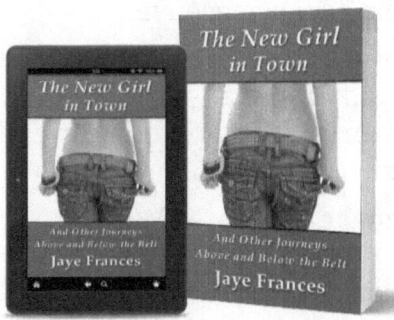

This special collection contains nine of Jaye's most heart-wrenching, mind-tingling, titillating, and thought-provoking stories. Here's a glimpse of what's inside …

- **Our Girl** – Every town has one, and there's always one guy who wants her for his own
- **Three Conversations** – Hindsight often brings wisdom, self-discovery, and a sense of closure—unless the heartache is too much to bear.

- **My First Girlfriend** – There's nothing like a first experience, especially when it brings respect, admiration, and unconditional surrender.

- **The Family Business** – Like mother, like daughter. Until the situation creates a dangerous legacy – and things have to change.

- **The Sighting** – Coming face-to-face with an urban myth can be exciting – and frightening. But when the truth reveals a surprise no one saw coming, it's time for a whole new perspective.

- **Avocados and Fruit Salad** – New beginnings are all around us, if we're willing to recognize the opportunities and take a few risks

- **Younger by Ten** – When love is about the numbers, a few hearts are bound to be broken, especially when you realize your choice of lover had nothing to do with you.

- **A Lie I Desperately Want to Believe** – Trust is often part of the collateral damage when the unquestioning bond of marriage is ripped to shreds.

- **The New Girl in Town** – Sometimes it takes a while to figure out what you want – and build the confidence to go for it!

The New Girl in Town is available in eBook and paperback at **TheNewGirlBook.com**

The Beach

Alan loves the beach. More than a weekend respite, it is his home, his refuge, his sanctuary. And for most of the year, he strolls the sand in blissful solitude, letting nature—and no one else—touch him. But spring has given way to summer, and soon, the annual invasion of vacationers and tourists will subdivide the beach with blankets, umbrellas, and chairs, depriving Alan of his privacy and seclusion—the fundamental touchstones of his life.

Resigned to endure another seasonal onslaught of beach-goers, Alan believes there is nothing he can do but prepare for the worst.

But fate has other plans.

Delivered to him on the crest of a rogue wave, the strange object appears to have no purpose, no practical use—until Alan accidentally discovers what waits inside. Now he must attempt to unravel an ageless mystery, unaware that the final outcome will change his life, and the beach, forever.

In the companion novella *Short Time*, you'll meet a respectable but bored middle-class executive, who exchanges his future for six months of excess and extravagance, only to discover out the price he must pay for his hedonistic indulgence is beyond anything he could have imagined.

The Beach is available in eBook and paperback at **BewareTheBeach.com**

The Kure

John Tyler, a young man in his early twenties, awakens to find a ghastly affliction taking over his body. When the village doctor offers the conventional, and potentially disfiguring, treatment as the only cure, John tenaciously convinces the doctor to reveal an alternative remedy—a forbidden ritual contained within an ancient manuscript called the *Kure*.

Although initially rejecting the vile and sinister rite, John realizes, too late, that the ritual is more than a faded promise scrawled on a page of crumbling paper. And as cure quickly becomes curse, the demonic text unleashes a dark power that drives him to consider the unthinkable—a depraved and wicked act requiring the corruption of an innocent soul.

The Kure contains mature content
and is intended for an 18+ audience

The Kure is available in eBook and paperback at
TheKureBook.com

Love Travels Forever

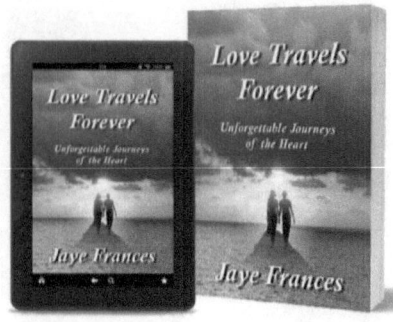

In *Love Travels Forever*, Jaye Frances captures the reader's heart with an inspiring collection of seventeen stories filled with romance and passion, the hopeful innocence of youth, and a love so strong that it transcends the mortality of life. Here are just a few of the people you'll meet:

Evan and Frankie, a loving couple traveling through life hand-in-hand, are unaware that the shadow of fate is about to tear them apart. Helpless to change their shortened future together, one of them makes a promise—a promise of devotion and courage, honoring a love that surpasses the boundaries of time.

Mark and Janice, the perfect couple with the perfect life, are on the threshold of finally seeing their dreams come true—until an unexpected circumstance changes their lives forever.

Danny, a young soldier fresh out of boot-camp, is desperate to find a way to travel home and marry his sweetheart before being shipped overseas. Stranded in a train station on a three day pass with no hope in sight, Danny meets Wanda, an incredible woman who vows to find a way to bring Danny and his fiance together.

Nora and Georgia are two eight-year-old best friends who share giggles, dolls, and secrets. But when one of them faces sudden danger, the other responds with an unconditional act of love and forges a lifelong bond between them unaffected by fear or prejudice.

So find a quiet spot, get comfy, and grab a box of tissue. You're about to take an unforgettable journey of the heart, to a place where compassion and hope have no limits, and where love continues to travel forever.

Love Travels Forever is available in eBook & paperback at **LoveTravelsForever.com**

Jaye Frances Books are Available in eBook
and Paperback at:

JayeFrancesBooks.com

JayeFrances.com